Days *in the* Diaspora

Days *in the* Diaspora

Kamal Ruhayyim

Translated by
Sarah Enany

The American University in Cairo Press
Cairo   New York

First published in 2012 by
The American University in Cairo Press
113 Sharia Kasr el Aini, Cairo, Egypt
www.aucpress.com

Dar el Kutub No. 11526/11
ISBN 978 977 416 537 5

Dar el Kutub Cataloging-in-Publication Data

Ruhayyim, Kamal
        Days in the Diaspora/ Kamal Ruhayyim. —Cairo: The American University in Cairo
    Press, 2012

            p.   cm.
            ISBN 978 977 416 537 5
            1. Arabic fiction
        I. Title
            892.73

1 2 3 4 5   16 15 14 13 12

Designed by Fatiha Bouzidi
Printed in Egypt

Chapter 1

I didn't board the plane with the rest of the passengers.

I heard them calling all passengers for the Egyptair flight to Cairo to proceed immediately to Departure Gate 20. Like the others filling the seats around me, I'd been waiting for that call. They all got up, and so did I; they hurried for the gate, and so did I. But the minute I got to the gate—the minute I caught sight of the airport officials standing there in their blue suits, peering intently at the documents of the passengers filing past, I turned on my heel and went back the way I had come.

That's just the way it was! It all happened in the space of a minute, maybe a second, maybe more, maybe less. I have no idea.

Was it temporary insanity? Was I possessed? I have no idea what came over me.

Naturally, my absence did not go unnoticed. They called me, once, twice, a dozen times. I just sat there, sprawled on a seat at the far end of the waiting lounge, unmoving. What on earth was I doing? I had no answer.

My name rang out through the airport speakers. A tremor went through my hands; I could see it, see my entire body gripped with tension, my fingers drumming on the bag that lay in my lap. It was leather, and it held my passport, my wallet, and the boarding pass with my seat number.

A little while ago, the girl at the counter had asked, "Smoking or nonsmoking?"

"Nonsmoking, please."

"Which seat would you like, in these rows here?"

"This one," I said. "By the window, so I can see Cairo from above when we land."

"Have a safe trip," she said.

The call for me rang out again, impatiently, almost threateningly. "This is the last call," they said.

I still didn't move. I was lost, empty inside. It was as if I didn't understand that they really did mean me. Or maybe I understood, but had lost the power to move my feet.

I couldn't bring myself to go and board with the rest of the passengers, but I couldn't bring myself to march back home either. My self just forced me to stay where I was; the pores of my brain were clogged and useless. Nothing made sense any more, not one little bit.

After a while, they extracted my luggage from the belly of the plane, and it took off without me, soaring up into the sky.

I'd been preparing a whole week for this day.

Only all my preparations were in secret! Neither my mother nor my grandfather knew of my intentions.

The thing is, I was afraid of being talked out of it if I came clean and told them of my plans. I knew exactly what my mother would do: she'd wrap a towel around her head and take to her bed, announcing that she was now in mourning! Her tears—and I'd do anything in the world to keep her from crying—would have made up my mind. As for my grandfather, though I look up to him, though he's got a great head on his shoulders, though he knows that the best thing for me is to go back—his eyes always pleaded, "Don't go, don't leave me."

I'd borrowed the airfare from Sheikh Munji al-Ayyari, the Tunisian who lived in the same building as my grandfather. This was in Barbès, a suburb north of Paris. My grandfather lived on the fifth floor, and Munji on the first; he owned the butcher shop in the building next to ours. The man's love for me was equal only to his hatred of my mother's family. He was always astonished to see me vacillating over whether I should stay or go. He would say in disapproval, "How can a good Muslim boy like you, who fasts and prays and obeys God, live with a Jewish family! Good Lord above! The mother, Jewish! The grandmother, Jewish! The grandfather, the aunt, the uncle—all Jewish! Whatever are you thinking, Galal? Aren't you afraid they'll seduce you away from your religion? Why, my boy," he always intoned, "they may corrupt your very faith!"

I would reply, "They raised me and took me in, Sheikh Munji."

He'd say, "Even so!"

I'd repeat, "My father died in the Suez War when my mother was still pregnant with me, sir, and I had nobody else in the world."

Insistently, he'd say, "Even so! Even so!"

He was a man who clung steadfastly to the trappings of religion: a beard, a rosary, a set of prayers he knew by heart, a white gallabiya for praying. It was his firm belief that the exercise of caution and circumspection when dealing with Jews was dictated by Holy Writ, a religious duty, and his principle in life was the old saw, "No peace nor truce with this unjust ilk, but Holy War until the Judgment Day!"

Not even my grandparents were spared—and as for my grandmother, she never showed him any mercy either! My grandfather was a kind and tolerant man, but her? Good Lord above, how the woman loved to fight! She was the world champion of insults, head-butting and kicking. I suffered terribly at her hands when we were in Egypt. Our relationship was never grandmother to grandchild; it was a battle between an aged cat and an orphan mouse! And don't think I was her only victim; her old neighbors, as well, got so fed up with her that they called her Old Beaky.

Anyway, my grandmother took my grandfather out of the equation entirely, giving herself free rein to stand there, hands on hips, and pick fight after fight with Sheikh Munji and his wife, Zahira

Bu Saf. What with insults and cursing and fisticuffs and one thing and another, not to mention bumps and bruises and things getting smashed, the French police had to step in. They frequently ended up in court, and quite a few rulings were issued in favor of both parties.

My grandparents, you see, were never what you could call Parisians. They'd never even seen Paris, except on TV. They were Egyptian to the bone. Most of their lives they lived in the Daher district, in a building in Abbas Street. But they left Egypt eventually, like all the other Jewish people who were no longer at ease and began to trickle out. They stayed longer than most, though. They didn't leave with the first wave, nor even after the Palestine war, nor yet with the second wave of emigration after the Suez War; they emigrated at the end of the sixties. They left the country for good, taking my Uncle Shamoun and Aunt Bella and her daughter Rachel, leaving just me and my mother, alone in my grandfather's apartment; God was with us, and that was all.

It wasn't that my mother had any kind of burning desire to stay; the thing was that she couldn't leave, because I was forced to stay. I was still a child, in primary school, and Egyptian law decreed that, as an underage child, I could not travel abroad without the express permission of a member of my father's family. "The male line," the law calls it. My Uncle Ibrahim, my father's brother, was that "male line." My mother begged and pleaded with him to give his consent, sending intermediaries to his village of Mansouriya in Giza, and his answer was always the same: "No and a thousand times No." It wasn't that I meant anything to him; he refused just to spite her. And me? I was just a ball kicked around by both teams.

And so I stayed until I came of age; I graduated from secondary school, and was accepted into the faculty of medicine. How bright my world seemed when I fell in love with Nadia, the girl next door! She and I would sit for hours, dreaming of the future. We'd discuss where I should open my practice when I became a doctor, and where we would live when we were married. I would suggest Nasr

4

City, and she Mohandiseen, but we'd always come back to Daher. "And why not?" we reasoned. "There's a building under construction next to the Collège des Frères; the owners are lazy and only build one story every year. We might make it in time," we'd say, "to get two apartments, one to use as a clinic, and one to live in."

My mother, though, was dead set against it. She wanted to go be with her family in Paris, as soon as possible and by any means necessary. She didn't mean to go alone, of course; she wanted me along. Although she claimed it was just for the summer, she was secretly planning for me to stay with her and never come back.

I stalled as much as I could. Fate, however, conspired against me. Nadia's mother found out about our secret little romance, and she disapproved of it; more to the point, she disapproved of me! How could a creature like me, with a Jewish mother, presume to think of marrying her daughter? Her daughter, whose parents and grandparents were God-fearing Muslims, to marry a boy whose mother's brothers were Jews! She decided to cut out the disease at the root: she up and left the whole building—just took Nadia and left, without telling anyone her new address.

My mother followed suit. She took me to Paris.

The summer vacation of 1974 crawled by, month by month, while I vacillated, unable to make up my mind to stay with my mother or go back. Finally, the day came when I was overcome with homesickness for my country, and for Nadia, and for my place in Dimerdash Medical School, sitting there waiting for me. I poured my heart out to Sheikh Munji, who gave me no time to think; he surged to his feet, saying, "What is this shilly-shallying? Your country needs you more!"

With that, he took me by the hand, marched out of his butcher shop, and climbed into his Citroën, still dragging me along, and drove off, heading for the Egyptair office on the Place de l'Opéra. So I was swept along, all the while saying, "Hold on . . . Just a minute . . . Can't we stop and think about it?" He didn't even answer; I believe he was feeling gleeful at achieving a victory over those accursed Jews!

On finding out I couldn't afford the ticket, he immediately paid for it himself, looking delighted.

"I'll tell my grandfather so he can pay you back," I told him as we sat in the Egyptair office.

He leaned back, waving a hand in disgust. "What? Me accept money from that buffoon! God forbid I should do such a thing! Galal, you're like a son to me. I'll take care of whatever needs to be done to get you away from that damned riffraff, back to your own country with your own people, where you belong." He squeezed my hand. "You don't owe me anything; there are no debts between father and son."

I spied my bags being wheeled out of a doorway, headed for the left-luggage area. I jumped up and reclaimed them, then went back to my seat and sat staring into space.

Yesterday, Sheikh Munji had advised me: "Wake up at the crack of dawn and perform the dawn prayer—prayer casts out all indecision—then get your bags. Don't wake anyone, just tiptoe out of the house without a sound. I'll be waiting downstairs in the car, God willing, to drive you to the airport."

"However could I do such a thing, Sheikh Munji, sir?" I exclaimed. "My mother—my grandfather—how can I creep out of the house like a thief in the night, without so much as a goodbye?"

"I'm just afraid they might make you stay, son," he said.

They were sleeping. I woke them to the sight of me fully dressed, airline ticket in hand. My grandfather rubbed his eyes in astonishment; my mother swayed in shock, and would have fallen had we not seated her quickly on the edge of the bed. She clapped her hand to her forehead as though I were going off to the wars, or saying some sort of last goodbye. My grandmother, though, yawned approvingly and smoothed down her tousled hair, well pleased. If she could, she would have let out an ululation of joy, left us to it, and gone back to bed.

My grandfather alternated between sitting in his chair and jumping up again, lamenting, "God's will be done!" My mother just kept on mopping at her eyes.

"How can you leave your poor mother?" she wailed. "How will you manage all alone out there? You don't know a living soul! You'll have to depend on Umm Hassan to feed you and take care of you!"

She was right, in a way. After all, there was no one from my mother's family left in Egypt. As for my father's family in Mansouriya, not only had they cut us off, they'd appropriated the three feddans of land that my grandfather had left me in his will, as though I didn't exist. But Umm Hassan, our neighbor from the old days in Daher, had helped my mother give birth, and was like a second mother to me; I knew she'd always stand by me.

My grandfather took up the conversation, wringing his hands together with a dusting motion, in the traditional gesture of complete disbelief. "But son, you know, you really should have . . ." he kept starting to say, but trailed off every time.

My mother's methods of persuasion became more forceful. She latched onto my clothing, trying to force me to get undressed again. I wriggled out of her grasp, her tactics only strengthening my resolve. Eventually, I lost patience and wrenched the door open, effectively cutting off her attempts at stopping me. My grandfather took her in tow; they both threw on their clothes and followed me out of the apartment in a rush.

And so we arrived at Orly Airport.

I didn't dare hug either of them before I went in, not wanting a repeat of the scene my mother had made back home. I strode quickly through the gate. Every time I looked back, I saw them behind the glass partition, my grandfather waving at me until I was out of sight, and my mother looking like a piece of flotsam that someone had discarded by the wayside.

To look at me this morning, all stern resolve, you'd never think I was the same person, lying like a limp dishrag on a seat in a corner of the airport. The about-face was so radical that I started to think

7

that perhaps my desire to return wasn't as firm as I had thought. Perhaps a part of me, from the very start, hadn't wanted to go.

Should I talk some sense into my *self,* or not? Should I feel sorry for myself, or not?

But talk is of no use any more.

Chapter 2

My mother's movements stilled when she saw me standing at the door in the flesh—flesh, shirt, trousers and all. Not a whisper, not a twitch—no motion at all.

I stood facing her, as silent as she. I have no idea how much time passed as we stood like that, perhaps a minute, but that minute felt like an hour, in length, breadth, and quantity. She stood, unmoving, and so did I. Her eyes glistened, gazing at me with a joy filled with reproach and blame.

All of a sudden, she sprang back to life, flinging herself at me and punching me in the chest. "Naughty boy! You gave me such a fright! I was going crazy! I couldn't believe you were heading off like that, leaving for good!" She looked behind her, calling for my grandfather. "Dad, Dad! Come quick! Come and see who's knocking at our door!"

Then she looked at the bag by my feet, saying in low tones, "The minute you left my sight, I almost died! If it wasn't for the one who stood by me and helped me . . ." In a softer voice, as though she were muttering a prayer to someone else, she said, "Blessings be upon you, Saint Abu Hasira! Bless you, with your great power! Bless you, protector of the miserable and unfortunate, the one who stands by the luckless like me!"

She pulled me close again, brushing aside the lock of hair that hung down over my forehead. As though she were fixing its appearance, she pushed it this way and that, as she used to do when I was little, while I ran a hand over the black scarf covering her hair, the one she wrapped about her head when the world dried up before her and took from her without giving.

Silence enfolded us once again, and still I gazed at her, paying no attention to the stuttering cough that emanated from the bathroom, nor to the old one-eyed cat, one of the strays that hung around Sheikh Munji's butcher shop, which had followed me up the stairs and slipped past us through the open apartment door.

My mother seemed to be somewhere else entirely, unable to believe that I was back, that the world had for once treated her fairly rather than cheating her. She started contemplating my features; she seemed about to speak, but did not. She just gazed abstractedly at me, not even aware that her fingers were playing with one of my shirt buttons, idly buttoning and unbuttoning it.

I stared tenderly at her as she kept repeating the same action. Once more I thought that she might be about to speak, but she didn't. A wan smile played over her lips, disappearing as soon as it appeared, giving way to a broader smile. Then I saw her cheeks returning to the way they were before: calm, except for a slight frown that covered them, that covered her entire face. Her lips were pressed together tightly, and it was as though her eyes were clouded, about to burst into tears. Her joy was marred with discomfort and confusion, as though a bird had flown from her hand and returned to alight on her palm; unable to believe it had returned, yet unable to shake off the shock of its flight.

She'd covered her hair with her scarf and prepared herself for parting, just as my grandmother Yvonne had done when my Uncle Isaac left Egypt, roaming God's earth until he finally settled, now, in Israel. My grandmother never took off the scarf until she got her first letter from him, after over a year. But my mother had worn the scarf for just half a day!

Her heart forever filled her with the fear of parting, telling her:

"It is coming, inevitable." Its winds blew over her whenever she would find me quiet and abstracted, or whenever I said something that led her to think that I still longed for what she had thought was gone. Her heart would give her a pang then, and she would be overcome with confusion; now she would throw my cousin Rachel at me, now make my grandmother talk to me, forever entreating me with her eyes. And here I was, back after a few hours, before the sun had even set—and here she was, bewildered, disbelieving, unable to credit that the world had done right by her!

I was in another world as well: my heart was empty. There was nothing left in it, nothing—or rather, it now beat as other people's did—like a machine, like the old wall clock my grandmother had bought for a few francs, or the alarm clock with the broken second hand that my grandfather kept beside his bed to help him tell day from night. My heart was a mere machine, performing its functions that doctors understood, not what people know about hearts. It had broken down. The rot had started in the airport, after it learned that there would be no travel, no airplane, and that all hope of meeting Nadia was lost. Even the hope was lost.

I had been reassuring myself, saying, "I'll go back. I'll definitely go back, and search for her, and find her, even if they've hidden her at the ends of the earth." Her perfume would flow into my nostrils again; once more I would feel her touch, whose smoothness I still felt, even now. But I had failed.

Strangely, I had trembled when they announced that the plane had taken off. At that moment I felt it was she who'd left me, not that I'd abandoned her. If the pilot's patience hadn't run out, I wouldn't be here now. I might already have finished the arrival formalities and already be across Abbasiya Square, the taxi almost turning toward our old house. I'd needed a push—just a push— someone to take me by the hand to where the plane was waiting. I would have responded. I'd have placed my fate in his hands if he had taken the trouble to do that. I was on the edge, and all I needed was a push! A word, a straw! But they were in a rush, and let the plane fly off without me.

I gently pushed my mother aside, out of my way. She went inside, and I heard her go back to her muttering, speaking to Abu Hasira: "Thank God! Thank God! I called on you and entreated you, and you didn't delay. The Lord will be bountiful to you as you lie in your grave, even as you brought him back to me."

This Abu Hasira is a saint in the religion of my mother's family. When one of them calls upon him for help, that's how I know he or she is in real trouble. There was an old palm-sized picture of the man affixed with four tacks to the inside of my grandfather's closet door in his bedroom in the Daher apartment. Next to it, on one of the shelves, was a copy of the Torah, books on Judaism and the prophets of the people of Israel, and several booklets, some printed in Egypt and others in the Levant, written in a strange language, which I later learned was Hebrew. There were news clippings and articles from old papers like *al-Celem* and *Israel* and *al-Ittihad* and *al-Saraha*, the newspapers that used to be issued by Egyptian Jews in the 1930s and 1940s. But I didn't care about any of that—only Abu Hasira.

In the picture, he looked drowsy and harmless, with a white beard that came to a point and a black cloth wound around his head, topped with a bright white shawl. And whenever my mother or grandfather asked me to get them something from the closet, I would recite the traditional Muslim blessing to myself, "In the name of God, the Merciful, the Compassionate," and I wouldn't fully open the closet door—I'd take the precaution of leaving it ajar, and spy on his photo with curiosity mixed with a bit of awe and exaltation. I never let my fingers touch his photo, for fear that he too might reach out and grab me. My heart would pound, and often, overcome with fear, I'd push the closet door closed and return to my grandfather empty-handed. He'd ask me where his glasses were, or his watch, whatever he'd sent me for, and I'd stammer, "Huh? I forgot."

That was my first acquaintance with Abu Hasira. I gradually started getting used to him, but I never abandoned my precautions, and still didn't dare to fully open the closet door. Sometimes, especially when I went into that closet in the evenings, I'd get the feeling he was about to speak. It was as though I were surrounded by noises; just noises, not spoken words, gentle and soft in my ear, insistent as the buzzing of bees. They had a rhythm of their own, almost like a melody; and although I had no idea where it was coming from, something in my heart told me it was coming from that man in the picture. In those moments, another voice would come to me with a flavor that had always enchanted me when I was younger: the voice of the well-known Quran reciter, Sheikh Damanhouri, reciting the Quran. I would be overcome with awe, and something invisible would overpower me, as though I were hanging onto it as it took me on a journey to another world, far from the one beneath my feet. Nothing seemed to make sense, and for quite some time I would stand there, distracted and perplexed. I was young then, but not young enough to believe that something like a whisper would come out of Abu Hasira's lips. I knew that could never happen. Still, the thought never quite left me; my soul remained captivated by something like a divine melody and a recitation of the verses of the Holy Quran, and when I finished my errand—if I remembered it—I would close the closet door gently, feeling it was only respectful and polite. If he was mentioned in conversation, I would speak well of him, as my mother's family did.

For a long time, I thought he was the prophet Aaron, who went into the wilderness in the company of his brother Moses, accompanied by the Israelites. That was a story my mother never wearied of telling me. She would tell it, and the Prophet Moses would sweep into my imagination, young and strong, powerful and determined, and when she mentioned the name of the Prophet Aaron I would immediately remember the face of Abu Hasira, imagining them to be one and the same. It was my grandfather who made me understand that he wasn't Aaron, nor one of the prophets of the Israelites, but a good servant of the Lord, a holy man who could convey blessings.

I would listen avidly to what my grandfather said, my eyes finding comfort in the familiar lines of his face, filled with calm and the acceptance of Fate, as he told me that Saint Abu Hasira had the power to visit different lands in a single stride, and that he kept the Lord's secrets. When he had faced disaster, with no help or hope in sight, his faith had inspired him to spread out his straw mat upon the waves, sit upon it, and humbly and abjectly entreat the Lord to bear him through his domain; he did, and so it was: the Lord bent the sea to his will and it bore him to his destination.

When my Uncle Isaac's absence had gone on too long, my grandmother prepared a basket full of cakes and biscuits and menein, and my grandfather put on his white, smocked gallabiya, paired with his navy-blue suit jacket and his tarboosh, and they embarked together on the journey to Abu Hasira's tomb, on the outskirts of the village of Damituh, close to Damanhour.

My grandmother said that the nasty little boys who lived close to the place came out to meet her; they started out by welcoming her, but as soon as they'd devoured the good things in her basket, they showed their ill breeding by mocking the black hat she wore, exchanging nudges and winks about her appearance and her gait, and comparing her to an upside-down water pot. One of the boys wore running shoes and a gallabiya with nothing on underneath. He had kinky hair that he scratched constantly. This little hellion, after eating his fill, took it upon himself—for no discernible reason—to warn the other boys against her, yelling that she was an old witch, a wily, cunning genie who could come out in broad daylight, while my grandfather was nothing but an old run-down dog she'd found panting, asleep at the foot of a tree, and transfigured into human form to show her the way. This lowlife even swore that under my grandfather's gallabiya they'd find a tail hidden in his underpants! He cried that my grandmother's food, which they'd eaten so greedily and now filled their stomachs, was enchanted! The boys leaped up in fright, some running off clutching their stomachs and screaming, the braver ones starting the search for dry sticks and palm fronds to strike blows upon my grandmother's shoulders. She snatched up an iron bar that was lying on the ground by her and waved it about to fend them off, and it was only by the grace of God that she took my grandfather's advice and avoided getting into a fight with the boys, and instead beat a hasty retreat with him, or they would surely have been hurt.

I said jokingly to my mother, an unexpected tear trickling from my eye, "So it was you, Mother dear, who set Abu Hasira on me?"

She answered firmly, "Yes. Yes, I begged him and pleaded with him. Who else brought you back but him?"

Suddenly, from inside, we heard the loud ring of Grandmother's disembodied voice: "Yes, it was he who brought you back, boy! Or do you doubt it?"

We were still by the door; it wasn't even closed yet. Where was her voice coming from? I looked at my mother in shock, and our eyes roved over the hallway and the rest of the apartment, until she called again: "I'm in here, in the bathroom. I'll be right out."

That infernal Old Beaky! Were you following our conversation from where you lurked inside, old hag? The Lord has seen fit to ruin your bladder since we left Egypt; you give us hell every time you go to the toilet; and yet, you unholy woman, you never let up. You keep arguing and spoiling for a fight even sitting on the pot!

Seeing my face go red, my mother squeezed my hand, eyes fixed on the door of the bathroom. We could hear Grandmother drawing the bolt from the inside. Mother raised a finger to her lips asking me to control myself, not to be the one to start the fight. Why Negma Ibrahim, the movie star, came to my mind at that precise moment, I have no idea. I said to myself: Wouldn't it have been fairer to us all if Grandmother had gone to do her shopping in Zanqat al-Sittat, and met our grande dame there, or even her sister Sikina, and they had borne her off with them and dealt with her like any other woman who fell into their clutches?

Finally she emerged, hair wild, wearing blood-red pajamas adorned with pictures of long-extinct animals: a dragon, a dinosaur, a two-headed creature, and some other thing with jaws that could crush iron. She looked like one of those scary dolls they make especially to frighten naughty children and strike terror into their hearts. She raised her left eyebrow like the famous movie villain Farid Shawqi, and prepared for battle. "Do you not believe, boy, that your master, and the master of your family, Abu Hasira, was the one to bring you back?"

I answered angrily, "I have no master, and don't say a word about my family."

My mother stepped between us, and my grandmother waved a dismissive, contemptuous hand at us both. "No master, he says. No master. Who cares? You don't deserve the privilege!"

Just then, I glimpsed the one-eyed cat peering out of the kitchen, a scrap of meat in his mouth. Seeing us deep in discussion and paying no attention to him, he came sauntering out of the kitchen as though he owned the house. I have no idea why the rascal stopped right by my grandmother, who had her back to him, and took to sniffing at the heels of her great flat feet, which bulged out of the back of her slippers—but he suddenly arched up his hindquarters and started to urinate.

He let it flow with astounding copiousness and enviable aplomb, as though he'd been holding it in for ages and now, with no choice but to let go, simply peed without embarrassment. He produced a truly impressive stream, what seemed like gallons and gallons of urine, spraying onto the hall rug as though it would be his last chance to urinate on this earthly plane. Splatters kept hitting my grandmother, splashing onto her slippers, showering her heels, and wetting her pajama pants.

The sight of me stifling my laughter was too much to bear: she went berserk! In the blink of an eye, like a kung fu master, she whirled full circle, delivering a precise kick that sent the cat flying into the wall. The second, harder kick caught him on the rebound. She bent and picked him up by the tail as he mewled in pain, blood drippng from his face. He'd at least lost a tooth, and had possibly even been crippled, his spine crushed; my grandmother's blows never failed to reach their mark, never failed to yield devastating results. She turned to me, her face warning me to get away from her unless I wanted her to commit a crime. Then she hurried to the stairs with the cat, and threw him from the stairwell, where he plummeted to the ground from the fifth floor. All the while, she cursed the cat and its father and Sheikh Munji and his wife Sitt Zahira Bu Saf, cursed Tunisia and all who came from her. Then she came striding back to me, rolling up her pajama sleeves, as if I'd let the animal into the apartment on purpose, somehow knowing it would pee on her.

My grandfather came rushing out of his room, bringing the thumb and fingertips of one hand together to indicate that she should settle down and shut her mouth. She ignored him, and charged out in search of Sheikh Munji's wife, who appeared to have heard the insults, and stood looking up at my grandmother from the bottom of the stairwell with her four daughters, all spoiling for a fight.

My grandfather looked disturbed. There had been joy on his face when he first saw me, but he soon sobered as he gestured to my mother to catch up with my grandmother and bring her back. I hurried over to him; he gave me a quick hug and said, eyes on the door and face worried, wary of what my grandmother might do, "I knew you'd come back. My heart told me so. Why, if you'd gone, I'd have . . ."

I placed my hand on his shoulder. He trailed off and placed his hand on mine, smiling; then he added, face growing serious once more: "Yes, if you'd really gone and left us, I wouldn't have taken it lying down. Everything that's been bottled up inside me would have come out, and tomorrow or the day after I'd have gone to the embassy, and said, 'My boy's gone, all you kind folks, I need to go to him.' They'd say, 'So you want to apply for a visa?' I'd say, 'Never! I won't enter my own country with a visa. Am I an Italian or a Pakistani or a foreigner from America, to need a visa to get in? I'm Egyptian, people!' I'd point at them and tell them, 'You gentlemen, you high-class people sitting there all superior, dressed in the latest fashion, sipping tea and coffee—do you think I'm coming to beg you for a visa? Visa, indeed! Visas are for strangers, but I'm an Egyptian. Egyptian since before you were born. Tell me, everyone, is there such a thing as someone who asks permission to enter the door of his own house, to be admitted or not as they please? Make everything the way it was before, and give me a paper, stamped and signed from the big boss the ambassador, saying in writing that I'm an Egyptian, and so was my father before me. For shame, people, don't make me ashamed to face myself!'" He caught his breath. "And if they didn't like what I had to say, and threw me out, I'd send a telegram to Sadat! Yeah! Sadat himself, just like that!"

Overcome with pity, I drew close to him, enfolding him in a comforting, kind embrace—it seemed that something had befallen him in those hours I had left him. He felt light in my arms, fragile and weightless. His face, which I had always known as kind and smiling, seemed dulled, extinguished, suffering. His eyes, behind the lenses of their spectacles, had no shine to them, as though they belonged to a sick man. When he pushed his glasses up to brush away something on his lashes, I noticed that his eyes had started to bulge slightly. He suffered from hyperthyroidism; when my mother and I were in Egypt, my grandmother had taken him to an Algerian doctor who had told her that it would only get worse and that his eyes could not help but be affected, or at least one of them. The days had gone by, though, and we had forgotten about it.

"But Grandfather, I wanted to say—"

He interrupted me. "Don't you dare say you don't believe me! Yes, I'd have sent him a telegram, and said, 'Will you stand for this, Mr. President of Egypt? Will you stand for it, depriving a boy of the family that raised him and in which he grew up? Have you no compassion, no humanity? Him in one place, us in the other? I'm an Egyptian and my father and grandfather before me, and all the way back to my great-great-great-great-great-great-great-grandfather, and maybe more, all born and lived and died in Egypt. Not only that, Mr. Big, Mr. President—my uncles, on both my mother's and father's side, are all buried in Basateen. We have nine family plots in the graveyards there. Why, my grandfather was a teller in the holdings of Ibrahim Pasha,* and they traveled many a time to tally up the earnings of his endowment in Greece. As for his grandfather before him. . ."

I stood before him, silent and unsure what to do; I couldn't do anything for him, nor even comfort him or make him feel better. He was in such a state of unhappiness and bitterness as I had never seen before. He added, "I'd tell him my whole story from start to finish. I'd tell him, 'I'm Zaki al-Azra', born in Egypt in the reign of Khedive Abbas,† raised in her bounty, and even if Egypt has forgotten him, he never will forget her!' He'd apologize and say, 'I know, Zaki, I know you've done nothing wrong, and we haven't been fair to you.' He'd pat me on the back and say, 'Come back, Zaki. Gather all your family and come back.'"

The hubbub on the stairs grew louder. We heard my grandmother screaming at my mother, saying that she wouldn't listen to my grandfather and go back into the apartment, because it was my grandfather in his misguided naïveté who had brought these people upon them, and that even if her father, Sawaris, and her mother, Zuleikha, were to come back from the grave and entreat her, she would not change her mind. It was now that she would put a stop to this conman of a butcher, him and all his family, this layabout with no conscience, and it was today that she would either kill or be killed!

As if that wasn't enough, my grandmother took off one of her slippers, and leaned over the banister waving it threateningly; she was so worked up that she dropped it, and Sitt Zahira Bu Saf caught it and held it as evidence of my grandmother's breach of the truce

---

* General Ibrahim, with important military conquests to his name, was the son of Mohamed Ali Pasha, Sultan of Egypt.
† Abbas Hilmi the Second, last khedive in the family of Mohamed Ali Pasha, ruler of Egypt from 1892 to 1914.

between the two families. In a smooth, poisonous voice, she told my grandmother that the one thing Sheikh Munji, the theologian well-versed in the Holy Book, would never allow was this breach of our truce, and that he was on his way immediately to declare what the Lord's judgment was on people like us, and it was not at all far-fetched that he might come up to our apartment and execute us all with a meat cleaver.

My grandmother only burned hotter and fiercer; she'd started to look like a cat whose tail someone had stepped on. She did everything she could. She spat from above onto everyone in the crowd congregated downstairs; aiming carefully, with her left eye closed, she scored a bullseye on Sitt Zahira's head with her other slipper. All the while, she kept up an artillery barrage of heavy-duty insults, insults not confined to the family of Sheikh Munji, but aimed as well at Tunisia, Algeria, and indeed the entire Maghreb region.

Sitt Zahira, whose daughters had leaped to her aid after Grandmother's skillful shot had knocked her face-down to the floor, rose to say, in the same tone, "Fine, you old harridan, just you wait! I swear, we'll tell Sheikh Munji and he'll tear you to pieces and then throw you in the garbage! Sheikh Munji's family, the cleanest, nicest, sweetest family, to be struck by filthy slippers hurled down from above? And from whom? You, you filthy old woman? The family of Sheikh Munji, a respectable, pious man, a man of prayer, on good terms with his God, a man who only leaves his house to go to his store, and his store to go to the mosque? You're a walking catastrophe!"

She motioned to her daughters to take a better look at the pajamas my grandmother was wearing, adding loudly and mockingly, "Look, look what she's wearing! A dragon's head! A dinosaur, a bull, a wolf—and what's that animal with two heads? God help us! She's an ogress, that's what she is! Curse you on Earth and in Heaven, you scourge!"

My grandmother, of course, was returning her fire twofold. When things got worse, my grandfather came out himself to pull my grandmother away from the battlefield. The fight moved to the interior of our apartment, between my grandfather and grandmother; he accused her of imprudence and recklessness; she called him a spine-less coward, and said he should have brought a club or a knife and supported her. My mother and I couldn't begin to shut them up.

The one who finally did was Sheikh Munji.

We all fell silent. My grandfather, especially, held his breath when we heard him shouting at us from downstairs in his thunder-ous tones. "What filthy neighbors! Curses on you and your parents, you vulture!" He meant my grandmother. "I spit on you. May God take you from this world, you and that white-haired old cur,"—he meant my grandfather—"that doormat, with no will of his own!"

My grandfather stood there helplessly, unable to do a thing. Even I was annoyed and angry with the sheikh. My grandmother was the most daring and savage one in the household—she charged into the kitchen and brought out a knife to answer him, but my mother and grandfather grabbed her firmly by the collar of her pajamas.

We could hear the sheikh screaming again, challenging my grandfather to come downstairs and wrestle with him; when he found his screaming was falling on deaf ears, he resumed address-ing my grandmother: "The best thing you can do, you miserable old batface, is gather up your odds and ends and take your little old white-haired manikin and get out of here. Since the day you came, God has withdrawn his blessings from the whole neighborhood! Praise be to God that Galal took my advice and left, went home to his own country and got rid of your miserable old faces! He"—he meant me—"is a decent boy, a good boy! I don't know how he came to be yours, you curs!" The sheikh didn't yet know that I hadn't gone and was standing there listening to his insults.

My mother whirled around to me in a rage, addressing me in a low voice, for fear of being overheard by the sheikh downstairs. "Oho, so *that's* it! Now it all comes out! So it was that lazy, feckless butcher pushing you to go back to Egypt! Oh, you rotten meat-cut-ter, you've got no conscience! It's true what they say in the proverb, your worst enemies are those who hate your religion!"

I gave her a look of reproach.

Chapter 3

I didn't think I'd be able to sleep that night, but I was wrong.

My alertness slipped away bit by bit, as I watched my mother sitting on the edge of the bed. Before my heavy, distracted eyes, one side of her face came and went, reflected in a medium-sized mirror she held in her hand. One eye, a bit of forehead, her thin right eyebrow, which met the left one in the center. She brought the mirror close, then moved it away again, then turned it over to the other side, where things appeared larger, and the thing she was looking for moved before my eyes.

It was a white hair. She was plucking at it with a pair of tweezers; in this motion, she would disturb the eyebrow, revealing more white hairs lurking in it; she was trying to pull them out, a frown on her face. In the mirror, I could see faint folds and light lines on her neck and on the surface of her face; things like wrinkles, becoming more pronounced with stress.

My eyes closed to the creaking of the bed and its sudden shaking; I must have dozed off for a moment. She turned to me and smiled tenderly. In return, I gave her a lazy smile. The last thing I felt, fuzzily, was her motions as she walked toward the closet.

Then sleep drew me in and I fell as if from a great height into slumber.

Sleep pulled me into the depths of its world, that magic world where we become puppets with no volition, mind, or understanding.

I seemed to be sitting in an examination hall, a hall in a strange style: high-ceilinged and slightly dark, no light coming in from the outside, except from a casement no bigger than my palm. The walls were unnaturally high; the blackboard at the head of the room seemed to be at the end of the world. However, the room was barely wide enough for two people, each sitting at his desk, between them an aisle wide enough to let one person through. It was more like a long train carriage, completely blank-walled; with no windows or even any door that I could see. Although many fans hung from the ceiling, working at full speed, they brought no hint of a breeze to my face, nor could they dispel the oppressive smell of decay that permeated the place and tightened my chest.

When they handed out the question sheets, I stared at them in disbelief: the test today was supposed to be an Arabic test, not a French-language test.

I raised a hand in protest; a tall man came to me from the very end of the room, a line of proctors trailing behind him. He was clearly their boss. I spoke with him, or so I thought; my mind was aware of the error that had occurred, and that they must correct it, and replace the question sheets in our hands with the correct examination sheets.

The problem was with my tongue: it stopped working whenever I tried to speak. The words came out of my mouth in fits and starts; if the words managed to make their way out, they sounded broken and strange, like a cassette tape being played at slow speed. I realized I was in a quandary; I didn't trust that tall man one bit, nor those people with him, who seemed to be forming a circle around me. My tongue remained the same: no use to me, never producing one comprehensible word.

When the man tired of my failed attempts at speech, he waved a dismissive hand in my face, asking, "Are you dumb, boy?"

My heart lurched when he spoke, for the voice coming from his throat was a woman's, not a man's. When he left me and turned back, I noticed that he was wearing women's shoes, high heels clicking on the tiles of the hall, as though something was telling me in the dream: "You are not in a dream, he actually is a woman, a woman who knows you all too well!"

I sat there afterward like someone who had been murdered. My mind froze: I saw myself as though I occupied a moment outside the time of the people around me—a time that was mine alone!

The boy on my left was the only one who paid any attention to me. He patted me kindly and offered to help. I felt I could trust him and gave in to him completely. He said loudly, unheeding of the proctors, "Come to me, never fear! Take the knowledge you lack from me!" And he started dictating the answers to me word for word. One of the nearby proctors was watching us, but his eyes were saying, "It's all right, it's all right," and encouraging us to keep going. When this boy had finished his task, he rose quickly to hand in his answer sheet. I was shocked to see that he hadn't written a single word on his paper—he handed it in completely blank, and then I found out that everything he had dictated to me was wrong, all wrong, and God now inspired me with the correct answer—only the paper in front of me was completely full, and there was no more ink, nor any more paper!

I asked for help. The tall man screamed at me from far away, by the blackboard, in the same woman's voice: "No answer sheet! No paper! Doctor's orders!" And he told me to come and write the answer on the blackboard.

I did. I remembered the entire Arabic language curriculum: grammar, syntax, poetry, composition. I started writing on the blackboard, and when I was done, I looked around. No one was there. No students, no proctors, not a living soul. I stood there asking myself how they'd gotten out. There was no door, no opening, nothing. What was I to do now with all these words I'd written?

And I woke up.

It was early morning, a thin ray of light piercing the room from the casement looking onto the stairwell. There was no movement coming from inside. It seemed my grandparents were still asleep. My eyes soon became accustomed to the place and recognized things: the satin robe my mother had been wearing at the beginning of the night, thrown over the chair, sleeves hanging down and fluttering gently in a persistent breeze coming from the casement, which was ajar; one of my shoes, overturned; and a little cockroach, which appeared to have come in through the skylight, crawling down the wall in my direction. My mother had fallen asleep next to me, her eyes closed and her face calm and at peace.

Chapter 4

Sheikh Munji was standing on a wooden pallet in the bowels of his store, making him taller than his already tall height.

He looked like a giant with his white butcher's apron tied across the chest, his rolled-up sleeves revealing arms like a man out of myth, while his mighty beard and his humorless countenance made him an awe-inspiring figure in the eyes of his customers. To his right was a medium-sized portrait of Habib Bourguiba,* in a wooden frame with worn edges; the photo appeared to be the cover of a magazine, *Le Point*—the name and logo of the magazine were indicated on the top. Nearby was a small wooden shelf with a tape recorder on it, from which a melodious Oriental tune issued. Farid al-Atrash was singing:

Land of nymphs, olives, and wheat,
O green Tunisia, for whom burns the heart,
Your white gazelles melt the hunter's heart!

I watched the sheikh bobbing his head to the music and the words, and said to myself, "He must be dreaming of his youth

---

* Habib Bourguiba, national hero of Tunisia, was a Tunisian liberation activist; he secured its independence from French rule in 1956 and became its first president in 1957.

and his early days, where—doubtless—he played in the fields and woodlands of Tunisia, barefoot and bareheaded, armed with a stick or other sharp instrument to hurt whichever of God's creatures he could reach."

The sheikh was cheerful indeed: humming along with Farid, his hands and apron moving lightly as he wiped a cotton cloth over the face of the block, itself an awe-inspiring wooden presence before him, with its solid body and thick legs. He rearranged the knives and choppers, one after the other, after giving them a quick wipe with the cloth, and returned each to its usual place, except for a large knife. He took a long look at its sharp edge, then placed it in a leather strap that hung about his waist.

I soon caught the fever: my heart carried me to the end of Farid's song, where he sings:

Magic Carpet, all the while
I have longed for the Valley of the Nile.
I've been all around the world, it's true
But too long have I been away from you.

I was overwhelmed with nostalgia for my far-off homeland and its kind folk. My eyes were overcome with a burning sensation, as though I were about to shed tears.

The sheikh was as yet unaware of my presence. I remained standing in a corner by the door of the shop until he finished with the customer who was with him. He was a drifter off the streets, a man I had often seen coming and going, loitering on the road. He wore a dirty hat and a jacket with a worn collar, tight around the armholes. As for his jeans, their color and condition bespoke a long lifetime of labor in the service of this unfortunate, and hard labor and difficult service at that; the man himself could only be a street sweeper, a garbage collector—someone in a low-class profession. He stood for a long time, his eyes roving over the legs of mutton and shoulders of meat and the generous bounties hanging here and there from metal hooks, while the sheikh looked at him silently. Finally, he screwed up his courage and gestured to a hefty leg of beef, the blood still dripping from it; apparently, it had just arrived from the slaughterhouse, and the sheikh was saving it for one of his privileged customers.

The sheikh paid him no attention whatsoever, and did not even look to where he was pointing. He cleared his throat abruptly, turned toward a wooden refrigerator in the corner of the store, and pulled out a piece of dark, discolored meat, covered with a thick layer of fat and gristle. It had clearly come from an old ox, or a bull broken down by age and infirmity; it was run through by a pipe of bone that could only be cleft by steel.

The man's face showed his dismay, and he gestured with a forefinger, "Sheikh Munji! We don't like such meat! Give me some of that leg I pointed out to you."

The sheikh again paid him no heed, not even the flicker of an eye.

He turned the piece of meat over in his hands, staring at it with a frown, then raised it aloft and threw it down again before him, the man's eyes rising and falling uneasily as the meat bounced on the surface of the block. I don't know why the sheikh was doing that—whether it was to convince the man that the meat was fine and there was nothing wrong with it, or to give him to understand that it was all he was going to get, no matter what he said or did.

He burped and withdrew the knife from his belt, and ran it several times over a sharpener hanging from the wall by a thick cord. Mashallah, his eyes were sharp and focused, his hands flying skillfully, the sparks never ceasing to fly from the edge of the knife. I must say, he was good at what he did and skilled at his work. When he was done, and the knife was finely honed, he started pressing the piece of meat repeatedly with his fingers, preparing to cut it, while the man remonstrated, "Come on, Sheikh! Sheikh! My dear sir! Really, my good sir, my dear sir, listen to reason, you good and respectable man from a good family, now really!" Then he added, "My dear Sheikh, I know you are aware of the teachings of our Lord and of the Prophet. I didn't ask for this. We like fresh meat, like the piece I pointed out to you, not the one in your hand that's been lying in your fridge for a month and has grown stiff as a donkey's tail!"

He went on muttering in a tone full of annoyance. He didn't stop until the sheikh fixed him with a terrifying glare that scared him into silence, then brought his huge cleaver crashing down onto the long bone with a number of powerful strokes, sending splinters of bone flying in all directions, some of which hit the man's face and spectacles. Some even flew all the way over to me and struck my clothing. The man reared back, taking off his glasses and wiping at his face, resentment plain in his expression.

It was then that the sheikh caught sight of me. His face filled with surprise: he frowned, staring hard at me. "Galal! As I live and breathe! What are you doing here? My boy, you didn't go then? Good Lord in Heaven!" But then he gestured for me to wait a moment. "Just a minute. Don't go, wait until I get done with this piece of filth."

The man whirled toward the sheikh in protest, but he soon came to his senses when his eyes met the sheikh's blazing ones. He turned toward me, face black and resentful at the humiliations heaped upon him; I gave him an encouraging smile to hearten him. He ignored me, however, and bent to the belt at his waist. He appeared to be tightening it, although it looked fine and not in need of any adjustments. Then he raised his face to mine and tried to smile, but failed. Poor man! What was he to do? He was powerless, helpless against this gargantuan creature who stood before him! He must have had previous experience with the sheikh, and knew that fighting with him was hopeless, and had disastrous consequences, and thus preferred peace.

The sheikh, meanwhile, was in another world. He scooped up in both hands the pieces he had cut up, and pushed them together into a pile toward the edge of the block, brushing them off it into a plastic bag: a few pieces of dark meat, then a large quantity of bones and chunks of fat as big as a man's hand, and in the end a great many chunks of gristle, the kind butchers normally throw to the cats. After that, he rolled back his shoulders and put the bag on the scales. When the needle stilled, he nodded. "*Quatre*." That meant four kilograms.

The man watched, his face gray as ash. When the sheikh pushed the bag toward him, he took a step back, refusing to take it. "My dear Mr. Munji, you who are familiar with the Holy Book, Mr. Munji, you who know the teachings of religion, it is a shame what you're doing to me. Every time we buy meat from you, my wife throws it back in my face." His tone became wheedling. "By your mother's head, have pity on me this time, and give me tender meat, man, that we can make into breaded escalopes like everyone else! We want escalopes, Mr. Munji! We don't like fat or gristle or bone!"

Taking pity on him, the sheikh placed his hand into the bag and extracted a chunk of bone as big as a fist, replacing it with a smaller piece of meat, saying in a friendly tone, "Man, fat is good for people like you, weak as sick goats, and bones are for soup! Don't you make soup in your house? And gristle is something that must go in the bag for people like you, who don't pay in cash!"

The man remained unconvinced, and went back to demanding red meat for escalopes. The sheikh burst out at him, "What are you talking about, escalopes, you riffraff? Have some shame, God damn you and your ilk! You're a fine one to talk about escalopes, you shameless creature! That's what the French eat, with their delicate stomachs! You, you're Algerian! Your ancestors lived on the Aurès Mountains and ate raw meat! But when you came here, this corrupt land made you forget you're men! Behave, behave, God damn you and your parents!"

The man answered in a rage, "Listen, Sheikh, you who know God's word and the Prophet's. Since it has become a matter of coercion, I shall take nothing from you. I shall go to another butcher."

"Oh, really? Is that so? Come here and I'll tell you a thing or two, you dog. Come here and I'll tell you. I weighed out four kilos for you and *c'est fini* (it's over). Take your meat and get out of here. Curse the day I saw you, you harbinger of doom! Isn't it enough that you always give me a hard time before you'll part with your meager francs?"

The man only became more steadfast in his refusal to accept the bag of meat. The sheikh raised a threatening forefinger. "Take the meat, or you won't know what I'll do to you." And with an unconscious motion, he turned toward his stick, hanging beside him from an iron hook: it was as thick as the leg of a bed.

The man watched him do this, and slapped his hand against his right thigh, saying, "By God, this is the last time I ever buy meat from you! O God, Beneficent, Merciful, Compassionate! What is this? A man without any compassion at all?"

The sheikh bellowed at him, reaching for the stick, "What? What? What was that, Mr. Garbage? The last time you buy meat from me? Say it again, just repeat that! Let me hear what you were saying, swine-face!"

Snatching the bag off the block, the man turned his back on the sheikh and rushed out of the shop. "No, no, no, sir, no, Sheikh . . . I didn't say a word."

I was the only one who saw him spit on the floor and rain down maledictions on humankind, on meat, on escalopes, and on the world that had such people as this villainous sheikh in it. He bumped into my shoulder deliberately, fixing me with a burning glare; if I'd so much as opened my mouth to say a word, he'd have hit me in the face with the bag of meat and exacted his revenge upon me instead of the sheikh.

So I hurried inside.

The sheikh was bending over a small refrigerator, getting out two bottles of juice for us. He turned to speak to me, worry etched on his face. "Galal, my boy, what's the matter with you? Why didn't you go home to your country?" He gestured again and again. "Why, my boy? Why?"

I told him what had occurred, and he only looked more uncomfortable, shaking his head. "It's not right. Not right that you should leave your country where your father and grandfather are buried, to live here with these damned curs!"

We talked, a word here and a word there, until the subject of the cat my grandmother had thrown off the stairwell came up. He said, "Your grandmother just will not get us out of her head and leave us alone. By God, if she weren't a woman, I'd have slit her throat and thrown her to the cats. I spit on her and her face. My boy, if this grandfather of yours can't put a stop to her behavior, I'll step in and teach him how to be respectful and mind his manners with Sheikh Munji! God damn this family of dogs."

Despite the annoyance I felt whenever the sheikh spoke ill of my mother's family, I always found myself drawn toward him and never tired of seeking out his company and conversation. I always forgave his slips with regard to my grandparents, saying to myself, "Perhaps he thinks he's closer to me than I am to them." For my part, I looked to him for the thing I sought and lacked, and found in him: the male line, from my father's side. I viewed him as a relation who cared for me, perhaps a paternal uncle. Not like my uncle in Mansouriya, of course, but a beautiful uncle I made for myself, who loved me as I loved him.

So it was that when he invited me to dinner, I agreed immediately.

I spent most of the evening with him and his wife, Sitt Zahira, and his eldest daughter, Khadija, in the company of his three other daughters, Aisha, Zeinab, and Umm Kulthoum, all veiled and religious girls. The youngest, his prized only son, Zein al-Abedeen, lay in his mother's lap, gurgling to her and slapping at her if she failed to pay him enough attention. Whenever I looked at him, he would smile at me; his eyes would disappear into the depths of his fat, round face, and I would stare at him and go back in my heart to our old apartment in Daher: the balcony on whose cool tiles I would crawl, sticking my head between the its iron railings to look at the street and hear its noises: the old whistle, the bottle caps and empties I would roll before me on the woolen kilim outside my grandfather's room. My thoughts drifted to our old neighbor, Umm Hassan, who had so often held me in her lap and nursed me at her breast; I had gurgled to her and put up a finger to the edge of her lip; she would tickle it, sucking it in, just as Sitt Zahira was doing now with her son.

Sitt Zahira broached the subject of my grandmother. She said to the sheikh, in suspicious, inflammatory tones, that my grandmother's activity had increased these days on the stairs: that she climbed up and down the stairs with a thick walking-stick in her hand, the kind used in fights! And, she said, she feared for Zein al-Abedeen because of it . . .

She had hit a nerve and knew it. She was well aware that when it came to Zein al-Abedeen, the sheikh would turn the whole world into a fireball, and so it was: he shouted, "If that old bat should so much as touch a hair on Zein's head, I'll go up there and by God, the One and Only, I'll make her see stars in the daytime, her and her little old fool"—he meant my grandfather—"and . . ." But then he fell silent. I think he wanted to bring my mother into it, as one of those to be punished, but held back for my sake.

He took up his speech again, pointing a finger. "No, and it won't end there, either! Even her son, Shamoun, who lives in the Vingtième Arrondissement"—he meant my uncle—"we'll crush his bones and show him what real men do!" He relaxed the forefinger, slapping a hand on his knee. "We know where he lives. Yes, we do. Never let it be said that I don't know anything about this family! No, no, no. I know everything about them." Confidently, he went on, "Oho! I've been investigating them for a long time, and God only knows how it will be when war finally breaks out between us. It may be worse than the war in Indochina,* and that's when nobody will be safe from me. Not young, not old, nor he who walks or crawls, and we won't rest till we've brought down all four walls!"

Sitt Zahira had succeeded in getting the sheikh worked up; his expression bespoke a man at the end of his tether, a man on fire, especially as my grandmother had been the one to violate the truce on the day of the cat incident. What worried me was his intention to expand the territory of the battle to include my Uncle Shamoun, and that he had conducted investigations and found out his place of residence—neighborhood, street name, house number! My fear and apprehension increased that he might conduct a pre-emptive strike to abort my grandmother's plans, which would place me in an awkward position: should I take my grandmother's side, based on family and blood? Or side with the sheikh, who loved me? Therefore, I tried to calm his rage, and make him understand that my grandmother had grown enfeebled, that I doubted that she was capable of hurting anyone, and that the stick Sitt Zahira mentioned was a walking-stick to lean on, not for fighting; not to mention her awareness that there were "red lines" that could not be crossed, and that touching Zein al-Abedeen would cost her her life. He listened to me and nodded, but I doubted he was convinced of my words. He closed the subject by telling his wife that I should be an intermediary between the two families, and that if they rejected the mediation and failed to submit to the will of God, well, then he had other plans.

Then Khadija took me aside and took to showing me correct French pronunciation, while the sheikh gazed upon us contentedly.

She was just about my age, and I was struck by her height, no doubt inherited from her father, and the rounded fullness of her

---

* In the 1950s Indochina (now Vietnam) was occupied by the French, whose military leaders would place their soldiers of Moroccan, Tunisian, and Algerian origin on the front lines of the violent guerrilla warfare launched by the Vietnamese in search of independence. Hence, the phrase remained in use by North Africans living in France until the late 1970s to indicate extreme violence.

breasts within her light housedress. I stared at her lips as they produced the sounds slowly and seductively; her upper lip looked slim and delicate, unlike the other, which was plump and pulling slightly downward. Her eyebrows were natural, thick and connected, as though they had never been touched by a tweezers, and yet her face was comforting, reassuring with its God-given color, free of paint. When her scarf slipped back a little, a few locks of hair showed, coal-black, making her face even more beautiful; but I took no pleasure in it. I felt a pang in my heart and Nadia was there in my mind, as though I were touching her fingers and smelling her perfume, even at this distance.

Khadija asked me if anything was wrong. "No, no," I answered, "nothing at all." I took my leave of the sheikh and went up to my apartment, head bowed.

Chapter 5

The family held a council to decide my future.

My mother was lounging on a couch in the hall, her legs stretched out before her. Her dress was gray with a wide neckline; on her shoulder was a shawl with the maker's name on the edge, Philippe Lacroix. She pulled playfully at the sleeve of my pajamas as I passed, inviting me to sit by her on a cane chair. She placed what she'd been reading in her lap, the French fashion magazine *Burda*, with the latest fads and the smartest fashions.

Her appearance caught my eye. She was striking in these clothes, which my cousin Rachel had bought for her; she was perfumed and wearing much too much makeup, and her white feet were nestled inside black velvet slippers decorated with Chinese patterns and drawings. She looked like a fine lady who found the Parisian atmosphere to her liking.

My grandfather came out of his room, his hair unkempt, his small form lost in too-big pajamas, under which he wore a woolen sweater rolled at the neck. He was disgruntled, which was unusual for him; we were used to him being cheerful and energetic first thing in the morning, laughing and joking and directing any conversation to times gone by and the good old days; his energy would gradually wane, and by the time darkness fell he would start to be depressed.

My mother vacated the couch for him, and he sat down in her place, muttering two incomprehensible words, which we took to be "Good morning." We answered him loudly. He ignored us, pulled his pack of Gitanes out of his pocket, and started to open it.

"Have you given up Gauloises and taken up smoking Gitanes now, Grandfather?" I asked.

"Gauloises, Gitanes; the one's as bad as the other."

"Don't say you're missing your old Belmonts, Dad!" said my mother.

"Belmonts! Where, oh where, are my Belmonts now!"

My grandmother was sitting on a small wooden stool by the kitchen. She wore a long-sleeved blouse, its chest decorated with a dog's head, its open jaws devouring a hot dog the size of an ear of corn. My grandfather turned to my mother in disdain, fanning the air in front of his nose: "What's this loud perfume, Camellia?"

"Loud?" She looked over at my grandmother, but he caught her.

"My dear girl, I don't mean the onions and muck that's in Mother's hand. I mean the perfume you're wearing."

My grandmother looked at him with her left eyebrow raised, while my mother said in surprise, "Dad, how can you call this perfume loud? It's the new scent from Yves St. Laurent."

"What's that, what? What are you saying?"

"Yves St. Laurent. He's one of the very big ones, Dad."

He cut her off. "One of the big ones? Fine! Charmed, Mr. Yves I-Don't-Know-Who! You're very welcome, I'm sure, make yourself right at home." He pursed his lips and made a sucking sound of disapproval, then said, "I hope that girl Rachel didn't buy it for you. It must be her. She'll ruin you as well. A plague on her and her father and mother."

My aunt stopped eating and turned to him in dismay; he quickly lit his cigarette and prepared for a fight.

Things didn't get worse, thank God! We were saved by the doorbell, which heralded the arrival of my Uncle Shamoun.

It was only the third, or perhaps the fourth, time I'd seen him since I came to Paris. It hurt to see him: every time we met he was paler, more preoccupied, and thinner than the last. Good God, he was dressed like a beggar! He greeted us with a dark expression, never meeting anyone's eyes. The only healthy thing about him was his handclasp: as though his fingers had swelled up and grown calloused from long years gripping his broom and pushing it through the streets of Paris. My uncle, a graduate of the faculty of commerce at King Fouad University, a former general manager of the Dawoud Ades department stores in Azhar Street, had never managed to find suitable employment here, going from job to job, each progressively worse, until he finally found a place as a street-sweeper for the Parisian county council on a temporary contract.

My grandmother asked him to sit, but he said in low tones, "Sorry, Mother. It's nearly time for my shift and I'm in a hurry. I just wanted a word in private with Father."

My grandfather took him by the hand and they went into his room.

"What's the matter with Shamoun, Mother?"

My grandmother sighed. "He's probably flat broke, my girl, and wants Dad to tide him over until the end of the month."

"Till the end of the month? Why, it's still . . . ?" She looked at me questioningly. "What day is it, Galal?"

I didn't know what day it was, and I don't think anyone else in the household did, either! We ate, drank, and slept, and each day was like the other. "I don't know," I finally said. "The tenth or the twelfth, maybe. Or perhaps the twentieth."

My grandmother sighed again. "The start of the month or the end of it, who cares? It's his wife's fault! Ruthless woman from a ruthless family! She's reduced him to a mangy dog, going round begging for alms, now from your dad, now from his Uncle Nusseiri—that's not counting the loans he gets from the banks." In a pained tone, she went on, "No, no, this can't be my son Shamoun. What a pity! I raised him in the lap of luxury, and now I see him waiting for a crust of bread, for charity?" My grandmother was scowling and upset; her tone showed exactly how far she felt my Uncle Shamoun had fallen. My mother gave her a worried glance as Grandmother commanded me, "Go and find me my smelling salts, boy, on the bedside table or wherever the hell they've gotten to!"

I answered her defiantly. "First, I'm not a boy, I have a name. Second, Grandfather's in the bedroom with my uncle and I can't barge in."

"So you mean to just sit here in our midst eavesdropping on the ladies' talk, then?"

My mother sighed, "Mother! Just talk to me, never mind him."

"Come on, girl, he's hardly a little boy. He should have some consideration and leave of his own accord—maybe we want to say something that's only for women's ears!"

My grandmother's wanting me out of the room only strengthened my resolve to stay. I said coldly: "What am I to do, Granny, so early in the morning? Go and lock myself in the bedroom, or go into the bathroom?"

She waved a hand in my face. "Stay, then. Stay and make us uncomfortable!" She turned to my mother and took up the thread of their conversation. "As I was saying, that woman's got the 'Gimme's!' A pox on her! And your poor brother only makes a pittance! A street-sweeper—what do you expect him to take home at the end of the month?" With visible emotion, she added: "Has Sarah, Zikri's daughter, forgotten herself? Has she forgotten where she came from? Her father used to scrub toilets in the Nessim Eshkenazy synagogue! And now, all she can say is, 'I wish I had that frock, Samson!' or 'Oh, Samson, if I had that handbag we saw at such-and-such a store! Wouldn't it go beautifully with my shoes with the bow on them?' And on and on, till she's worn 'Samson' threadbare. Don't you see how much weight he's lost, the health leached out of him? Why, if you picked him up and rolled him into a ball he'd fit into a handkerchief in the palm of your hand!"

"Samson, Mom? Who's Samson?"

"It's her pet name for him, the bitch!"

My mother's voice dropped and she spoke slowly. "Oh, Sarah, you little dishrag, you really have come to a pretty pass, haven't you? Do you think you're a 'lady' or something? And you, 'Samson'—Shamoun wasn't good enough for you? Heaven help you, you were so much better off in Egypt!"

"Not a word—about Egypt or anything else! He's a fool, is all! If he'd taken my advice and gone to your brother Isaac's in Haifa, he'd be much better off today."

My mother took up another thread of their conversation. "But does Dad even have the money to help Shamoun out? He's not well off himself, the poor man . . ."

She trailed off, eyes on my grandmother's mouth. And sure enough, Grandmother cut in quickly, "No, no, my girl! He's plenty well off, and he's got a respectable bank account! Isaac sends money, and so does that little sprout Rachel. Why, she puts a thousand or two into his account every month, not to mention the social security check he gets at the start of each month."

My mother nodded. "Ah. Something to ease my mind, toward the end."

My grandmother's suspicion glands were activated, and she turned to my mother belligerently. "Ease your mind? What d'you mean, ease your mind, girl?"

"Nothing," my mother said quickly. "Nothing at all."

"You know, Camellia, that low-down wife of his, may she never prosper, she said she wants to go—get this—to that whatchamacallit, the Lido, and she tells her 'Samson' to tell Rachel to scrounge her up two tickets. The little bitch wants to go to the Lido like the tourists and the fine folk! Why, the tickets alone cost a fortune, and a woman has to be dolled up in this and that and a man has to be dressed to the nines. These things aren't for the likes of us, my girl!"

"I know the Lido, Granny," I said. "Rachel showed it to me when we went to the Champs-Élysées. It's a very smart theater, and even the seats way back, right at the end, cost a mint!"

"That's what I'm saying, sonny. Is Sarah, or even Shamoun, cut out for these places? She wants, the silly idiot bitch, to put her hand in his and walk into that classy theater with the great and the good! Imagine! Abu Zikri's daughter! Am I right? And I bet that's not the last of her airs!"

Our conversation was cut off by the reappearance of my grandfather and Uncle Shamoun, who stayed with us at my grandmother's urging.

The conversation resumed, this time about my Uncle Isaac, who'd sold his supermarket in Haifa, and gone into the import/export business full-time, and about Haroun, my Aunt Bella's husband, who'd moved up in the world and suddenly looked like a man-about-town. "I'm not convinced of a single word of all this stuff you're saying," my grandmother insisted. "He's smart, you say! A good businessman, you say! I don't know what, you say! Well, I just don't believe it. The long and short of it is, he's shady! I bet he's dealing in heroin!"

"Lord! What are you talking about, Yvonne, heroin? Where do you get this stuff? Think better of people. He's your son-in-law after all!"

"You're just naive, Abu Isaac, and everyone's an angel to you. Tell me then, where Mr. Elephant-Trunk got the money to buy an apartment in this . . . in this . . ."

She looked to my uncle for help. "It's called Enna Street, Mom. Enna Street."

"Enna? May you meet your Ennd-a one of these nights, Aaron, Freiha's son! And is this Enna Street anything like our street, then?"

"What, are you kidding me, Mom? Oh, no no no! There's no comparison. It's a classy street, in the best neighborhood. Why, it's just steps away from the Champs-Élysées."

"Oh, Aaron, you son of a bitch! And he paid cash, I suppose?"

"Yes, he paid cash. You can ask Rachel."

"You hear that, Zaki? Hear what your son is saying?" She made a sucking sound with her lips, leaning over to pick up the hairpin that had fallen from her hair. "And the car he's driving! The clothes, the evenings out, the fripperies! Fate's certainly smiled on you, Mr. Elephant-Trunk. Why, when you first came here, you used to go to bed early because you couldn't afford a full supper!"

My grandmother was right to give him that nickname, for he did indeed have a most impressive nose, a truly stupendous proboscis; it was rare indeed to find such a nose on a human face. It had a protuberance on the bridge, whence it came I knew not, nor what use it was. If you were to see my uncle, even at a distance, you would notice his nose immediately, and say to yourself, "Heaven help us! God save us!" You could never stop yourself from staring, or stop thanking God for not having given you one like that.

When my grandmother once, in a slip of the tongue, said to him during one of their fights in Egypt, "Shut up, Elephant-Trunk!" he walked out of the house in a huff and didn't speak to her for a whole year, until some kind people played intermediary. After they made up, he became very sensitive about this, and woe betide any of us if he caught us staring at his nose: it would start an argument at the very least, and sometimes he would stop speaking to the culprit entirely, which would lead to solemn vows that it had all been a mistake.

His visits to us at our old Daher apartment always turned the place upside-down, and we would plan a thousand times for them. Even my grandfather would take the precaution of dropping his line of sight to a plane below Aaron's nose; he would only raise his eyes if absolutely necessary, and admonish us all to follow his example.

The problem was . . . well, me! I was little back then, and couldn't control my eyes and glance quickly at his nose as the older folks could. My mother would often heat my ears with pinches, admonishing me not to look at his face. I would feign obedience and nod, and she'd say, "If you stare at his face, tonight will be ruined and we'll have a miserable evening!" She'd stand there, not knowing what to do with me, then say, "Or should I lock you in your room? Should I? You remember the last time? You nearly made us all look rude! Remember, boy, when I nudged you in the shoulder, that time

Uncle Aaron had that handkerchief over his nose? Remember? You're a naughty, inconsiderate boy!"

My grandfather didn't like the way my grandmother was speaking ill of her son-in-law, so he changed the subject. Getting ready to light his cigarette, he turned to me. "And you, Gel-gel, what are your plans?"

I looked at him without a word, so he started to talk. My grandmother butted in, maliciously suggesting I take up street sweeping alongside my uncle, or go into the garbage business with Habib Aslaan, the husband of her relative Hanouna. I leaped out of my chair in a rage; my mother hurried over to me, while my grandfather gestured for me to stay, scowling at my grandmother.

My uncle intervened. "What are you talking about? Garbage and street sweeping? Good grief, Mother! It's demeaning, backbreaking work. And all day, either the rain or the cold beats down on the back of your neck." He swallowed. "Are you serious?"

"Of course I'm serious. He'll be supporting himself, won't he? What's good enough for you isn't good enough for him, is that it? Poor fellow, you're pushing a broom, and not complaining—"

My uncle interrupted her. "It's different for me. This is what I get. I was different back home in Egypt—I used to be a manager, with employees under me!" His eyes filled. "Please, let's drop it. The whole subject depresses me."

My grandfather was worrying his lower lip with his teeth, eyes on my grandmother. When my uncle finished speaking, he put his palm up toward her. "Yvonne, let's have a peaceful day. Either you think before you speak, like a good girl, and have some consideration, or I'll thank you to go to your room."

She leaped up and stormed off to the kitchen, muttering vague words that didn't quite reach us. My grandfather waved a hand at her retreating back, saying, "Madness! Her Excellency wants the whole family to end up as street-sweepers. Isn't one enough?" He looked over at my uncle. "No offense, son."

My uncle ignored him. He gripped my wrist, saying with repressed indignation, "You should have gone back to Egypt, finished your education! You'd have made it easier on your family, and easier on yourself. Is my life so attractive, then?" He pulled his hand from mine. "If I only knew what made you turn back at the airport . . .! Come here, smart guy, and I'll show you ten or twenty Jewish guys just like us, who would love to leave their jobs and go back to Egypt! They've got no love for croissants, or pâté, or *bonjour* and *pardon*! They're saying koshari and white cheese and semeet are good enough for us! And 'Ahlan ya Hajj,' and 'Izzayak ya Bey'!"

My grandfather craned his neck to follow my uncle's words— swept up by enthusiasm, he was almost shouting. "Yes, they'd go back! If they could, they'd go today, not tomorrow, and I'd be the first! Yes, I've got French citizenship, but only a liar would say that I'm comfortable here, that I'm living among my own people! My language isn't theirs, my habits aren't theirs, my lifestyle isn't theirs. I feel like I'm lost, looking around me wherever I go. Where are the days when I lived in Sakakini Square and drove a Fiat 1100, and came and went every day . . . ?"

He didn't finish. We heard my grandmother growling from the kitchen, and my mother waved a hand in his face. "Wake up and watch what you're saying, Shamoun, and stay away from my son! Galal is staying here, by his mother's side. And the people you're talking about are the failures like you."

"Failures? Heaven forgive you!" And he and my mother started arguing.

My grandfather didn't bother to hide his disapproval of the relent-less arguing, and when it grew too much, he shouted at them both. My uncle quieted, while my mother went into the kitchen, accom-modating his request for tea. He didn't stop scowling, though, staring at an old wound in the heel of his hand, tracing the rough folds in the wrinkled skin gathered about his finger joints. When I looked closely, it seemed to me as though a tear was forming at the edge of his left eye. My suspicion was confirmed when I saw his thumb wiping there. I think he was moved by my uncle's words; no sooner was Egypt mentioned in conversation than he went wild with longing for it. If it had been up to him, he would have packed up immediately and gone. As for my uncle, he sat there staring down at the tongue of his shoe, which was hanging out.

My grandfather suddenly asked me about his old tarboosh, which he had left behind in Egypt over seven years ago, and about the picture of Abu Hasira; had we brought them with us? I told him that I didn't know; Mother was the one who did the packing.

"Mother?" he said irascibly; he called on her, but she didn't answer. He called again, louder, but she still didn't hear him. He bent over, righting his overturned slipper, then leaned over to talk to Uncle Shamoun.

My grandfather's hearing wasn't a hundred percent. That was why he didn't notice that my mother hadn't answered his calls because she was occupied, having a muted quarrel with my grandmother. The latter, despite her annoyance with my uncle's nostalgia for Egypt, supported his view that it was better for me to "get lost" and go back to Egypt, and my mother couldn't stand her talking that way. Apparently the quarrel escalated, and my mother was struck a blow with something in my grandmother's hand. My uncle and I heard a thud, followed by a muted cry of pain, after which we all fell silent.

My mother came in, a tray of tea in her hands, her face livid with fury, a fresh bruise above her right eyebrow. My grandfather never noticed; my uncle, on the other hand, took in the bruise with a fleeting glance, but held his tongue to avoid complicating matters.

My grandfather took the cup of tea from my mother's hand, took a sip, and pronounced, "Tasteless. Where did you buy it?"

She offered no answer, and he didn't wait for one. He turned to my uncle and asked if he visited his sister Bella; Shamoun answered that he didn't see her any more. Grandfather shook his head, saying, "Oh, well . . ." After a moment, he asked me to go to the kitchen and bring him a pinch of the nutmeg he'd bought yesterday.

When I came back, he placed it under his tongue, saying, "Got to get a better taste in my mouth, wash out your mother's disgusting tea."

She looked at him.

He started to talk about a dream he'd had, forgetting about the tarboosh and the picture of Abu Haseera. He said that his Great-grandfather Ezra had come to him in a dream, sauntering up in a wide white gallabiya, hiding something behind his back; Grandfather had run to his great-grandfather, believing it to be a bag of sweets like those he used to buy for him in the good old days, but it turned out to be a broom of rough brown fiber; he brought it down on my grandfather's head, then spat on him.

He asked us what the dream might mean. Each of us said something, and he listened, irritated by our narrow perceptions. When we were done, he said that we were all ignorant, that we knew nothing about the interpretation of dreams. The whole point, said he, was that his Great-grandfather Ezra was incensed with him because he had left his homeland.

My uncle threw up his hands in astonishment. "How would he know we left Egypt? He's been dead for a good seventy years!"

My grandfather looked at him in amazement. "Know? Know, you say? If he didn't know, why would he have come and shamed me in my dream? Of course he knows!" After which, overtaken by a sense of grandeur, he started to chain-smoke and told story after story, all sixty years old or more, dating from his days as an apprentice at Susu Mizrahi's store in Muski. He'd start with an anecdote, then segue into another, leaving the first unfinished and at its climax. When any of us would call his attention to the fact, or to any error he'd made in place names, street names, or dates, he would fall silent for a few moments, staring us in the face, then say, "Ah, yes . . . just be patient with me," and start the first story all over again, as we yawned, my uncle the most bored of us all.

My mother took the opportunity of a pause in his speech, as he was occupied with dusting off a chunk of cigarette ash that had fallen into his lap, to tell him, in a rush: "Let's stick to what's important, Dad. I know how much Galal means to you. I'm asking you to help him finish his university education here." He craned his neck lower, inclining his head toward her. She went on, in a low, shy voice: "Medicine, I mean, or architecture."

My uncle was the one to speak. "University, *here?* Medicine? Architecture? Either you're living in a dream world, or you have no idea what you're talking about!"

"You stay out of this, Shamoun!" she screamed at him.

But my grandfather, who was truly in a tight spot, motioned for her to quiet down and hear my uncle out. "Listen to me, Coucou! Education isn't easy. It takes money, and it takes good French, and it takes all sorts of other things. It's a huge undertaking, much too big for any of us to handle."

They argued for a while, until finally my uncle yelled at her, "Will you please wake up and admit to your limitations? Do you think your son's from the Sawaris dynasty, or perhaps a grandson of Qattawi Pasha? Dad's a poor man, he's just getting by as it is!"

My grandfather had lowered his head, stealing glimpses.

My grandmother leaned out of the kitchen door, in support of my Uncle Shamoun. "So you want him in medical school, do you now, Coucou? I hope you drop dead, and him too, at the same time! And just tell us, apple of your mother's eye, who's got the money to pay for him, huh? It's not like we've got anything to our name. Tell her, Zaki! Why don't you speak up?"

My eyes crept without my volition to my uncle's dirty olive pants, his worn tennis shoes, and his cheap, many-pocketed sweater; Amm Tolba, the street sweeper back home, came to my mind, in his ragged government-issue uniform, sweeping our old street in Daher.

I imagined myself holding a broom too, following in the footsteps of these two great street sweepers.

Chapter 6

My grandfather took to going out.

When winter came, he would either be in his room, reading his Torah, cross-legged on his bed, or sitting on his favorite chair in the hall, smoking and leafing through old magazines or the Egyptian newspapers that some people kindly donated to us—Rachel, sometimes, or Uncle Shamoun, especially if we were at the beginning of the month. If someone came to visit with something to read about Egypt, my grandfather would take it from him.

He'd grow bored; casting aside whatever he'd been reading, he'd start to yawn. This was the prelude to his dozing off repeatedly for a number of short naps, which would take him through till lunchtime. Between naps he'd stop anyone who passed by, asking about anything and everything: the wall clock, thinking it was out of order, whereupon the answer would come that it was working fine; it was only the second hand that wasn't working, and the pendulum, which, "as you know, is broken." My grandfather would nod his agreement. Every member of the household had been subjected to this question before. I had been asked it twice: once a few days after I returned, and another two months after.

He might also ask about a smell of burning that reached his nostrils, or jerk up out of his naps, rubbing his eyes and calling for us to open the door. "The doorbell didn't ring!" we'd say. "We didn't hear it."

He would accuse us of deafness and get up himself to open the door, finding no one there. He would return, astonished, saying: "Strange! I heard it with my own two ears!" We wouldn't say anything.

He'd fall into a doze; a little while later, he'd awake, asking about the sound coming from the kitchen, thinking it was coming from a cat playing in the pots and pans. "There are no cats in the house," we'd say. "It's the wind coming in from the kitchen window, moving around the empty pots and pans."

"Close it."

"The handle's broken," we'd tell him.

He would fall silent, feeling in his pocket, then ask for a matchbox. We'd point it out to him; it would have slipped behind the seat cushion, a corner of it protruding.

If he found nothing to say, he would ask whoever was passing him where they were going. "To the bathroom!"

"The bathroom!" he would reply. "Ah. Well. All right, then."

And he would stare after them till the bathroom door closed behind them.

On very cold days, he would shut himself in his room after lunch, and sleep for ages. He would only wake up if we woke him to have dinner with us. We would notice how puffy his eyes were from too much sleep, and say, "He'll surely be awake all night." But he'd have dinner and surprise us all by going to bed before we did.

A whole week passed with us watching him wake early and get ready to go out. To look at him, you'd have thought he was going to the land of the Eskimos; pants of the heavy wool we call "soldiers' wool" in Egypt, with cotton long johns underneath; a jersey underneath his shirt and another over it, then a waterproof jacket of artificial leather over that, and then, over it all, an overcoat!

That coat, I swear to God, was an artifact in its own time; it had no equal, either in its extreme length, like the coats of the mounted police or the rural caretakers of the Egyptian countryside, or in the style of its breast, or the cut of its shoulders. I would not believe for a moment, no matter what fervent oaths anyone swore, that its brother was to be found anywhere in Paris. It must have been a relic of the World War—the First, not the Second. Its original color was impossible to discern; it may have been black at one time, or perhaps slate gray, with a cheap fur collar now threadbare and rough as a loofah. My grandfather complained of it, saying, "It pricks like nails!"

As if that wasn't enough, he'd reach out and draw a woolen scarf off the coatrack, winding it about his neck, and then place a dark blue beret on his head. And out he'd go.

After a time, he'd come back, hungry, with a copy of *Al-Ahram* under his arm. If his food wasn't prepared immediately, he'd get impatient and raise his voice. My grandmother would ask him where he'd been, and he'd hide his resentment of the question behind repeated coughs, and then become preoccupied with trivial things. She would ask again, and he'd mutter, "Errands."

"Did you drop by the bank on your way?" she'd ask.

"Yes," he'd reply ungraciously, "and nothing's arrived from Isaac yet." After a beat of silence: "Rachel's the same. She transferred in a check for two thousand."

"Bless her."

"Right, I'm going in for a nap."

"But your meal?"

"Where's Galal, then?"

"Downstairs, with Sheikh Mud."

"Sheikh Mud, I'm sick of him."

"Your lunch?"

"Ah! Lunch. What's for lunch?"

"Okra with meat and tomato sauce."

"Bring me some, quick!"

After savoring his lunch slowly, with great enjoyment, he'd start his regular routine: lying down on the couch, he chain-smoked until his bowels started to move. Then he would leap up, asking my grandmother to fetch him the tin box with the enema apparatus, snatching it out of her hand as he hurried into the toilet.

Rachel finally graced us with her presence, after a long absence. Tight jeans, a white silk blouse with raised embroidery on the chest, finished off with a dark blue Dior jacket. She cut an eye-catching, if boyish, figure, and she was fun to be with. If she'd had her hair straightened, she'd have been hard to resist.

She wanted to spend the day with us. "Now that fall is over, there are fewer people in Paris. There's not much work until the New Year. Happy New Year in advance! The Gulf Arabs have gone, and they won't be back till the beginning of summer. Not many people are coming in for Christmas, and most of those are from the Levant or from Egypt."

"Be careful of those people, Rachel," my grandmother warned her, "and watch out for yourself." It was understood that she was warning her to guard her virginity against sexual predators. Despite my many reservations about my grandmother, she was an upright woman who didn't like loose behavior and wouldn't stand for any immorality. If she glimpsed a steamy scene on television, she would turn it off, cursing the actress and the actor and the director and anyone else involved, perhaps even including President Valéry Giscard d'Estaing himself. What she was absolutely crazy about, what made her boil inside like a ball of fire, was action movies and wrestling matches, where two muscular men faced off and beat each other without mercy.

"Be careful of what, Grandmother?" Rachel replied. "They're the ones who should be careful of me. I'm a tour guide and I do respectable work. Service for money, that's all."

"Still, be careful. They're not to be trusted, especially the ones from the Gulf. They pretend butter wouldn't melt in their mouths, but they're bold as brass!"

"No, no, Granny. There are a lot of good people. The ones who do want more, well, I can deal with them." She put on the character of the old actor Tawfik al-Deqen, and making her voice low-pitched, she repeated his famous line, "Honor, there's nothing sweeter!"

I turned my head toward her, stunned. She just said, "I adore Arab movies, Gel-gel! Every couple of days I turn on the video and watch a film or two. Did you think I was a Frenchwoman? I'm an Egyptian all the way back to my great-grandfather!" She threw her head back and reached an arm out in the cliché pose of Egyptian fishwives from the streets. "I'm Rachel, as God is my witness!" She said it exactly like the girls in films and on TV.

She asked to borrow a housedress from my mother, putting it on inside and then reemerging wearing it. It was light blue and came down to her feet, with long sleeves and a high collar; despite all this modesty and decency, it was slit up the side to mid-thigh. My grandmother, seeing it, yelled angrily at Rachel: "What's this indecency! Take it off at once! Don't you see your cousin among us?" And she took my mother to task. "And you, Coucou, are you a young girl, to wear such things?"

My mother shrank a little into herself. "Yes, I think you're right. I'll get rid of it. Throw it away, even."

The problem was solved with another dress; Rachel took the seat by my mother, leaning her head over to her, and they conversed in whispers about my Aunt Bella, who had had it with her husband. Rachel said softly, her eye on her grandmother, who was coming from her room with a box of smelling salts in her hand, "He'll stay away all day, sometimes for two days, and nobody knows where he goes. And sometimes he has Negro visitors from Africa, with kinky hair and chains around their necks and their wrists. They come in carrying packages and they leave carrying packages, and they look like criminals."

My mother listened.

"Why, he once came home to Mom in the wee hours, with two men holding him up! He was limping, poor guy, and he'd taken such a punch to the nose—it kept him crying for a whole month!"

My mother looked uneasy, and she made a noise with her lips. "And that's not all, Auntie—he's found himself a woman, from Tunisia! He spent a week with her in Nice, running around and playing, and Mom was here weeping and wailing!" Rachel lowered her voice even further, saying that her mother had said that if her grandmother wasn't crazy, she'd have come and complained and asked for her help.

The whispering stopped when a muffled whistle issued from my grandmother's nose. She'd just finished sniffing a pinch of smelling salts into both nostrils, and the dose must have been higher than usual, inflaming her upper respiratory system and making her eyes tear up. In spite of this, she'd heard everything Rachel had told my mother.

Fanning her nose to ease the burning, she said, "Where does he go, girl? Where does he go, Mr. Greasy-Shirt, the son of Freiha Effendi? And what was that you were saying about his nose? It's like the Sphinx's nose: if they keep punching at it from here till tomorrow, nothing's going to happen to it!"

Rachel's eyes flickered across my face, and I likewise stole a glance at her. She had gone pale with shame about what had been said about her father and grandfather, Freiha Effendi. She didn't dare answer back to my grandmother, though, for she knew what might happen to her if she tried. She bit her lip in frustration, and tried to change the subject, telling my mother that she'd be coming by tomorrow to take her to the rue de Rivoli, as C&A had just opened a branch there, and they were offering up to 50 percent off on the occasion of the opening.

My grandmother, though, insistent on following the news of her son-in-law, shouted at her, "Where does he go, the buffalo? Where does he go? Talk!"

"Oh, Granny. I told you before, the Tunisian girl's turned his head. It looks like he goes to her."

"A plague on Tunisia and everyone from Tunisia. I know all about them! One of them is called Sheikh Mud, and he makes our life miserable here in our own building, and here there's another one from Tunisia making my daughter bitter over there! Just wait till Zaki gets here. I'll take him and we'll go to your father's, and I'll have a thing or two to say to Mr. Elephant-Trunk!"

Rachel's irritation with my grandmother grew; she was upset by the appellation 'Elephant-Trunk,' but what could she do? She knew she was dealing with a rash, reckless grandmother, a grandmother whom no one could control, her constitution iron although she was approaching eighty, who could leap upon her if she said something that was not to her liking, and sit on her and smack her senseless, or throw anything at her that happened to be in her hand, even if it were a sharp object, a scissors, or a saucepan lid. So she held her peace. Trying to close the subject without any trouble, she asked my grandmother not to worry, and even kissed her head, saying, to reassure her, that if her father's treatment of her mother continued, she would take her mother to live with her in her apartment in St. Germain.

"What-what-what-what-what? Leave her apartment and live with you? Leave the new apartment to Freiha's boy so he can have it all to himself, him and his slut?"

Realizing it was no use, as my grandmother wanted to keep the subject wide open and jam the doors, and Rachel had no energy to talk to her, she took her leave. I walked her to her car; as usual, she took the initiative and kissed me. It wasn't the usual sisterly kiss on both cheeks; she kissed me on the mouth. She even pinched my arm teasingly, before flying off in her car.

We found out where my grandfather had been going.

About an hour after Rachel had left, he came home to us, exhausted like all the other times. He ate and drank, and smoked two cigarettes, then disappeared into the bathroom with the enema tin, emerging contentedly a while later.

We told him that Rachel had been to visit; he paid us no mind. When my grandmother told him what she had said about her father, he warned her against going to see Elephant-Trunk, for he was ill-bred, as she knew. He, my grandfather, would take care of things his own way. In any case, he didn't put much stock in the words of a silly girl like Rachel.

To me and my mother, he said that after calling in favors and much pleading with our Jewish relatives, he had secured a job for me in a fabric store.

My mother's head slumped.

"It's respectable work, Camellia," he said. "Galal will meet people, make money, learn the language." When she remained silent, his voice grew more tender. "Don't worry, Umm Galal. Believe me when I tell you that Galal is dearer to me than you, and Shamoun, and even absent Isaac. Why, I'm the one who raised him, and every day I watched him grow before my eyes." His voice faltered. "All my children are grown and self-sufficient. He's the only one left. I don't want to worry about him. This thing with his education, I haven't forgotten about it! Let's just be patient, and God will provide."

I bent and kissed his hand, and he let me, enjoying the gesture, then pulled my head to his chest and smoothed my hair with his hand. When the access of emotion had run its course, the phrase "Umm Galal" that my grandfather had used rang in my ears. Here they called her Coucou—my grandmother, my uncle, my aunt, and all our new acquaintances. When my grandfather had called her by her old name, Umm Galal, he whisked me back to Daher in the blink of an eye, and I couldn't help thinking of my second mother, Umm Hassan, when she would come over to our place in her housedress and invite us to iftar on the first day of Ramadan. She'd finish her invitation with, "Don't you dare stay home, Umm Galal, or I'll be upset and that won't do!" Sometimes she would come to our place, bearing trays of cakes for Eid, and there were other times, so many of them. I felt a pang; I had left Egypt without saying goodbye to her, and here I still hadn't written her so much as a line.

That night, before I fell asleep, I daydreamed of Rachel. In my bed, in my thoughts, I dared to do with her what I didn't have the courage to do awake. While I lay there, I didn't think of the new job I was about to start, didn't think of my grandfather's promises of further education. I thought only of Rachel's body. I did not think of Nadia that night, nor for many nights after that.

Chapter 7

My mother insisted I go to bed early.

"Your mother's right, Galal," my grandfather said. "Off to bed with you, dear boy. First day at work, you've got to be bright and full of energy!"

I didn't sleep, though. I lay in bed awake, thinking of this new burden that lay before me. Early the next morning, I would have to go out and make a living and support myself, as my grandmother said.

Starting tomorrow, I would become a shop boy in a fabric store. Although there was still an idea, a remnant in my head, a thought of going to college . . . "although," indeed! I must rub it out with an eraser: my grandfather's promises were nothing but words . . . words and empty hopes.

A shop boy!

It was foreign to my ears; it had never occurred to me before. The price for staying by my mother's side, God forgive her, was abandoning my country and my university and the beautiful world I had been looking forward to, to become one of the boys who make their living in stores and stalls. I might even fail to satisfy my superiors and get kicked out, like what happened to Uncle Shamoun, and have no choice but to pick up a broom and push it through the streets and alleyways. Like uncle, like nephew. Or maybe clean toilets like the minorities and the black Africans—or I might take a liking to underground life, become a *clochard*,* and live on alms!

But talk is of no use any more . . .

In any case, this wasn't unusual for the graduates of our high school, especially Class 13. Didn't Khawaga Marcus Effendi, the vice-principal of our school, tell us one day when we asked him that he didn't recall a single graduate of Class 13 who'd been blessed with the chance to go to college? For decades, Class 13 graduates filled the streets. They were laundrymen and grocers and salesmen in feseekh stores, while some had made quite a name for themselves in illegal trade.

Well, Marcus Effendi, you can add to your spiel that one of the Class 13 grads once got high grades, high enough to make a doctor of him, only he'd refused and gone away to the land of the Franks—not to worry, don't let your imagination run wild! He's like the rest of you after all, loyal to the cause: a salesman in a fabric store.

When my grandfather sat us down with him and told us what he'd arranged for me, my mother was the one who bowed her head, while I let the words just slip by. I didn't speak a word, a syllable . . . silence! My face remained impassive, unconcerned, as though the conversation was about someone else. All I could think about was Rachel's kiss. Her ripe body stirred things within me, not things of the spirit, but physical, animal things, buried deep within me. It's not that I was unfamiliar with these sensations—I am a man, after all—but my heart had been postponing them, shunting them aside. Nadia and I had been preoccupied with days to come, not with the brief bursts of pleasure brought by joining bodies. I was lost in her soul, not her breasts; captivated by her keen, soulful eyes, not her waist and shapely legs. We were not concerned with orgasms, but with a full-dimensioned life, with aspirations, with children

---

* *Clochard* is a French word for the homeless who live in the Métro underground, making their home on subway platforms. They generally wear stinking rags, shouting, drinking, and trading insults, and occasionally breaking into fights that cause an unbearable din.

and grandchildren. A life in which, when I took her in my arms, I would be seeking her tenderness, the comfort and sanctuary of her embrace. When I saw her tongue-tied, I still knew she was speaking, and when she noticed that I wasn't talking, she heard what I had to say without words.

We talked and dreamed, never knowing that the world was conspiring against us. . . .

Now Rachel had landed out of the blue, returning me to my primitive state in which there were Male and Female. I stayed that way for two days, or maybe three, never coming out of it until they said to me, "Off to bed with you, for tomorrow you shall become a shop boy!" What a dizzy, immature boy I was!

I did nothing. I didn't think, or even dream, of a miracle to come and rescue me before it was too late, a miracle to lift me back onto the bird of good fortune headed back to Egypt, to sit me in my empty seat at Dimerdash Medical School. I remained silent and quiescent, distracted by the fullness of Rachel's calves, and her breasts that invited me to steal a glance, following their motions whenever she bent or leaned over.

Wasn't I pitiful? All I deserved was to accept my fate in silence, like the widows and orphans.

But even if I did accept it, I didn't speak the language, which might have been a help; nor did I even know anyone in this strange land, except for Sheikh Munji al-Ayyari, and a few of my mother's relatives, and the street we lived in and one or two others. . . . This was all I knew, and now I was required to enter the ranks of the working class, to become one of the struggling proletariat.

From the moment I went to bed until the night enveloped me, I felt I was on a precipice, the edge of something . . . something devouring. One step and my foot would slip, and I would fall into it, into a dark and no doubt deadly void. A new world awaited me. A world without anatomy books and stethoscopes, with bales of fabric to carry to and fro on my shoulders, and "Come here, boy!" "Go there, boy!" and "Now look what you've done, boy!" A dry, coarse world where I would wake at the crack of dawn and rush to the Métro so as not to get a harsh rebuke or an angry stare from Mr. So-and-So. I would become one of the people on the margins, the riffraff, the helpless and powerless who filled the Barbès-Rochechouart Station at this early hour, knowing nothing of fashion and etiquette, kicking and elbowing as they swarmed onto the train, choked with the sweat and odors that practically clawed at the nose, giving lie to the thought that you are in the City of Light and Perfume!

And at the end of the month, my salary, no doubt small. To cover my clothing, my food and drink, and so month would follow month, and no room to grow, as I advanced in age.

Dear God!

I was lost that night, pitiable, the part of me called Hope officially dead. I was afraid of something about to pounce on me. Something cold, something heartless, something called the Future, the coming days and nights. Something hateful and gloomy, with no pity for the weak, with iron claws that would lock about my ankles, denying all hope of escape. Something that you are aware of, although it cannot be felt by the senses. You think it distant, yet it silently draws near! I was aware, fully aware, that I was more hopeless and pitiable than poor Uncle Shamoun.

As the old proverb says, misery loves company: in this case, the company of other unpleasant memories. The old troubles: the ignorant, accursed boys who would refuse to play with me and taunt me over my mother's religion, both in our neighborhood and at school. The humiliations and the fights. Nadia, whom they thought too good for me.

I felt my eyes prickling with tears—a sour combination of my profound resentment against this world, and the bitterness that floated in my veins. It felt like something in my blood, impeding my circulation, stagnant, glutinous; while my body remained still, inert. It produced resentment and hatred, I know not of whom. Hatred of myself for refusing to leave when I had the chance, of my mother for seducing me back, chaining me to her by the ankles? Of my mother's entire people, here and everywhere, garnering suspicion and wariness everywhere they go? Of my father, perhaps, for dying, for abandoning me. . . .

Wouldn't my father have done better to look to his lessons and his study? His own father, Sheikh Abdel Hameed al-Minshawy, had sent my father off to law school to become a lawyer or a judge. He ought to have spent the whole day in the classroom, listening to his professors and lecturers! He should have devoured his books to make his father's dream come true! Studied day and night, and quit this foolishness! But no, what did he do instead? Romance! Love! Marriage! Ensnared by the charms of a beautiful Jewess, he fell in love with her and she with him and now I was paying the price! Better if they'd never met and I were deferred—God knows where!

Chapter 8

As luck would have it, I didn't get to go to Bouchard's Fabrics the next day; Paris was hit by a killer cold wave. My grandfather said, "We can wait till the weather improves. Old Bouchard's isn't going anywhere."

The snow fell like butterflies, tirelessly, with the temperature at ten below zero. The thunder had its way with us at night; my mother and I, especially, felt that we would never live to see another day. Naturally, we gave up going out of the house, or even getting out of bed, except for the essentials, namely, eating and going to the toilet. The heating was useless; each of us loaded up his or her body with all the clothing it could possibly carry. I wore three sets of underwear on top of each other and two jerseys, one a turtleneck, in addition to my pajamas and woolen socks, and then wrapped myself in a towel. The grand prize, though, had to go to my grandfather: he wore so many clothes that he ballooned out, looking like he was wearing a space suit.

It was an opportunity for him to gather us around him and tell us stories. He started out with one that occurred in his first youth, when he played defensive back for the Sakakini Youth Soccer Club. His team played an unknown team from the provinces on a pitch in a poorer area; Cairo had once been full of these. They played and played, the spectators screaming and cheering. The match ended with a painful 2-0 defeat for my grandfather's team. After the final whistle was blown, all the team members ganged up on my grandfather and showered him with blows and kicks, joined by some of the spectators, for his general incompetence in play, not to mention the fact that it was he who had inadvertently scored those two own goals!

Another story concerned his childhood in the city of Damanhour, when one of his companions threw a stone at a short-tailed dog that was known for its frequent barking. The dog chased them from street to street until my grandfather stumbled and fell onto the very edge of a manhole. Story followed story as we sat around him, teeth chattering, ceaselessly blowing on our nearly frozen hands, and hardly paying attention to what he said. It was my grandmother who reminded him that he had told her the Damanhour story at least seventy times before, and that he hadn't fallen onto the edge of a manhole as he said now, but had landed face-first in a garbage dump and gotten his head stuck in it, and been dug out of there with difficulty, and been a laughingstock that day. He retorted sharply and angrily that it had been a manhole and that she was making it up; after all, it was not plausible that she should know better than him what happened to him in his youth or childhood! He appealed to my mother and me, wringing his hands, and we nodded our assent. My face in particular showed my disapproval of Grandmother, crossing the line like that, making up false tales about God-fearing folk! His mood was changeable, though, and he would quickly grow bored with us, throwing us out of his room with the excuse that his head was heavy and he wanted to go to sleep.

On many nights, we would watch painful images on television, of what Nature was doing to people, in the form of weather-related automobile accidents on the southbound highways to Marseille and Toulouse, or the northbound route to Lille. We heard them saying on the news that a large truck had crashed into dozens of cars, scattering them this way and that. On the next report, they would tell us that the driver of an elephantine lorry had lost control, brakes useless on the ice, destroying the front of a gas station or a number of huts on the side of the road. And so it went every day, with the dead numbering in the dozens.

The sun disappeared completely, so we could no longer tell if it was day or night. Snow and ice covered practically everything: the cars, the buses, the Métro station entrances, the facades of cafés and shops; even the umbrellas over people's heads and their coats, waterproof or valuable fur. Snowflakes covered everything and piled up in drifts so high you didn't know if you were looking at something familiar or a cold, dead thing shrouded in white.

It was a killing frost, the like of which had not been seen in fifty years, or so they said. It was the topic of the hour, that fantastic beast called Nature, with the violent hand and the incontrovertible orders; indeed, in cafés and bars and sometimes on the radio and television stations, there would be debates between believers in God—and these were many—and atheists, Heaven protect us, as to who was the real author of this: Nature alone, or the Almighty?

Our hearts went out, in particular, to the *clochards*; more and more would be found dead every morning, frozen, on the edges of platforms, under arches, and in corners. The town council of Paris was obliged to establish emergency taskforces to give out blankets, food, and bottles of wine; they also opened up the subway stations for them to sleep in instead of in the open air.

When the cold had abated somewhat, my grandfather took me to Bouchard's. It was early, and I couldn't stop yawning, the cold stinging my ears. My grandfather was wearing *that* coat, and had taken all protective measures from scarf to beret to gloves. Steam flowed out of his mouth whenever he spoke or exhaled. We left the door of the building and headed with heavy steps to the Barbès Métro station, without a word. Grandfather seemed helpless. He'd failed to present me with any other choice, and now took refuge in silence. I was silent, too, like a lamb being dragged by the ear to the slaughterhouse; the time for speech was past. I thought then of the first day I went to primary school; I'd been as scared as I was now, looking like a cartoon character in clothes at least two sizes too big for me, with my grandfather walking by my side smiling and keeping up an unceasing flow of encouragement—not vacant and used-up, as I saw him now.

We went in through the door of the subway station. The crowds at this hour were at their peak—people running to work, life flowing gradually into the veins of Paris. Most of the passengers were simple people like us: low-level civil servants, craftsmen, and workers young and old. Their pace was fast, their shoulders broad, and their height impressive; they were impatiently looking out for the train's arrival, as though being on time for work was a matter of life and death for them. This hour of the morning was only for the dedicated; no place for loiterers, the lazy, or the unemployed. Schoolchildren, in clumps and clusters, added a note of cheer and fun to the platform; their faces free of any deceit or guile, their antics painting smiles on faces, occasionally causing laughter, reminding us of the delightful past. Smells and moisture and blasts of cold air squeezed in through the cracks, and escalators groaned under their human burdens.

The *clochards*, heaven protect us from their ilk—all covered up, nothing visible except a toe or perhaps a hand, and still asleep— were occasionally stepped on, or unintentionally kicked by some hurrying man's shoe. The victim would then jerk up out of his slumber, raining curses down upon the son of a so-and-so who had done such a thing, but the perpetrator would have already fled, swallowed up by the crowd.

The cleaning staff of this station, and most of the stations, consisted mainly of Arabs from North Africa, accompanied by Africans, Indians, and Portuguese; they were all busy removing the detritus of those dreadful *clochards*: empty wine bottles, some broken; paper cups; empty cigarette-boxes and tins; and things strewn about here and there. They seemed to avoid the spaces occupied by the *clochards*, fearful of waking them and starting trouble and fights at the beginning of the day. They preferred to leave them alone, sucking their lips disapprovingly or raining silent curses down upon them. This state of neither peace nor war between them would soon be upset should one of the workers discover that a *clochard* had decided to urinate or defecate in his place during the night instead of going to the toilet; said worker would then shout out to his colleagues, who would start to punish the *clochard* in question, insulting his mother and father and cursing at him, poking him with their brooms in the back and legs. When he opened his eyes in a panic, they would point out the evidence of his transgression in disgust.

Some of these Arab workers knew my grandfather; they would smile at him as soon as they saw him, along with some other Arab passengers. "Good trip, good trip," they'd say, or "Have a nice day," or "How are you doing, elder?" The answer would generally be "Fine, how are you?" or "Things are fine," or sometimes the well-known French phrase "*Ça va, ça va,*" which means, "Going well."

After speeding from one station to another, we finally emerged onto the surface again, into the Gare Saint-Lazare with its large basalt stones, spacious and filled with shops and two- or three-star hotels. The sky stayed gray, with scattered showers starting to fall. Despite this, the motion never stopped, and the water never gathered into puddles. The drains had built-in pumps that automatically drew the water inside. The cleaners appeared in their orange jumpsuits, bearing brooms of differing lengths and sizes, small devices, and flasks of corrosive liquid to remove the dirt clinging to the lip of the sidewalk.

Everyone wore coats and hats and carried umbrellas as they walked swiftly to work. Several of them were walking even faster than their fellows, almost running toward the Gare Saint-Lazare railway station, not to be confused with the one we had just emerged from; rather, this was a station to transfer people to distant suburbs such as Saint-Cloud and Versailles.

My grandfather and I turned into a café in the square and sat there having two cups of espresso and watching the people go by. When the rain stopped and a ray of sun appeared in the sky, we left. It was still early, so my grandfather suggested we take a little walk. We started at the rue de l'Arcade, a small street off the Place Saint-Lazare, where, off to the right, after a few steps, there is a modest three-story hotel named after the street. My grandfather made me stop outside this hotel and went inside, then hurried back out, complaining, "Your Uncle Saul is not a man of his word! He said he'd meet me, but he wasn't there! They said he'd be here at the end of the day."

"Do I have an Uncle Saul?" I said, stunned.

"Your maternal uncle, boy—your maternal uncle, your maternal uncle! True, you don't know him, but he's a distant relative, from your Aunt Esther's side, who . . ."

My grandfather was very precise about whether a man was your uncle on your mother's or your father's side. Everyone who was related to him on my mother's side was, in Arabic, a khal—maternal uncle—and could never be called amm—paternal uncle—as long as my father was a Muslim. The word khal for someone in my position meant that I and this khal shared a paternal bloodline. You see, I was a Jew, to my grandfather and other observant Jews, as long as I was born to one of them; Jewish, no matter how much I fasted in Ramadan or said Islamic prayers or even memorized the whole Quran. They had no truck with what was in my birth certificate, or my verbal or written protestations that I was a Muslim, a Muslim, a Muslim.

My grandmother and my mother believed the same, similarly deluded into thinking I was Jewish. On the other hand, Uncle Shamoun, Aunt Bella, and Rachel were more laid-back, and such things didn't matter to them.

The problem, as far as my grandmother was concerned, was that she didn't believe me to be a worthy grandson. She didn't see me as worthy of being related to her, and always said in private and public that the reason my mother hadn't made good was, first, because of the marriage she had made to my father, and second—and more important—that she had given birth to me, a thankless, useless child, and that the world would have been a better and more pleasant place for everyone if it hadn't been for me. The sticking point wasn't whether or not I was a Muslim—my Jewishness was firmly established in her mind, no matter what I said or did—but rather it was a matter of personal chemistry, and, as luck would have it, mine and hers were completely incompatible. For my part, I couldn't meet her revulsion with charitable forgiveness; perhaps, if I had done so, time would have dulled her resentment of me, and she might have accepted me. Instead, I did everything I could to spite her, insisting on doing all the things that filled her heart with rage and made her feelings toward me even blacker.

My grandfather kept on telling the tale of my Uncle Saul since his birth in Berket al-Ratl, a neighborhood near Daher, and up to his emigration to France directly after the Suez War and position as manager of the Hôtel de l'Arcade.

My grandfather was speaking, but I only heard one out of every ten of his words. From street to street we walked, passing Maxim's. The famous restaurant was still closed, two men darker than black coffee standing at the door in the restaurant's uniform, with its logo, looking at the passersby with a reserved expression, not—God's honest truth—a haughty look that bespoke the unworthiness of people like us to walk on the same sidewalk and so much as look at where our betters dined! Another step or two and we arrived at the Église de la Madeleine. The church was closed too; heaven preserve us, it was cold, chilly, nay, freezing! The priests and curates were doubtless fast asleep under the covers, "eating rice pudding with the angels," as we Egyptians say! The only one there was an old woman in raggedy red and black, her face adorned with loud makeup, a large straw hat on her head. I think she might have been a female *clochard*, and one who liked to relax as well: she was listening to soothing music that emanated from a transistor radio in her lap, her eyes dreamily fixed on the cloud of smoke rising from the cigarette in her fingers, utterly heedless of the two security men urging her politely to remove herself from this place where tourists congregate.

Our feet took us to Havre Street, then to Aubert, then Londres Street. When my grandfather felt we had gone far enough, he took us back by a shortcut.

"Are you sure, Grandfather," I said to him, "that they're going to give me a respectable job, not one of *those* jobs?"

"You mean sweeping and mopping and that kind of thing? No, no, is that any job for people like us? I've got your Uncle Saul's promise that you'll be a salesman, and that's no small matter!"

"So Uncle Saul is the one who . . . ?"

"Whoever else? Isn't he your uncle, your own flesh and blood?"

I nodded, giving in. "And what does this store sell, Grandfather? Cotton batting and castour and eyelash lace and that kind of thing?"

"Bless your soul, what are you talking about? Castour and batting, indeed! They don't sell that stuff here! Use the brains God gave you! Why, this is the very heart of the city, the classiest neighborhood there is! Those things you'll find in the stores behind the Sacré-Coeur, or in the alleys of Barbès or in Le Châtel. Not here, Galal! Bouchard is a big-time fabric trader—all you'll find there are expensive furs and silks and satins and ladies' evening fabrics, all the things the high-class folk wear."

We were nearly at the Place de l'Opéra; it appeared before us with its historic building, and immediately Alexandre Dumas' *The Three Musketeers* popped into my head. I came to know the Opéra de Paris from that novel, having bought it—in translation—for a few piasters from Azbakiya. He described the Opéra from outside and in: its staircases, its pillars, its great auditorium, the royal box where Louis XIII sat surrounded by his retinue in their loose cloaks, their large hats and shoes with pointed toes, and the schemes engineered by the crafty Cardinal Richelieu to ruin the Queen, foiled at the last moment by the brave musketeer D'Artagnan, who risked life and limb to pull victory from the jaws of defeat.

Dumas described it with quick phrases, and I filled in the rest with my imagination, creating an Opéra quite different from the one before me now. An Opéra made by myself, for myself alone! With auditoriums grander than those described by Dumas, and domes, and a musical chorus in embroidered clothing, and a scowling, somber king sitting in his box, and a crafty cardinal stealing glances through narrowed eyes with all of France in the palm of his hand. With costumes and movement and whispers and tension, and a Queen with a worried expression and a beautiful neck. . . . All things woven by my little-boy imagination, woven without haste, remaining alive in my memory until now, as though they had actually taken place, as though I had seen them in reality and not in my imagination.

Nadia suddenly crossed my mind.

Perhaps it was because of the girl crossing the street in front of me with a scarf on her head. I don't know why she would have reminded me of her, though: Nadia didn't cover her hair with a scarf! Was it because she was holding her bag to her chest the way Nadia used to carry her schoolbag? Perhaps.

She came and cast a pall over my heart. I hadn't smelled her perfume or seen her in my mind's eye for days, not since my urges were diverted toward Rachel.

Damn Rachel! And damn the opera! Damn everything!

What have I to do with the opera? What have I to do with France in the first place? I was infatuated with it as a boy, dreaming of what I read in the words of characters in books: Cosette, Jean Valjean, Esmeralda, Cyrano de Bergerac, and Quasimodo, the poor hunchback . . . I learned what they said by heart, and added to it from my imagination and took away what I pleased . . . and dreamed.

I had loved Paris when it stood dumb, knowing nothing of me. But when I came to it, it took away Nadia and gave me Rachel!

And as if that wasn't enough, it recommended me for a menial job, because being a shop boy in a store is hardly better than a servant.

My grandfather took me by the hand suddenly, shaking me with an ecstatic expression. "You know, young Galal, I walked the soles of my shoes off in Opera Square!" Afraid I'd misunderstand, he added loudly, "Not this Opera Square! The Opera Square in Cairo! See, there was a place that sold spare parts for watches behind the Khazendar Mosque, and I was always going back and forth to that store by way of Opera Square. I'd look and there the booksellers would be packed, packed, along the fence of the Azbakiya Garden, and the people, masses, masses of people, Galal! 'How much is this book, man?' 'Five piasters, sir!' 'How about that one over there?' 'Ten piasters, Hajj!' 'And this one here?' 'Those are the Pocket-Books sir, one for two piasters, two for three piasters, and four for five piasters!' And the way they'd say, 'Just stand over to one side, sir, take your time looking through the books.'"

He took a moment to get his breath back. "And the statue of Ibrahim Pasha!" He repeated to me the story of our great-grandfather, who worked as a teller in the holdings of Ibrahim Pasha, and traveled by sea with his coworkers to Italy to undertake a census of his properties there. . . .

"You mean Greece, not Italy, Grandfather," I said.

"Greece! Greece, of course! What do you mean, Italy? Why aren't you concentrating and listening properly to what I say? Really, now!" Silence, then a sigh, long and wistful, before he returned to the silence that had claimed him ever since we set foot outside the door of our building. We walked for a while, each lost in his own thoughts.

He stopped suddenly. "Where are we?" He looked around him, astonished. "Goodness gracious! Isn't that Haussmann Street? Yes, yes it is! Why, that means we've gone past Bouchard's!"

He turned back, looking for it, and his eyes danced with childish joy as he pointed: "There!"

Patting me kindly on the shoulder, he told me the name of the man to whom I was to introduce myself.

When I walked into the store, I felt like my legs wouldn't hold me.

I asked shyly after Monsieur René, who turned out to be the manager. They showed me into his office.

He scrutinized me unhurriedly, then invited me to take a seat. He spoke slowly so that I would understand him, and when I spoke to him in my stumbling French, he seemed to understand some of what I said. He called for a towering Lebanese man called Akram Abul Shawareb, and handed me over to him.

Several months passed. My French improved daily, and I learned the skills of salesmanship and the ins and outs of the trade.

Chapter 9

I was just coming back from Bouchard's, when, turning toward the house, I glimpsed Sheikh Munji sitting on a chair outside his shop, his legs stretched out before him. On a chair opposite him sat one of his customers, an African with a printed shawl around his head, in a flowing abaya with a satin ribbon around the neckline and the sleeve openings, and multicolored ribbons adorning the chest. Such a comical garment! And he wasn't even sitting up straight, but curved sideways in his chair, swinging his age-worn sandal from the arch of his foot—the thing had a rusty buckle, to say nothing of the broken rear strap. And the way he spoke, heaven preserve us! Haughty, with his nose in the air, as though he was one of Africa's patriarchs, her great elders.

I knew him.

His name was Abdou Lahi Mamadou, and he was unusually, shockingly tall. He was a plumber with the sanitation department by profession, and I had never seen him before without his dark-blue jumpsuit and his knee-high rubber boots, which always made me think of the old tale of the genie who came out of the bottle. I had always been surprised at him, for I had never seen him going to work without being in a huge rush, looking at his watch every two minutes as though he had a weighty responsibility to fulfill. During breaks, he was always fighting with the street urchins, who loved to tease him, or standing before the street vendors, contemplating their wares and scratching his head.

It was sale season. Bouchard's was a hive of activity, and I was exhausted, my head ringing like there was a train-whistle going off in it, so I had no desire to walk toward Sheikh Munji and this Mamadou. I waved at them in passing and made for the door of our building, but the sheikh stopped me. "Galal! Come over here, my boy."

Something in the rhythm of his voice worried me. It was vacant, distressed, lacking all its usual fire and ringing timbre. I went to him and he rose to greet me, sadness showing on his face. The Mamadou moved backward, looking me up and down as though I were a thumb joint, or something not human at all.

I was jolted by his visage. I had not thought his face so unkind, his nose so broad and spatulate. I did not hide from him my distaste at the sight of the two discolored front teeth in his upper jaw, which had been gold, but were now covered with rust, or at the scar that still covered a major portion of his neck. No doubt someone had deliberately splashed him with acid or burned him because of some deed he had done!

He, too, examined me at leisure and looked away from me in distaste, then pulled a handkerchief as big as a baby blanket out of his garment, and took to blowing his nose in it with such a din, louder than a trumpet, that Sheikh Munji looked disgusted and looked at him sharply as if to admonish him to cease what he was doing.

The sheikh asked me to get myself a chair from inside. I did, and as soon as I sat down, he said, "Don't you know what's happened, my boy?"

Mamadou took to blowing his nose even more violently, then spat out a glob of spittle at the feet of the sheikh, who exploded.

"What is it with that mouth of yours? What's in there, damn you, an airplane engine or a donkey braying? Go fix it somehow. Go find a doctor instead of harming those around you. What is this, for God's sake?"

Meanwhile, I was staring into space, wondering what had happened that the sheikh was asking me about. The first thing that came to mind was that my grandmother had broken the truce again, and attacked the sheikh himself, or had lain in wait for his wife, Sitt Zahira Bu Saf, on the landing and hit her on the head with her stick, carrying out the vow she had made the day of the cat incident. Instinctively, I scanned the sheikh's face, neck, and wrists for the impressions of my grandmother's scratches, while he leaned over and said, unhappily, "He's done it, he's gone and done it! May he never be blessed, may God never forgive him."

"He?" My confusion increased. The only member of our household who could conceivably cause trouble with the sheikh was my grandmother! If it wasn't her, but a 'he,' then there must have been some sort of mix-up! My grandfather couldn't have 'done' whatever the sheikh had in mind! He couldn't have done anything! My grandfather was pretty ineffective, and he'd never be so impulsive as to throw himself into harm's way like that. He knew how puny our resources were next to this ogre of a sheikh. So, to resolve the matter beyond any doubt, I said to him with bemusement, "My grandfather did something? My grandfather minds his own business, sir! He wouldn't even—"

He cut me off. "Your grandfather! What's your grandfather got to do with anything? That one, he just sits there like a sheep. We're not talking about that grandfather of yours." He dusted his hands off in disbelief, clapping them loudly as he did so, as though to absolve himself of the deed which he was bemoaning. "Sadat, my boy! Sadat's the one who's done it!"

"Sadat?" I asked him, stunned. "Sadat who? Sadat, our president?"

"Yes, my boy, Sadat. I heard today on France-Trois that he's off to Israel! All packed and ready to go to Israel! Who'd ever have thought it?"

"Israel."

"Yes, indeed! Israel!" He dusted his hands off in disbelief again, face bursting with indignation. "Is it possible, O Prophet? Can this be? I swear to God, I didn't believe the news at first. And the bastards here, applauding and cheering and saying how daring a step it is! A brave step! What's the world coming to, everyone? When this Sadat goes off to Israel, it doesn't mean he went all alone. All of Egypt went with him. And not just Egypt, but the Arabs and the Muslims. Can this be? God damn the unjust, one and all."

He leaned toward me, his hand trembling unsteadily before my nose, fingers splayed, and said in hushed tones: "And you know who's meeting him at the airport? Menachem Begin!" He bowed his head after he said it, Mamadou looking down at him curiously.

"Did you say Menachem Begin?"

"Yes . . . Menachem Begin!"

When Mamadou joined in the conversation, Sheikh Munji spoke to him in French. They spoke together for a long time, raining down curses on the Jews, and Golda Meir, and Levi Eshkol, and Yigal Allon, and Shimon Peres, and anyone who had ever extended a helping hand to Israel. However, I noticed that the sheikh seemed uncomfortable with the man's company and wanted to end it, which he did; he closed the conversation by shouting at him, irritation plain on his face: "And just what has Theodor Herzl got to do with Sadat visiting Israel! True, he's a major Zionist, but he's been dead for more than seventy years, you ass. How can you say that he's still alive and living in a villa on the outskirts of Tel Aviv, and that he's controlling everything and that it's he who issued the invitation to Sadat to visit him and stay with him there in Israel? Have you no brain?" He turned to me angrily. "God, spare me! Why does no bolt of lightning come from the sky to remove this donkey from my sight?"

The sheikh leaped out of his seat when he caught sight of a lady customer coming into the shop, leaving me and Mamadou face to face.

I smiled at him, but he ignored it; he looked at me with dislike, sticking out his lower lip. It was clear that he had his own views, and that he was not comfortable with this visit. What worried me was that he seemed to want to involve me in a matter like this that was the province of heads of state. For my part, I was careful not to engage him in conversation during the sheikh's absence: I knew this Mamadou well, and I wasn't a match for him—he was street-smart, a professor of fighting and screaming in every known language: French, Swahili, Arabic sometimes—and that's not counting the rude gestures! He was a true master: able to insult and deride with fingers and tongue and parts I didn't even want to think about! But what could I do?

He gritted his teeth as he scratched himself with his fingernails, digging deep into the coarse hair at the sides of his face, then called my name loudly, although the distance between us could be measured in inches: "Zalal. You, boy, Zalal."

No sooner had I looked at him than he screamed at me in Swahili, waving both hands in my face—if not for the grace of God, he might have poked my eye out with a finger! Of course I didn't understand a single syllable of what he was saying! All I did was scoot my chair back a little bit to put more space between us—who knows what this black giant might do? And his fists were the size of camel's hooves!

I said in French, as politely and respectfully as I could, "Ça va, ça va."

This seemed to soothe him somewhat; I guess he was rebuking me for Sadat's journey, berating me. Speaking that single, simple phrase, I had told him he was right to do so, and that calmed him down.

My mind returned to the name that the sheikh had mentioned: Menachem Begin. I knew that he was the prime minister of Israel, and had heard his name mentioned before in our home; not these days, but long ago, when we lived in Daher. I remember that one day my head was lying on my mother's thigh, and I asked her about this man whom my grandmother never stopped talking to her about. She smiled and said, "Your grandmother adores him. He's a star to her. She keeps his picture among her things." Later, I saw my grandmother fingering his photograph, among other pictures: one of her twin sister, Dalal, who lived and died in Cioccolone Street in Shoubra, and of her father, Sawaris, who started out in life as a carpenter in Damanhour, and her Uncle Hazzan, who was active in the Communist Party;[*] when the government had had it with him, they threw him into jail. The photo of Menachem Begin, as I recall, was clipped from an old foreign-language magazine; he looked thin in the photo, his cheeks sunken; you might take him for a late-stage diabetic. As I sat there, I saw in my mind's eye again his thick spectacles that filled half his face, and the barrel of the gun sticking out from behind the top of his shoulder, and the six-pointed star on the cap on his head, his shirt sleeves rolled up to above the elbow.

I couldn't remember my grandfather saying anything in front of me about this man; it was my mother who said to me one day, in the presence of my grandmother, "I wish you could grow up to be like him!" And when I looked at her with acquiescence, she stroked my forehead and added, "He's a Jewish hero. He took his life in his hands and fought with his comrades to find a refuge for our poor relations migrating to Palestine." She motioned to my grandmother, saying, "She keeps his photo hidden from your grandfather, because he doesn't hold the same opinion of him." My grandmother sucked on her lips in disapproval of her uncomprehending husband, and warned me, as did my mother, not to mention Begin's name in front of him.

In those days, I was too young to completely be aware of what they meant; my imagination made me think, at the time, that there was something between this Menachem Begin and my grandmother: perhaps they were related, perhaps they'd had a love affair, a romance, a burning passion, or perhaps he had been one of those who had asked for her hand, and they both warned me not to mention his name because Grandfather was jealous!

---

[*] The Egyptian Communist Party was founded by a wealthy Jewish gentleman named Henry Corell.

Sheikh Munji pulled me out of my reverie. His loud voice came to me, quarrelling with the woman. He was saying, "I don't sell the best cuts of meat to the likes of you, you and the lowest of the low, but to respectable people who pay cash!" And he pulled out of the fridge—yes, *that* fridge—a piece of meat that wouldn't be good enough for a dog in the street if you tossed it to him; said dog would not only refuse to eat it, but would pee on the door of the shop as an indication of his displeasure.

The sheikh finally returned, after having completed the transaction on his terms. He got straight to the point before even sitting down. "Do you know what this Menachem Begin did? He's the one who slaughtered the Palestinians. Young and old alike fell to his slaughter."

Distracted, I said, "I know him, Sheikh Munji. I know him, I know him."

"You don't know a thing about him, not him nor his Zionist comrades. I know their life story, each and every one, those damned Zionists, starting with the short man, Ben-Gurion, all the way up to Yitzhak Shamir." He poked me in the knee. "That Yitzhak Shamir, whom they call the Head of the Knesset, is no better than Menachem Begin. He's a big terrorist, too. Yes, my boy! He killed, slaughtered, and spilled the blood of our women and children in Palestine. He did all this, my boy, and thought nothing of killing our relatives there. And in the end, Sadat goes to the Knesset and sits with him."

He sighed deeply, ending in a groan. "Oh. Oh-h-h . . ." He went on: "We were children, then, in Tunisia, and we heard that the Jews had done terrible things to Arabs. We read the *journaux* and saw the photographs of them slaughtered like sheep. And French people, standing with them, and giving them assistance—if it wasn't weapons, it was money or volunteers!"

His heart was clearly consumed with bitterness; his voice was faint and its rhythms unhappy. I fancied that his face had darkened as well, and that his beard was no longer mighty. He had lost his freshness, and much of his awe-inspiring quality; and when he pushed back his dark blue beret, it showed his well-shaped, shiny, bald pate. True, it belonged to a man with a skull of steel, but in the end, it was a bald pate on the head of a beleaguered man.

Something was wrong with him; something significant. He was unable to grasp what had happened. He couldn't believe that Sadat was going to meet Menachem Begin and the Israeli generals, and that they would welcome him with open arms. He would greet them, and they would greet him in return; they would spend pleasant evenings together; they might even kiss each other on both cheeks!

The news had confused him; had confounded his expectations. Sheikh Munji, you see, was not like any other sheikh, or indeed like any other person, in his enmity toward our kissing-cousins the Jews. His scuffle with my grandmother and her family were not the scuffles of neighbors, summer clouds soon to dissipate; to him, it was a matter of sin and righteousness, of principle and religion, and the Lord had given us permission to wage war upon those who had driven us out of our homes.

When my eyes crept toward Mamadou, I caught him surreptitiously watching the sheikh as well. He grimaced as soon as our eyes met. His face darkened; it made me uneasy. I said to myself, "Please God, don't let him start something; I don't have the strength to argue with him."

I decided to keep an eye on him—a legitimate line of defense!—so as not to be struck with the first blow unawares. My fears were not unfounded; he was a burning coal indeed, rocking back and forth in his chair, twisting his neck this way and that. He pulled his handkerchief from his collar for the third time and started blowing his nose, drowning out the sheikh, who stopped speaking and shot him a warning look. Mamadou ceased and returned the handkerchief to its hiding place, but he never took his red eyes off me, following my every move with such indignation in his gaze that you would think I, and not Sadat, had gone to Israel!

I found myself spontaneously rising, picking up my chair, and moving it to sit close by the sheikh; he gave me a fleeting glance as I did so, then resumed his speech, addressing his words this time to Mamadou.

"*Mon frère*," he said, "the issue is not with Menachem Begin, but with ourselves. What should we go to this terrorist for? Why dissolve our unity? Why would Sadat ruin the victory he achieved! Sadat and our brothers in the Levant achieved something huge. They made us proud! What's happened to this Sadat? Has he gone mad?"

Mamadou listened, his eyes on me.

Chapter 10

Being in a strange land, I found that my enthusiasm for following up on the news of my homeland and its issues had waned; I didn't even care any more about events outside of my own little world. I'd become introverted, occupied with my own problems, my own migrations, my own burdens. I no longer knew anything about my country except what I gleaned from a stray newspaper I happened to pick up, a news item I chanced upon on television, or whatever people talked about here—people who loved, who hated, and who concealed poison in honeyed words: Sheikh Munji and his folk, my mother's Jewish relatives, and fleeting conversations with the Arab customers at Bouchard's, sometimes Frenchmen or Levantines.

Palestine too had been shunted into a far corner of my mind; not of my feelings, or of my being, but of my mind and word and deed. When I was back home in Egypt, how brightly that mind had burned for Palestine! How often had I said that the Zionists owed me two debts: the debt of the homeland that was lost, and the debt of the father who had died? If some blabbermouth boy had approached me back then, saying with black humor, "Aren't they your mother's people?" I'd have said, "God damn you for an ignoramus! Who said so? My mother's relatives are Jews; the other ones are Zionists, not Jews."

And yet the words would cut deep, and I would feel a pang in my heart; meeting my mother afterward—the mother who brought me into this world!—I would contemplate her in silence. I would contemplate her, and in my heart I would ask, and answer, and reach dark, unspeakable conclusions, until I would calm down and come to my senses. Then I would approach her guiltily, kissing her forehead, being kind to her, kissing her hand again and again, and she would look on, bewildered, not knowing why I'd stayed away and remained silent for so long, nor why I now curried favor after avoiding her for so long.

Palestine had been shunted aside, and with it, great words. Arab Unity, the Strategic Dimension, the Homeland from the Gulf to the Ocean, and so many other slogans that enflamed our passions, words we used to hear in the Egyptian media, day and night.

Oh, that Arab Unity! The Leader planted it in us when we were still chicks, and we clung to it; I savored it, our hearts absorbed it slowly, and I felt I was the most steadfastly attached to it of all the children. Arab Unity flowed out of me, warm and abundant, as though it were visible, with a pulsing soul. It came out of my heart, from the deepest parts of me, not just from my tongue repeating the phrases. How many times had I entered into a dialogue because of it—indeed, into an argument that bordered on a quarrel—with my neighbors at home, my playmates in the street, and my schoolmates.

I argued so much about it with my professors in the classrooms, my Arabic teacher and my Arab Homeland teacher in particular, that one of them nicknamed me "Arab Citizen No. 1." I still remember him: Mr. Ahmed Abbas al-Tawil, with his shiny bald head and smiling face. They all ended up calling me that, whether seriously or in jest I still have no idea! They'd say, "Come here, Arab Citizen No. 1." Or, "Step up to the board, Arab Citizen No. 1," or "Answer this question, Arab Citizen No. 1," or "How can this be? Whoever heard of the Arab Citizen No. 1 falling asleep in composition class?" When I rebelled at first against this title they had conferred upon me, they said, "It's an honor, you ninny! The only

person who ever held that title before was Shukry al-Quwatly,* the
Syrian president. The Leader conferred the title on him to honor
him and his national pride." This would only increase my attach-
ment to, pride in, and defense of Arab Unity, and what was then
called the Greater Arab Homeland.

What I didn't understand at the time, though, was that all I
said and did, although it came from the heart in good faith, had
another face to it: that Arab Unity, without my knowledge or planning, had been the straw I was clutching at, the shelter I sought
in order to prove to those around me that I was half Egyptian and
that my other half was Arab, not Jewish as they thought! It was a
line of defense, a way to tell them that I was as good as they were,
nay, better—a weapon I could grasp in my hand as I called out all
this and more.

And here I was, now that everything was gone: the Leader was
gone, I myself gone from Egypt, with no more other children or
classmates that I needed to be wary of, to fear. Here I was, now
that the world had changed, and I found I'd become someone else:
someone who could listen to Sheikh Munji without caring about
the subject that was causing him such pain, who could say neu-
trally to him, my heart cold and steady: "Calm down a little, Sheikh
Munji. What's wrong with the Arabs making it up with Israel? Why,
as the old proverb says, making up is good."

His voice was strangled, the light in his eyes concealed behind
drooping eyelids: "What good, what evil, my boy? You're still a
child! You don't understand anything yet! How can you say the
Arabs can make up with Israel? Did the Arabs give Sadat a power
of attorney to speak for them? My boy, the Syrians don't trust
Sadat! They say that he let us down by not escalating the attack!
He contented himself with the kilometers he won in Sinai! His
men in the media call them liars, say it's Syria's fault, because we

---

* The Syrian president during whose administration the union between Egypt and Syria was
founded in 1958. It lasted for two years.

did what we'd agreed to do, we did what was written down in the plan. And Palestine? They don't trust Sadat either! And now you say he's here to solve the Palestinian question? No, no, my boy, he only cares about the Sinai!"

He asked me to give him a moment, mopping the sweat from his brow, then said, "He who solves the question has to find a solution for the Palestinians — they're the ones who can't find a handful of dust to be buried in. They're the ones rotting in the tents, living like dogs. If a girl wants to get married, she can't. If a boy wants to get an education, he can't. The mothers and fathers are helpless! He who wants to resolve things must solve all these problems and return the Palestinians to their homes, and Sadat isn't even thinking about any of that!"

I tried to argue with him, saying that this was Sadat's intention, and that the things he was so concerned about were surely on Sadat's mind, but he wouldn't hear a word of it. "*C'est fini*! The Arabs no longer speak with one voice, and it'll be fifty years before there's maybe a hope of coming together again! Go, my boy, and turn on the television, and listen to what the news agencies are saying. The Arabs are rejecting it: demonstrations everywhere, from Morocco to the Gulf." He leaned in to me, saying wretchedly: "Look, my boy, all my life we have considered Egypt the kind and giving mother of the Arabs, and Palestine is given to her as a trust to safeguard and to keep." He moaned. "Oh, for the days of Abdel Nasser! Back then, he used to say, 'The Golan and the West Bank first — then Sinai!' Now that's what you'd call a *father*! Galal, my boy, I'd like you to be an adult, a man who understands how things are! A child of Abdel Nasser, not of Sadat!"

I listened until he was through. I preferred not to respond, though, so as not to draw out the conversation. However, it was Mamadou who spoke. He burst out at me all of a sudden, with words like electric sparks, sharp and fast, in a voice that could shift from tenor to bass in less than a second. All the while, his eyebrows never stopped going up and down and his nostrils flared as though he were a mule in a fight. I was astonished by how wide his mouth opened; I could see his wisdom teeth and the top of his throat.

I placed my fate in the hands of God first, and Sheikh Munji second; the latter was trying to calm the man down, but it was useless. He defeated both of us, and rained spittle upon us. The wretch forced us to listen to him until the very last word, then curled up on the chair, resting his chin on his hand, awaiting my response to what he had said. Naturally, I didn't say a word—I hadn't understand a word of what the Mama-Mud had said, and even if I had, I had no desire to respond.

Sheikh Munji came to my rescue: with a crafty smile on his face, he said, "Your uncle, Mr. Mamadou, was saying I should tell you that you should be ashamed of yourself for what Sadat has done!"

"Me?"

"Yes, you! He says, if he were in your shoes, he wouldn't dare show his face to anyone again! If he were you, he said, he'd lock himself away, and never be seen again!"

I bolted up out of my seat and started to stalk away from the place, but Sheikh Munji stopped me, grabbing me by the hand and saying slyly, "Why be angry, my boy? You must forgive your Uncle Mamadou! He's just recently become a respectable human being, you know, and now he talks politics, too! And, you know, he's a Muslim, so he's familiar with the teachings of God and the Prophet! It's impossible for him not to care about an issue where Muslims are getting the worst of it. So what if you've never seen him set foot inside a mosque, sonny? So what if you've never heard of him fasting in Ramadan?"

Mamadou was gazing at us with satisfaction, for he imagined that Sheikh Munji was telling me off and taking his side. The Sheikh warmed to his theme. "This one, my boy, has no conscience. All he knows of Islam is the time when zakat is handed out! That's when he tells me, 'I'm more deserving than this person or that,' and who is 'this person or that'? Weak and old people! And he comes to the Zakat Committee to ask us for more, and he harasses us beyond endurance! There was this one time, Galal, my boy, we had an Algerian sheikh on the committee called Bu Allam. He had a long beard, and was an imposing figure. He handed Mamadou his donation, and it was a little bit less than what Mamadou had in mind. So this rotten creep, he grabs Bu Allam and pulls him by his beard! And if I hadn't stepped in and slapped him in the face, he'd have killed Bu Allam! It's God's will, my boy, what can we do? You tell me what we're to do with him! This is a trial from the streets, placed upon me by our Lord!"

When a smile crossed my lips, Mamadou's expression changed and he poked his head between the two of us suspiciously. The sheikh gave him to understand that he was still taking me to task, and that he had conveyed his, Mamadou's, point of view to me, and extracted a promise from me to be ashamed of myself from this moment on; furthermore, I was giving serious thought to locking myself indoors.

Mamadou nodded happily, clapping the sheikh on the back; the latter was holding back his laughter with an effort, and so was I.

Then the sheikh said, "You know, Galal, my boy, this wretched fool has been harassing me endlessly. What's come over him? About a year ago, he suddenly became interested in politics. First he wanted to leave for Kashmir and become one of the mujahideen, and then for the Philippines, to be with the Muslims there. Then he wanted to join the IRA and carry out bombings in London— and he doesn't understand a thing! Just the day before yesterday, this wretch comes to me and tells me he wants to leave for the Soviet Union and see how the Muslims are doing over there, and organize them into militias! I said, 'Leave them alone, cockroach; if the KGB gets hold of you there, your life will be over, and they'll shove a skewer up your rear end."

I glanced at Mamadou to find him perplexed and suspicious, as though some instinct told him we were playing him. The sheikh was still talking. "This Mamadou comes to me straight from his shift in the sewers, and sticks close by me, and he stinks, my boy!

He stinks! And the stink hits me and it's enough to knock me over! I have to hold my nose, for God's sake! Anyway, he comes and says, 'Give me the newspaper with the politics in it.' I give him the old newspapers we wrap the meat in for him to read, *Le Monde* and *Le Figaro* and *L'Humanité*. All out of date, two years old, five years old, I mean *really* out of date, my boy. This ass reads them, then comes and messes up my mind with events that were over long ago. One time he read a paper at my shop with an analysis of the Indo-Pakistani War of 1971, and this nincompoop was walking around believing that the war was still going on—and no sooner did he see an Indian man in the street than he picked a fight with him, and put his hands round his neck, because they're fighting the Muslims in Pakistan. And that poor Hindu kept yelling out, 'Man, the war's been over for ages! For six years! They've made peace already! Are you living in another world? Besides, I'm a Muslim like you! My name's Ghulam Abdel Rasoul!' It took all I had just to pry them apart! What am I to do with this fool? My God! Why, a chicken has more sense than he has."

I couldn't help myself. I laughed out loud. Mamadou, his suspicions that we were indeed making fun of him justified, leaped at me, but the sheikh grasped him threateningly by the wrist.

"Listen, Mama-Muck, I'm warning you! You stay away from Galal. Galal is like a son to me. He minds his own business and wouldn't hurt a fly—and he has enough troubles already. If you try anything with him, you'll have to answer to me. Do you remember the Syrian girl you tried to molest outside the Barbès Métro station, you filthy cur? Remember what I did to you then, or have you forgotten? Have you forgotten the beating you took then, Mr. Donkey, so that even the little children couldn't stop laughing? Do you want that again today?" He turned to me. "Don't pay him any mind, Galal. He's a lightweight, a nobody. Compared to other men he's not worth a gob of spit."

I left, obeying a gesture from the sheikh, leaving them still locked in a violent argument.

Chapter 11

My Uncle Isaac called to congratulate us.

I was coming upstairs from Sheikh Munji's, where I'd bought a whole sheep and asked him to give two-thirds of the meat to charity through the Zakat Committee, and send the remaining third up to us here at our apartment with one of his shop-boys.

Everyone was gathered around the television, so intent that they didn't even notice my arrival. My mother and grandmother were huddled together, whispering, my grandfather was leaning forward, eyes riveted on the screen, and the whole apartment was hushed, except for the voice of the French announcer, ringing and loud as though it was the Judgment Day.

The president's plane landed.

An "Ah" of contentment issued from my grandfather. The camera panned quickly around the VIPs come to greet him: Golda Meir, who had been away from Israel and summoned back in haste, Moshe Dayan, Yitzhak Shamir with his head that weighed half his body weight and his untrustworthy face, Chaim Hertzog, Weisman, Abba Eban, statesmen, and generals, all ranged in what looked like a queue.

The camera then moved to Menachem Begin, following him everywhere he went; it was clear that he, more than anybody else, had a presence that commanded respect. Perhaps it was because of his position as prime minister, or his person, shrouded in silence and awe-inspiring mystery. He walked unhurriedly, and his word was law; you never knew where his hooded eyes were looking or what they were scrutinizing. My grandmother followed him with her eyes, staring dreamily at his face. It looked like the face of an old fox, seasoned by many days and many schemes.

He approached the stairs of the airplane with steady steps, his head raised toward its still-closed door. As for me, without meaning to, my eyes gravitated to my grandmother, mooning over Menachem Begin! Apparently, my mother expected this of me; she blocked my path, fixing her eyes on me as a warning not to speak or comment or make any gesture to anger my grandmother or draw my grandfather's attention, so as not to cause a scene.

The president appeared at the door to the plane. He was well turned out, confident, strutting like a peacock. My grandfather burst into fervent applause, looking at us and expecting us to follow suit. We did not and he trailed off, but said hotly, "A man! You're a man, by God, Sadat, and you walk the walk! Yes, *that's* it, you big-hearted man!"

My grandfather ignored the television in favor of turning to us ecstatically and launching into a story of the oppression suffered by the Muslims and the Jews at the hands of the Goths in ancient Andalusia, how they had clung together and migrated, banished, to the Moroccan coasts, and how they had subsequently scattered among different countries. My grandmother, though, gestured to him to be silent and watch what was happening on the screen.

I too turned my attention back to the screen, watching with curiosity, as though I were watching a play or an action movie, until my grandmother said, "Now that's what I call a sensible man, a real politician. He went there to beg them to give back the Sinai because he knows how weak Egypt is. A defeated nation, poor thing: all they could do was cross the Suez Canal! Then what? Then nothing—they just stopped there and never accomplished anything."

My grandfather shot her a bemused look, but, as if that wasn't enough, she went on, "Isn't that right, Zaki? Sadat should just stay out of things like Gaza and Palestine and Syria and I don't know what and the other. Those things ruined his country, and maybe Israel will give him a slap on the wrist and forgive him and tell him to behave."

My grandfather lost it. "You just can't let us be without making trouble, can you? You'll never change. What do you know about politics—and what do you mean, Egypt defeated? Are you blind? Do you live in another world? Don't you read newspapers? Don't you watch television? Lord give me strength! You're driving me insane! What am I going to do with you?"

My mother showed her disapproval; I went berserk myself, and exploded into a fit of anger and blame. I said a lot of things: I cursed Israel, even Sadat himself for going to these people! And the Jews everywhere! The Jews here, and in America or Britain or Argentina, filling the nooks and crannies of the world like cockroaches.

I don't know precisely what came over me in those moments, transforming me so drastically. What was this latent thing inside me that this old hag had unleashed?

This thing had lain dormant as I spoke the day before yesterday with Sheikh Munji and that riffraff Mamadou; indeed, it had lain dormant not a minute ago, allowing me to sip my tea with milk from the cup in my hand, calm, and enjoying the scene unfolding before me as though I were watching one of the plays they used to broadcast on television back home during feast days.

The thing had been buried deep, but it was pricked by my grandmother and immediately weighed down on my chest, taking me in the blink of an eye to where my father and his comrades had set sail one day, bearing arms, heading for Port Said during the Suez War; to where the merciless currents had taken hold of them and pushed them this way and that, leaving them motionless, dead. I had always mentioned my father in my prayers, and had often thought of him in times of trouble, when I needed help and support. I had never seen his face, so I crafted it for myself. Eyes, brows, forehead, thick black hair. I never knew his stature or build or way of speaking; my heart built them all, so that even my subconscious had come to believe that this image before me was my father; in dreams and visions, he came to me in this imaginary form. The thing that had never come to my mind, what I had never dared to imagine, was how he looked as he died, until my grandmother said what she said. It was then that my heart began to rage, and I screamed at her as my father came nearer to me, his last breaths rattling, his soul all but rising from his body. His uniform was hanging open, the buttons undone, the fatal water, its mission accomplished, pushing his body lightly this way and that.

I leaped to my feet, tears bursting from my eyes, and left the room.

My grandfather caught up with me as I reached my room, sobbing in earnest now. He comforted me and took me in his arms, even bending to kiss my hand to console me! He kept saying, sincerely and tenderly, "Don't pay any attention to anything your grand-bitch says! I'm at my wits' end with her! You, you live with her, you know what she's like! The last thing I expected her to do is shove her oar in where she doesn't know what she's talking about, and slander our homeland. If she had a shred of sense—a glimmer of light in her heart!—she'd know it's Egypt, not Israel, she should be proud of! She was born on its soil, her sons and grandparents are buried there, and she and her children have long enjoyed its fruits and blessings."

"It's not just that, Grandfather," I said. "I remembered my father."

"I know. Things are connected."

After I'd calmed down, he resumed. "I forgive you for everything you said out there. It's true that your grandmother offended you, and gravely. But you went too far as well, you said much against us! Don't be unfair to the Jews, Galal. Jews are like everyone else God created: there are good and bad people among them. There are those whose hearts are filled with justice and goodness, as the prophet Moses taught us, and there are those who have distanced themselves from their creed and their religion and think it their right to usurp the property and the land of others. Very soon I'll take you on a little errand, and show you the Jews who live here, show you how they wax nostalgic as soon as somebody mentions Egypt."

He patted me on the shoulder. "Anyway, son . . . heaven help us all. Let's go."

I rose, feeling somewhat guilty for what I had said, and he took me by the hand and seated me by him. My grandmother looked at me with something like regret in her face and said, "I'm sorry, Galal. Forgive me, dear."

I nodded silently, and we went back to watching TV.

The president was now shaking the hands of the VIPs meeting him. He stopped for a moment before Moshe Dayan, with the eye patch covering his left eye; they exchanged a few words and smiled at each other. At a gesture from Menachem Begin, the portly form of Ariel Sharon jogged onto the red carpet, to where the president was walking, and we saw him nod a greeting to him. The president returned the greeting, all smiles, whispering a few words to him, raising his forefinger in his face.

My grandfather turned to me. "You know, young Galal," he said, "that Sadat is not a man to be trifled with in the least! Why, the first I ever heard of him was the day of the Amin Osman [*] trial, and you should have seen him! There he stood in the dock, cool as a cucumber, confident, not a bit of fear!"

Then my grandfather launched into one of his tales about Sadat. It went on and on. When all efforts to silence him failed, my grandmother bent in search of her slippers so she could leave the room, while my mother leaned her head against the back of the chair and started yawning.

---

[*] Pro-British Egyptian statesman assassinated in 1946. Sadat was among those accused of the crime.

We were saved by the telephone.

It was my Uncle Isaac calling from Israel. They all leaped up to exchange congratulations with him. I had never seen him, for he left Egypt before I was born, and it was the first time I had ever heard his voice. In the blink of an eye, as I closed my hand around the receiver, I had formed an immediate mental image of him: short and fat like my grandmother, clean-shaven, with patches of white and yellow skin around his mouth, the legacy of an old bout with vitiligo, while his palms were smooth and slipped out of your hand when you shook hands with him. He spoke to me in limping Arabic, the way foreigners speak, in a voice smoother than running water. "Galal, my dear boy, by God I wish I could see you and look my fill of you. What is your face like? Are you beautiful like your mother? I'm sure you are."

I didn't answer him.

"Galal, dear heart."

I coughed, repeatedly.

There was a loud knocking on the door. It was Bu Said, Sheikh Munji's nephew and his shop boy as well. Tall and broad, he stood there like a lion; like his uncle, he wore a knife tucked into his belt, and in his hand were the bags of meat. My grandmother bristled, ready to defend us, imagining he meant us some harm. When I told her what was going on, she withdrew and they all bid me a happy Eid al-Adha.

It was the first time I had chipped in and bought something for the house.

Rachel came to visit the next day, in the evening.

The event didn't mean a thing to her, except she was irritated by "these Arabs, who can understand them?" She was asked by a tour company to accompany a package tour from Iraq. They looked poor, and it was clear that they had scrimped and saved for ages to be able to afford this trip. She felt sorry for them, so she went above and beyond, taking them here, there, and everywhere, directing them to cheap places to eat and shop for clothing, and preventing anyone from taking advantage of them. She had worked "with heart," as she called it, with professional ethics and more, and in spite of this, they had suddenly gone to the company today and asked for a different guide!

"But why, dear girl?"

"Because of Sadat's visit, Gran! Imagine that! What's one got to do with the other? I've been working with them for four days and it's not like they don't all know I'm a Jew through and through."

"Those miserable worms!"

When she came to leave, she took me by the hand and we walked down the stairs together. "Are you pleased with the initiative like Grandfather, or . . . ?"

"I don't know," I said.

"I bet it made you think of your dad, may he rest in peace, didn't it?"

I hugged her, I was so grateful.

Soon after, my Aunt Bella suddenly descended upon us, accompanied by Uncle Elephant-Trunk. They appeared to have patched things up, or maybe there was a temporary cessation of hostilities.

Elephant-Trunk, with his business acumen, was eager to be a step ahead of everyone else, and imagined that my mother and I would be a treasure chest out of which he could scoop up great armfuls of information about the Egyptian market: what enterprises would yield the quickest reward, what was the most profitable trade, and so forth. But we disappointed him; we were "cleaner than a washed plate," as the saying goes: we had nothing to give him.

As soon as he came in, we noticed his striking—no, not his nose, that was old news—the striking set of false teeth that now occupied half of his mouth. My grandmother feigned concern. "I'm so sorry for you, Aaron, my boy! You're too young for such things! Why, your Uncle Zaki still has teeth like iron, and he doesn't spare them, either! Crusty bread, peanuts, all kinds of nuts, he crunches up everything in sight!"

My grandfather looked at her with displeasure, while the man responded, "It's the diabetes, Aunt. You know I've had it for ages. The damned disease rotted my teeth and the doctor said there's nothing for it but dentures." She nodded agreement. But from my position in our circle, close to my grandmother, I could hear her whispering into my Aunt Bella's ear: she doubted Elephant-Trunk's words, and wanted to learn the truth from her. Had his teeth really fallen out because of diabetes, or had there been a fight, and someone knocked them out?

Bella answered her haltingly, her eyes on her husband for fear that he might overhear something. When he went to the toilet, though, my aunt's voice grew louder. This thing with the dentures had thrown her husband into a tizzy at first; he'd been so mad about it, he'd wanted to flush them down the toilet. "When he takes them off for bed or any other reason, his mouth collapses inward and his nose hangs down nearly to his chin, so that if the poor man smiles or speaks, he seems about to cry."

Elephant-Trunk returned; to be on the safe side, Aunt Bella changed her seat to go sit next to him, and my mother took her empty seat. He and my grandfather were soon deep in conversation regarding Sadat's initiative, while my grandmother took to whispering again. She told my mother to take care with Elephant-Trunk, for he was no doubt planning illegal enterprises in Egypt: hashish, heroin, confidence tricks and schemes, and so on. To quote her to the letter, she said, "Let him get caught there and beaten within an inch of his life, and lie down and never get up."

Elephant-Trunk appeared to sense that he was the subject of all the whispering. It was my grandmother who was to blame; she had unconsciously turned her eyes toward him at the end of her whispering to my mother, and he was paying attention, unfortunately, and surprised her with a sudden, "Everything all right, Aunt? I hope you're not talking about me."

"Is there any bad blood between us, that we should talk about you?" she said. "You're a respectable man, the best there is! We're talking about the world and the dreadful people in it." She paused to catch her breath. "So tell me, Haroun, my boy, are you thinking of going to Egypt?"

He pulled a pack of Dunhills from the inside pocket of his jacket, unwrapped it and took a cigarette out, tapping the butt on the back of the pack to settle the tobacco, the way lower-class men and blue-collar workers do, before he lit it. "Why not? It's a market after all, and soon it'll open up."

"And then what will you do, my boy? Start a company, build a factory, or what do you mean to do?"

"A factory!" He smiled. "Why not a school then, or an orphanage? What factory, Aunt? My system is like the vultures': grab and run!"

My grandfather was clearly disapproving. As for me, my tongue ran away with me. "Uncle Haroun," I blurted, "I swear I'd be the first to go back with you if you really did think of opening a factory or any enterprise there."

"That's enough, Galal," said my grandmother, "that's enough, my dear! This kind of thing is none of your business. You'd do best to mind your own P's and Q's."

I had the feeling, in that moment, that my grandmother feared for me from Elephant-Trunk. It was her firm conviction that he was a criminal of some sort and she didn't want us to have anything to do with each other. Was I then closer or dearer to her than he was? Truly, I didn't know what to make of this grandmother of mine!

"As for me," said my grandfather, stretching his legs out, "first thing tomorrow morning I'll be at the Egyptian Embassy."

"Whatever for? Is something wrong?" gasped my grandmother.

He did not answer her, but turned to my mother. "I'll tell them I'm going back to my home, to my apartment. You've still got the keys to the apartment, don't you?"

She just stared at him.

"The Daher apartment! Go on, go bring them and I'll pack them this minute!"

"Just slow down a minute, Zaki!" Grandmother yelled at him.

Chapter 12

One evening, my grandfather took me to the apartment of Mr. Yacoub Abu al-Saad. It was a Saturday evening; the weekend. He asked me to accompany him to J. Moquet Street, where this man lived.

He was about ten years younger than my grandfather, and his face was the first thing that caught your attention: perhaps because it was scarlet and florid, unlike the Egyptian Jews I knew, or because his blue eyes looked long and hard into yours, staring you down, when you spoke to him. My eyes were also caught by his full head of wavy silver hair, his slim figure, and the clothing he wore to meet us: stylish and classy, almost like evening wear: a white silk shirt with gilded cuffs, black pants and shoes, a bowtie, and a waistcoat.

I had learned from my grandfather that he had been one of the largest exporters of onions in Egypt, and had lived in Garden City in a building behind the famous Shepheard Hotel, until he came here with the second wave of Jewish emigrants. He lived alone now that his wife had passed on, and his children had scattered to Argentina and Israel.

The moment we walked into the apartment, I was stunned by its opulence. My grandfather's apartment, by any standard, would scandalize anyone who compared the two. The foyer had several pairs of wrought-iron chairs, with a chandelier in a modern style from which three attractive globes were suspended, giving off light that was neither dim nor glaring. There was a coat rack upon which my grandfather hung his coat and beret. The rectangular mirror in a corner of the entrance caught my eye; I went in for a closer look, and found myself staring at a lowlife wage-slave who worked at Bouchard's, dressed in nothing but jeans and a cheap sweater.

Mr. Yacoub led us into a long, rectangular hall with four pillars of black marble, one at each corner. The sofas and chairs were in the Louis XVI style, and so were the two chandeliers and the antique piano with the closed lid, the grain of its expensive wood visible. Crystal vases were scattered about in niches and corners.

My eye was drawn to two large photographs, prominently displayed. The first was of a woman in the bloom of youth, wearing a small hat that came to a point in front, and earrings. I learned later from my grandfather that it was a picture of his dead wife Liliane, who had been from the Nadler family, the wealthy Jewish clan that used to live in Alexandria. The second portrait was of Mr. Yacoub as a young man; he was dressed for the beach, with three children around him. One was building a sand castle.

Hung in the corners of the room were other pictures, of famous Egyptian singers and movie stars: Abdel Wahab, Umm Kulthoum, Leila Murad, and the Jewish artist Camellia, the darling of the picture palaces in the 1950s. They were all young, and the pictures were all the same size, in wooden frames painted a light gray.

There was another picture that I hadn't noticed at first, although it was just above the piano. It was larger than the others, a black-and-white image of a man in his seventh decade, wearing an old-fashioned suit, a tarboosh on his head, a monocle covering his right eye. A chain hung from the slightly prominent pocket of his waistcoat and disappeared into his jacket. He was not standing straight; he stood hunched over, leaning on a stick with a crook at the top.

I gazed at the picture. "My father," Mr. Yacoub said to me, "Sarouf Abu al-Saad."

My grandfather approached us, saying, "Sarouf Bey Abu al-Saad! He was an actual Bey, Galal, my boy—the title was conferred upon him in the reign of Sultan Hussein! The crème de la crème: a real aristocrat worthy of the title!"

Before we sat down, Mr. Yacoub bent over a recording device on a small marble-topped table. He turned it on and Umm Kulthoum's voice filled the room, singing Khayyam's *Rubaiyat.*

Unseen is the morrow; today is all mine.
The future has let us down many a time.
Am I so unfeeling as not to rejoice
At the beauty and splendor of this world so fine?

It appeared that we had arrived early; my grandfather had told me on the way that we were going to meet some of his friends at a gathering, more like a party; only I found no one there, and spent a while looking around me, slowly eating an apple from the plate of fruit offered to us by an old French maidservant, followed by a cappuccino. I was overcome by the feeling that something was passing between my grandfather and this man; perhaps it was because of the looks they exchanged behind my back, or because of all the surreptitious glances the man gave me, thinking I didn't notice.

The guests started to arrive. Their dress was pitiful: disreputable old sweaters and pants; plain, flat shoes; shirt collars worn at the edges; and woolen caps and hats with no connection whatsoever to our era. The coats were in the style of my grandfather's, no color or cut to them, worthy one and all of a prize in an ugliest coat contest.

Their faces were mostly dark, marred by trouble and unhappiness. They took their gloves off as soon as they entered, throwing their weary bodies onto the chairs, some resting their heads on the edges, panting. They were old, some coming from far away—St. Cloud, Versailles, and even Fontainebleu. All were Jews who had lived in Egypt and then left. Some had lived in Jews' Alley in Bilbeis, or by the Jews' Wholesale Traders in Damietta; others had occupied clerical positions in Damanhour, or owned textile workshops or stores in Mansoura or Rosetta, and so on. They came together in a strange land, never meeting until they arrived here, and the credit for this went to Mr. Yacoub. He adopted them one after the other, making his apartment a refuge for them on the first Saturday of every month, to reminisce about the good old days, and find solace for their own pain in sharing it with others. Yacoub would prepare a sumptuous supper for them, and never withheld his charity from the poorest among them: money, old clothes, what was left of the food after the dinners.

The life they lived here had left no impression upon them; they still unconsciously behaved as they had in Egypt. They spoke loudly, interrupted each other's speech, gesticulated in each other's faces, and guffawed occasionally for no reason. They ruined the carpets with their dirty footprints and blew their noses with all their might, with no regard for etiquette or politeness; indeed, one of them was sitting opposite me and appeared to be struck by a thought while blowing his nose, so he paused and started to speak, handkerchief still held to his nose, and resumed blowing it when he had finished speaking.

Heaven help Mr. Yacoub. They turned the gathering, as closely as possible, into an approximation of a vulgar scene at a lower-class street café in al-Zawya al-Hamra or Boulak al-Dakrour. The French maidservant's disgust was obvious. She was muttering in French and cursing the circumstances that caused her to have to serve these lowlifes.

The conversations mingled. Someone was telling the latest joke he'd heard from a visitor from Egypt, told by a toothless old man, one foot in the grave, and the joke was so obscene it made me blush! Someone else was cursing Abdel Nasser for being the author of their current predicament, and another was waving a hand in his face, saying it wasn't Abdel Nasser, but that lousy Israel that was the cause: that they had been living with their Egyptian countrymen in peace, and if not for Israel, none of this would have happened. Yet another was complaining that, but for the grace of God, he would have died alone in his bed last night. Another was tearing up as he recalled his boyhood in the Gumruk neighborhood of Alexandria, another in Kamel Sidqi Street in Faggala, another mourning the loss of his apartment in Daher, a big five-room place for under four pounds in rent!

Mr. Yacoub, the maestro of the session, was calming one, telling another to go wash his hands after eating instead of wiping them on the fabric of the chair he sat on, and reminding a third that politeness dictated that he tap his cigarette ash into the ashtray instead of letting it fall onto the Kashan rug. Sometimes he had to speak sharply to control the situation.

When the conversation turned to Sadat's initiative, rosy dreams filled the air. Most of them, my grandfather the first among them, thought that all their problems were now resolved and that they would be going home in a matter of months, back to their old jobs and houses.

Mr. Yacoub looked from one to the other of them, then asked one, "Didn't you sell your house and your workshop in Rosetta, Ma'allim Nessim?" Nessim looked at him without speaking, and Mr. Yacoub's voice grew sharper. "Did you sell them or didn't you? You sold them! So how are you going to get them back?"

Ma'allim Nessim scratched his head. "I'll buy them back."

"Oh, really! Are people going to obey your whims, buying when you want to sell, selling when you want to buy? And there's another thing: do you have so much as a franc to your name? I know your finances better than anyone else!"

The man fell silent. Mr. Yacoub stared him down, and he looked away. "Besides, whom do you have back there? Your son Yusuf's in Canada, and here you haven't seen him these ten years. Your daughter's married in Greece. You've got no brothers, no cousins or anything in Egypt. Who are you going to go home to, Abu Yusuf? To Mohamed and Mahmoud and Khalil from Rosetta, whom you don't know? Wake up, Ma'allim Nessim! You've got to know that the people from the good old days you're thinking of aren't there any more! They'll have been dead and cold for years now."

Another man said, "But it's our country, Mr. Yacoub, where we were born and grew up. Did you ever hear of an old tree that bore fruit when it was uprooted and planted in different soil? Maybe our children and our children's children won't understand this, because they weren't born in Egypt, and those who were left it young; they never knew its streets and neighborhoods, never sat at the cafés with their friends. It's our country, people! When you're alone with your thoughts, and you turn on the tape recorder and play the songs of your youth, who among us doesn't break down and cry like a child?"

To them, Egypt was a kind of Paradise Lost. They were completely cut off from the world in which they lived now. It was strange to them, and they were strangers to it; all they knew of it was the face of the bank teller who paid them their social security at the start of each month, and the grocery store where they bought their necessities, and Mr. Yacoub's apartment to which they would hurry whenever they were invited. Their relationships with their children had dwindled; they had emigrated and left them behind, wandering through God's earth and only asking after them as an afterthought.

She, Egypt, was the only one left: she was solace and longing, the prick of pain and the shadow of hope. She was the sun that had set, leaving them unable to feel warmth any more. She came to them when they were alone in their houses, speaking to them as they spoke to her. She seduced them, and they believed. She beckoned to them, but she was only a mirage. They dreamed of her, as they dreamed of their friends who had died; they called to her as they called to them. They all knew time had passed them by, they all knew they would never attain her, and yet they never gave up their burning passion, their thoughts and their longing. The sensible ones among them realized that their strength was sapped, their lives gone by, their hopes dashed, and contented themselves with letting her live in them, since they were deprived of living in her.

The doorbell rang. When the man at the door was revealed to be Ibrahim Abu Kaff, a cheer went up; even Mr. Yacoub forgot his dignity and applauded, then hurried inside and brought him his lute.

Ibrahim was different. In Alexandria, he'd played the lute in folk ensembles; after his wife's death, one of his fellow Jews had lured him away from Egypt. He had a married daughter there, whom he visited occasionally. He made his living now playing the lute in the cheap nightclubs where Arabs from North Africa, in particular, congregate.

Luck had smiled upon him: he had written a number of fair-to-middling tunes, which were very popular and had become famous in the circles of the Arab poor—those invisible men—as "Abu Kaff's pieces." Perhaps it was their sentimental melancholy, their grief over exile, their nostalgia for days gone by.

Abu Kaff took the lute in his arms and began testing its strings with his right hand; the instrument responded with notes, high and low, which changed as he tuned it. The wooden keys grunted under his fingers as he adjusted them and checked their flexibility.

Silence reigned. Even the angry French maid, who resented these evenings, came in on tiptoe and placed a small tray before him, bearing a coffee cup and a glass of hot anise tea. Everyone was suddenly on their best behavior: not a sound, not a breath. Their eyes were locked on him and his lute. They knew what he was going to sing, for there was no room for choice with the first song: it was a long-held tradition that they always started their monthly gatherings with this song.

Abu Kaff cleared his throat like the famous singer Abdel Wahab. Then the words flowed from him, speaking to the gathered company.

Loving my homeland is a duty! I would give my soul and my eyes for her!
Why, oh why did the nightingale sing? He made me think of my dear
homeland.
I spent my dearest youth with her, she holds my lovers and my foes.
If she should suffer cruelty or dishonor, I would give my soul and my
eyes for her!

He stopped to take a sip of his anise tea, then occupied himself
with adjusting an errant string that had almost caused him to sing a
false note. The company sat, eyes half-closed in ecstasy, some nodding and some exclaiming "Beautiful! Beautiful!" or leaning over to
their neighbors and whispering in their ears.

The French maid, cigarette in her mouth, placed a cane chair
outside the kitchen door, and sat in it to watch this mania more
closely. Abu Kaff started up again.

O Egypt, your love is my mother's milk,
There I nursed when young; it runs in my blood.
I love your Nile and love your sky.
You are father and mother to me.
You are my only love, O Egypt,
In this world, you are all I see.
You raised me on your bounty.
Could I forget my love of country,
The clear sweet waters of your Nile?
I would give my soul and my eyes for you!

When he had finished, they all applauded, and some rose to
kiss him on both cheeks. The disputes raged as to his next song,
until they agreed on "Wanderer," first sung by the Nightingale. He
started:

I'm a wanderer, wandering from land to land
And each step of the distance

That separates me and my love
Is a journey in itself.

My grandfather and I took our leave, leaving them all to their
joys and sorrows.

On the way home, my grandfather asked me what I thought of Mr.
Yacoub. The man seemed to me to be generous, yet someone who
liked to hold his generosity over people's heads; a compassionate
man who was haughty. "He's all right," I said.

"All right? He's the best of men. A respectable gentleman, son of
a good family."

We talked and talked, until my grandfather got to the point. "To
tell the truth, son, the man has asked for your mother's hand in
marriage."

We had reached the Barbès Métro station and were just getting onto the escalator. I stopped and took a step back, stunned.
"Mother? Whose mother? My mother?"

"Yes, my boy."

"And does she know about it?"

"Yes she does, and she's met him a few times, and she says yes, on
condition that you agree."

"That son of a bitch!"

My grandfather looked at me reproachfully.

Chapter 13

The war was on between me and my mother.

I couldn't get my head around the idea that she could get married. The idea had never so much as occurred to me. I had never thought a day would come when she would disappear into the bedroom with another man. And with whom? With this strutting peacock, this superannuated old coot!

Is this part of the rules of being a good host? Is this your hospitality, Mr. Yacoub, son of the aristocracy, descendant of beys? You offer me an apple and a cup of coffee and leave me sitting blithely in the midst of your inane sycophants, while you're plotting and planning to steal my mother away? You homewrecker!

The villain spirited her off to his pied-à-terre in J. Moquet Street so she could console him and massage his stiff limbs, and come and go bearing bowls of fruit and glasses of wine for his unfortunate friends, taking the place of the old French maid.

The onion salesman had taken me by surprise; I couldn't open my mouth or say a word, for he had in his hand a paper called the 'katubah,' a Hebrew word that means 'marriage contract.' He shook my grandfather's hand and agreed upon what they called in their religious law 'shetar tana'emm,' Hebrew for engagement. My mother had become a morsel for him to chew upon! When night fell, his breath would mingle with hers, and his fingers would creep into her bra. Was not this the clawing of a predator?

And you, Grandfather, have you no mercy in your heart? Were you plotting this behind my back, though you know I love you? Did your fingers do your bidding as you signed this katubah? Did your heart not tell you that it was a contract to dispose of my mother, of Umm Galal?

What relation am I, Grandfather, to this doppelganger that you are marrying off to Mr. Yacoub? What have I to do with this woman whose name has become Madame Yacoub?

I don't know this new woman, Grandfather, and I don't want her. She is not my mother.

And you, Umm Galal, what happened to what lies between us, thick and deep, tender and compassionate, joyful, cheerful, silent, eloquent? Where is all of this? It's as though it never was, never happened.

You always told me, Mother, that all my father did was place a seed inside you and leave. Just a seed! Blind, deaf, helpless, with no mind to understand, and you were the one who made it a person, raised him, and cured his hurts, loving and giving. I am a part of you, as you say . . . part of you, whether I am lost in your womb, lying in your lap, or older and blessed with a mustache and children. And I listened to you! You found it strange when I fasted and prayed, for you imagined—God forgive you—that I was Jewish like you. And you wondered at my disloyalty should I disobey you even a little; up to now, I never realized that we possessed—excuse me, you first, then I—possessed one mind, one heart, one religion.

The mind, of course, was yours. The heart was yours. The religion was yours. I was the sailor and you the captain. That was what I understood, not explicitly, but it was hinted at. You spoke of it when you were happy and when you were mad, as though, as much as you gave, that much you owned, that much belonged to you.

I listened, too, and pitied you sometimes. I would say to myself, "Is it a religious thing? I don't think so. Is it because she found herself prematurely deprived of love? Possibly!" Sometimes the Devil would lead my thoughts astray, and I would say, "There's nothing to be done about this mother of mine. She needs a psychiatrist!"

This is what I used to think about my mother, what made me pity her. I had no idea that some of it lurked inside me as well. Lurked silent, quiescent, while I remained unaware of its presence. For when my grandfather said what he said, I took it hard; not just because she was going to leave me and get married—what was worse was that she would marry a man not of our religion, not of our creed. Something inside me imagined her to be a Muslim like myself! A Muslim with no right to even consider such a thing! I had no idea that my thinking was in fact the same as hers: I really had no idea. But who said that not knowing a thing means it doesn't exist?

Each of us, it seems, unwittingly, had created an image of the other to please ourselves. I saw her as a Muslim; she saw me as a Jew. I saw her as my mother, all that I had, all mine, to do with as I pleased; and she, my dear mother, why she was just the same. Again, I apologize—she made me, after all, so I should say that I was the same as she. She never thought of me as anything other than part of herself.

Do we hold things unknown deep inside us? Things that only make their presence known when provoked?

To be fair, she tried to speak to me, many times. I was the one who refused to respond. What was in my heart would not allow for arguments and counter-arguments and justifications, and would not be satisfied with half-measures. She began to lose patience with me, while I seethed with resentment. Gradually, we stopped speaking, and then war broke out.

It was a war of eyes, not of tongues. She would be sitting before the mirror, or arranging her things in the closet, and I would look at her from behind. Sensing my presence, she would turn her head toward me, and I would let my eyes bore into hers until she looked down. Then I would leave her and occupy myself with something else. Or she would be coming into the house after going out with my grandmother, followed by Rachel. My grandmother would let the bag in her hand fall onto the nearest chair, and head, panting, for the bathroom, both she and Rachel groaning at the weight they were carrying: bags of clothing, a hatbox, and another rectangular one containing a frock, and breakables, and things for a trousseau. . . .

I would watch them setting their purchases down, and when they were finished and getting ready to talk to me, I would rise, and leave the room. If we were to come together at table or spend an evening together, I would avoid looking at her, unless she wasn't paying attention to me; in that case, I would follow her with my eyes: her earrings, which shook whenever she tilted her head to right or left, and her hair, which she had started to wear in a hairdo like a young girl's, and the blood-red lipstick, like a whore's, and eyebrows that were now very thin, in accordance with the fashion of the moment. When she said something funny, I would not laugh. When she smiled at me, I would not return the smile. If I were absolutely obliged to, I would measure it in millimeters. My grandfather noticed, but could do nothing about it. As for my grandmother, she was under strictest orders to remain neutral, and, wonder of wonders, she did.

My only solace in all of this was Rachel. She would pick me up in her car, and drive all through the length and breadth of Paris, or take me to sit at a café in the Champs-Élysées or Montmartre, or Saint-Germain, then to a disco where we would dance like crazy people all night long.

She left the house. All that was left in her room were her old things and a photograph on the wall. My anger at what she had done couldn't douse the flames of my loneliness or dull the pain of missing her, and I was overcome with loss, as if I'd been orphaned anew.

When everyone was asleep, I spoke to myself incessantly, asked myself, Was I sinned against, or sinning?

In my more peaceful moments, I would say: Doesn't my mother deserve, after all she's done for me, a life? Isn't my grandfather to be forgiven as well, for setting her up in a home of her own before he dies?

But, I never thought of paying her a visit in her new home, and I could never stand to look in the face of that Yacoub.

Chapter 14

I received a letter from Egypt, from Hassan, whose mother had nursed me, and whom I thus counted as my half-brother. He started out his letter by roundly insulting me, calling me a louse, and saying that if his mother hadn't made him, he would never have written to me! After all, we'd surely forgotten him and his mother and all that was between us, leaving so suddenly, without bothering to tell them or even say goodbye, sneaking out like thieves in the night! And here we'd been away for four years, and not a word, not a peep out of us! We hadn't so much as picked up the phone or licked a stamp!

He went on to say, "Well, I have all the respect in the world for Aunt Camellia, so I can't say a word against her, but what about you? You didn't tell us! Mom is really cut up about you in particular, and she says, 'Why, I nursed him, and how many times did I hold him in my lap? What a sneak, to hide that he was going, to leave without telling me!' I said to her, 'See, Mom? The guy has a Jewish streak in him as wide as the Nile! He puts no trust in anyone!' She shooed me away and said, 'For shame, boy! Keep a civil tongue in your head! Don't you dare speak ill of Galal.'"

I didn't appreciate Hassan's jesting, and found it strange that he hadn't said a single word about Nadia. I picked up my pen immediately and wrote a letter to him, begging him for God's sake to tell me any news of her.

The answer arrived, fast and brief. Nadia, he said, was back, living in her old apartment with the man she had married. Hassan saw her almost every day, but he had refrained from telling me in the first letter so as not to make me unhappy in a strange land.

He urged me to take care of myself, and not to think about anything except my future: Nadia was part of the past now, and thinking of her would only bring confusion and pain, especially as there was no hope on the horizon; she was a married woman now, and was soon to become a mother, for she was pregnant.

What Hassan had called Nadia—a married woman—gave me pause. I bent my head over the letter, bemused, anxious, in denial, as though they had said of someone dear to me, not only that he was dead, but that his dead body had been mutilated.

Nadia . . . like a breeze . . . daughter of the moon and of roses . . . Nadia, with her braids and the bag clutched to her chest, and her bountiful heart . . . a maiden no longer? Spending the long night in the arms, in the bed, of a man who was a stranger to her heart?

About to give birth?

Did this world of ours have no morals, no heart, no eyes? Wasn't it even ashamed of itself? Was it chivalrous, was it even fair, to enlist two men? One to have his way with my mother here, and the other, defiling my truest love, far, far away?

Days passed as I came and went to Bouchard's like an automaton. I ran errands for my grandparents, and answered the phone: now Uncle Shamoun, now Rachel, now a friend of my grandmother's called Samaka, an unpleasant woman with a deep voice like a man's. I did all this with a scowl, speaking only when spoken to, and only as much as necessary, not one extra syllable or flicker of emotion: "Yes," "All right," "Thank you." Monsieur René, the manager of Bouchard's, would look at me sometimes and say, "Why are you so unhappy, my boy?"

"Nothing," I'd say, "it's nothing. Thank you, sir."

I would nod to him, or smile, if I could manage it.

My direct supervisor at work, Akram Abul Shawareb, was forever comforting me. He would clap me on the shoulder, saying, "Why so sad, man? What has the world done to you?"

I would say a word or two to him and get back to work.

My problem, though, was distraction, was lack of concentration. It was the shadows that came, uninvited, to haunt me: Nadia's, and those two damned shadows that weighed down on me suffocatingly, from whom I couldn't excape: Mr. Yacoub, my stepfather, and this Bishri who had married Nadia.

I would try to push them out of my mind and occupy myself with showing pieces of fabric to customers, but they never left. If I thought they had, it would only be for a moment, and then there they would be, exactly as they had been. I would sit with Sheikh Munji, occasionally accompanied by Mamadou, who would make our gathering into a comedy, putting the sheikh into a good humor, laughing out loud, so hard that he shook the chair. I would do the same, looking into the face of Mamadou, but then the shades would ambush me, changing everything, so that I would leap up and bolt, as the others looked on in astonishment.

When alone in my room, they would have me all to themselves; I would never be rid of their importunate presence unless I pulled out the small copy of the Quran I kept under my pillow and sat reading it.

What's strange is that I had never seen this creature that had married Nadia, nor even heard him described; despite this, his features and build were clear as day before my mind's eye. The nose, the eyebrows, the blue eyes, the pinhead mole in the curve of his ear, and a stocky, healthy body clad in pants, a shirt, and an old-fashioned jersey, somewhat tight at the armholes.

This happened in the blink of an eye, without my imagining it or intending to think about it. I saw him before me the moment I read Hassan's words in the letter, saying that Nadia was another man's woman now. For a long time I stood before myself in confusion, asking myself where I had gotten this face, this build, and this clothing.

The answer came more than two months later.

My grandfather was returning from a visit to my mother, with a small photo album. He and my grandmother were flipping through it as they were drinking their tea. Most of the photos were of my mother and this Yacoub, one in the Place Trocadéro, my mother in jeans and a low-cut blouse, he in a hat and casual attire, and another photo with this shameless beast kissing her in the street, where all the world could see! There was a third in front of the Pantheon, and another during a short trip to Cannes, in the south. The last stiff card in the album held an old black-and-white photo of a thin man in a short-sleeved shirt and pants, standing outside the Gumruk building in Alexandria, with a cigarette in his mouth, pointing to some distant object.

"Who is that man?" I asked my grandfather.

"Don't you recognize him?" he smiled. "It's Mr. Yacoub as a young man."

Great heavens, I said to myself. It *is* him! I swiftly remembered the photo where he was sitting with his children on the beach in Alexandria, in which I had seen this taunting face. The photo hung on the wall in his apartment, and I'd seen it fleetingly the first time I visited him, that night with my grandfather.

His was the face that came to me in the guise of Nadia's husband! It was practically the same, with only minor details to differentiate one from the other. Good Lord! I had completely forgotten that photo of Mr. Yacoub! But a part of me, clearly, hadn't forgotten. It had captured the image and preserved it, added those few details, and sent it from time to time, to torment me, giving Yacoub's face to my archrival, to the man who had won Nadia's hand while I remained trapped here, a stranger of no importance.

The build, though, was not his; Mr. Yacoub was tall and thin, while the shadow that haunted me was of a heavyset man. It was then that I saw in my mind's eye the image of Sheikh Mustafa,

Nadia's uncle. Even before I came here, they said back home that he sought to claim Nadia as a bride for one of his sons. I had often met this Sheikh Mustafa outside the door to our apartment in Daher, or as he was coming up or going down the stairs. He used to come to visit his sister, Madame Sobki, Nadia's mother, nearly every week after Friday prayers, and visit till after the call to afternoon prayer had sounded.

Good Lord, good Lord! His build was the build of that man I saw. And I had remained haunted by this persistent shade, which borrowed the face of an old man's youth, and the form of a sheikh that my mind had for some reason retained! What is this thing inside us? What is this silent, mighty thing that inhabits our bodies, and yet thinks, acts, and forms things quite apart from us! Indeed, it schemes against us, torments us at its whim!

My days were depressing, washed-out, meaningless. One night I awoke, terrified, to a hand shaking my shoulder and a voice loudly calling my name. It was my grandfather. "I heard you from my room," he said, clearly concerned, "moaning and talking, shouting to yourself."

He sat down by my side, feeling my brow and slipping a hand under my jaw to palpate my tonsils. "I'm not sick, Grandfather," I said. "I'm fine. It was just a nightmare."

He read some prayers for me, then kissed me on both cheeks, tucked me in, and turned to go. As he was closing the door to my room, he asked, "Shall I leave the light on?"

"No," I said as I piled the covers up over my head.

"Call upon God to protect you from evil spirits before you go to bed," he said, "so you won't get nightmares."

I nodded from beneath the covers.

Despite the precautions, I had another nightmare. It was as though I were walking cautiously down a dusty path, bordered on both sides with thick intertwined stalks of greenery that hid what lay behind them. From a distance, from among the bushes, the shadow of a man wearing a hat appeared before me. He seemed to be bending to the ground and pushing things toward me. I couldn't make out what they were from where I was, but I could hear the dry leaves crackling under their weight. At the moment I was distracted by this shadow, I was set upon by a number of turkeys, raising their beaks and gobbling in my face. Each of them had a long wattle. I was in a terrible state, unable to shoo them away or even call out for help. Nearby, a tall man gazed at me. He was wearing a long flowing garment, a pointed cap on his head; he looked like a dervish. He was not alarmed as I was by the turkeys, or even concerned by them; in his gaze I saw his judgment: I deserved what I got from these gobbling birds.

Chapter 15

I grew closer to Akram Abul Shawareb.

The first thing I had noticed about him had been his massive height and girth: he looked like a wardrobe. He had a white mustache, yellow at the edges, or rather, amber-colored, stained by the cigarettes that were always between his fingers. His thick hair was the main thing, as they say: parted in the center as though with a ruler, and so diligently oiled with special oils that it didn't seem to be divided into individual hairs like other people's, but stuck together in sheaves or clumps, in such a way that it was impossible to muss it; impossible, indeed, even to move a single hair. The entire mass moved as one. In the back, a large lock hung down, wrapped with a plastic clip or sometimes held in place with a hairpin, as was the fashion in Paris at the time.

As for his features, they too were striking: nose, ears, mouth, and eyes. All were of an absurd size, and the size of his fist rivaled that of a healthy young gorilla's. He was nearing sixty, but his appearance belied his age; he looked young, his face healthy and pink. Although he had been living in Paris for several decades, his clothing was old-fashioned, sixties at the latest. He was also an attraction in the shop, especially for elderly French ladies. They would ask for him by name as soon as they walked in the door, and watched him more closely than the fabrics, and bought from him under the spell of his charm and attractiveness, not necessarily because of the quality of the fabric or its reasonable price. For this reason, he had special status with Bouchard, the owner. His requests were granted, his salary was on the rise, and he was the emblem of the shop.

Despite all this, he was dissatisfied with his lot. He would say that he had wasted his life serving in this shop, and got only the crumbs.

When M. René first handed me over to this Abul Shawareb, I had reservations about his massive build and his unfamiliar Lebanese dialect. But the barriers between us quickly melted. He withheld none of the tricks of the trade from me, so that I grasped them in a few months. I found out that he was softhearted, tender as a leaf of lettuce. Day by day our friendship grew stronger, in spite of the age difference, and we started to go out together. Since he was the teacher, the professor, in the world of fabrics, and I the apprentice, I deferred to him and went where he pleased, not where I wanted to go.

He was mad about Oriental music and singing, and I felt there was no harm in my enjoying what he enjoyed. Many times we would go to the Place de Clichy in the heart of Paris, finding groups of young men and women from North Africa sitting on the sidewalks with musical instruments in their laps: lutes, drums, the tambour, and the reed flute. Most of their songs were emotional and rhythmic. They sang covers of all the famous Arab musicians: Farid al-Atrash and Uleyya al-Tuniseya and Abdel Wahab al-Dukali, and Algerian rai, which I enjoyed without understanding what it meant, and naturally the session always ended with a verse or two of Kulthoum.

They would always draw a crowd of passersby, French people and foreign tourists drawn by curiosity. They would form a circle around the group that was playing, and there would be such singing and clapping! Sometimes one of the girls, in a transport of ecstasy, would snatch a scarf from someone and tie it around her hips, and there would be more dancing and fun! The increasing noise and merriment was infectious: I would enjoy the moment with them, forgetting my stepfather Mr. Yacoub, and his evil doppelganger who had long played with me, giving ghostly form to my archenemy, the man who had won Nadia, the man who was running and playing with her now.

Abul Shawareb, filled with enthusiasm, would suddenly rip off his jacket and throw it down, then bend and take off his belt, tossing it into the air, accompanied by the shrieks of his admirers who knew him from his frequent visits. People would turn their backs on the band and start clapping in time to the music, as he gyrated and wiggled his hips. One of the girls would eventually come close and tie a scarf round his hips; he would burn hotter, and gesture to the assembled throng to clap harder.

The band would stop, and then play a tune more suited to his colossal dimensions. The drummer would draw so near to him that he was kneeling nearly between his legs, and beat ever faster and louder, setting him aflame, and Abul Shawareb would present such amazing belly dancing that he put Taheya Carioca and Samia Gamal, the famous belly dancers, to shame!

I would pick up his things; his jacket, his belt, and the little things he'd dropped, his key ring, his wallet, and a few francs, and take him aside when he was done, while he mopped his brow like a little boy.

If a Lebanese band should happen to appear on one of the sidewalks, he would be filled with a new surge of enthusiasm, and pulled me by the arm to run toward them. He'd stand there dreamily, lost in the songs they sang, covers of Wadie al-Safi, Mahd Balan, Sabah Fakhry, Fairuz, and Sabah, "the Blackbird." Their sessions were enjoyable as well, and they never broke up their celebrations before they had sung, and us along with them, their famous folk song:

O Levant, my Levant, it's been so long, come, my love so true,
O Levant, my Levant, your love is on my mind, the sweetest times have been with you.
You said goodbye and promised never to forget me, nor I you.

Sometimes we would go to other gatherings: at Saint-Germain, and opposite the Louvre, and at the Place Saint-Denis: huge congregations and groups of people, mostly French, around bands playing all kinds of music: some staid and sensible, playing smooth, calm tangos or high waltzes, their audiences of respectable older people; and others playing pop and rock, to say nothing of jazz and the music of the gypsies and Martinique, and the one-man bands, musicians sitting alone with their guitars or violins, trying to draw a crowd.

These we watched without participating; the watching itself was empty of enthusiasm and curiosity. We felt that they were one breed of human being, and we quite another.

One weekend, Abul Shawareb took me—for the first and last time—to a nightclub in the Pigalle district, called Le Cirmillou, which as I recall meant a rat or a small mouse.

The cabaret was a dive, where Arab capital paid Lebanese managers. The patrons were mainly working-class Arabs, especially the Lebanese, who had made tracks for Paris when the civil war broke out in their country. Here you could find Tony and Remon, the Christians, rubbing shoulders with Mohamed, Rafik, or Waleed, the Muslims (or Druze), clapping, nodding their heads to the music, and blowing their hard-earned cash while their Lebanese brothers and sisters spilled each other's blood and fought up and down the alleyways. Other nationalities filled the neighboring tables: Africans, Portuguese, some Indians and Chinese, and some working-class French, consumed by curiosity but unable to afford a ticket to the upscale clubs like the Moulin Rouge and the Folies-Bergère.

Waiters circulated with glasses of wine. Wandering around were a number of emaciated Arab and Portuguese girls, half-naked in spite of the bitter cold, searching for someone to spend the night with them in exchange for dinner and a few francs. There was also a lying, unscrupulous MC, who would bellow at us periodically, "And now, the fiery goddess of dance with the alabaster skin and the fabulous figure, with the slender, swaying hips!" So we'd look, and there she would be—a rhinoceros of a woman, dripping with sweat under her extravagantly painted face, her shoes—I swear I'm not exaggerating—a size 11, while the drunken patrons applauded and swayed and belched when the wine stung their bellies. Only one of our Lebanese brethren was paying any attention to her, and he swore up and down, by everything sacred and profane and by his misspent youth, that the dancer before him was no woman nor any member of the female sex, but a man, yes, a man, he swore by God, a man in drag, and that he was fully prepared to conduct an examination and prove it to everyone.

Then the MC's voice called out, "And now I present to you the silver-throated singer whose dulcet tones have brought music to Lebanon's hills and vales, her valleys and dales!" The curtain went up to reveal a man with a face like a mule's, with a positively criminal countenance, a porter if we were to be very charitable, or in all probability a highwayman.

As if that weren't enough, he withheld his dulcet tones from us at the start, imagining—this buffoon—that this would whet our appetite, so he kept winking at the band to prolong the musical introduction, until one of the patrons, a fellow countryman from Lebanon, hollered, "Get a move on, will ya? Keep dawdling and we'll go home! Who do you think you are, Wadie al-Safi or Fahd Ballan? Sing already, you son of a bitch!"

So he opened his mouth to sing. It was the fatal blow. He started a slow ballad that immediately turned the place upside-down. One erstwhile patron was howling for blood from the innermost depths of the bar, calling for someone, anyone, to bring down the curtain instantly upon this braying brute, or else he would climb on the stage and take his revenge himself as a public service to the rest of the patrons, while others condemned such hasty calls, saying that justice must be tempered with mercy, and that there was no harm in giving him his chance, two full minutes, before justice was done. Abul Shawareb had had one too many, for his face was blood-red, and his expression showed a man at the very end of his tether. I feared that there might be bloodshed soon, especially when he started pounding on the table, bawling for the manager of the filthy dive to attend to him right that very minute.

"Come on, Abul Shawareb!" I beseeched him. "Calm down! We don't want a scandal here!"

"No!" he bellowed. "Right this minute! Right this minute!"

He repeated it several times, then his head fell to the table. When I elbowed him, all he did was raise his red eyes to mine and resume slurring, "Right this minute! Right this . . . minute . . . And he'd better pay me damages for what his croaking raven did to my ears!"

I finally paid the bill and dragged him out.

Chapter 16

I entered the business world.

We were having a leisurely stroll, Abul Shawareb and I, in the Luxembourg Gardens, each of us unhurriedly licking at an ice cream cone. After a long, comfortable silence, he stopped me.

"Are you satisfied with the way we are now, you and I? How long are we going to go on like this? What are we? Just salesmen, working for Bouchard! Wage slaves, getting a few francs every month that barely pay our bills. We toil and sweat and it's that petit-bourgeois who reaps the profits!"

For a moment I thought that Abul Shawareb had socialist leanings, or perhaps was a supporter of Marchais,[*] who was quite famous in France in those days, and never tired of yelling in the media about the injustices suffered by the workers, threatening dire consequences for the owners of factories and department stores and capitalists. I didn't comment, though, just rubbed my nose and stared at him.

"Yes, man," he resumed with feeling. "I want to be rich, to have lots of money like *les riches*. I don't want to stay poor and not be able to help my family out. I want money, francs, lots of francs. Don't you know what francs are?"

---

[*]   Georges Marchais, head of the French Communist Party at that time.

Something in my face must have provoked him, for he squeezed my shoulder. "I'm not kidding. I'm telling you, it's not that I want a lot of money for my family here. If you think it's for my wife and children, you're wrong. And I don't mean my parents in Bent-Jbeil either. By the grace of God, I send them money every month. I mean the young guys in Bent-Jbeil and Maroun-al-Ras and Debal-Ein and 'Edeisa and Sheba'a* too. I want to send them money and help them."

I had known that he was from southern Lebanon, from Bent-Jbeil in the very southern tip of the country, on the border with Israel. He had often told me of the good folk there, with their big mustaches and puffy black pants, their agals on their heads, living in peace all their lives as their forefathers had, never bothering anyone or being bothered by anyone, until Israel had come to be their neighbor, and appropriated some of their lands after the war of 1967. They had fought back, and so had Israel, killing the young and kidnapping the elders, and they retaliating in kind. The IDF and Saad Haddad's† men had underestimated them. They had classed them as no-account, ineffectual farmers and shepherds, but they had proved to be stalwart opponents with a strong sense of honor, who would die before being used by the Zionists or by Haddad's men.

Abul Shawareb's voice softened as he leaned over to me. "There was a man who came from the south and told me how they lived over there. They're suffering, Galal, suffering. They need someone to fund them with arms so they can fight back against the Jews and against Saad Haddad. Don't you hear in the media about the youth groups called the Hope Movement?"

---

* Tiny villages in southern Lebanon.
† A well-known Israeli collaborator who split from the Lebanese army and formed militias that settled in southern Lebanon to serve Israeli interests, to the detriment of the local inhabitants.

I nodded, and his face became enthusiastic. "There's fresh news about other groups as well!* They're preparing themselves to fight back against Haddad and Israel. They're young people of faith, taking their lives in their hands, not afraid to die. And the people like us, away from home, here or in America—we're the ones who ought to help them, and give, if not our lives, at least money so they can arm themselves." After a silence, he looked at me. "That's good, isn't it?"

"Yes," I said. "Yes, it's good." I said it from the heart. We started walking again. A few steps away, we glimpsed a vacant bench. A boy and a girl were walking toward it, so he grabbed me by the wrist and ran toward them.

"Quick, let's grab the vacant seat before those two!"

We sat down. He caught his breath and changed the subject. "You know who our boss used to be? A traveling salesman, in the streets of Marseilles in the days of the war with Hitler. Little by little, his business grew. He came to Paris, and worked day and night till he made his fortune, and now he owns three stores—one in La Défense, another in Montparnasse, and the third in Saint-Antoine—besides the one where we work." He lit a cigarette and stretched his legs out, exhaling a plume of smoke with satisfaction. "Galal, my boy." He said it lovingly, so that I was reminded of Sheikh Munji. I looked at him, and he added, "You want the truth? You're very dear to my heart. More than that, you're like a younger brother to me, and you remind me of my youth, when I first started work at that store. I was poor then, and I had to live. Now I've been working for thirty years, and the boss still isn't paying me what I'm worth. I swear, all I have is ten thousand francs in the bank here, and yesterday I transferred them to the south."

---

* These were the fledgling Hezbollah, although Abul Shawareb didn't know them as such; they only called themselves that two years later. At the time, all that the Lebanese living in France (particularly those from the south) heard was that there was a new political resistance party forming in secret.

125

He sighed. "I swear, you're a good boy, a kind boy, a trustworthy boy. Give me your hand, and we'll go into business together! We can build something good, something fine, for both of us."

"But, my brother Akram . . ." He liked it when I called him that. I had tried before to call him Uncle Akram, due to the difference in our ages, or Monsieur, because he was technically my boss, but he wouldn't let me. He was young in spirit, and he wanted me to call him by his name without any prefixes. Finally we had reached this compromise. I said, "I'd love to help you, and help myself as well, but how?"

He patted my shoulder. "Let's put our trust in God and go into business together. We'll go into trade, because it turns a good profit. You'll get your share, to do with as you please. And I'll get mine, and send it to the kids down south."

We started by going to rue du Caire in Montmartre. How well I remember the day I went there!

President Sadat had been martyred on the reviewing stand a few months previously. Abul Shawareb got out at the Métro stop by the Wax Museum, which isn't too far from that street. We thought we'd start by going to the museum. We bought two tickets and entered through a long passageway with thick red velvet ropes on either side, affixed to brass poles on the ground. There were life-size wax statues of prominent statesmen, artists and celebrities: Queen Elizabeth II, JFK, King Hussein, Maurice Chevalier, and in an appropriate place, a freshly-made statue of President Sadat, with a big bouquet at his feet and flowers all around him.

Abul Shawareb and I stood there, reciting the Fatiha over his soul as it is customary to do. I lingered, looking at his outstretched hands, and his broad smile for which he had been famous while opening a People's Assembly session or greeting crowds in public places. Behind us was a French girl with her family; I saw her cast a white rose on the pile, wiping her eyes. The visitors to the museum—the French ones especially—seemed to pause before his statue more than any other, gracing it with a sad glance before leaving.

The museum also held a Hall of Mirrors. We went in there; it was medium-sized, its four walls covered from floor to ceiling with giant mirrors, convex, concave, and normal, all shiny and smooth, as though your eyes saw straight through them to the other side. When it was judged to be full enough, the doors to the room were closed and the lights extinguished. All at once, the mirrors lit up with blinding floodlights coming from within, making the world before us look—I have no idea how—like a tropical forest in Africa, filled with the squawks of predatory birds, the roars and howls of wild animals, and waterfalls cascading toward us as though they were real and would sweep us away in a moment.

The scene changed. Calm reigned; now we were on a green hillside, with gently waving wildflowers. They would suddenly raise us up to snow-covered peaks, which we were told was the formidable Mount Kilimanjaro itself. A cheetah spied on us from on high with its great eyes. All the while we were treated to subtle, ravishing music by Ravel and Debussy, followed by the sweet melodies of Tchaikovsky's *Swan Lake* and *Sleeping Beauty*.

Finally we emerged into the rue du Caire, rubbing our eyes. It was a bustling trading center, not unlike Muski Street in Cairo. Most of its stores carried clothing, women's apparel in particular, and they only sold wholesale: "Six pieces minimum, sir, or else you can go to a place that sells retail." The street was full of foreign traders: from the Levant, the Maghreb, Asia, every country there is. They were all here to buy, and it was a wise man who knew the secrets of how to buy.

Abul Shawareb's plan was for us to come every week, to find out what was selling well, and snatch up the newest colors and trends, buying twelve or eighteen of each piece, instead of six, because the price goes down the more you buy, going down to 50 percent off, sometimes even less. Abul Shawareb said, tapping his pack of cigarettes, "Our main customers will be the Gulf Arabs who come to Paris in the summer. We need someone who can tell us which hotels and furnished apartments they stay in. Those people are very rich, and a lot of them are gullible. We're guaranteed a profit!"

Rachel immediately came to mind. I said to myself, "No doubt about it! She's a smart one! She'd be the best helper we could hope to have! If she puts her heart into it, we'll be raking it in."

Abul Shawareb was finishing up what he had to say, namely, that he would be able to unload the remaining stock on the tourists from the Levant and Iran on whirlwind tours of Paris, who had no time to shop around in stores.

But where would we store the stock?

Abul Shawareb wagged a finger in the traditional gesture of negation, adamant that his house was completely unsuitable for the storage of any clothing; his wife, Umm Bahloul, couldn't keep her hands to herself. She would raid the stock and take what she pleased, whether he liked it or not! Moreover, she had a gaggle of female neighbors, all without the slightest shred of conscience or feeling, and he expected his *femme formidable* to invite all of them to invade the apartment as well, to look, try on, and model the different sizes! And they'd have no qualms about borrowing them for a few days, only to return them with a grease stain or a snag!

When I offered the use of my apartment, he agreed.

My grandfather didn't let me down. He welcomed the idea and said that I could do as I wished with the whole apartment. He also extended a loan of five thousand francs to get me into the business, to be repaid at my leisure. My grandmother agreed after some persuasion, in the hope of receiving a long-sleeved blouse or a coat, or even a dozen pairs of socks, which I would give her willingly to shut her up, and if I was slow to deliver, there would be nothing for it but force and fighting.

Abul Shawareb started to come by almost every week; either to store some new stock, or accompanied by a customer. He would sit at a café in the street, and I would come and go with the bags of clothing, and deals would be struck.

He met Sheikh Munji, and they gradually became friends. However, he never trusted Mamadou, and felt uncomfortable around him. He said that he stank; that he'd smelled pigeon droppings and this Mamadou smelled just like them.

Chapter 17

Sheikh Munji invited Abul Shawareb and me to dinner. When we arrived, we found a man there, a Palestinian sheikh, complete with turban, who told us as we were shaking his hand that his name was Sheikh Ekrema, from Nablus in Palestine.

It was toward the end of Eid al-Adha. The mellifluous, tender rhythms still rang in my ear, tripping off the tongues of the Muslims gathered at prayer. I dreamed with them, lost in the grace of God, as they chanted the traditional prayer, "God is the Greatest, God is the Greatest, God is the Greatest, God is the Greatest, all Praise is due to Him, and Glory to God, in the eventide and in the morning."

I craned my neck upward as they called out with pride, "He has fulfilled His Promise, and made Victorious His worshiper, and made Mighty His soldiers and defeated the confederates." I bowed, humility in my heart, as they said, "There is no god but He, Him alone we worship, with sincere and exclusive devotion, although the infidels hate it; O God, have Mercy on our Prophet Mohamed, and on the family of our Prophet Mohamed, and on the Companions of our Prophet Mohamed, and on the Helpers of our Prophet Mohamed, and on the wives of our Prophet Mohamed, and on the offspring of our Prophet Mohamed, and bestow upon them much peace."

We had repeated this prayer the day before in the Mosque of Paris during the Eid Prayer: Abul Shawareb, Sheikh Munji, and I, and Mamadou, and Ghulam Khan, the Pakistani barber who lived with us in Barbès, but it still didn't steal my heart, nor did it make my blood surge as it used to back there, in my far-off homeland!

When I was in Sheikh Khalaf's prayer hall, these moments—especially the moments when we chanted the prayer—used to make me feel that I was no longer in command of myself. Every pore in my body would be filled with something ethereal, making me light, pliant, yielding; it was as though I were floating, as though something were taking my hand and lifting me from the ground where I stood. I would never manage to end the prayer without a tear, remaining after everyone else had left, alone, abstracted, and unsure: was I praying, or was my troubled heart reaching toward the Lord?

This wasn't what I felt the day before yesterday. The prayers rolled off my tongue while my eyes wandered between Mamadou, who had no shame before his God, and was looking at his watch while praying, and Sheikh Munji, lips moving in words of thanks and prayer, for all the world as though he were as observant of God's law in the shop and in the street and in the marketplace as he was now in prayer. And Abul Shawareb, pushing sixty, still didn't know whether the Eid sermon came before or after the prayer!

Was the fault in me? God was the same here and there. Or were place and time and self and the people around me also movers of faith? I didn't know—God forgive me, for the fault is mine. Why had I not noticed all the people with whom the mosque was now bursting? Africans, Asians, Arabs, blond, blue-eyed Frenchmen, all kneeling and bowing, giving themselves over to their Lord!

When we came out of the mosque, Sheikh Munji took advantage of Mamadou's preoccupation with his sandal, which had a hole in it, and invited us to dinner, urging us not to tell Mamadou; if he came, he would leave us not a morsel or a scrap, not a single dish with food in it. To accompany him was doom: not even a sip of water would come your way.

I had a craving for meat broth, and fatta with vinegar and garlic. I had always celebrated Eid at Umm Hassan's, especially Eid al-Adha; Hassan and I would pull the ram by the collar round its neck, while behind us Amm Idriss the doorman waved his stick. Said, Hassan's elder brother, would stand at the top of the stairs, calling us stupid, saying the sheep would surely escape. We would look up, rolling our eyes, saying, "You're the stupid one!"

We would stand right next to the butcher as he slaughtered the sheep, delivering it to its recipients according to the list, handwritten by Hassan's father, Hajj Mahmoud al-Attar. I also remembered Sheikh Salamouni Abu Gamous—I ask Heaven neither to forgive his sins nor bless his soul—the nasty Quran reader who threw our meat back in our faces when he weighed it in his hand and found the amount to be not to his liking, and then hobbled after us in pursuit, leaning on his stick, insisting on coming himself to the site of the ram.

And then there was Umm Hassan, who would swear on the souls of her late father and mother and every member of her family who had died, that my mother and I were not permitted to leave until we had dined with her. She would dip her hand into her neckline and pull out her little purse, and give me my traditional Eid gift of money, just as she gave her son Hassan. God grant you good health, Umm Hassan. How I mourn the loss of those days!

After dinner, there was mint tea and talk.

Sheikh Munji started out by telling us of the health inspectors who had descended unannounced upon his shop, heading straight for *that* fridge. They had looked here and there, and taken samples. "Ah, if I only knew who that dirty, irreligious cur was who keeps reporting me!" he cried. "It's the third time those riffraff have stormed my shop, with their white suits and clipboards!"

I smiled surreptitiously, my mind's eye conjuring the poor Algerian man who had entreated the sheikh for a piece of meat suitable for escalopes.

We also spoke of the accursed Arabs, pockets bulging with francs, who spent the nights in the clubs, staggering and weaving out into the streets in the wee hours on the arms of loose women, getting into their Rolls-Royces and Citroëns, heading for their pricey apartments or big-name hotels, where a single night costs two or three thousand francs. Most of the talk came from Abul Shawareb, followed by Sheikh Ekrema. Fussing with his mustache, he said, "Even the poorer Arabs, my friends! Some of them don't have enough at home to support themselves—even those—heaven protect us—some of them stay out all night in cheap saloons in the Saint-Antoine and the Pigalle! There are two, the Rat and the Rabid Dog, and there's also the Shameless Monkey, and they go staggering home, for their families to see, and some of them have young children!"

I looked toward Abul Shawareb, thinking to myself, "Just where did this naughty sheikh find out all this?" and thanked God that Sheikh Munji was unaware of what Abul Shawareb got up to at the Rat, or else it would be I who bore the brunt of it; I would receive a disappointed lecture for having suffered this drunk womanizer to enter his pure and honorable abode.

When it was my turn to speak, I found I had nothing to say. The only thing that came to mind was the bunch of withered, doddering old Jewish men who came to spend the evening at Mr. Yacoub's, my stepfather's. So I spoke of them.

Abul Shawareb cut me off, protesting. "Man, those people are fortunate and well-off. Those . . . those are people who have food and drink and shelter, and they've nothing to worry about: the rich Jews here give them everything." Warming to his subject, he took out a cigarette and made to light it, but Sheikh Munji motioned for him not to; in his home, anything that would displease the Lord was prohibited—cigarettes, alcohol, and the like. Abul Shawareb put it away, disgruntled, but kept talking with the sheikh. "You've been living here for a long time, Sheikh Munji, and I'm sure you know of Samarta, Chison, and Jacques René, the rich Jewish men here who own the factories and the heavyweight stores. And you know how much they send to the Jews in Israel."

Sheikh Munji nodded, and Abul Shawareb resumed. "If you came to Lebanon, sir, and compared them to the Palestinians, you'd see how much poverty there is over there. The poor Palestinians are destitute, living in wooden hovels, in the camps at Ein al-Helwa in Sayda, and Sabra and Shatila in Beirut. Nobody helps them. Every one of those families has eight or nine people in it, all alone, living in one room, nobody comfortable, no room for so much as a guest. Poor folk—back home those people had real estate, homes, shops, and were living high. They were well-off, not like now, waiting for assistance so they can eat like beggars awaiting alms." He turned to me reproachfully. "Those are the ones you should talk about when you think of the unfortunate ones, not the Jews who have money and houses, Galal!"

Sheikh Ekrema took up the thread of conversation. "I am a Muslim, my boy, and our laws teach us to have pity upon the weak, be it a cactus in the middle of the desert. Therefore, I . . ." He paused. "Remind me what your name is, young man?"

"Galal."

"Bless you, Galal. Your name is derived from the Exalted Nature of our Lord, who forgets and ignores nothing." He looked around at the assembled men. "My honorable brethren, I bear no ill will toward these Jews of whom our son Galal speaks. They are created by God like you or me, and they too have the right to compassion and pity. However, in the end, they left their homes by choice. Their means may have been strained back there, but nobody forced them to migrate. The evidence is that there are still Jewish people in Egypt until now." He looked to me. "Am I not right?"

I paused, then nodded. He took off his turban, brushing off its dark red top with the wide sleeve of his caftan. He dried off his bald pate with a cotton handkerchief, as the sheikhs in Egypt do. He craned his neck toward me, saying in moving tones: "Go, my boy, and sit with the unfortunates who left, banished, with their women and children and beasts, in 1948. They migrated from Jaffa and Nasira and Megedel and Kuikat and Wadi al-Nisnas and Damoun.* Some were born in the wilderness, some died on the trail without even the time for a prayer; those who did were thrown into a pit with the clothes on their backs, the shoes on their feet, and the hats on their heads. They were covered up with dirt, and the migrants rushed on, afraid of the Jews trailing some distance behind them, as if to say, "The living are more important than the dead, and it is enough that he lived and died and was buried in Palestine, for who knows what shall befall us and in what land we shall die?"

He turned to Sheikh Munji, saying, "We had our dignity, Abu Zein al-Abedeen. We had homes, trees, and wells. Afterward, we wandered, lost, like the moths and rats in the night; we lived like dogs foraging through garbage dumps, and received provisions like beggars." I watched in shock as he said, "Perhaps you don't know, Galal, that after the people of Haifa were gone from their homes, the Jews entered them, and found the tea and coffee still freshly poured in the cups."

When my face showed astonishment, he shook his head regretfully and said, "Yes, my boy, that's what happened. The owners left their homes in such a hurry they didn't have time to drink it. Perhaps you don't know, as well, that all they cared about was hiding their possessions and locking them in. For the mother, it was the pantry; the lentils, sugar, rice, and tea. For the little boys, the toys, pencil sharpener, eraser, pens, and copybooks; for the little girl, the dolls and little mirror and the new dress she was saving for Eid. The father took the keys to the house with him, for it was only days—or weeks, at the most—and they would be back. The poor folk were afraid that the Jewish gangs' hands might extend to their food and drink and linens and the clothing in their closets. It had never occurred to them that they had lost the houses themselves; the houses and everything in them."

---

* Villages and towns in Palestine where the inhabitants were subjected to forced migration.

A gloom settled over us all. He added, "They destroyed our villages. Tamra, Maloul, Shafa Amr, Eblein. Even the names of our towns they changed. Sahat al-Hanatir, in Haifa, they named Paris. Marg ibn Amer they announced was no longer called that—they renamed it the Plain of Azrael. Ain Jalout! Do you know what that is, Galal, my boy?"

I responded, "I know it, sir. It is the field of battle where we triumphed over the Mongolian army."

"Yes," he said, "that's it, and now it's called Ain Haroud. Haroud is a Jewish name." Sadness filled his face as he added, "Shouldn't you, you Egyptians, have retained that proud name, which is now erased by Israel? Shouldn't you have named some great street for it, some square, and made the day when you triumphed over the Mongolians a national holiday? Isn't it a day of victory like the Sixth of October? Wouldn't it have been your right to protest against Israel—Israel that never lets the whole world rest if one of her little boys' toes receives so much as a scratch—and tell them to return the name to what it was before, and stop playing around with history?"

We drew nearer to Sheikh Ekrema, consoling him and saying comforting words. "We did what we could," he said, his voice breaking. "We resisted. We were killed, and taken hostage, and our bones broken, and our property confiscated. They took away everything, except our love for Palestine. Even the Palestinian women, weak and gentle, changed. They're not like other women any more. Oppression, the loss of their land, of their children, of their lovers, has transformed them. Their hearts are like iron and rock. Their eyes are neither young nor old, but ageless with suffering and unshed tears. Some of them have died martyrs, with nursing infants waiting at home. Some of them have bared their heads and borne arms, each on the chance that God will reunite her with her child, consumed by the Jews. You will not find a woman, young or old, who does not teach her children how to fight; she will ululate with joy if she sees one of them bear arms and go into battle. If the child is young, she rocks him to sleep and sings to him, 'Hush-a-bye little Mahmoud, Daddy's gone to push back the Jews.'"

I said to Sheikh Ekrema, "My father's name was Mahmoud. He died going to war with the Jews."

Chapter 18

Our business venture flourished.

The profits came rolling in, richer than we had expected, thanks be to God—primarily—but thanks also to our Gulf Arab brethren with their heavy purses, who came to spend the summer in Paris. Not all of them, of course, but a number to whom money meant nothing, or who had no other use for it than fun and games and throwing it under women's feet.

It was Rachel who'd hooked us up with these heavyweights. We would visit each of these customers in his hotel suite, or his apartment on the Seine, rented for the summer for a sum that was enough for five families back home to live on for a year. Abul Shawareb would wear an Armani suit, or a Lanvin, and shoes from Bally or Michel Jourdain, his mustache oiled with perfumed oils from Cosmetique. In his inside waistcoat pocket was a shiny gold monocle, which he placed over his right eye when he had to look at something closely, or when it came time to pay the bill. He leaned on an ebony stick, and there was a flower in his buttonhole, a silk kerchief in his jacket pocket.

Rachel had engineered this new image. She had whispered into my ear that Abul Shawareb, in his outmoded clothing, looked more of a period piece than a businessman, and would not impress our customers from the Gulf; they went out, after all, and walked in the streets, and saw how people dressed, and understood how things were; and since we were going to sell things to them in their homes, with long sessions and discussions, he needed a new image, as well as some culture and information.

And so it was. She and I spent a long session planning and refining his new image; or to be precise, Rachel, the little minx, was the artiste behind it, and my role was confined to convincing Abul Shawareb—and thank heaven he said yes! He even agreed to several sessions with her, in which she taught him the rudiments of etiquette and gave him the fruits of her experience about how these potential customers thought and behaved.

To see him in this new persona was to be instantly impressed by the striking figure he cut, and silently say, "Dear Lord! This is not a tradesman offering his wares, but an important minister in the Levant, a consul or an ambassador here on a mission to conduct negotiations!"

As for me, I wore jeans, running shoes, and a waterproof jacket. I would keep my eyes down, and never speak unless spoken to, and not sit down unless given permission, and walk three paces behind Abul Shawareb. Whenever he spoke, my only response was, "Yes, sir," "Whatever you say, sir." The plan was for me to appear before the Gulf customer like Abul Shawareb's servant, carrying the goods for him and obeying his orders and driving his Jaguar—that year's model—which we'd have rented just for the day, after lengthy and protracted bargaining.

The Arab sheikh welcomed us, his face wreathed in smiles. They always call themselves Sheikh So-and-So, while usually their names are Khalfan, Durgham, and sometimes, Shackboot. "Welcome, welcome, welcome!" he cried out, "A thousand welcomes to the genuine son of the Levant, the Mujahid, son of Mujahideen, the leader of all the Druze!" This was all due to false information planted beforehand by Rachel into the ears of the sheikh, giving him to understand that this Abul Shawareb was not a man to be trifled with, the grandson of the al-Atrash clan, who had long fought the French for their freedom, and that he was on good terms with the most important families of Lebanon, such as Rami, al-Sulh, and Arsalan—but that he had, unfortunately, fallen on hard times.

The sheikh's chivalrous side would inspire him to ever more effusive and fulsome greetings, which Abul Shawareb received with decorous and refined gratitude, his face tinged with sadness, as though at the fate which had reduced him to this. But his head remained high and proud, his nose held slightly higher than usual.

I don't know how Abul Shawareb achieved this balance. He executed it perfectly, so much so that I was almost taken in by it sometimes—the customers didn't stand a chance!

It wouldn't seem like a matter of trade or bargaining at first, but a meeting of good friends, of equals. As a precaution, Abul Shawareb would feel out the sheikh to find out how knowledgeable he was. Finding him a tabula rasa, he would shoot me a confident look, sit back, legs crossed, and start talking—and all he talked of was trivialities, made-up hooey, filled with errors. The sheikh, thinking himself to be gaining valuable information, would nod his head sagely. "Good! Good! God bless you."

Unless politics or Arab leaders came up. That was when the sheikh would look around him cautiously. Nobody was ever at their ease as long as the bag at my feet, the one containing our wares, remained closed. They always thought there was a tape-recorder concealed inside it. If the conversation was about jokes, women, or things to do with sex, the sheikh would be positively alight with interest; upon noticing that their voices had risen and that they were laughing uproariously, he would glance at the connecting door between us and his womenfolk, and lower his voice, motioning to Abul Shawareb to follow suit, so that the talk would not reach their ears.

Eventually, he would run out of patience. "What do you have?" he'd say, looking at his Rolex. "Let's hope they're things that gladden the heart and make one's mouth water!"

This would be a signal to get down to business. Abul Shawareb would command me to open the outer pocket of the bag and get the bottle out. It was no bigger than two fingers, and had an indecent picture on it. They didn't sell it in any shops—in fact, I think that if found on anyone, it would doubtless induce the French authorities to detain the holder for investigation while they subjected the bottle itself to tests and analyses.

We got them from the poorer Indians who worked in the shops and streets, and sometimes from Thais; they smuggled these in secretly from their own countries on the way back from holidays. They would peer at us and say, "It's a ball of fire, extracted from wild animals, lions and tigers, crocodiles and horned rams!"

Suspiciously, Abul Shawareb would ask them, "Are you telling the truth, man?"

They would assure him that its effects were extraordinary, and that it could make a hopeless man as virile a stud as had ever been seen.

I didn't like to trade in this kind of thing: it was asking for trouble. My worries had become more acute after an incident a few months before with an incorrigible senile old Gulf Arab, who styled himself a sheikh like the rest. He had bought a bottle from us, along with a number of other things, and a week later we came to show him silks he had requested for his wife Umm Salboukh. We found him enraged, shouting, "You lied to me, you swindlers! You tricked me! You gave me a bad bottle—it didn't do anything!"

Abul Shawareb drew near to him. "My dear sheikh . . ."

"Stay away from me, damn you! You embarrassed me, made me look like a failure in front of my wife Umm Salboukh! You dragged me through the mud. May God never forgive you, may you never prosper!"

The argument grew more heated as they exchanged words, and Abul Shawareb's tongue ran away with him. "There's nothing wrong with the bottle. The bottle is guaranteed and stamped with the stamp of virility from the province of Punjab. It's your parts that aren't working, sheikh; either they're past their expiration date, or they broke down for some reason."

The sheikh, unable to take this, in the heat of his rage, took off his slipper and threw it at us. Then he bent over his stick, cursing us and our parents and grandparents. We decided that getting the hell out was the better part of valor, and took to our heels as he chased after us.

That was why my heart pounded when Abul Shawareb opened another bottle and with a matchstick touched a drop of it to this new sheikh's hand. "Please," I said to myself, "let this not be another disaster."

I stared at him, and started back when he sniffed at it. It was like a mixture of hot spices and chili peppers, cooked together with some oil. He turned the bottle over in his hands, unable to understand it, skeptical that it could hold such secrets. He bought it, however, Abul Shawareb giving him the thumbs-up, assuring him it would be "A-Okay."

It had cost ten francs—or, as we we told him, eighty. He nodded and placed it gently in his bag, saying, "Do you have something for me for Umm Helal?" We naturally understood that this Umm Helal was his wife. "I want something to please her," he said, "to delight her heart."

Abul Shawareb commanded me to open the bag of modest clothing. Long-sleeved, high-necked blouses, maxi-length skirts, light perfumes, and extremely conservative underwear. The sheikh looked at these in consternation, appearing extremely disappointed. "What's this?" he said in dismay, fingering a thick pair of pajama pants in basic black. "Is this what they make in Paris?"

"Yes, you of the long life."

"Who do they make it for?"

"For modest, God-fearing ladies," said Abul Shawareb.

"Ah. You really mean women who wear full-body veils and those who have no use for this earthly plane or the delights of this world? I don't want that." And he tossed the pants on the floor. "I don't want modest clothing! I want indecent garments! Obscene, you understand? For the bedroom!"

Wasting no time, I opened the left side of the bag, and we started to show him things that were a delight to the eye. He took them, one after another, fingering the fabric, passing his hand over them, holding them up to make sure that they were see-through. "Mashallah, Mashallah! Now that's more like it!"

Knowing he liked the wares, Abul Shawareb and I exchanged glances, while he scrutinized a brassiere that was barely enough for a belly dancer. "How much is this?" We told him—three times the price we had bought it for. He nodded in agreement. "And this one?" It was worse than its predecessor! We followed the same pricing policy.

At one garment, he reared his head back slightly, and raised his voice, trying to play smart. "No, no. This is too expensive. I want discounts. This would be much cheaper back home."

We were surprised; we had no idea why he was bargaining this time, although he hadn't before. However, to make him happy, we cut the price a little.

He went inside to show Umm Helal the goods so that she could choose what she wanted, she and her grown daughters and her Filipino maids. He returned, well pleased, and paid up. As we were getting ready to leave, he asked us, "How are you getting home?"

We told him, "Our car is downstairs."

"Where?" He went to the window and saw it. "A Jaguar? Mashallah! Mashallah! I have the latest Mercedes-Benz." He pointed at a fabulous vehicle, resplendent in its slot like a crocodile. Wonderingly, he said, "The engine is good, I'll say that for it. I shift into fifth and step on the accelerator and it flies like a pigeon!"

We laughed politely and hurried off.

I would ask myself afterward: was what we were doing a sin? I wondered at a gentleman like this, who reaped sins with the wealth God had seen fit to give him.

I began to have real money.

I started to buy things for the house: I tried to pay a fixed sum every month, but my grandfather refused staunchly on principle, saying that if I did so our positions would be reversed and that would never do. When I insisted, he grew firmer and we nearly quarreled. He said to me reassuringly, "My financial affairs are healthy, thank God." Then he took me by the hand to his bedroom, and took an envelope out of the closet that contained his will.

He had left everything to me, my grandmother, and Uncle Shamoun—a third to each of us. The surprise was that he had a very large bank balance.

"Why do you begrudge yourself, then, Grandfather?" I asked.

"I was worried about you all. I thought, maybe they'll need these francs one day. Now my mind is at rest with regard to your mother. I only worry about you, your grandmother, and your Uncle Shamoun."

I started to invite him and my grandmother to dine out, and bought things that would please them: a watch or a gold ring for my grandmother, or a pair of shoes that caught her eye as we went walking. As for my grandfather, smaller things made him happy, and he would be delighted if I came in bearing a packet of cigarettes, or some newspapers and magazines.

One time he asked me to take the initiative in inviting my mother and her husband to dinner at a restaurant. "Yes," said my grandmother. "Yes, please do invite them out." But I refused, despite their urgings. I wanted us to move to a new home.

"Leaving us, Galal?" said my grandfather sadly.

"Leave you? Who else have I got in the world? We'd move together! I'll take you and Grandmother to live in a new apartment."

"What kind of talk is this? You want your grandfather, an old man, to pack up, kit and caboodle, and go live with you? The correct thing is for you to live at my place, not for me to live at yours."

"But Grandfather!"

"My boy, this is how we were raised in Egypt. I'm never going to leave my apartment, not till I die."

He thought I would leave him when my financial situation improved, so he added reproachfully, "Unless you think it's better for you to live somewhere else, in which case, go ahead. We won't mind."

"Who will you leave us for, Galal?" my grandmother chimed in. "Nobody visits us or looks in on us any more."

It's true—Aunt Bella, Rachel, and even Uncle Shamoun hardly visited. And my mother, heaven forgive her! It was as though she had been trapped in a box and had broken free, to enjoy life and regain her lost youth. Last I heard, she'd actually gone with her husband to spend two weeks in the Netanya resort in Israel!

Chapter 19

I married Rachel, just to spite Elephant-Trunk.

Nadia was gone; I didn't see her any more. With the passing days, what was between us had waned and withered. Or so I thought, for I had not known that my heart, part of me, had hidden her in its folds, and, upon sensing that the days had carried me away, never thinking of her or remembering our old promise, it started to revive old wounds and release her, so that I would see her shade in daydreams, or in dreams. How many times, in the belly of the night, after long absence, did I start to toss and turn, sleepless, aching—I had become my own worst enemy!

And yet, I married Rachel.

Rachel, Rachel, Rachel. The girl meant nothing special to me; she was just a girl. One of the family, a sometime business partner, at the most a cousin whom I visited. Her attempts to get closer were wasted, for I ignored them.

The funny thing is that the idea of marrying her didn't ripen gradually in my head; I didn't spend any time thinking or calculating like sensible people, asking myself if this girl, alluring, flirtatious, very nearly a loose woman, was suitable material for a wife and mother. It happened all at once.

It popped into my head, so I did it.

I was taking the Métro home one night, after an evening out with Abul Shawareb at the Chat Noir, and another club in the Pigalle district, and a third, the indecent one called the Rat. They were all the same, nightclubs, late nights. Nothing good could ever come of them! Bare shoulders, sexual heat, curves that enflamed my passions, whetted by long deprivation.

The wheels of the Métro pounded on the metal tracks, a perfume wafting across my nostrils from a woman who seemed to be a lady of the night. She had just gotten on and was sitting opposite me, legs crossed.

Most of the passengers—if not all of them—were minorities: from the Maghreb, Tunisia, Southeast Asia, black Africa, and Portugal. Their bodies were exhausted from the toil of making their living, and from serving merciless bosses and business owners. Some were yawning loudly; a few had stiffened up completely where they sat or stood. Their eyes, too, were fixed, staring unblinkingly ahead: you might think them corpses! Some had dozed off, heads hanging down or resting in their hands. The carriage itself, unusually, had very little light; some of its neon tubes were burned out, and the rest gave off a feeble glow. I was tired, sick at heart, filled with an overabundance of restless energy, an energy that refused to decrease, and I was unable to do anything about it. It pushed me irresistibly toward that woman. I wanted to molest her.

I turned away from her, taking refuge in the glass of the closed window. There was nothing outside, except lamps surrounded by metal grilles, unable to dissipate the gloom of the tunnel through which hurtled this monster in whose belly we rode.

I returned once more to the woman, and plunged anew into the delirium of my sensual urges, which gave me no respite. She stood; I stared at her, from her bare knees to her neck, then at her buttocks when she turned round. Another man turned his head, joining me in my pursuit. I think he may have been a mechanic or a painter; he wore an overall that indicated his job. Our eyes remained on her until she passed through the door of the train and was swallowed up by the platform.

I yawned, and so did he. Our eyes met briefly, then each of us went back to his own thoughts.

I bent my wrist as it lay on the windowsill, laying my head on the palm of my hand. Rachel came slinking toward me in a nightdress of translucent silk, barefoot, with nail polish the color of henna. She tossed her hair with a flick of her head; the column of her throat was white, with a faint blush of underlying pink. The train whistled loud and long, and with every beat of the wheels pounding on the tracks, I became more and more mad for her.

When I got back to the apartment, my grandmother was still sitting in front of the television, watching a French horror movie about a murderess who picked up men in front of bars and clubs, seducing them with her body, then killing them. She would kill them horribly after they had had their way with her; with a stiletto in her handbag, she would cut off each man's forefinger and keep it in a wooden box padded with red velvet as a souvenir of the deed. In cold blood she killed, while the police were beating their heads against a brick wall. They were desperately picking up whatever threads they had dropped to solve the case, and that she-serpent was leading them down the garden path. Murder followed murder, and my grandmother was on the edge of her seat, slapping her knee in encouragement each time the woman got away with it and gave the men hell!

Not wanting to interrupt her—she wouldn't have paid me any mind, and would probably have said something that would annoy me—I waited until she was done, and sat watching her without her noticing. She stretched, her face glowing with pleasure at the deeds of this daughter of Eve! When she pulled the scarf off her head and scratched at her hairline, she looked grim; as though her skull had expanded a little, especially at the brow. I had not paid any attention to her recently, and I hadn't noticed the changes in her. I was overtaken by curiosity over what had befallen her.

Dear God! Her hair was no longer capable of forming locks; her head was islands, patches of hair. The part in front was the only place still covered with hair; another, at the back of her head, was completely bald. Something like peach fuzz was scattered all over the rest of her scalp. On the top of her brow were two prominent bruises, each the size of a Coca-Cola bottle cap.

As she was putting her scarf back on, she noticed my presence. "What are you looking at, you monkey, son of monkeys? And what's that smell coming from your mouth? What the hell have you been drinking?"

"So I'm the one who's drinking now, am I?"

Anyway, we had words, but I told her what I wanted to in the end.

"What is it you're saying, again?" she answered me, eyes sweeping my face. "You want to marry Rachel? Hmm . . ." She made a grunting noise that signified that she was thinking. "Rachel and Galal . . . Galal and Rachel . . . I don't know whether the dime-a-dozen cheap cord will weave well with the silken cord whose every gram is dear!"

"Cord? What do you mean, cord, Grandmother? Do you mean I'm . . ."

She waved me aside, laughing. "Just be patient, let me think about it."

"Oh, Yvonne, Yvonne!" I said, laughing too, "Let's have none of your sly tricks!"

I'd never kidded around with her like this before, never called her by her name to her face. Even more alarming, "Old Beaky" had been on the tip of my tongue, and I might have gone on to say it, but for the grace of God. Heaven only knows what punishment I would have incurred if I had!

Thank God, she accepted my teasing and welcomed the idea.

After breakfast the next morning, we told my grandfather. He didn't like it, though, and appeared nervous, glaring at my grandmother, thinking this was her doing.

I took him aside to find out why he was against it.

"You deserve better than Rachel!" he said.

"I don't know anyone here but her," I said. "Rachel is my cousin, and there's nothing wrong with her."

He shook his head mockingly without speaking, and half-stood, saying he was going into the bathroom to shave. But I took hold of his arm and urged him to sit back down. He acquiesced, and sat looking at me for a while, nibbling at his upper lip. "Marriage is a big undertaking, Galal; it needs careful thought and planning. I advise you to hold off; you're still young. If you insist on getting married, it would be better for you to choose another girl, one more suitable for you."

"What's wrong with Rachel, Grandfather? She was raised by you, just like me."

"Raised by me?" He took offense at that, turning away so that I couldn't see his expression. He caught himself. "I mean that you should choose a girl of your own religion."

"My religion? You mean . . . ?" I fell silent.

Looking very serious, almost harsh, he went on, "Yes, that *is* what I mean. And in plain Arabic: stay away from Rachel, she's nothing but trouble."

His words silenced me. I looked at him, puzzled.

"Yes, trouble. You're a stranger here, my boy. You aren't among your own people. If you get on well together—that's *if* you do . . ." he said mockingly, waving a hand in my face, "I'm saying, you know, if you're blessed with a child or two, they'll live a different life from the one you lived in Egypt, and they might grow up Jewish!" Passing a hand over his chin, he added, "There's no *might* about it. For certain, they'll grow up Jewish. How'd you like that, boy?"

"What?" I said, incensed. "What am I, then?"

"What will you be able to do?" he snapped. "Do you think there'll be anything you can do?" He pressed my hand tenderly, softening his voice. "My boy, it's not about the father being the master of his house and what he says goes. Take Mahmoud Effendi, your father—he died when you were just a helpless baby. If it was only about the father, we'd have made a Jew of you and it would have been over a long time ago. You were too young to know a thing, and you had no father to judge us or quarrel with us." He gestured in my face. "Wake up, Galal. It's about the world and the people we live among, and the law of the land and its customs that rule us and force us to obey."

He was seized by a long bout of coughing, while I stared at the wrinkles at the sides of his face as they tightened and smoothed out. He put out the cigarette in his hand and said, in a voice that started out a little choked, "Where were we? Ah. Why do you think you stayed a Muslim, huh?"

I stared at him.

"Because we were afraid of your grandfather and your relatives in the countryside, and all our neighbors in Daher. Umm Hassan and Hajj Mahmoud and every Tom, Dick, and Harry, this, that, and the other. We took them into consideration; we knew that if one of them had caught a whiff of anything, they'd have called the police, and the police would have given us hell. True, the father is important, son, but the world we live in is too, maybe more."

We stayed silent for a moment.

"Here, kid, you're in France, not in Egypt. Look at the world around you, son! Religion and religious law don't enter into how things work. There'll be no law or custom on your side. You're too young to bear such a burden." He patted me on the shoulder. "Find yourself a nice Muslim girl and marry her; she'll be better for you than Rachel, and your kids won't grow up confused, not knowing if you're a Muslim or a Jew."

"I'm a Muslim, Grandfather."

"I know, I know. But there's a bit of Jew inside you. And that little bit is what makes it impossible for any of us—Jews, I mean—to admit you're a Muslim. And no matter how you try to get around it, swear on your Muslim Bukhari, it won't matter one bit."

"And you, Grandfather?"

He smiled into my face. "I'm your grandfather."

I was utterly infatuated with Rachel. This she-devil had appropriated my urges; I was half mad. I pushed my grandfather to agree to the marriage, but he was adamant. When he grew sick of me, he interrupted, saying, "Listen, my boy. I'm an old man and I don't have the strength for long arguments and useless debate. I've said what I have to say and that's all. Suit yourself." He rose, muttering, "There's something else, too, something more important."

He stopped me when I made to speak, heading for the bathroom.

I tried to find out what the important thing was, but he refused to tell me, contenting himself with restating his disapproval of the marriage.

I spent long weeks, torn between my grandfather's words and my urges, which only wanted Rachel. One moment I would be insistent on marrying her, and another I would awaken to what my grandfather had said, and I would grow more and more curious about what my grandfather refused to tell me.

My grandmother was something else again.

She completely ignored the confusion and turmoil I was going through, likewise with my grandfather's disapproval of the match, and his repeated warnings to her to mind her own business. Old Beaky cast all this aside and appointed herself my matchmaker. Without our knowledge, she called up my Aunt Bella and Rachel, pleading my suit to them, deluding them that my grandfather and I had asked her to speak for us, and that she alone had the final say in any and all decisions related to this matter.

It followed from this that my aunt started to ask my grandmother a few things she needed to know before she, too, said yea or nay. The telephone never stopped ringing between the two of them, and they ceaselessly discussed everything, down to the minutest detail: the dowry, the prenuptial agreement, the ring, which my Aunt Bella insisted must be a real diamond, and where we should live—Rachel said it was okay by her if we lived in her Saint-Germain apartment—and my salary from Bouchard's and my earnings from my business and my bank account at the Crédit Lyonnais, and had we told my mother, who was currently away in Israel with her husband, Mr. Yacoub? Rachel even sent me a message with my grandmother, conveying her surprise and dismay that I hadn't asked her myself. Rachel even stopped visiting us, out of embarrassment, waiting for me to speak out and voice what I thought.

My grandfather and I had no idea about any of this, until my grandmother came home and said, "The girl says yes, she wants Galal, and her mother does too. The miserable Elephant-Trunk's the hard-headed one."

My grandfather set his newspaper aside and turned to her in surprise. "What girl? Elephant-Trunk who?"

"Elephant-Trunk who? Why, our Elephant-Trunk. If you please, His Excellency doesn't agree, and says he's not prepared to give his daughter away to a useless, no-account boy like our Galal!"

I was offended. My grandfather dusted off his hands in disbelief. "Good God!"

My grandmother thought that he was upset by Elephant-Trunk's rejection, not by what she had done, so she said, "Don't think I took it lying down, oh no! I gave him such a tongue-lashing!"

"Do you mean to tell me that you opened the subject with him?" my grandfather screamed, cutting her off.

"Opened it? Of course I opened it, not once but many times. And I kept telling him, 'Really, come on, Haroun, my boy,' and he was stubborn as ever. So I thought, there's no hope for it, and I lit into him."

My grandfather clapped a hand to his forehead. "Lit into him?" he quavered.

"You bet I did! And I told him, 'Who do you think you are, you heroin dealer, you black-market seller of forged passports? Why, back home in Egypt you were a raggedy street urchin!' And, Abu Isaac, we kept on yelling until he hung up on me."

"We're all doomed."

"Why? Are you scared of him? I hope you're not taking him into consideration! Have you forgotten Freiha Effendi, his dad, who was scared of his own shadow, who jumped if you said 'Boo' and peed his pants? Who's this Haroun?"

Things escalated between my grandfather, who was floored by what my grandmother had done and wanted to eat her alive, and me, no more, in Elephant-Trunk's eyes, than a silly no-account boy. Immediately, my final days in Egypt came to mind, and Madame Sobki, who had thought Nadia, her daughter, too good for me, and considered me beneath her.

My insistence on marrying Rachel grew, in spite of this Trunk. She took my side, defying her father, and Aunt Bella took the opportunity to settle her old scores with her husband.

The family burst into flame. Shuttle diplomacy was employed—my grandmother and I on the one side, Rachel and her mother with us, and Elephant-Trunk alone on the other side. Veiled threats were exchanged, and we engaged in something akin to psychological warfare. As for my grandfather, he played it safe and distanced himself from the conflict, not speaking or commenting on what was taking place before him. He looked at me with reproach, though, whenever our eyes met.

Uncle Isaac called us daily without fail from Haifa, and called Elephant-Trunk to melt his resolve. My mother suddenly called in the middle of the night from Eilat, in Israel, where she and her husband were staying with his married daughter. She said she had just heard, and was arriving on the first plane!

My mother's arrival dampened the raging battle.

The issue was instantly resolved when Mr. Yacoub, at my mother's urging, paid a visit to Elephant-Trunk. Apparently, nobody in the family meant anything to Elephant-Trunk, nor did he attach any importance to any of us, except for this gentleman. Perhaps they shared business interests, or things of which we had no knowledge.

My grandmother commented on this, saying she had "heard—heaven only knows if it's true" that Elephant-Trunk's maternal grandfather was a servant in the household of Sarouf Bey Abu al-Saad, Mr. Yacoub's father, and that he mentioned this during their meeting, thus guaranteeing his acquiescence!

"What idle talk!" my grandfather rebuked her. "For shame! For heaven's sake, stop gossiping."

And so Rachel and I were married.

We wrote out a document, which we both signed, and for witnesses we had Sheikh Munji and one of his followers called Bu Mikhla'.

It was no small matter to get Sheikh Munji to mount the stairs to my grandfather's apartment, where the ceremony was to be conducted. I badgered him continually; now he would say his foot hurt and he couldn't climb the stairs, now that Khadija, his daughter, was sick in the hospital. Finally, he acquiesced and climbed the stairs with ill grace, accompanied by Sheikh Bu Mikhla' in his Moroccan abaya, a turban on his head and his face and beard lit up like the full moon, and Abul Shawareb, resplendent in his full get-up as though he were the groom, bearing a box of Patchi Swiss chocolates.

Sheikh Munji stepped over the threshold, right foot first, muttering all sorts of blessings and prayers to ward off evil, as though he were entering a nest of devils! My grandfather was waiting, beret on his head, feet encased in high-topped patent-leather shoes with buckles. Sheikh Munji cleared his throat to announce his arrival, as if to tell his enemies, "Here I am!" He held out his hand to my grandfather with reserve, but my grandfather was having none of it! Seeing it as an opportunity to let go of old hostilities and normalize relations, he held out both hands, palms up, beaming, and flung himself at the sheikh, kissing him on both cheeks and patting him on the back. "Welcome, welcome, your presence lights up our home! Your presence blesses our home, honorable friend! How are you and how is your good wife, Zahira? Welcome, welcome!"

The sheikh stiffened at first, then relaxed in my grandfather's embrace, and reached a hand out to the others: Elephant-Trunk first. They exchanged lukewarm smiles. The sheikh seemed to have crushed the man's hand in his grip of iron; a fiercely scowling Elephant-Trunk could be observed shaking his hand violently in pain, then opening and closing his fingers to restore circulation. Meanwhile, the sheikh moved on to Uncle Shamoun, then Mr. Yacoub. The latter, with his white scarf, silver hair, and thick cigar, looked more like Don Juan, immortalized in the Hollywood movies of the 1940s and 1950s. My mother rose languidly, haughtily extending the tips of her fingers. Nonplussed for a moment, Munji hesitated, then produced a woolen glove from his coat pocket and put it on to touch her fingers. My grandmother, though, didn't budge from her seat, nor did he glance at the chair she was sitting in!

The next day, Elephant-Trunk insisted upon another family gathering, this time at his apartment, so that Rachel and I should stand before all assembled and perform a teqi'at kaf, which is a traditional Jewish handshake according to the religious engagement ritual. "What on earth for, Haroun, my boy?" my grandfather remonstrated. "They're already married. It's not like they're just going to get engaged!" But her father stood firm, and so my grandfather relented. "All right then." We performed the teqi'at kaf. Everyone applauded and they called for a kiss! We gave them a kiss, and they asked for another. We gave them another, and then my father-in-law threw dignity to the four winds and bellowed, "This isn't the kiss we expected of you, Galal! And you, Rachel, give him a hand, won't you? His shyness will be the death of him! We want burning passion, like when Tyrone Power kissed the girl in *Blood and Sand!*"

I was embarrassed at their relentless yelling and egging on. Meanwhile, my grandfather had retreated into a corner, wanting no part of this madness.

All of a sudden, my mother opened her mouth and a joyous ululation split the air—the air of Elephant-Trunk's apartment, just off the Champs-Élysées!

And that had been just the signal to start, apparently. A number of ululations split the air, among which my ear could make out my grandmother's immediately: a heavy bass rumble, a braying, howling sound, as though some dangerous beast had received a fatal shot in the gullet!

Not a few days had passed before Elephant-Trunk came to visit, wanting me, my grandfather, and the whole family to get ready to go to the synagogue near his house the day after tomorrow, where a religious ceremony would be held entitled the Sheva Berachot, the Seven Blessings. He launched into an explanation, saying, "It consists of seven blessings and it is conducted in accordance with such and such religious rituals . . ." and concluded by saying that this ceremony would be attended by a group of his Jewish acquaintances numbering no less than ten, as per their religious laws.

"Slow down, slow down, Haroun, man!" my grandfather said, astonished. "You know quite well that the bridegroom is a Muslim and we didn't have a Jewish wedding. Why these last-ditch measures, then?"

I refused to attend, my grandfather backing me up, until Elephant-Trunk said, "Have it your way, but the prayer will take place, whether you like it or not! The groom doesn't have to be present!"

"As for me, I feel a cold coming on," said my grandfather, "so I shall stay home with the groom, and you may do as you please!"

And that wasn't all.

Elephant-Trunk wanted me to sign a document saying that I would have to pay a compensation of fifty thousand francs if I were to divorce Rachel.

I asked Sheikh Munji, who answered angrily, "No! The settlement agreed upon in the prenuptial agreement I witnessed is quite enough for them! If you sign anything of the sort, you're an infidel, untrue to your religion and its laws, and you'll never set foot in my house or speak to me again! What is this? Have they no decency? God damn these accursed people!"

My grandfather resolved the issue by signing the document himself. When he was done, Elephant-Trunk said, "One more condition, gentlemen."

"What?" we asked.

"If you should move back to your country permanently," he said, "you don't get to take Rachel with you. She stays here with us, and you can come and go."

"What on earth for, Haroun?" my grandfather burst out. "If only we *could* get to go back to Egypt! It's a dream for us. Isn't it her country as well, and your country too, where you were born and bred?"

"Hah! What's that you're saying, Abu Isaac? My country? Ha! My country, indeed!"

My grandfather's eyes dropped. "Not your country?" he whispered. "God forgive you, my boy."

Chapter 20

It was as though we had never gotten married. Rachel and I separated on our wedding night.

Since the evening I had spent with Abul Shawareb at Le Chat Noir, I had been nothing but a ball of energy, churning inside a machine of flesh and blood! Mindless energy, emanating from an almost-enchanted source of lust, whose only concern was to snatch up Rachel and quench my thirst for her lips and smooth cheeks. I was like a bubbling pot, suddenly uncovered! A stallion who, confronted with a mare with a fair brow, slipped the reins!

That was what I was like, for since I arrived here I had never sinned with a woman, or even thought of doing anything that might displease God. I was afraid—afraid of myself. I was afraid my inner self, anticipating my sin, would wait until we were alone and start tormenting me, or perhaps push some imagining at me in the form of a man hurting my mother! Many times had this happened before in Egypt, when I was still a teenager. She and I were all alone there, without a man: a woman of flesh and blood, still-soft flesh, her heart broken, exhausted by care and sleepless nights, and a boy who had been young and now was grown, for whom the world consisted of Man and Woman, each of whom would inevitably get what they wanted from the other.

It was then that I began to fear.

I began to fear my mother was the target of treacherous eyes and unscrupulous men. Thank heavens, there were none living in our street, and all of our neighbors, Mr. A, Mr. B, and Mr. C, saw my mother's honor as their own, and me as their son, and her as their sister.

And who could forget the waiters at Abu Ouf's café, on the corner of our street in Daher? I remember once when my mother and I were coming home, on foot, from Tor Sinai Street. I was little, playing with a toy in my hand. She was carrying a bag of spices. Two street hooligans followed us, verbally molesting her and openly harassing us with obscene words as we reached Saka-kini Street, then on to al-Khaleeg al-Masry Street, which they crossed with us, and followed us until we reached our street. The waiter, Abu Wedn, saw what was happening and yelled for his colleagues, who all rushed out of the café, armed with tables and chairs. Hajj Saqr, God bless him, ran out after his waiters, taking off his gallabiya, a long, thick staff in his hand to defend us. He swore by God that these two boys should not be allowed to leave the street as they had come in, and called to his waiter al-Hanash, standing at the preparation counter, to pour boiling water on the napes of their necks. But for the grace of God, they would have died.

In spite of this, that fear remained a phantom that never left me. I felt that what I did would come back upon my mother. Every time the devil tempted me into some wild deed, I would, that night, dream of a man, presented differently each time; now in his underpants, now completely naked but for the thick hair that covered his private parts.

In the dream, I would be sleeping by my mother's side; he would poke me roughly in the chest to wake me, and his eyes and his frown showed me what he would do to her! I'd growl in anger and fear, gasping for air as drowning men do when they feel the shock of swallowing water. But my throat would never manage to form words; I would be reduced to a pitiful state, neither able to speak nor in control of my body, with no hope of defending my mother.

I would never know how he'd gotten in. He would simply appear before me, pushing me away with a hand, and head for my mother, asleep, insensible, defenseless. He would mount her, bending her body to his will if she struggled, his hungry lips feeding on her upper half, by now laid bare. The only thing that saved me, or my mother, would be for me to wake in terror, disbelieving, dripping sweat. I would swear to God, fearfully and sincerely, never to do it again.

Something inside me always rebuked me, standing between me and my youthful desires.

That night came.

Abul Shawareb, God forgive him, never stopped tempting me with a glass of wine, and a second, and a third! He beckoned to a Portugese lady of the night to sit with us. She seemed to be of gypsy origin, wild and voluptuous. She was wearing a dark bandanna, a pointed nose beneath it, her eyes shining with a bold light. Her body was soft and healthy, like just-set bread dough. At a wink from me, she began to coax me with debauched abandon, her questing fingers knowing no modesty. I squirmed in mortification, so over-whelmed with pleasure that I was on the brink of orgasm.

After that, things happened without planning. I could see no answer before me but Rachel. It wasn't about love. I didn't desire to settle down and start a family; from start to finish, it was lust, physical desire, and sexual pleasure.

It may have been a mistake—no, it *was* a mistake. It's wrong to trifle with respectable girls.

But who said that Rachel was respectable? Heaven knows who she really is and what she really does; I was certainly ignorant of her life at the time!

I was overcome with lust, so I turned a deaf ear to my grandfather's advice, and to Sheikh Munji's angry, mocking words. I didn't even take advantage of Elephant-Trunk's rejection as a pretext to back out! Instead, I only grew more stubborn—indeed, stranger in a strange land though I was, I didn't even stop to think about, or fear, this man and his criminal record! So many times Uncle Shamoun had warned me against him: "You mustn't marry into that family, Galal! There's no telling what that man will do; he's got no religion and no conscience." It would only make me cling on harder. "My boy, he's a criminal, and I wouldn't put it past him to harm you!" I wouldn't answer, and he'd say, "Listen to reason!"

But I didn't listen, not to him or to anyone. The only thing that reined me in and brought me back to my senses was a gene I got from my father, Mahmoud Effendi, and my grandfather, Hajj Mahmoud: a weightless gene, only visible under a microscope.

On my wedding night, Rachel turned out not to be a virgin.

In the blink of an eye, I slipped away from the whole world. As though I had died a little inside, the blood stagnating and pooling in my veins and arteries and even the smallest capillaries, in every part of me, seen and unseen.

I came to myself. Part of me became aware of myself, as though seeing it all from above, from all around me. It saw me defeated, vacant, ashamed of myself under my own gaze. No vestige of thought or volition made me whole or gave me life.

I experienced that fatal moment: its length lay in its depth, its time not like ours. Rachel, as far as I could see in my confusion, seemed stunned, upset, trying to shake me out of my stupor. She could not believe that I, having lived all these years in Paris, placed any importance on such a thing as this. Was I a boor, a country bumpkin, within whom my father's clergyman's turban and caftan still lived?

When some of my energy filtered back, I leaped out of her bed, stung, searching for another refuge. Before the next day dawned, I was knocking on my grandfather's apartment door.

I was embarrassed to say anything, but my grandfather soon guessed, and comforted me. "God will provide, my son. I told you from the start."

I nodded silently and he went on, in a softer tone: "Forgive me, Galal; it's true, I knew she was a loose woman, but I couldn't break it to you." And he bowed his head. "She's my girl too, after all."

All night, I tormented myself, wondering how many times Rachel had done this thing, and with whom? With the Arabs she guided around in the streets and the stores? With her Jewish lovers? Or perhaps with the Moroccans, the blacks, the dregs of the street!

How, in a moment, had all the fire within me been extinguished, fizzled into useless ash? Gray ash, not a single coal that promised to burst into flame? And would that fire have been quenched if Rachel had given herself to me without marriage? Are we, then, deluded to think that desire itself—even the ability to deny it!—is in our hands at all? Or does it have its own set of rules and laws—hidden laws we must abide by, whether we accept them or not?

Again I blamed myself for letting desire run away with me, for imagining this strumpet could be a virgin—or even suitable material for a wife!

Chapter 21

I spent two days in my room without going out.

Most of the time I lay on the bed, silent and unmoving, my eyes staring at anything in their path. Anything: a doll's head peeking out from on top of the wardrobe; a single sock dangling out of the mouth of a shoe; an old photo hanging on the wall, in which my mother's eyes appeared drawn to the camera lens, and I, two years old, sat relaxed and trusting on her knee. Or my eyes would be drawn to a fly landing on the edge of the dresser or the door handle. I would stare at it as it stood still, then bent its head to clean its feet, or raised its wings, preparing for flight, after which I would stay inert and useless. I yawned, repeatedly and often; I sought sleep, but it didn't come.

I heard a knock at the door, so I dragged myself upright.

It was my grandfather. He looked inside with the door ajar. My mother was on the phone.

I motioned to him in apology. His eyes insisted, which strengthened my resolve. He said she was worried about me, and wanted me to go spend the night at her house.

I said, "Sure, if God wills it," but I didn't go.

He left me, headed for the kitchen, and occupied himself with making a dish of beans with linseed oil. He came in bearing a tray with the plate on it, a deep dish of pickled vegetables next to it, just like we used to have back home: turnips, carrots, green peppers, and limes.

All this was common enough; my grandmother made the pickles herself here at home, and she bought the beans dried and cooked them over a slow flame in a special pot as she used to do in Egypt. What was new was the linseed oil! "Where did you get it, Grandfather?"

He smiled proudly. "I was poking around yesterday, looking for a spice store where the Chinese keep their shops in the Quartier Latin. And all at once, what should I find but this scratched old bottle, tossed aside! I asked the shopkeeper and he said, "It's oil for your cough." And it turned out to be linseed oil! Where did those sly foxes get it?"

That dish of beans with the linseed oil was like an antidote. I started to slip out of the depression that surrounded me, and began to go outside to where my grandfather sat. I found him as he had always been: sitting on his customary chair, a pile of old newspapers and magazines tossed in front of him, on top of which rested his glasses. He was usually asleep, eyelids slack, head leaning over the edge of the chair. I called on him two or three times before he raised his head. He gazed at me for a moment, eyes wide, as though he didn't know me. Then he made a shooing motion at me and looked at the wall clock. "Goodness—I've missed the afternoon prayer!" It was his customary way of speaking. He never noticed what time it was, but knew what period of the day it was according to the traditional Muslim prayers—it was the way he'd been raised with the common people in the streets of Cairo. He and my grandmother would often say things like, "Come on, Galal, it's noontime," or "Good Lord, it's night-prayer time already, it's gotten dark."

He made room for me to sit by him, saying, "Come here, next to me." Not waiting for me to speak, he said as soon as I sat down, "Don't think that your grandmother Yvonne approves of what's gone on. I swear, she could drive a whole country to distraction."

He glanced warily at the kitchen door. "Yes, by God! And every now and then she'll embark on some ruinous enterprise. But she won't stand for what's not right. And when What's-her-name called her—what is her name, anyway?"

"You mean Mom?" I asked helpfully.

"Your mother? Of course not! Silly woman. I mean What's-her-name. Yes, yes, I remember! When your Aunt Bella called her and complained to her of what you'd done, she lashed out at her." He paused, peering into my face. "I bet you don't believe me. No, really, son, I heard her with my own ears, telling her that we've been honorable people all our lives, and to keep an eye on her daughter, and not to forget that her family and ours were all raised in old-time Cairo, and her Grandfather Isaac used to wear a caftan and a gallabiya! We've got the same traditions, the same notions of honor and dishonor!"

"Did our great-grandfather really dress like that?"

"Of course! A gallabiya and a caftan and high-topped shoes, and a shawl about his head like a turban, and he spoke like a regular son of Egypt. He was a big-time feed-trader, son, and he sold beans and lentils and doum and nuts and dried fruit in Ramadan." He fell silent, surprised. "But what's your Great-grandfather Isaac got to do with the matter at hand?"

"True," I smiled, "what brought him into it?"

"Yes, my boy, concentrate on what we're saying and don't go all over the place with digressions."

After we talked, he would usually—if he were in a good mood—open the subjects dearest to his heart. Talk and more talk, subject following subject, without stopping; he didn't stop speaking even while he was blowing his nose, with the handkerchief held to his face. If he was feeling down, that would be written clearly on his face; he would remain silent, never speaking a word, only sometimes he would spring questions upon me for which I had no answer. One time he leaned back in his chair and asked after an old friend of his called Besah. I looked startled, whereupon he flapped his hand impatiently. "Yes, Besah! What's so unusual? Everybody knows Besah, don't they?"

My grandmother would come to the rescue. "Besah is a spice trader, dear. He had a store in Tor Sinai Street, over by Sakakini, and was your grandfather's dearest friend. He only ever really enjoyed himself when he was sitting with him outside his store. Ah, Besah, where are you, and where are the good old days when we used to be friends! Your grandfather would come home positively *laden* with carrier bags from his store, and he'd say only, "Your Uncle Besah says hello." She turned to him. "What reminds him of you now, Abu Isaac?"

He looked surprised at the question. "He's my friend, isn't he?"

"I know he's your friend, but this was thirty years ago, maybe more. You went your separate ways when his son Shoulah proposed to Bella and she refused him." She looked at him wonderingly. "Besah, my goodness. Besah indeed!"

Once, my grandfather asked how Abul Shawareb was treating me; he didn't think much of him, seeing in him a wild man who didn't act his age and who was a little crazy besides. No sooner did I start to give an answer than he interrupted. "I don't think I'll ever go back to Egypt, will I?"

I was struck dumb at the total non sequitur. I went along, though, saying, "Why not, Grandfather? You can go now, at any time. You have a French passport; there's nothing to stop you entering or leaving Egypt."

"No," he said, "no." His tone was firm, and he made a gesture with his hand that sent his coffee cup flying; the ashtray in his lap overturned, scattering ash and cigarette butts everywhere.

My grandmother came rushing in from the kitchen. We spent a while dusting off his dressing gown and tidying up. No sooner had he settled back into his chair than he started again. "It's not that, my boy, bless your soul. Do I have to repeat it? I don't want it to be just a visit. What are you talking about, visit? What visit? I want to go back for good, go to the street and reopen our apartment.

People coming and going, 'Uncle Zaki this, Uncle Zaki that...' And 'How much are the tomatoes today, my girl, Zakeya?' and 'Give me a pack of Cleopatras, Uncle Eleish.'" He stopped as though remembering something he had forgotten. "Tell me, do you have the key to the Daher apartment?"

He had insisted on taking the key back from my mother a while back, before she left us to get married. "The key is with you, Grandfather," I reminded him. "Would you like me to tell you where, exactly? In the old spectacle case you keep in the bottom drawer of the bedroom dresser."

"Yes, yes, that's right!"

He sat there, staring at a fly that had landed on his knee. He turned back to me, saying, "How about you come back with me? You'll keep me company there, at least. And when I die, bury me next to my father and mother—and if you want to come back to France, why, you can."

"God grant you long life, Grandfather. God willing, what you want will come to pass one of these days."

His face changed. "One of these days? You take my words for senile ramblings, do you, and you're just humoring me? You can come if you please, and if you don't, don't. I'll go back on my own, and I don't need anyone, not you, not Shamoun, not Yvonne, none of them."

"Be patient, Grandfather. You know that my business is here."

"Business?" His ire rose. He made to leap to his feet, but I caught his arm and kept soothing him and apologizing until he calmed down, and made him a false promise that I would close up my enterprises soon, in a year at most, at which time we would go back together.

Afterward, I joked with him. "So, Grandfather. Suppose we were in Egypt and war broke out with Israel, what would you do?"

"Why should they fight? They've made peace, haven't they?"

"I just said, suppose. What would you do then?"

"Do? I'd fight as well. Fight and a half, and quickly, too."

"Fight Israel?"

"I'll say!"

"Grandfather, come on!"

"Grandfather? What's this 'Grandfather'? You think I'm fifth column? I'm Zaki, son of Isaac, son of Yusuf, son of Haroun, son of Shamoun al-Azra', and all of those were born and bred in Egypt, and never left its shores. They never went east nor west; the farthest they went was Abu Hasira's birthday celebration, and then it was back to their homes and their jobs. How long do I have to spend crying in the wilderness and saying, "Hey, everybody, hey everyone, hey you, this country is my country as much as it is yours?"

A tear had formed in his eye as he spoke. "You ask me if I'd fight, Mr. Galal? Why shouldn't I fight? Am I somehow less than the Muslims in India who stand at the border with Pakistan, and do battle in time of need?"

He was a few years past his eightieth birthday, and I think he meant every word he said.

Chapter 22

Abul Shawareb and I gave up being door-to-door salesmen, as well as all the other trifling sales we had engaged in. We stopped selling retail by the piece and luring in customers, and going to our customers' homes and hotels, especially after the incident with Sheikh Da'ess, who had chased us out one day, brandishing a slipper and swearing a thousand oaths to deliver us to the police!

We had outgrown that, as well as striking deals in cafés and bars as we used to, putting on a show for the customers like circus clowns, and all the rest of it. We were businessmen now, and we had been blessed: business was booming.

We started out with a small office, a one-room apartment in Versailles, with a dark, damp storeroom a few miles from Paris, which we rented from a farmer. It appeared to have been used as a barn for sheep and goats, or perhaps beetles and pigs. The musty odor, to say nothing of the smell of dung and refuse, lingered, however much we cleaned it. I would get allergy attacks, sneezing incessantly the moment I stepped into the place.

Step by step, we registered as a business; our company was now registered with the Paris Chamber of Commerce. As a result, we quit our job at Bouchard's, and bought a used Renault truck to move our stock. We hired an office boy, an old Tunisian man, over seventy, called Bu Lehya. Abul Shawareb said he wasn't suitable; he was hard of hearing, while his face and figure indicated that he was a walking disaster. However, I insisted on him, because he came on a recommendation from Sheikh Munji; and, I must say, he proved himself in time. He was light on his feet, and ran like the wind, here and there and up and down, with the agility of a monkey. The only problem was that when I spoke to him, he would hear me fine, even if I spoke low—but when Abul Shawareb addressed him, he would feign deafness and step closer, asking him to repeat what he had said.

We also hired another employee, an Egyptian like me, called Fouad. His parents were from Markaz Abu al-Matameer. We sat him down behind a computer and charged him with doing our accounts. Last but not least was the Lebanese driver, Harfoush, who drove the Renault. We took our lives in our hands every time we sat in his cab. He drove so fast and recklessly that we would always say to ourselves, "He's driving us to ruin, not to deliveries and customers!"

The Lord gave generously of His bounty. We soon moved to a larger office: three rooms and a reception hall, with a balcony overlooking rue Saint-Michel itself! We acquired more warehouses. In addition to the old one, we added two more, one in Saint-Cloud and the other in the Vingtième Arrondissement. Our sales multiplied, totaling hundreds of thousands of francs, and our clients were now big businessmen: heavyweights from Turkey, Libya, and Pakistan. We grew famous for accepting credit, and our profit margin was reasonable. We operated on the principle, "More sales, more profit."

We concentrated on clothing that had become outmoded here in Paris, which had usually been on display in boutiques or department stores for a season or two, three at most. We didn't buy from just anyone, but from the big fashion houses, after they had withdrawn their stock from stores and placed it in storage when the new designs hit the stores. We bought them at a quarter of the price. They wouldn't let us take possession of the stock until they had removed any identifying tags that bore the name of their fashion house: Dior, Armani, Cacharel, and Pierre Cardin wouldn't let their wares go to liquidators like us with the labels still on. That would be a scandal for the house, especially as they had no way of knowing where the stock would be displayed and where it would end up selling. High-class stock, they felt, should only be sold at prestigious stores, and at prices that reflected its quality and its label.

The transactions between us were based on the fact that these were unidentified, unsaleable wares; it was up to us to sell them, whether in the alleyways of Paris, or to small traders coming from towns and villages in France, or by exporting them. We could do with them as we wished, the only condition being that we not replace the original makers' tags; that was a violation under law, and they would have the right to take us to court. We would take these lots, hundreds and sometimes thousands of T-shirts, skirt suits, skirts, sweaters, belts, and handkerchiefs, place them in our warehouses, and start looking for customers. This was where Abul Shawareb came in; he took it upon himself to perform this task. Not a week went by, or a fortnight at the most, without him coming into the office accompanied by a businessman from the Levant, Libya, or Palestine; or sometimes from Korea or Brazil, accompanied by an interpreter.

The most famous of all, and the one with whom we did the most business, was a Turkish businessman. He came in the first time in smart clothing, with an unusually thick mustache, the ends curled up distinctively, curving upward in a manner that defied all divine laws, never mind gravity! He was exceptionally large, noticeably so, so that you would wonder upon first meeting him, "Is this all man, or was his grandmother a walrus?"

We helped him seat himself on a wide leather sofa, as he panted. After he felt he was stable, he pulled out his pipe and lit it, puffing the smoke in our faces. He started to speak of everything except what he had come for: the problems in Turkey, especially those caused by the Kurds and their leader, Abdullah Öcalan, and the conflict between Syria and the Turks over Iskenderun, which had nearly burst into war, gradually moving on to the glories of the Ottoman Empire, which, but for Kemal Atatürk and the fall of the caliphate, would have changed the face of the Islamic world. He refilled his pipe and took a number of quick puffs, wreathing us all in a veil of smoke.

He spoke of himself, telling us his name back to the fifth generation, and his mother's name, and the girl he was in love with before he married, and a few words about his three wives, and that he was a descendant of Sultan Abdülmecid II, the last sultan of the Ottoman line, and that if things had gone as they should, he would have now been caliph of the Muslims, or a ruler of a country at the very least.

Our patience, mine and Abul Shawareb's, was running out; we exchanged a glance, but what could we do? He was a customer, and the customer is always right.

He was the one who took action! He looked at his pocket watch, which he still kept as an heirloom, saying that his time was valuable and that it had been wasted, and that this was no way to run a business! A business, he said, was give and take, without gabbing or unnecessary words.

In a dissatisfied tone, he asked, "Where is your stock? That's how you are, you Arabs—too much talk and too little action! I'm an impatient man, and I have no time for talk and gossip!" He made to leap up and storm out, but couldn't quite manage it. His bottom dragged him down to the couch in spite of himself.

We hurried to him, having exchanged baffled glances. Abul Shawareb rushed into the neighboring room and brought out the samples, only to find that he had launched into a long monologue about thyme, black cumin, and marjoram, and how people in the Anatolian valleys lived, and so on. This time, though, Abul Shawareb cut him off by the expedient of placing the samples in his lap, saying, "This blouse costs fifty francs wholesale; wholesale rates start at 120 pieces. This costs X, these men's shorts cost Y, they come in four colors, and we only have small sizes in stock right now."

The man turned the samples over in his hands and took to bargaining. "No, no, sir," we said, "our prices are fixed, we don't bargain." He looked at us with displeasure.

We said, "If you go to Maxim Ekhwan's, you'll see that we sell dirt cheap. Or Awlad Boume-Klab, the Moroccans, or David Saul the Jew, or anyone else you please."

He would, of course, have gone to all of these before coming to us, and he knew that our prices were reasonable, so he relented and agreed.

Now he began another maneuver, to find out the identity of the maker. We told him, "That comes at a price, too."

After coming to an agreement, signing the contract and taking his check, Abul Shawareb and I, as one man, hoisted him up off the couch, and helped him leave our office safely.

And so it went.

I was rolling in money. I now drove a BMW, and had a fat bank account, and stocks and shares. Without noticing it, I had come to love money. I was careful to amass and hoard it. I never tired of picking up my calculator, urging it to show that I had made my second million francs. I don't know if it was in my nature, or if I saw money as a refuge, a safe haven to protect me in a strange land. Who did I have, after all? An aged grandfather, a mother who had emigrated to her new world, and a city where I had no one at all. Abul Shawareb was the opposite: he never cared at all about money. He set aside a portion to spend on his pleasures, and part for his family in southern Lebanon. The remaining portion, and there was a lot of it, he sent to his brethren in Hezbollah. A summer storm had arisen between me and that worthy gentleman, for I had suggested that we take my Uncle Shamoun into the business with us. Not as a partner, of course, for everyone knew he didn't have a penny to his name, but as an employee, or even a modest worker like Bu Lehya; he refused adamantly, though, saying, "No Jew shall ever work for us! We should never put our trust in one of those people. They kill our women and children in Lebanon and Palestine, and if it weren't for those devils living with us in this world, it would be free of ill will, blood, and vengeance."

Sharon's invasion of Beirut and the massacres of Sabra and Shatila were still fresh in our minds, so I forgave him. However, I said to him that my uncle was a Jew and not a Zionist; that being a Jew was one thing, and being a Zionist was another. One was a heavenly religion; the other politics, crime, and everything else he spoke of. However, he was adamant, saying, "No and a thousand times no."

We sought an arbiter in Sheikh Munji; he took the side of Abul Shawareb, and warned me against being charitable to Jews, even if they were my uncles. "Abul Shawareb, God bless him, sends all he can to his kinfolk in Lebanon so that they can defend themselves," he said angrily to me, "and if that one called Shamoun does that and sends part of his money to Israel, will it not be money that you have helped him earn? Will this not be treason toward your people and your relatives? God has seen fit to shower you with his blessings, Galal, so do not fritter them away on the unjust or those who would lead you astray. Enough of this, my boy, and ask God's forgiveness."

I believed otherwise. In my book, a Jew was one kind of person, a Zionist another. My grandfather was a living, breathing example in flesh and blood of a God-fearing Jewish man who had taken in and raised a needy, orphan Muslim boy like me, and helped him get on in life as best he could, even privileging him above some of his other, purely Jewish, grandchildren. My grandfather had made no distinction between his religion, which he loved, and his homeland, where he was born and raised. Both were sacred to him, and worthy of respect. Uncle Shamoun was the same; I had never once heard him say a word against his country; in fact, he had long been consumed with the yearning to return there. Zionists were Elephant-Trunk and my Uncle Isaac, and my grandmother, of course—she topped the list—and perhaps Mr. Yacoub was one, too.

I could find no help for it but to give assistance to Uncle Shamoun in secret. I gave him a thousand francs a month, and sometimes two, and also whenever there was a Jewish holiday: Passover, Yom Kippur, Purim, Shavuot, Chanukah, and so on.

I shall never forget the look on his face the first time I held out my hand, offering an envelope containing money. He was taken by surprise and took a step back, waving his hand in demurral. His face was ashamed, confused, wanting it and yet not, and the light in his eyes went out. But he was poor and needy, and with slight urging from me, he extended his hand. I was overcome with embarrassment as well, so that I looked at the floor, avoiding him, and indeed myself. It was the first time I had given anything to a man older than I was, of my own flesh and blood; the first time I had been the stronger and he the weaker.

I put my arms around him and pressed his back and shoulders softly, tenderly. I loved him: my uncle.

Chapter 23

"Galal? Who's Galal? No such garbage. I just told you there's no one here by that name."

"Your Aunt Yvonne? What on earth? My name's Wezza, darling."

"Now really, Miss, or is it Madam?—we're not Egyptians, we've never been there in our lives. We're from Sudan, ma'am, Sudan."

"Zaki who? Zaki al-Azra'? No Azra' here, and no Akta' either, and I'll thank you to quit bothering us by phone."

My ears picked up these phrases, and I woke. They were followed by the receiver being slammed down, then there was movement in the hallway. It was as though someone was dragging a chair, opening and closing the fridge door, and little by little, the smell of burning tobacco reached my nostrils.

The night was almost over; the small window in my window wasn't pitch black as I was accustomed to seeing it in the deep of the night, but tinged with light, telling me that there remained only a little while before daylight. Although I wasn't fully alert, I realized that the telephone had rung while I was asleep, and that it had been my grandmother who had been speaking.

But to whom? And why did Grandmother, whom no one could control, insist that her name was Wezza, not Yvonne, and that she was from Sudan? And why was she denying that this was my grandfather's home? And my name that had been mentioned in the conversation: Galal, no such garbage.

My suspicions were roused, naturally; I was also consumed with curiosity: why had my grandmother performed this telephone gambit? Why had she wanted to delude this poor woman? "Old Beaky," I said to myself, "surely wants to spoil something or other!"

I rose and emerged to find her chain-smoking, a tall glass of ice before her, with a chipped plate containing two pears and an uncapped bottle of beer with a fly buzzing around the opening. My grandfather was still asleep, his snoring coming to us, soft and repetitious, suddenly reaching a crescendo of honking that would make you think he was in a life-or-death battle with his windpipe. After a while, he would return to his previous state.

She covered her head with her scarf as soon as she saw me, and said in a sweet, soft voice, "You're awake? I hope you slept well, Gel-gel. Go back to sleep, dear boy, dawn still hasn't broken."

"The . . ." I gestured to the telephone.

"No, no. It was a wrong number."

"Wrong number, Gran? I heard you saying such-and-such."

"It was a wrong number, I'm telling you!" she grumbled.

I finally extracted from her—the effort nearly killed me—that the one calling had been Khadija, Sheikh Munji's daughter. She justified herself by saying that she hadn't wanted to wake me, and anyway, those were low-down people from whom no good ever came.

I dialed Sheikh Munji's number, biting my lip in frustration, as she poured herself a glass of beer, muttering all the while: "We can do without Khadija and the rest of the trash. She's just a bitch like her mother, acting all helpless on the phone, like she can't even get the words out. She must have gotten a beating from her wretched old father! What are we to these people? They're nothing but trouble, best to stay out of their affairs!"

Five or six times I dialed the telephone and nobody answered. I threw on my clothes and rushed downstairs like the wind. I found the door to the apartment ajar. Broken French came from inside.

I rang the doorbell repeatedly, and got no answer; my terror and urgency pushed me forward, and I burst in. The place was dark, empty. In another moment I was at the door to the inner room, from which a dim light emanated.

It was Khadija's bedroom. She lay on the bed, breathing rapidly, face deathly pale. Droplets of sweat were clustered on her forehead and behind her ears, some trickling in a thin trail down toward her neck. Her dress had fallen open, exposing her legs.

I didn't even look at the people gathered there. I quickly bent to pull her dress over her, joined by a woman who was bending to assist me. She was the caretaker's wife. When we were done, I asked her in hushed Arabic to tuck back in the locks of hair that were hanging out from underneath her scarf and tie it securely around her forehead. Despite Khadija's condition, my eyes couldn't help noticing her cheeks, whose sweet roundness always attracted my attention when I saw her by chance or visited her father's house.

Her eyes followed our motions. I looked at her encouragingly, but was disturbed to see that she wasn't really responsive. Her soft whimpers pained me, as did the way her hand clutched at her chest as though there was an excruciating pain in that particular spot. I have no idea why it occurred to me, in the depths of this crisis, that she paid more attention to me than the others; perhaps because when I pressed her other hand she gave me a grateful glance before her eyes closed.

All this had taken no more than a minute. I sprang erect, seeing the caretaker of the building, Bu-Bakr Weld Kharoub, a naturalized Frenchman from Mauritania, and next to him a man in pajamas and a robe. This was M. Raoul, the Frenchman who lived opposite Sheikh Munji. They were on friendly terms. Now, in worried tones, he told me, "Mademoiselle Hadija is having a heart attack. As soon as she called for help, I called the ambulance service at the municipal hospital."

"I called Sheikh Munji," Bu Bakr chimed in, "and he said they were coming immediately."

"Coming?" I asked. "Coming from where?"

"From Marseilles," he answered. "He went to attend a funeral there with all his family; a cousin of his was killed in a traffic accident." Taking a step closer to me, he resumed in Arabic, "Sheikh Munji told me before he left that he would only be gone a couple of days and asked me to take care of Khadija. I was doing so, and my wife, too! Every hour she rang the doorbell to make sure she was fine, and we . . ."

I wasn't really listening. My eyes roamed Khadija's face, fading moment by moment, somehow smaller than the face I knew.

I came to myself as the Frenchman bent to pick up Khadija, saying, "We'd better get ready and go outside; the ambulance should be here any minute."

Leaping toward him, I shouldered him aside, not roughly but indecorously. "I'm the one who'll carry her."

Looking startled, he stepped aside.

There were three of us in the ambulance riding to the hospital, Khadija and I, and a young, serious-faced doctor who laid her out on the stretcher. When I made to help him, he shoved me aside, snapping at me to stand aside or else he would have me removed from the vehicle. He bent over her, attaching wires and clamps to her chest and around her wrist, then knelt by her, worriedly perusing the numbers that fluctuated on the device before him.

The streets at that hour were practically empty; it was between four-thirty and five a.m. The sky was filled with menacing dark clouds, and Paris still slept, except for the odd car whizzing by, or a lone pedestrian going hither or thither, swaddled in a thick coat, umbrella at the ready under his arm for any sudden fall of rain. I was gradually slipping away, back to that day when I'd seen Khadija hurrying across the street to tell me, "My father wants you to come to his place right now. He's got a visitor from Tunisia called Boushnaq, and he wants to introduce you to him."

"Boushnaq," I laughed. "Isn't he the young singer who just got very popular?"

"Don't you ever stop kidding?" She gave me a little shove. "He's a cleric with a beard as long as your arm, and his every sentence is peppered with 'God says' and 'According to the Prophet'!"

"Let's forget about this Boushnaq, and sit at this café." I gestured to it, gently guiding her toward the door, but she ducked her head shyly and pulled me by the hand to return with her.

That day, I kept her hand in mine for a long time, and she didn't seem to mind. Walking back, we crossed the street, and I put my arm around her waist. There weren't any cars coming at high speed—indeed, there weren't any cars at all, nor anything else for me to protect her from, but I did it anyway, and she accepted it gladly.

Another time, I ran across her in Saint-Germain. We sat at the Deux Magots café. I tried to converse with her in French to keep in practice, but she insisted on hearing me speak in Arabic. "What for?" I asked.

"Because I like the way you talk," she said.

Seeing my sudden embarrassment, she added quickly, "I mean your Egyptian dialect! It's fun! Smooth! It trips off the tongue gracefully and enchants the ear!"

"The ear," I said, joking and not flirting, "or the heart?"

She thought it was flirting, though, and blushed and told me to stop talking like that.

The doctor subsided a little, looking at me. "Don't worry, as soon as we arrive she'll receive an injection to dissolve the clot." Shaking his head sadly, he added, "Unfortunately, this is the second time. I know this patient. I came for her three months ago when she called for an ambulance. She spent two weeks with us under the supervision of my professor, Dr. Marc Dasou."

"And is she in danger now?" I asked, my face dark.

"I don't know. When we get to the hospital we'll know more."

A beat later, he looked at me over the top of his glasses. "You're her brother, I take it?"

"No."

"Ah, her husband, then."

"Yes."

I said it without thinking, without hesitation!

Chapter 24

My grandfather and I arranged to go out together behind my grandmother's back.

He stood in the hall waiting for me until I came out. My grandmother was in front of the TV with a cup of coffee, watching an interview on France-Trois with Brigitte Bardot, who was gesticulating and objecting strenuously to the inhumane slaughter of animals perpetrated by Muslims during feasts.

Face flushed, half-naked bosom jiggling with anger, she was saying, "What is this that these barbarians do? Such cruelty and barbarism and violation of animal rights! Aren't they ashamed of themselves, to be slaughtering these helpless creatures while fully conscious! They don't even drug them first! Is there no mercy in their hearts? And what's worse, some French Muslims slaughter animals in the bathtubs, in front of the children, and blood and fur are washed into the drains, and they get clogged, and the city has to spend days, sometimes weeks, cleaning them up! Aren't these people ashamed of what they're doing?"

Meanwhile, the devious director of the program was showing scenes on screen from Egypt, Algeria, and Pakistan, and some Gulf countries as well, of people grasping knives and slaughtering sheep and goats outside their homes and in the stairwells of apartment houses and in the open air, with crowds of men, women, and children encircling them and watching. The cameras zoomed in on their watching eyes, pupils dilated and fixed on the neck of the sheep at the moment of slaughter; some inclined their heads, some bit their lips or stamped a foot in exultation or perhaps pity, and then the cameras focused on those who raced to dip their hands in the fresh blood and make handprints on doors and walls, and, as if that wasn't enough, naughty children were competing as to who could set off the most firecrackers, the sound mingling with the cries and yells of "God is Great!" that went up from the crowd.

"She's right, by God," said my grandmother, shaking her head sorrowfully. "The sheep is a helpless creature, it doesn't deserve to have all that done to it."

I was in her line of sight. I turned away, indicating my displeasure at what she was saying, so that she might understand and be quiet, but instead she ingnored me and continued, "Yes, by God, it's good to show mercy! Poor sheep! Poor, poor sheep—don't you think so, Galal?"

Now I got it. She wanted to pick a fight. But I decided to hold my peace and turn a blind eye to her antics for now, thinking, "Spare me! Burdened in a strange land with a harebrained grandmother who never tires of combat!"

It was my grandfather, though, who fired up. "Sorry for the sheep? Them and you, too, Madame Yvonne! Well, since those sons of bitches are all angelic and showing us this stuff, they ought to speak out as well about what they used to do in Algeria!" He gave me a nudge. "Why, they killed and massacred and looted and pillaged! Land, money, trade, all of God's bounty that fills Algeria." Another nudge. "Oh, Galal, my boy, Heaven preserve us! Whenever a company of French soldiers got the notion, they'd lay siege to a village, and what kind of village? A tiny little village in the shadow of a mountain, or in some remote location, its people destitute! Then what would those sons of bitches do?" With that, he lightly tapped my chin to turn my face completely toward him. "Listen up! By force, under armed threat, they would march the men out of the villages and lead them far, far away, and place them under guard. Then they would go in, to the women. And they didn't discriminate! Married women or virgins, even old women with one foot in the grave, they'd do their dirty work! And when they'd gotten what they wanted, they'd call out to one another, 'Hey, Jack!' 'Hey, Mark!' 'Hey, Philippe!' 'Hey, Mud!' And the swine would hop into their Jeeps and double-time it back to their camps. Have you ever seen anything more indecent, more criminal?"

He waved a hand angrily at my grandmother. "They should have shown those things, my fine lady Yvonne! Is that all they're good for, filming the Eid sheep? And that female, posing and preening and all come-hither, what's her name again, Galal?"

"Brigitte Bardot, Grandfather."

"Yes, her! The one who makes all the seamy, steamy movies, who strips for the camera! Her father or grandfather was one of those soldiers, I'll bet."

My grandfather and I were now so worked up that my grandmother backed down from starting a confrontation: she sensed that we were just waiting for an excuse to start, and that we outnumbered her. "I didn't say anything, did I? All I said was that it's good to have mercy," she said in peaceful, submissive tones. "There, now." And she turned off the television. Noticing we were dressed, she asked, "Where are you off to?"

"Going for a walk," said my grandfather, already turned to go. "Going to Japan! Going to Karachi! Going to hell! What business is it of yours?"

She jumped up angrily, but we hastened to close the door and fled downstairs.

My grandfather stopped by a woman selling flowers in the street and bought two roses wrapped in cellophane, and we went to visit Khadija in the hospital.

Sheikh Munji was there, sitting with three men in their forties, all in Moroccan burnooses, with beards as impressive as that of the sheikh himself, if not more. They wore thick socks under traditional leather slippers, and the women surrounding Khadija's bed were concealed under burqas.

As soon as my grandfather and I poked our heads round the door, Sheikh Munji leaped up to greet us, all smiles, while the women also leaped up, flustered, trying to hide. "Stay where you are! They're my relatives!" he bellowed at them. Then he grabbed my grandfather into such a bear hug that he almost crushed him, kissing him on both cheeks and on the forehead as well, telling the men with him, "This is my neighbor, Mr. Zaki al-Azra', a respectable and compassionate man, from an old and venerable family, the clan of al-Azra'!" He looked at me, his eyes saying, *Isn't that so?*

I was flustered at Sheikh Munji's exaggeration, but went along with him and confirmed what he said, while the sheikh's Moroccan guests nodded with the appropriate "Mashallah! We're honored," and so on. My grandfather, meanwhile, was embarrassed and gratified by the warm welcome and the praise, looking at the floor shyly. When it was my turn, the sheikh gripped my wrist and raised my right hand high, bellowing, "And this is his grandson Galal, who's like a son to me. However much he loves me, I love him more."

Khadija smiled at me when I bent over her in greeting. I pressed her hand and her eyes lit up, quickly veiled by her lashes. I was slow to withdraw my hand; and apparently this triggered some sort of radar in those veteran veiled women, for they all raised their heads toward us and took to exchanging secret code with their eyes.

On the way home, I unburdened myself to my grandfather.

I'd thought he would have some objection, perhaps because of our old disagreements with Sheikh Munji's family, or out of respect for Rachel or because my grandmother would raise hell if this marriage took place, but he gave the lie to my fears and said at once, "Go right ahead, son, with God's blessing. If you feel comfortable with her, don't hesitate. Also, that way you'll be moving on with your life and Rachel will know where she stands." With a note of reproach, he added, "I said from the start—Rachel's no good for you, and you should look for a more suitable girl. You just didn't listen. Did you have to go all hardheaded and bring about all this? You were so much better as brother and sister."

"You mean I was hardheaded when I walked out on her?"

"Of course not, of course not, God forbid! You think I'd stand for you living like that? I meant the marriage itself." He waved a hand lightly. "Tell you what, this is no time for such talk—I'm just glad that God led you to Khadija; she's a sweet girl, and she's always been upright and respectable."

"And oh, Grandfather," I responded enthusiastically, "if you knew how much I loved her . . ."

He eyed me. "Do you love her, or Sheikh Munji?"

"What? What do you mean, Sheikh Munji, Grandfather?"

"Yes, Sheikh Munji. Listen, my boy, I've lived for a lot of years, a long, long time, and I'm telling you that what's between you and Khadija is something else, not love. It's an important thing, a fine thing. But not love."

"Grandfather!"

"Your old grandfather, who loves you, has only one thing to say: Khadija is the most suitable one for you, and in our present circumstances, you won't find a better girl."

"But Grandfather, why don't you believe I love her?"

He laughed. "Hey, I love her too!"

We had alighted from the Métro carriage and the crowds pulled us apart. As soon as we came back together, he put a hand on my shoulder. "But first, sport, you've got to finish it with Rachel."

"Let's leave that till later, Grandfather."

"Later? There's no such thing as later! Are you out of your mind? You must separate from Rachel immediately, and officially, too, before you take any steps regarding Khadija. You're no match for Haroun!"

"Elephant-Trunk again?"

"Yes, my fine fellow, Elephant-Trunk again, and again, and again! He's an evil man, and I wouldn't put it past him to report you to the police and take legal action."

"Legal action! What kind of talk is this, Grandfather?"

"Yes, legal action, what did you think? They'd even be within their rights to put you in jail. That's the law of the land here, you can ask Sheikh Munji. Nobody in this country can marry more than one woman at the same time; if he marries another woman, it's bigamy, and that's against the law. In plain Arabic, there's no legal provision for polygamy, and if Your Excellency should go marry Khadija while Rachel is still legally your wife, according to the law you'll be a criminal, and they'll drag you to the police station and there'll be all kinds of questions and hell to pay."

"But Khadija and I are Muslims! Do those jerks have the right to dictate to us and control our religious laws?"

"I'm with you, but don't forget that Khadija is a naturalized Frenchwoman and so is Rachel, and in this country they make their girls abide by their laws. And since you're set on marrying one of them, you have to abide by their system, so I don't want to hear any more talk about 'our laws' and 'their laws.'" He dusted his hands, adding, "Hey, we've got polygamy too, in our religion, just like you lot, but the law that goes for us goes for you too. That's how things are over here. So get a move on, and try to finalize this thing by tomorrow or the day after."

We were about to start climbing the stairs to our apartment. He stopped and turned to me, forefinger to his lips as though he were addressing a small child. "Now, you don't breathe a word of this. Keep it under wraps until I soften up your grandmother first," he said. "By the way, does your mother know of this?"

"Not a thing."

"Right, we'll give it a day or two. I'll tell your grandmother and by then you'll have gone to see your mother."

"But Grandfather, you know I . . ." I trailed off.

"No, dear boy, go and inform your mother, it's your religious duty. Doesn't Islam teach you to be kind and compassionate toward your mother and father?" I looked at him, surprised and pleased. "What?" he added sharply. "You think I don't know anything about your religion? Shows how much you know—why, I've read books and books by the great Islamic theologians, Sheikh Ghazali, Sheikh Tag, Sheikh Makhlouf, may he rest in peace . . ." and he listed a few more. He raised a hand for emphasis. "And many's the time I listened to Sheikh Shaltoot."

"Sheikh Shaltoot?"

"Yes, my boy; he was the head of al-Azhar, but it was before your time. He was a good man. He had a radio program where he used to speak every morning, and nobody went to work without listening to it! Anyhow, go to your mother, my son, and ask her for her blessing, so that God may bless you."

"But Grandfather, since you're familiar with all these Islamic clerics, why don't you think about becoming a Muslim, to set my mind at rest?"

I bit my lip as soon as the words were out, afraid I had hurt him. My love for my grandfather was something I held sacred, and I didn't want right then to say something that might directly or indirectly tread on forbidden territory. I speak of the territory in the heart of hearts, to which neither wishing nor hoping holds the key. Its secrets and tranquilities are closed to all but its owner.

My grandfather was aged by now. He had grown old, was at the end of his earthly life, and yet he still read the Torah bound in green felt that he kept by his bed. From time to time, tales of the Jewish prophets would trip off his tongue: Abraham, Isaac, Jacob, Jonah, Elijah. . . . Was I wrong to say what I said? Had my heart led my tongue astray behind my back? More to the point, was what I had said any use? Had it had any result at all? What on earth drove me to say it? Just like that, with no premeditation, no awareness, no intent!

I had taken myself by surprise, and now I leaned on the banister, looking into my grandfather's face, fearful of his reaction. Was what I had said a mere slip of the tongue? Were they just words with no meaning or purpose, one of those insignificant things one says that one doesn't really mean and that the listener doesn't really pay attention to? Or was it a slip of the tongue motivated by a heart preoccupied with this matter, unbeknownst to its owner? Did something inside me want this, but was suppressed by another part of me?

Part of me wanted my grandfather just the way he was, while another wanted him another way, and it was a case of never the twain shall meet.

Thank God. Again I say thank God, for my grandfather burst into uproarious laughter, and laughed until he cried. He started to mutter prayers and invocations to God under his breath as the Muslims do, then flung his arms around me, still chuckling. "My God, Galal, you're a character!"

My grandmother rolled up her sleeves as soon as she saw us, for no reason; I imagine that it was an instinctive reaction to our arrival, given what my grandfather had said before we had gone out and left her at home, especially as we were laughing as we came in the house.

Her expression was black; she was spoiling for a fight with us, the kind of fight where you really did have to roll up your sleeves. By way of starting round one, she scolded, "And just where have you been, coming home in the middle of the night and laughing all over the place? Well, there's no supper. The electric heater's broken."

My grandfather winked at me. "Should I tell her what I was laughing at, Galal?"

"Grandfather! Spare me!"

Chapter 25

I wasted no time.

I got up bright and early and headed for a registry office my grandfather had directed me to, and thence to the Egyptian consulate, where I finalized my separation from Rachel completely; now I was "all legal and legit," as they say. Then I went to my mother's.

Her husband Yacoub opened the door. "Long time no see, Galal. What's up? Do you want your mother?" He left me standing there.

"Well, I'd like to come in first, Uncle."

"Yes, yes, come in, come in. This way." He seated me on a chair at the very end of the hall and said, "But your poor mother is tired, exhausted. We just got back from Haifa in the middle of the night." He suggested I leave and come back at six or seven o'clock in the evening—eight o'clock at the latest, because they had a business meeting at ten p.m.

I stared at him, suddenly overcome with the impression that it appeared to this Yacoub as though I had come to ask for charity, and that the woman inside was not my mother, but a thing that belonged to him. When I insisted on seeing her, he turned his back on me and walked inside, saying inhospitably, "All right, I'll have a look."

He returned, telling me to wait, and sat opposite me, crossing his legs. I was irritated at him, and my eyes drifted to the photographs on the walls and the Persian drawings decorating the Kashan rug beneath our feet, and thence to the ankle protruding from his slippered foot, and his lower leg; it was bare, and eye-catching. I had not imagined it to be so thin, and the whiteness of the skin around it was strange, striking, like an unlit neon tube. There wasn't a single black hair on it, but formless things like tiny insects everywhere, in a mixture of white and blond. He never ceased jiggling his leg, nor bothered to hide his displeasure.

He must have felt my eyes upon him, for he lowered his leg and pulled down his dressing-gown. I bent to tie my shoelace, which had come undone, something telling me that his gaze, too, was roving over my head as I bent over my shoe. I could hear my mother moving around inside. I would have liked to go to her, but could not; it was Mr. Yacoub's house, after all. Even if I had, would she have greeted me as she had before?

He started to yawn again, moving his hand back and forth before his mouth. He said, eyes red and teary from sleeplessness, "Excuse me, Galal. Long journey, running about all over the place—I only had two hours of sleep."

I didn't respond.

After a moment, he said, "We were visiting your Uncle Isaac."

I still didn't respond.

"Your uncle is a real brain."

I felt that if I didn't respond, I would appear ungracious, so I said, "You know, Uncle, I've never met my Uncle Isaac. I've never even heard his voice, except one time on the telephone."

He leaned over and picked up a packet of Kents from a small side table. He lit a cigarette, took a couple of puffs, then stubbed it out in displeasure. "My! If you've smoked cigars and gotten used to them, you don't enjoy a pipe or anything else any more." He gave me a shrewd look, scratching a small protuberance below his ear. "You say you've never met your uncle? Your uncle isn't far away, dear boy. It's just four hours by plane. And if you want to see him, I'm going back to Haifa in a month, and your mother will be with me. Give me your passport and I'll get you the visa. Come with us and see your fill of your uncle."

"Are you serious, Uncle? You want me to go to Israel?"

Although he could see the expression on my face, he said, "Why not? Your president himself went all the way there, and the highest officials in your country are coming and going all the time."

My ire rose, entering my voice. "So what? What are they to me? Israel? Me, go to a country that practices such injustice?"

Leaning on the sofa cushion and fishing for the box of matches that had slipped into the crack, he said, "Why did you take it so hard? It's just talk. If you think it could work, be serious, take it seriously; if you think I'm kidding, well then, say I'm kidding. If you can't say either, forget I said anything."

In a more conciliatory tone, he said, "Wow! You and your grandfather really are cut from the same cloth, aren't you? He lost his temper too when I opened the subject of Israel, when we told him to pack up and come with us, that we wouldn't be there for more than a week." He stretched out his legs in my face. "Your mother was so frustrated, she even said, 'Fine, you can stay, but no more whining, "I miss Isaac, I miss Isaac."'" His eyes roved over mine. "You, Galal, you've got the right; it's all new to you. But him!"

I made to interrupt him, but he didn't give me the chance. "I mean, you're thinking this trip is too good for you, you can't quite take it all in. But why should he refuse, and why should he lose his temper? And why should he get mad at your mother, and warn her not to open the subject with him ever again?" he said. "I wish I could understand exactly what's going on in his head."

With no little pride in my grandfather, I said, "My grandfather has integrity. He knows where he came from, and he stands by his principles and doesn't give up his position."

"Position?" he said derisively.

"Well, Uncle," I suggested, "instead of pressuring my grandfather, why not get Uncle Isaac to pay him a visit?"

"You think your uncle has any objection? If he were free, he would come here two or three times a year. He used to, you know. He's busy, son. He hasn't got a minute to spare. A factory in Haifa, and a business partnership with some Druze, not to mention the settlement he's building."

"He's building a settlement?"

"Yes! It's going very well, too."

"Which one? One of the settlements they build on the Palestinians' land?"

"For heaven's sake, dear boy, quit this talk, and politics, and 'our land' and 'your land,' and the things they say in the newspapers."

"If you build a settlement on another man's land, Uncle, by force, and force out the people who live there, and 'Get out of here, filty swine, you and her, and find yourselves another spot,' is that talking politics? Or is it God's law? Not Islam, never mind Islam. Does Judaism, real Judaism, condone that?"

"My dear, dear boy! What religion, and what law? You're terribly naïve; your thinking is limited. It's not like that at all for your Uncle Isaac. It's all business; business is business, and he'll make a pretty penny now his bid has won and he's got the contract."

"But Uncle . . ."

"But what? He's an Israeli, and what's he's doing is in his interests and his own country's interests. If you want to blame someone, how about the workmen under him? Half of them are Arabs. Some from Jaffa, some from Haifa, some from Gaza or Jericho. What, they don't know it's a settlement? And this isn't even another man's land—it's in their land, as you were just saying yourself."

He didn't wait for my answer, but went inside, returning with a tray bearing a bottle of mango juice. "Drink up, little boy, drink up."

I knew that he had gone into business with Uncle Isaac, which might be the reason for his frequent visits to Israel. So I said, "If I may ask, Uncle, are you a partner in this settlement deal?"

"No, no, I'm not into settlements. I have no business interests in Israel at all. I just go there for holidays, and to see my daughter, and we spend a couple of days at your uncle's. I have other plans, and business plans in Egypt, also with your Uncle Isaac, and perhaps your Uncle Haroun Bey, will join us,"—he meant Elephant-Trunk—"or one of our people here."

Curious, I pressed him for more information.

"We want to start a garbage recycling plant in Egypt, plus some other projects—maybe the most important one is the plot of land Haroun Bey has bought by Neama Bay in Sharm al-Sheikh, and your uncle and I would like to come in as partners."

"All this in Egypt?"

"Where else? A promising country; a penny invested will get you ten, if you've a good head for business and are flexible." Then he added, "This recycling project, well, that's so-so. What I've got my eye on is this land in Sharm al-Sheikh, and if Haroun would say yes and just listen to me, we would build a gambling casino on it. Not a regular casino like the ones here and there; no, no! A world-class casino! Something big and well-thought-out, like the casinos in Monte Carlo and Las Vegas, and it would attract heavyweights from all over."

"But that would cost tens of millions, Uncle."

"Tens? Hundreds! And that's the easiest part. Investors are there, and they're ready. The important thing is to have powerful protectors inside the country."

Apparently, he thought I didn't grasp what he was getting at, so he went on, "Protection, I mean. Important officials to help you get licensed, deal with the tax authorities and the customs officials, to get rid of the obstacles in your path and clear the red tape and protect you when necessary. All for a fee, of course. All it needs is a trip to Egypt, to test the waters and find out where the heavyweights are."

I couldn't find words to answer him, so I fell silent, and he went on to discuss other matters. He launched into a description of

Haifa: its architecture, its marketplaces, its beaches, its large port, and its tourist attractions: Carmel Valley and the Holy Mosque and the Clock Tower and the Tomb of the Virgin Mary, and that he and my mother had also visited the Baha'i World Center, and Abdel Bahaa's tomb;* they also listened to a lecture by Baha'i theologians from America, and Iran, and France, and Israel. I nodded, bored, saying, "Yes, yes" as needed.

"I swear, these people speak well and convincingly."

"Who?"

"The Baha'is."

"Ah."

"And the city, Galal! The streets are sparkling, and houses with tile roofs, and residential areas nicer than Europe!"

My revulsion must have shown on my face.

"All the disgusting stuff comes from the Arab quarters. And their names, eww! Preposterous names! Sahat al-Hanatir, Wadi al-Nisnas, and I don't know what and the other. Thoroughly off-putting. Poverty and dirty streets and, oh, it's just depressing! And if you saw the Jewish areas—clean, attractive, classy boutiques, and shops worthy of the name! Civilized people who know their rights and obligations!"

Provoked, I retorted angrily, "Those disgusting people you're talking about, Mr. Yacoub, are the natives, the owners of the land, and it's their great-grandparents who built Haifa. We do them an injustice when we judge them on their current state: they're under occupation."

"Under what? Occupation? Where did you get this stuff?"

"From what happened. Geography and history and events, sir."

---

* Real name Abbas ibn Hussein ibn Ali al-Noury. His father was Hussein Ali Mirzah, born in Teheran on 12 November 1817. He was the founder of the Baha'i religion, and was called Bahaa' Allah. Mirzah Abbas, also known as Abdel Bahaa, revived the religion after his father's death and brought together disciples and followers. He was buried and has a shrine on the side of the Carmel Hills in Haifa, where the Baha'i World Center lies, its central establishment visited by Baha'is from all over the world.

He held out a hand to interrupt, but I forged on. "And the people you call civilized, that's just the image that you and others get to see: they dress nicely, they speak nicely, they live in classy, clean places—you're right about all that, Mr. Yacoub. But if you examine who they are and where they came from, you'll find that in the end they're immigrant Zionists. Some from Romania, some from Hungary, some from Poland, and Yemen or Morocco: people who left their countries and came to stay in our midst by force. People who stole our homes and streets and money and things and everything they could get."

He stared at me. "Did you ever hear, Mr. Yacoub, of someone stealing a whole nation? Not a watch or a car, or even a house—a nation! An entire nation, Yacoub Effendi! With its land, its people, its sea and sky, its summer and winter."

"Listen, boy," he scowled, red-faced, "don't drag me into talk of politics. Not that I'm ignorant, but if I want to speak of politics, I'll speak to someone on my own level. Someone with the maturity and balance to do so, not an inexperienced kid." Louder and angrier, he added, "And what's this 'Yacoub Effendi'? You should address me more politely, don't you think? After all, you're sitting with a man who—I don't need to remind you that I'm the same as an uncle to you, but a man who has had an important career. And if you didn't know, I'll tell you that we were Beys and Bashas in Egypt, and people didn't call us 'Effendi'—they called our servants that."

I apologized, but continued to prod. "So Egypt did do good things for you, Uncle, did it? Egypt gave you grand titles, and let you in generously, and you must have enjoyed her bounty."

"Indeed. Indeed. Who could deny it?"

"There are those who do! Uncle Elephant-Trunk, for example— I've never heard him say anything good about Egypt.

"Elephant-Trunk, Garden-Hose, what he says is nothing to me. It's an ungrateful man who denies what Egypt's given us, and not only us . . . others, as well." He gave a long sigh. "Armenians, Levantines, Italians, Greeks, and people of countless faiths! And son, you know, they all came to Egypt penniless, and came to own land and factories and apartment buildings. Egypt is a wonder." He crooked a forefinger at me. "But you must know that we did much for Egypt as well. There were writers and artists. Yacoub Sannu', Dawoud Hosny, Togo Mizrahi, and many others! You won't have heard of them."

I shook my head.

"I don't blame you. They were before your time. My boy, there have been Jews living in Egypt for a long, long time. Some fled there from Spain after the fall of Andalusia. Some migrated from Europe and some from Turkey, and so on and so forth. Don't forget that we lived in Egypt, too, at the time of Joseph." He stared at me. "You know of him, I'm sure."

"Know him! Of course, and we have a sura dedicated to him in the Quran."

"That's good. Now you're with me. And that was in the days of the Prophet Moses, which means since the time of the pharaohs. Egypt has always been our country just as much as it is yours." He smiled, leaning closer to me. "What about the famous singer in the movies, Leila Murad? Do you know her or not?" He didn't wait for my answer. "Now *there's* a Jewess, born and bred. Find me a single Egyptian who doesn't like Leila Murad's voice, or her art."

"But she became a Muslim, Uncle!"

"A Muslim?"

"Yes, she became a Muslim, and fasted and prayed, and sang for the Prophet Mohamed, too. Didn't you hear her singing, 'You who are going to visit the Prophet, congratulations, I hope to join you'?"

He didn't answer. He turned his face completely toward the passageway leading into the interior of the house. Perhaps he thought my mother was approaching. Then he turned back to me. "And what about the Qattawi family? Who could deny what they did for Egypt? Yusuf Qattawi Basha reclaimed twelve thousand feddans all by himself, and founded the sugar refinery in the town of Kom Ombo. And he was a minister and a member of parliament as well. And the Sawaris family! They reclaimed countless amounts of land, and founded banks, and they founded the first public transportation line in Egypt. The government even honored them and named a famous square in the heart of Cairo after them—Sawaris Square—only it was later renamed Mustafa Kamel Square."

He leaned back, resting his neck and back completely on the chair, occupied for the moment with knotting the belt of his dressing gown, and afterward extracting a thick Cuban cigar from a gold box on the table beside him. He lit it, blowing its hot smoke into my face. "And the Menasha family, and the Dweiks, and the Nadlers, and the Nusseiris, and the Hararis, and the Semouhas, and the Mizrahis, and so many others. All these did so much for Egypt. And when you go back to your country, my boy, take a look at the names of the stores in the Sagha or in Muski: Mustafa, Hanna, Fouad, and Nassif. Those aren't the real owners: the owners were Jews who fled, selling their businesses and their affairs and what they had toiled and sweated for, dirt cheap."

I tried to stop the monologue or change the course of the conversation, but it was no use.

"In Alexandria, we founded the suburbs of Semouha and Torell, and Maadi in Cairo. And the big department stores, Shamla, Cicurel's, Omar Effendi, Dawoud Ades, and Simon Arzet, Gattegno, and the Salon Vert, and Ibn-Zion."

"Ibn-Zion?"

"I mean Benzion."

"You're right, Uncle," I said. "But those people who did all that, weren't they Egyptians just as much as they were Jews?"

"Egyptians? Really?" he said, offended and provoked. "Tell me then, if they were really Egyptians, why did the government constantly harass them? The government, not the people. The Egyptian people are kind; they won't turn on a neighbor or treat you cruelly or kick you when you're down. It was that damned government that kept at them until they hounded them right out of the country. Not a word of comfort, not a single reassurance that their businesses wouldn't be harmed—nobody told them, 'You're

Egyptians after all, and we will only punish you if you do something wrong!' Why, if you were Jewish, it didn't matter if you were a big businessman or a little clerk, if you said, 'I'm leaving' it would be 'Good riddance! You said it here first!' and he'd have to run this way and that to sell his house and his furniture and his shop. And those without conscience would gather like butchers around a dying beast, who won't so much as take out their knives unless you sell it to them at a quarter of the price." More sharply, he continued, "And anyway, tell me, my Galal, do you pigeonhole people as you please? When we build great enterprises that bring good to the country, you call us Egyptians. When we shrink into ourselves and look to our own interests, you say, 'Ah, those bastards. Once a Jew, always a Jew!' And when Israel comes up, you call us Zionists who deserve to be burnt at the stake! So, you decent people see us as creatures with no identity. Our identity is only as good as our deeds, and our deeds are subordinate to your whims and your interests."

We were heading inevitably toward a dead end. I fell silent; his enthusiasm waned, and gradually our conversation wound down.

After this, I didn't know what to make of the man. I had always avoided him, and pushed his image away in disgust when it entered my mind, like shooing a rat away with my foot. I had never felt comfortable with him; whether he was flirting with my mother in a way that made one's blood boil or taking liberties with her that were even worse, making my flesh crawl and eating at me as though the act were taking place before me, and as if it were a sin before God. And yet, now that I had been forced to spend time with him, I found him sensible and balanced, and my attitude changed. I found myself, indeed, sometimes convinced by his words. My eyes admired this mutton dressed as lamb. I admired his aspect and his clothing; he always, in my eyes, seemed to outclass those around him.

Perhaps my mind believed him; my heart, though, never ceased to reject him. When we were alone together that day, all that had been hidden burst forth; my words mingled with his, and our words

merged in my heart without my noticing or meaning it. I didn't real-
ize until afterward that my ego, which loved, hated, liked, resented,
had been my partner, moving the conversation along. It had made
me fancy that he had done what those Zionists, these strangers, had
done to Palestinian land. They had stolen the land, and made free
with it; he, too, had carried off my mother, and made free with her.
My mind and tongue were saying to him, "You did such and such to
us," and my heart meant that he, too, had done such-and-such!

What was it with me and that man?

And if my mother had married another man, a man who was
not Jewish, would I have treated him so coldly? Was my mother's
marriage to this Jew what pained me, or was the very act of her
marriage the root of the illness?

My mother arrived, unsmiling, making me more depressed. I
didn't want to waste time, either. I told her immediately of my
plans. I spoke, not as one asking for permission or approval, but
as someone telling her the news, nothing more. She stared at me
disapprovingly as she reached for her cigarettes, asking, "What was
wrong with Rachel?"

I didn't answer.

"I'm asking you, smart boy, what was the matter with Rachel? A
clever girl, and beautiful besides, and money in her hand." She looked
toward her husband, shaking her match out. "She went against the
whole world for his sake, Yacoub!" Then, to me, "Shouldn't you have
come to me for advice first? I'd have told you what was right, instead
of breaking the girl's heart and disappointing her mother."

I answered in a low voice, sneaking a glance at Mr. Yacoub,
"Mother, that was something that goes without saying. And this is
no time for such talk, you know everything."

"I know, do I? What do I know? You know the dumb talk I heard
that made you walk out on the girl on her wedding night?"

"Mom! What are you saying? What's the matter with you? Is
honor dumb talk now?"

"Honor?"

Seeing that things were getting heated, Mr. Yacoub stepped in as she continued, "Honor, that's rich, you ignoramus! You think you're still grubbing around in the alleys in Daher! And what's more, you hopeless boy, just you tell me, who has the energy to deal with Khadija and Khadija's family? She's ill, she's not healthy enough to marry. And her father's a street hooligan, all he knows is the knife and the cleaver."

She wrung her hands, talking and muttering. "Rachel! The pretty girl, making good money, what does he do? He leaves her. And for whom, pray tell? Ah, well. There's nothing for it. How unlucky I am! I marry his father, the effendi from the countryside, and waste my youth with him. He leaves me, and poof! Goodbye. And then I find out he married a woman from his village! Are these people who have any conscience? And the second one, well, he's a chip off the old block! Leave Rachel, a girl from a good family, and go marry into a family of garbage, no use in the world at all!"

"Shut up!" I screamed at her. "I won't have you insult Dad!"

"Your father, your brother, who the hell cares? He's gone."

She had changed. She was no longer the mother I had known growing up; she was not my mother who had come to France, thin and wasted, looking for a shelter for all of us, wanting nothing from the world but for me to make something of myself. Ever since she had married this capricious old man, she had rushed out into the world, drinking her fill like a hungry she-camel. Now in the Natanya resort, now in Capri or Cannes. Another time, I'd heard that she and her husband had been forcibly ejected from the Folies-Bergère because she had been drunk and wouldn't stop creating a disturbance.

Now she sat on the couch before me, a diamond ring on her finger of no less than three carats, and a Star of David in white gold dangling from her neck. She spoke to me, wagging her forefinger and frowning, as clouds of smoke emerged from her lips. Her face and breasts had been filled out with silicone and subcutaneous firming injections; as for her hair, she wouldn't dream of having it done anywhere but at Jacques Roissy's. And this great stork, her husband, had he no shame, bending over her cheek and kissing her right in front of me? Just like that, you son of a bitch, plain as day?

I ignored the insults she had heaped upon Sheikh Munji, for all her family said the same. What pained me was what she had said about my father. I stormed out, not saying goodbye or even looking her in the face. Before the elevator door closed upon me, she hurried out after me with her husband, but it bore me down and separated us.

Chapter 26

I married Khadija.

My grandfather was the only one who came with me to ask for her hand; they all refused, and even Uncle Shamoun avoided me, making the excuse of illness. When I reproached him, he said in shame, "I'm sorry, Galal, I'm in an embarrassing situation. You know how Mom is." He meant my grandmother. After a silence, he said, "What can I do, son? She's lost her mind. Imagine, she's threatening to ask for the return of the four thousand francs she lent me if I go with you to Sheikh Munji's. She gave them to me when my young son Saul asked me to buy him a bicycle last Passover." With a tone of astonishment, he continued, "This was nine months ago or more. I thought to myself that she meant to forgive the debt, or forgot about it or something. But . . . my goodness, Mother's a hard woman! She has no mercy!"

My uncle was right; if not for the financial embargo she had imposed upon him, he would have come with us willingly, instead of just my grandfather and me going in like orphans.

If only it had stopped at that! My grandmother made the house into a war zone; now talking to herself, now fighting with my grandfather for hours, in the hope of dissuading him from accompanying me. Sometimes she would launch herself at me with whatever she happened to be holding; her walking stick, the fly whisk, or the serving ladle. Once she even grabbed the ashtray, meaning to throw it at me, but overbalanced and fell to the floor along with her walking stick, and but for the grace of God would have broken her foot or cracked her hip. As I helped her up, I said, "You're not a young woman any more, Grandmother. This behavior doesn't become you. I'm a man, not a child. I have my own business and employees and workers under me, I'm not little Galal who used to play ball in the street. What is this, Grandmother? Can't you communicate in any other way but ear-pinching and screaming and punching and throwing things in my face?"

"Shut up, rude boy!" she said, puffing and panting. "You've dragged us through the mud! What am I to tell my friends, Samaka and Rika and Hanouna? That we're marrying into the family of Munji al-Ayyari, the miserable meat cutter whose dishonesty is broad and deep as the salty sea? When you left Rachel, we said, well, all right; but to marry this little lizard, you blind fool?"

I put my fate in God's hands. We went, my grandfather and I, leaning on one another for support. Sheikh Munji welcomed us and led us into the sitting room.

It was the first time my grandfather had been inside the sheikh's apartment. As it happened, he sat down opposite an old-fashioned photo on the wall, of a man with a short tarboosh on his head with a scarf wrapped around its base, wearing something wrapped around his body; it had a collar with huge flaps, like the ears of a large elephant. It was confusing, unlike either the gallabiya we wear in our country or the burnoose worn by Tunisians and Moroccans. The man himself was stocky, with a build both strong and muscular, as though he had been a porter or bearer in his youth, or perhaps an athlete—a wrestler or bodybuilder. The noticeable thing in the picture was the severe scowl visible on his features, and his strict, slightly narrowed eyes, as though he were planning to attack someone.

My grandfather wasn't comfortable with the photo. He asked me who this man was, and I said that he was Sheikh Munji's father. He had been a famous butcher in the Gerba district, from which the sheikh hailed. "Heaven protect us," he said. "Are there people in the world with faces like that? It's like he's staring at me and wants to throw me out of the house!"

My grandfather was right. I had been in this room many times before, and every time I had sat in the seat my grandfather had taken, I would feel that the man in the picture was staring at me with displeasure, as if to say, "Who are you and what are you doing in our house, you son of a bitch?"

There was a thick stick hanging on a hook next to the picture. It wasn't a walking stick like the ones regular people lean on, or sometimes just swing as they walk; it was the type used for fighting and inflicting bodily harm. "Sheikh Munji's?" my grandfather asked, eyeing it admiringly.

"No," I said, "Sheikh Munji's is a little smaller. This is his late father's, and he thinks very highly of it. It's an heirloom, and he only uses it at gatherings and important occasions."

My grandfather shook his head. "Heaven protect us!"

We heard the sheikh clearing his throat to announce his arrival; my grandfather straightened, and Sheikh Munji entered, followed by his wife, Sitt Zahira Bu Saf. She gave my grandfather a lukewarm greeting, and asked after my grandmother. "She's ill," I said. "She ate something that had gone off, and it gave her diarrhea."

After a moment, with suspicion in her tone this time, she asked after my mother. Was she well, or did she, too, have diarrhea?

The sheikh spared me; he closed the matter with a warning glance followed by several warning coughs. She bent her head and folded her hands in her lap, and refrained from asking me about any other member of our family; indeed, she never said another word.

Khadija came, and we recited the Fatiha. Sheikh Munji followed this up with a number of prayers for such an occasion. My grandfather bowed his head during the recital of the Fatiha, but his lips moved, murmuring something, perhaps prayers of his own; Sitt Zahira never took her eyes off him, until Sheikh Munji elbowed her in the side.

My grandfather spoke of the engagement ring and the gift of jewelry. The sheikh suggested that she and I go together to an Algerian jeweler's called Bu Zarzour, because the French gold traders, he said, were overpriced, and most of their wares were either precious stones or eighteen-karat gold. Bu Zarzour had Arabian designs in respectable twenty-one- or twenty-four-karat gold.

To my surprise, my grandfather put his hand in his pocket and produced an envelope containing a wad of fifty-franc notes, and presented it to Khadija. She demurred, looking at her father, who told her to go ahead, after which she took the envelope.

Things went as though we had been in Egypt or Tunisia; Arabs are the same everywhere.

In a week, we finalized our engagement with a simple reception. A month later, we signed the marriage contract, and had a wedding in the Tunisian style: old Tunisian folksongs to please the older guests of the sheikh, and girls singing in the style of Aleyya the Tunisian singer, and a young man from the sheikh's family who resembled the Tunisian singer Lutfi Boushnaq, in looks and voice. He took to covering that artist's songs, to resounding applause. Then there were traditional riding songs, and the musicians beat the tambours, and it was as though we were in green Tunisia and not in Paris.

Mr. Fouad, the Egyptian who worked with us at the company, was there. Apparently, he also considered himself a singer, for he took the microphone and sang us a Farid al-Atrash song. He wanted to follow it up with an Umm Kulthoum, but they revolted and snatched the microphone from his hand; one of them said he had a terrible voice, hissing like an old drake's! Abul Shawareb was occupied with eyeing the girls, and the sheikh watched him from where he sat. When we asked him to dance, he welcomed the opportunity. We tied a scarf round his waist, and he started to dance like an experienced belly dancer to Umm Kulthoum's "Inta Omri." The sheikh stared at me and whispered in my ear, "Your friend is not respectable. Isn't he ashamed of what he's doing? By God, who is the One and Only, if he were not in my home and the wedding was not that of my daughter, I would have gotten up and slapped him on both cheeks." He called on his wife and daughters and commanded them to stay away from him.

My grandfather could not stop laughing at what was going on around him. He asked them to sing him the old Mohamed Qandeel song: "If you're going to Ghoureya, bring a gift back for my sweetheart." They said they'd never heard of it, so he fell silent. A while later, he said, "How about 'You who give the Evil Eye, mind your own business' by the folksinger Mohamed Abdel Muttalib? Do you know it?" They sang a couple of verses and begged off, saying they didn't know the rest.

Uncle Shamoun, in flagrant defiance of my grandmother's directive, came with his children and his wife, whom everyone urged to bellydance for us; she was Egyptian, after all, and this art stemmed from Egypt. She did so, with her husband's and grandfather's permission; but she was nowhere near as good as Abul Shawareb.

Sheikh Munji paid special attention to us; whenever he passed my grandfather or my uncle, he patted their shoulders gratefully. When the party was over, Khadija and I repaired to our new apartment in the rue des Écoles in the Latin Quarter.

Chapter 27

My grandfather had been wise when he said that what was between me and Khadija was something beautiful, but not love. Else why did Nadia's shade still torment me?

How many times did I see her shadow as I looked out of the closed window of my and Khadija's bedroom at the rue des Écoles? Heavy raindrops pattered down, misting its surface, making everything before me look blurry and unfamiliar. Cars passed, driving slowly and carefully. Two women stumbled by in the wet, then turned right, seeking shelter in the entrance to a building. The streetlamps were slightly dimmed, droplets of water sparkling on their metal frames whenever the headlamps from a car washed over them. Little boys ran here and there, unheeding of rain or water. The whole world seemed strange, the wind and the misty sky and the wetness laying siege to everything and making it unfamiliar.

And then she'd come . . .

The nose, the eyebrows, the freckles on the column of her throat. Her schoolbag. Her breath, which enveloped me every time I put my arms around her. The sound of her footsteps as she hurried up the stairs of our building in Daher, fearful that someone would overhear us. I would be overcome by her voice, low, melodious, smooth. She whispered, then stopped. Catching her breath, she resumed her whispering. I came closer; she coyly pushed me away. I would relive a time we had experienced, preoccupied, my heart pounding, my eyes dreamy.

Except for one time . . .

One time, in the present, not the past. I was standing in my usual spot by the window. The water and the rain were the same, and so were the clouds; it was as though she were standing at the crossroads of the street I overlooked, a child by her side, his features indistinguishable. She wanted to cross the street, but couldn't, taking a step forward, then retreating.

"Not so fast," I said. "Where's your umbrella? Don't you have an umbrella?"

She stared at me, her eyes shining, as though she hadn't yet recognized me.

"I'm Galal."

"Ah," she said. Then: "Who? Galal?"

I inclined my head toward the child. "And who's he?"

"My son, Sameh."

I feigned surprise. "Your son?" Yes, feigned; for I knew. Hassan had told me in his last letter that she had gotten married, but I wanted to appear before her as though this was the first I had heard of it. I looked steadily, reproachfully at her, without a word. She understood my reproach, and dropped her gaze in shame. This was how I saw myself, and her, from above, from behind the windowpane.

"Give me your hand," I said, "let me help you cross the street." I hesitated, then said, "And Sameh, too. We'll take him with us."

She waved a hand dismissively. "Don't worry, sir. My husband will do it."

The appellation upset me; I followed her gaze, seeing the husband she had mentioned, standing close, watching us silently. What astonished me was that he didn't look the way he always had when he had come to me before. His face was not that of a younger Mr. Yacoub, nor his figure that stocky build I had long visualized: he was different. He wasn't smartly dressed, his tie not even tied correctly. His body was noticeably emaciated, as though he suffered from an incurable disease.

I felt Khadija come up behind me. She put her hand on my shoulder. "Come on. There's a Louis de Vigny comedy on Channel Four! Quick—I've made coffee, I'm afraid it'll get cold!"

"Leave me alone a minute."

And I drifted in a bygone world, where I had no hope of belonging any more.

A day, or part of one, would pass; finding me sitting in an armchair or lying in bed, Khadija would ask me what I was thinking of. I never told the truth. "I was thinking about my father," I would say, and rise.

"Where are you going?"

"I'll perform a prayer to ask for mercy on his soul."

"I will, too," she'd say.

She was a kindhearted, gentle soul. All she knew of the world was the good side.

I would kneel to God. I would pray for him to save me from my own evil, to allow me to be all hers, not just partly. Day by day, my tenderness toward her grew, as though something were happening between us. It wasn't the love that lays waste to everything, like a raging wave, or ripples clear and transparent until you see the sea bed; it was something I could watch growing, unlike the love that is born full-grown, where you never know how it will end!

We went out a lot. We would go to the Luxembourg Gardens near our house, and spend hours sitting on their wooden benches, chatting and watching the gardeners taking care of the trees and flowers like angels of mercy treating human patients. One time, an aged French gardener kneeling before a pansy caught our eyes. The position seemed painful for him; every now and then, he would sit up and bend and stretch his legs to relieve them. Curiosity made us draw nearer; he was caring for a small pansy bush with a twisted stalk. He wrapped plaster around it, after dosing it with several drops from a bottle of medicine that lay beside him, then pulled it gently toward the larger stem of the main bush. A magnifying glass lay at his side. I think he used it to determine the amount of damage that had befallen the stalk.

"It's just a flower," I said.

He looked at me. "If someone in your family got hurt in an accident, would you leave him to die, or take him to the hospital and treat him?" I understood then, but he went on. "It lives and breathes like you and me, and feels, and suffers. Some naughty kid pulled the stem and ran off. Should I just let it suffer—especially as I know this plant? I've been working in this park for forty years, and all these plants," he gestured around him, "know me, and I know them." He went on in low tones, "This flower that you think so unremarkable—who knows how valuable it is in the eyes of God? It might move Him to forgive one of my sins."

From our street, we'd walk through Saint-Michel until we reached the Seine, crossing the Pont-Neuf to the Centre Pompidou, to use the library or watch documentaries about nature or humankind. Or we would take the Métro to the Louvre, feasting our eyes on works by Renoir and Rembrandt and Cezanne, and the "Mona Lisa" with its special security, cordoned off to prevent visitors from getting too close; in fact, the area around it was so packed they had to institute a rule that no visitor was allowed to spend more than three minutes before it.

After this, we would go to the section on Greco-Roman art, seeing statues that seemed about to speak. When we finished, we would go to the Hall of Ancient Egypt. Khadija would be impressed, and I proud. This monumental art would lift us up; the pharaohs were kings in the true sense of the word, and we would boast vicariously of them as long as we lived. The lower we sank, the more we'd say to those who lorded it over us, "But we have something you don't!" When they scoffed, we'd respond, "Are you descendants of the pharaohs, like us?"

Khadija and I learned how to look at works of art, how to appreciate them and contemplate them. The first time we went to the Louvre, we hurried through the halls, casting a glance here and a glance there, content with our first impression of the beauty of the works, our eyes skating over their surfaces. We thought it strange that people stood before the works for a long time, moving forward, then back, perhaps taking a step to the right or left to view it from different angles. A viewer might notice something, and whisper to his companion, and the companion would, in turn, look closer, and either nod or argue with him in whispers. "Why don't we do as they do?" we thought.

We visited many times, especially on Sundays, and took to asking the museum guides, who would tell us, "Look at the use of color in this painting; the gray is expressive of such-and such, and if it had been a little lighter in tone, the meaning would have changed. As for this bright shade, it means something different." They would take us over to another painting by the same artist, to show us how he had developed his use of color or facial features, another phase where he favored symbolism, and so on. They would gladly explain to us the differences between Rembrandt and Renoir, or Van Gogh and Gauguin.

The same went for sculpture, and which of the great sculptors, for example, was best at facial features, which focused on the shape of the profile, and which concentrated on physical perfection and scale and dimension, and we began to understand.

One evening, I put on a black suit and bow tie. Khadija wore a long-sleeved evening dress and a silk scarf the color of the dress. We got into my BMW and set off for the opera.

When we got out of the car, the opera house towered forbiddingly over us, as though it were looking down at us, instead of us contemplating its ancient architecture. It had been looking down from above at us, and at others like us, for a long time. We were only a fleeting moment in its long life; how many inspired artists had stepped across the threshold of its great doors, their music ringing out within these walls! Verdi, Strauss, Handel, Bach . . . and up its sweeping staircases, the great kings of France had climbed, decked out in entrancing fashions; so had cardinals like Richelieu and Mazarin!

That night they were performing Bizet's *Carmen*, a favorite here. We passed the doors, Khadija and I, after handing the usher our tickets, and they had in turn presented us with the opera program for that year. Within its wide halls, we found a number of aristocratic patrons, still preserving the tradition of top hat and tails. Middle-class ladies and gentlemen, even young men and women, would come for an evening's entertainment in the company of this wonderful art!

Everything was reserved and restrained; there was no gesticulating or hand-waving except when necessary; conversation was hushed, nothing too loud or garrulous, no shouting or whistling; opera-goers know they are in for a treat for the soul, and that they are seated in a shrine devoted to art, not unlike those who go to houses of worship and shrines where God's name is spoken.

The women's dresses, especially, were a source of delight to us; here, fashion designers competed, creating short and long evening dresses, with sleeves and without; and tiny gold and silver evening bags; and mink and silk stoles, in addition to the expensive strands of pearls and diamond earrings and necklaces. I doubt that all this was a matter of vanity or fashion; it seemed to me to be a celebration of the place itself.

The lights were on, so I looked at the program. Next month, they were performing Tchaikovsky's *Swan Lake*, followed by Mozart's *The Marriage of Figaro*, and then Schubert's *Unfinished Symphony*. The lights went out, and silence reigned.

The curtain went up to reveal an enchanting gypsy scene: the opera tonight would be about the gypsies, their world, their journeys, and their loves. The sets depicted old-time Seville, while gypsy girls in full skirts and bandannas wore jingling bracelets and earrings that swung and shook whenever they turned their heads. And Carmen, gypsy legend, enchantress of hearts, breathed fire into everything; the audience, quite losing control, interrupted her several times with bursts of applause. She walked with her shoulders back and her head held high, proud and haughty, hands holding up the sides of her full dress, shaking it wildly and drumming her heels on the boards as she came and went, seducing her Spanish lover, Lieutenant Don José. I fell in love with her and with her voice as well, and with Bizet's music, which, despite its operatic nature, carried me back to our old street in Daher, with its crowds and the cries of its street vendors. When one of the brass instruments rang out, the Abbasiya tram burst into my imagination; it clanged and clattered too, and came and went before our eyes when we were children, as electric sparks flew from the trolley pole that reached up to the overhead wires.

Although Khadija was sitting by my side, and had reached out to enfold my hand in hers, I nevertheless followed the vision of Nadia. It was as though she were alighting from one of the cars of the tram and I was waiting for her; she caught sight of me out of the corner of her eye, and I hurried up to catch her. "Behave! People are watching!" she said.

We never finished. The final chords woke me, and soon the conductor was climbing the boards to receive his applause. He nodded his head calmly in response to the wild clapping, for he was truly a king and we his subjects.

Chapter 28

Mr. Fouad knocked on my office door.

It was my first day back at work, after my two-week honeymoon with Khadija. He told me that his annual vacation was due, and that he would be going to Egypt on the Monday flight.

"Egypt!"

I said it in hushed tones, full of longing, so that he smiled and said, "Do you miss it?"

"Do I! Come here, come here . . ." And I took him by the hand and sat him down and gave him our address and took to describing how to get to our apartment house in Daher, and the number of our apartment and the number of Umm Hassan's, and how to get into the street and the names of the stores, each and every one, and Abu Ouf's café and the neighboring juice place that sold sugarcane juice, and warned him about the deaf old dog with no conscience that usually loitered at the top of the street, for he didn't like strangers.

"I get it, I get it!" he cut me off. "Dog? What dog, Galal Bey! Do you think the dog's going to still be standing there after all this time?"

But I was describing it to him and going on and on, not for fear that he would lose his way—the way was so clear, a child could get there, never mind an adult—but because of the intense pleasure that flowed through my veins at speaking and reminiscing and describing. When I was done, I said to him, "Look here, what I'll do is, I'll give you a letter and a bag of gifts for Umm Hassan, and the key to our apartment too, so she can open the door and give you my grandfather's tarboosh. You'll find it in the big armoire."

"Tarboosh?"

"Yes, tarboosh. Don't you know what a tarboosh is? Plus, Mr. Fouad, do you know where al-Geish Street is?"

"Do I! I used to take that street to Abbasiya when I was a student in the faculty of commerce at Ain Shams University."

"Good. Good. Do you know where Cinema Misr is? You must have seen it before. Look, here, after you pass through Bab al-Sha'iriya, coming from Attaba into al-Geish Street, it's a little way down and you'll see it on your right."

"No problem; I'll ask for directions."

"You do that. Opposite the movie theater you'll find a tram stop with a platform—it's built with reinforced concrete. After you finish your errand to Umm Hassan's, I want you to stand at that tram-stop for half an hour or more, and keep looking around you at the stores you see, and the ones behind you, and the people getting on and off the tram."

"And then?"

"Then nothing! What do you mean, 'and then'? You do it and that's it!"

He looked at me, baffled. "I do it and that's it?"

"It's where I grew up, Mr. Fouad," I said, drawing near him, trying to gain his understanding. "This place holds so many memories that are dear to me. I entreat you to do as I ask, and when you come back, tell me all that you saw, and all that you heard."

He gave me another long, puzzled look. The next day, when he came to me, I gave him the letter, the bag of gifts, and the key to the apartment. "One more thing, Mr. Fouad. There's a haberdashery next to Cinema Misr. A little shop, with a refrigerator outside selling soft drinks. Its owner is called Uncle Abu Lehaf . . ."

"Uncle who? His name is Abu Lehaf? That's his name?"

"Yes, that's his name! He's an old man. Day and night, winter and summer, he's got a shawl draped over his head and never stops yawning. Tell him Galal says hello. He'll ask you, Galal who? Tell him, Galal from Daher who passed by your store every day going to school and coming home from school! Galal, who would sometimes be walking with a pretty girl with long straight hair hanging down over her school uniform! Galal, who . . ."

I held my tongue. He was staring at me, with no idea what to say or how to respond. If I hadn't been his boss, he would have rebuked me and gone already.

"So, do you know of Sheikh Damanhouri?"

"Damanhouri? Damanhouri who?"

"He's one of the big Quran reciters, Mansour al-Shami al-Damanhouri. May he rest in peace—he passed away some years ago. I wish you'd bring me back one of his tapes—or two, or three, as many as you can manage."

I started to tell him of my love for the voice of this sheikh when I was a boy. I told him how I would find any excuse to go out on Wednesdays, at eight o'clock on the dot, because that was when he used to start his recitations. I would keep coming and going and dragging my feet outside Abu Ouf's café, my ears glued to the radio on a wooden shelf in the depths of the café, all the while watching for any movement on our balcony, a few steps away, for fear that my mother or grandmother would see me and rebuke me, commanding me to come back upstairs.

When he said goodbye to me, I said, "You know, of course, that everyone has their secrets."

He stared at me uncomprehendingly.

"What I mean to say is, I don't want any news of my marriage to reach Egypt. Umm Hassan is going to ask you, for sure, whether I've gotten married, whether I've had any children. Tell her I haven't married, and that I'm always distracted, with a far-off look. Tell her you don't know what's the matter with me: 'It seems, Hajja, that there's some secret, something momentous, in his life.'"

He raised his eyebrows. "You want I should tell her that you're distracted, with a far-off look, and that there's a secret in your life?" He clicked his tongue. "But, I mean . . . I mean, what I mean to say is . . . Well, okay, sure, I'll tell her that, if it'll make you happy."

I don't know what drove me to say that. It was just something that occurred to me; I don't know how it came, or why I went along with my desire to say it to Mr. Fouad. Was it that I wanted to hide the news of my marriage, convey the idea that I was suffering in a strange land, so that the news would reach Nadia by way of Umm Hassan? She would tell her, that was certain; indeed, she would embellish the story and say how sorry for me she was. Did I mean for that to happen, so that she would still labor under the delusion that she alone had betrayed what was between us and married another, while I remained faithful to the pledge we had taken to each other when we were young—the grand words we had said to each other, that neither of us would ever belong to another, and neither of us would ever do this, that, or the other?

Did I mean to cause her pain? And why should I do this, when I, too, had married, not once but twice? I don't know. The human psyche is dark and mysterious sometimes, closed even to its owner.

A month passed. Mr. Fouad returned bearing a plastic shopping basket with two handles at the top, of the type used when buying groceries. I immediately smelled the hand of Umm Hassan. She came to mind, coming and going from the Waily food market carrying one like it. He handed me a letter from her, but said to me that she had told him to convey to me a secret about her son, Hassan. I drew nearer, listening. He said, "She misses you and says that when times are hard, she only has you to lean on, now that her husband is dead; the woman who nursed you has the right to make demands."

"Uncle Mahmoud al-Attar is dead? When did this happen?"

"I don't know. The problem is that her son Hassan has married and is living with her in her apartment. Seems she's not comfortable living with his wife, or even with him, and she wanted your permission, and Uncle Zaki's, to go into your apartment and stay there until you come back."

"Until we come back? She can have it for good. Why, I'd get her an apartment in the best neighborhood in Cairo. Why didn't you give her the key?"

"I actually did of my own accord, or tried. But she wouldn't take it. She said, 'Give it back to its owner, and when he agrees, he'll find a way to send it to me.'"

"Send it? What a waste of time! I'll call her and tell her to break in to the apartment, let herself in."

Then I asked him about the Damanhouri tapes. "Here they are," he said. And the tarboosh? "Here it is. But it made a spectacle of me in the airport on my way back. The customs inspector wouldn't stop staring at it, and kept me standing there by him for about an hour, turning it this way and that and pulling on the tassel and passing it around to his coworkers like it was something bizarre. Guess what? That son of a gun thought I was a magician, and it was my stage prop!"

But he hurt me when he said that he had found no trace of Abu Lehaf's shop, that it had been replaced by a videotape store, with a frizzy-haired, nasal young salesman. "Didn't you ask him?" I cut him off.

"Sure I did. He said he didn't know any Abu Lehaf, nor any Abu Mkhadda either."

He hadn't found a trace of the tram stop. They had wiped it off the face of the earth: the concrete roof, platform, concrete seats, and all. He had seen it himself: a group of workmen with crowbars prying up the tram tracks themselves, and a truck parked close by, into which they were loading them.

I was unhappy in the car going home, as though the Abbasiya tram that had died was a relative of mine. I was also irritated at Mr. Fouad's comment that "They did well to remove it. Let them take it to some other benighted place. It was just a dumb, stupid thing, no use anyway."

I remembered when Hassan and I were boys, and Uncle Mahmoud al-Attar would turn the dial on the radio, bored and discontented, in a fruitless search for Sheikh Saleh Abdel Hayy's song, "Why do you bring joy, O violets, while you are a melancholy blossom?," which they didn't play on the radio any more. In those days, with the ignorance of youth, we used to wink at each other and say things like Mr. Fouad had just said to me.

Chapter 29

My grandfather couldn't believe his tarboosh had been returned to him: his old tarboosh, which he had never taken off until he was obliged to leave Egypt and take up residence in a strange land. A cry of joy burst from him as soon as I took it out of its brown-paper wrapping, and he said without thinking, "Bless you, Galal, my boy! When did you get it? How?" He embraced it in his hands, tenderly running his fingers over the edges and fingering the threads of its black tassel, contemplating it and reminiscing of bygone days, before he and his tarboosh had been separated. The tarboosh, over there, enclosed in a dark closet, and him as though dead in a home with damp, still air, no world for him in the big world he lived in, Paris, which they called the City of Light, but a bed, a bathroom, and a table where he ate whenever they called him.

I noticed how dreamy he was, and watched him push the tarboosh aside and say, "Everyone had already left off wearing tarbooshes when we were living in our street in Daher, except for me and a few people you could count on your fingers: Malak Effendi who worked at the library, Mr. Eweiss from the traffic authority, Hajj Zanati who owned the halawa factory in back of the Bein al-Sourein district. You know, Galal, my boy," he leaned toward me, "the tarboosh is a respectable thing, it covers the head and gives you a kind of cachet. Look at Nahhas Pasha,

Makram Ebeid, Lutfi al-Sayyid, and many others—see how they looked in their tarbooshes! What a glorious sight! Prestige, cachet, something satisfying!"

"But, Grandfather . . ."

"But what, bless you? They got people to take off the tarboosh. What did they get them to wear instead, may I ask? Now the sun just beats down on everyone's heads, and some have frizzy hair, some have thin hair, some, heaven protect us, don't have a single hair on their heads . . . the tarboosh covered a multitude of sins! Why, before . . ." And he launched into long tales of the good old days, when an acquaintance of his had gone to ask for the hand of a girl whose family lived in the eastern part of Abbasiya, where the upper classes lived in the 1940s. They rejected him because he had come bareheaded, which clearly showed that he was flighty and lacked proper respect for the occasion.

"You mean Rustum Effendi, Madame Sadeya's son?" my grandmother cut in.

"Yes, why yes, that's him!"

"But they disagreed on the dowry and the jewelry, not about the tarboosh!"

And so story followed story, my grandmother correcting as he went. Frustrated by her refusal to allow him free rein, Grandfather said peevishly, "I'm hungry, and Galal hasn't had lunch either, I bet. Come on, let's go to the kitchen."

He was so pleased with the tarboosh that he tried to put it on his head and look at himself in the mirror, but he failed; the brim of the tarboosh, it seemed, had shrunk with lack of use and the passage of time, so that it no longer fit his head. But he insisted on wearing it anyway; I lent a hand, attempting to push it onto his head by force—to no avail, of course. It bulged at the sides, and the tassel nearly came off in my hand, not to mention the red line it left on my grandfather's forehead.

Hearing the noise, my grandmother came out of the kitchen. She looked at me with irritation. "What's this nonsense, Galal?

And you, Zaki, are you planning on wearing that benighted thing here or what?"

"Wear it here? What do you mean, wear it? Do you take me for a fool? I'm just trying it on. I'm going to hang it on the wall! Where . . . Hmm, where, Zaki, where . . . ? Yes, here, by the clock, so that everyone can see it as they come in."

As they come in? What's this, the tarboosh was reduced to an item on display for guests who come and go? What a terrible thing! I stood there and wondered at the ways of the world, asking myself how and when my grandfather had so changed as to become Monsieur Zaki. The ID, which they call here *carte d'identité*, shows a scowling face, a dark, preoccupied glare in his eyes, as though it were a photo of a prison inmate. And the data on the card: Monsieur Zaki Isaac al-Azraʿ, a Gaulish citizen, born in 1896, blood type such-and-such, married to Yvonne Sawaris, resident of No. 9 in such-and-such street, of such-and-such district, Paris. That's what his ID says. French law says, too, that this unhappy old man has become one of us; and its sibling, Egyptian law, is of course of the same opinion, and says that if this person—this human being—this one—wishes to enter our country, we shall review the matter and issue our decision in due course, yea or nay.

My grandfather had become one of the Franks. Louis I up to Louis XVI, followed by Charles X and Louis-Philippe and Napoleon Bonaparte and Charles de Gaulle and Georges Pompidou, and Giscard d'Estaing, these were his leaders now, his history and his past. Like any good Frenchman, his only concern should be to ensure that the French language reigned supreme, and that France should lead Europe, and if things grew serious, he must sacrifice his most valuable possessions, to say nothing of his cheapest. My grandfather, who knew nothing of the world but Daher, its alleyways, and the watchmaker's where he worked in Azhar; who, if he wanted entertainment, had only a game of backgammon at Abu Ouf's café, or a visit to one of his friends in Sakakini or Khalifa Street. If he happened to have a yen for a day out, then there was nothing for it but the zoo, or Fayoum, at the farthest.

Zaki Effendi al-Azra', who used to carry a basket of biscuits and menein, and visit his parents' graves at the Jewish cemetery in Basateen, on Saturdays and holidays. Zaki Effendi? Now his anthem was "La Marseillaise," the flag to which he pledged allegiance was the French flag, with its vertical lines of red, white, and blue! This is my grandfather, whose eyes shone with joy like a child's at the sight of his tarboosh! The tarboosh, which the French customs official was so surprised to see. Was it truly a type of hat, a toy, or a magician's prop?

Dear God!

We emptied out the contents of Umm Hassan's bag: a whole goose, several brace of pigeons, dried okra strung together, and two cow's hooves. My grandfather laid them out together in delight. "Now that's food that does a body good! That's real bounty! Not cheddar cheese and smoked meat and hot dogs and the tasteless, useless vittles here!"

I seized the opportunity to tell him of Umm Hassan's problem. "Why not, my boy? People were made to help one another, after all. Send the key to her." He thought for a moment. "But tell her it's only temporary—a few months, because it'll only be a little while before your grandfather comes back. Be sure and impress that on her, Galal, because it's a matter of months, at most, before I go back to Egypt."

I knew these were mere wishes; my grandfather's health no longer permitted him to move anywhere, not even to the next street, but I went along and reassured him that I would convey his words. My grandmother did the same.

Before I went upstairs to my apartment in the rue des Écoles, I sat in my car, opening the letter that had come from Hassan and reading it. It was all jokes and idle talk; I only paid attention to one line, where he said that Nadia had had a daughter!

Chapter 30

Spring had arrived. The south is charming at that time of year; the coastal towns, Nice, Cannes, Saint-Raphaël, Antibes, all along the French Riviera, are at the height of their unparalleled splendor. We remembered the invitation of Mr. Mustafa Bu Saf, Khadija's maternal uncle, to visit them; he had been insisting for months that we come and spend a few days at the Nice hotel of which he was the manager. The last telephone call had been a few weeks ago, and he had again urged us to come, saying that the bridal suite was at our disposal whenever we should come.

He was fortyish, a bachelor, lighthearted and easygoing to the point of foolishness. His bane—as I found out from Khadija—was his voracious appetite for the enjoyment of worldly delights; his principle in life was summed up in the philosopher-poet Omar Khayyam's verses:

Extinguish the heart's fire with cooling drink;
The days, like clouds, are gone ere we but blink;
Life's but a passing shade, so seize the day,
Ere fleeting youth into old age doth sink.

It was for this reason that Sheikh Munji was reserved toward him, and never ceased to show his disapproval of him, with and without any occasion for this. Every time they met—which was rare, of course, because of the distance—they had to start an argument. To be accurate, the sheikh lectured him and made his life a misery by asking him which of his religious obligations he had fulfilled, and what provision he had made for the afterlife. Then he would cross-examine him as to how many prayers he had said—not the regular five prayers, of course, but the Tahajjud, which lasted all night, and the extra prayers that the Prophet is supposed to have done at sunset and eventide, as well as invoking dire threats of the hellfire he would surely be cast into, and the horrible torments he would endure at the hands of its demons. The man would listen, saying, "Amen, Amen," and receive the sheikh's lecture with good grace, for the man was like a father to him, and had taken him in and raised him for a long period of time.

Khadija told me with a laugh that once when he had come to visit them, the sheikh had happened to be the one to open the door; the thing was, Mr. Mustafa was drunk at the time, slurring his speech and swaying. The sheikh had flown off the handle, especially as he had just given him a long sermon just a few days previously. He pushed her uncle with one hand, then rushed to the sitting room and retrieved the stick, while his wife tried frantically to get her husband off her brother. The sheikh screamed, "Let him taste my stick! It's like magic—everyone knows that, near and far! Let me go! Teaching manners to his kind is a great pleasure of mine, and a religious duty to bring me nearer to God!"

She didn't listen to him, taking her brother by the hand to the bathroom and pouring cold water over his head until he sobered up, then bringing him to the sheikh. But he didn't accept him as a guest until he had had a bath and purified himself of the impurity that clung to him, then performed his ablutions and prayed two prostrations outside of the normal prayers.

The sheikh never ceased to show his irritation and annoyance with the man whenever his name came up in conversation, and had advised us more than once not to accept his invitation. We didn't take his advice, though, and went.

He was waiting for us at the airport, carrying a bunch of flowers, pushing and shoving to get to us. Khadija hastened toward him, and so did I. After exchanging hugs, he accompanied us in his Citroën sports car to the Hôtel Monseigneur on 17 rue Malesnes. I still remember the number and the street name; they have never left my imagination.

It was an old hotel, with rectangular windows of heavy wood that required a great effort to move. Its rooms were wide and high-ceilinged, the balconies decorated with Roman paintings and urns. We were on the second floor, in the spacious bridal suite with every possible amenity, with crystal vases of fresh flowers on every table, and a fruit plate, which was refreshed every day, and a small fridge filled with juice and Birell and Vichy mineral water, and bottles of beer and spirits. I turned one of the bottles in my hand and said to him, "We don't drink."

"I know," he said. "They're not for you, they're for me when I come up to see you!" With a sudden glance, he said, "Is there any chance that Sheikh Munji is coming too?"

"No," we said.

"Ah, then it's all right. Nothing to fear. Let the bottles stay safe where they are."

We would go for walks every day; now in rue Malesnes, through Liberation Square; another time through rue Jean Madessa, window-shopping in boutiques and antique shops, and relaxing at cafés. We would continue in this fashion to Victor Hugo Street and Felix Court, until we were almost at the sea. Then, if Khadija were not too tired, we would walk along the Riviera, which they called the Côte d'Azur, the bay curving in a horseshoe, fantastical lights shining from tall lampposts the length of the promenade, lighting up the chestnuts and palm trees alongside them, making their proud green heads fresher, as though they had just been washed. The lights would also filter toward the water, mingling with the lanterns that twinkled in the dozens of charming boats and rowboats resting in their moorings, or carrying their owners over the sea. The water's surface was breathtaking, enchanting; with playful, joyful delight, it flirted and shimmered as if to say, "There is no beauty in the world greater than mine." You felt that it was inviting you to draw nearer, not just two or three steps, but to touch it with your fingers, plunge your hand into it, and dip your feet in too, even if you were wearing shoes.

On the opposite side, the streetlights shared our enjoyment, sparkling in the facades of shops, boutiques, cafés, and hotels: the Negresco, the Carlton, the Grand Hotel. These were all eighteenth-century buildings, with ornately carved entrances and facades; the sides and the balconies were decorated with marble columns and statuettes, even a few full-size statues. The people's faces were glowing, natives and tourists alike, shining with joy.

Mr. Mustafa Bu Saf gave us a great deal of his time. One time he took us on a visit to the cities of Cannes and Monte Carlo, neither of which was far from Nice, and once to the high hills that surrounded us. Green and interconnected, they were almost like mountains. In some of these, the primitive lifestyle survived: one could see scattered huts, shepherds and goatherds, and, at far-flung intervals, luxurious mountain houses whose rich owners stayed there in summer and sometimes spring, and mansions of various sizes with guards at the doors. We were enraptured by one of these in particular, and stood close by it, admiring its architecture and lush gardens and armed guards monitoring the luxury automobiles driving in and out.

"It appears," Mr. Mustafa said to us, "that the owner," and he mentioned his name, "the Gulf prince, is home. He's a billionaire, and only comes once a year. He spends a week here, then flies off to another mansion he owns, in the suburbs of Geneva." Then he added, "Do you notice how the street we took to come up to this prince's mansion is paved with asphalt and tar and has traffic markings on it?" We said we did. "Whereas a lot of the roads out here, as you see, are still unpaved dirt paths?" Again, we said we did.

"This," he told us, "is a story in itself. Look at these huts scattered over the hill from the very bottom right to the top." We did. "These huts are owned by poor French herdsmen. They keep goats and make a living by selling their milk and cheese, especially the cheese, as it's well known and well loved by the people here. For years, these herdsmen have been begging the town council, handing in requests and petitions, to deign to pave this road for them, sparing them the hard slog up and down, and the city council always refuses because they don't have the budget for it, saying, 'We have our priorities; your road is a side street; it's not in our current plans,' and so on and so forth.

"But necessity is the mother of invention. They said, 'Why not go to this prince? He's Mr. Big on this mountain, after all, and they say that the Arabs are generous folk who never let a request go unfulfilled, nor turn back those who seek a favor.' They asked the keeper of the mansion, who's a Frenchman same as them. He welcomed the idea, and told them of the prince's temperament and what would please him, and the time of his arrival.

"When the prince arrived in his dishdasha and ugal in his Rolls-Royce, with a security vehicle behind and another in front, making sure the path was clear—he was so surprised at what he saw! All along the path, the herdsmen in their simple clothing, some in rags, lined the path, bearing signs and waving at him, some calling out in comical, stilted Arabic, 'Long live the prince' and 'God bless the generous, charitable prince!' He asked one of his escorts, "Who are these? And good heavens, they're speaking Arabic, what—what are they saying—I don't understand a word!'

"He said, 'Just a moment, O Prince, may God grant you long life. . . .' The escort listened intently, then said to the prince, 'They are praying to God to grant you health and long life, Your Highness, and saying, "Welcome, welcome to the land of the French."'

"The prince smiled, and said, 'God bless them, they are people of taste and discernment.' And he took to waving at them from inside his car. When he arrived at his mansion, he found another group of them congregated at the door, bearing a large placard with signs welcoming him in both Arabic and French. Their applause and cheering reached a crescendo as soon as he alighted from his mighty street machine, and some of the boys started whistling (which, as you know, is a positive thing with the Arabs) at a sign from their elders. He smiled again. 'Good. Good. What do they want?'

"A palace official leaned closer and said, with all courtesy and respect, 'They are desirous of imposing upon your generosity, and would like it if His Highness would command that this road be paved, for the city council of Nice has long failed them, and His Highness is their neighbor and the lord of all he surveys, and they have no one to turn to—besides the Almighty, of course—but His Highness.'

"And he said, as he turned to go inside, 'No problem! Have it paved at my expense.'"

Afterward, we made a detour to one of the herdsmen's huts.

They welcomed us, offering wine. Khadija and I demurred, but Mr. Mustafa wasn't one to waste the opportunity, and drained every glass they offered him. Khadija and I drank goat's milk, which the herdsman's wife presented to us in earthen cups, only she asked us why we refused to drink her wine. We explained that we were Muslims, but she did not understand. Her husband, though, said, "I've heard of that religion. I know it prohibits drinking alcohol."

"But why, then," she asked, "is that gentleman drinking? Isn't he a Muslim like yourselves?" And she gestured to Mr. Mustafa, engrossed in conversation with her husband, the entire carafe resting in his lap.

"He's a bad Muslim," Khadija said softly, "and he's so confusing! He does things that are contradictory: what Islam commands, and also what it prohibits!"

They refused the money that we offered them, maintaining that it would be a slight, and saw us to our car. Afterward, we drove up to the top of the mountain. We saw Nice below us, tiny, its houses no bigger than matchboxes, the sea as wide as though it were the whole world; enthralling, glorious, wakeful, alert, its waves flinging themselves upon the shore, their white foam remaining on the sand without returning with the receding water.

When Khadija felt her breath becoming tight, we descended in a hurry.

We were due to go home to Paris by air the next day. Mr. Mustafa had made reservations for us at one of the nightclubs on the water, but Khadija cried off, saying she was slightly dizzy and wanted to go to bed early.

I wanted to stay with her, but she wouldn't hear of it. "Whatever for? I'm going straight to bed. Go with my uncle, and the two of you have fun for me." She insisted that I wake her upon my return, though, no matter how late it was.

Mr. Mustafa and I spent a long time at the nightclub, sitting and talking; he listened to me, and I to him. I drank different kinds of juice and finished off with a cappuccino; he drank till his head was heavy, and we left.

He drove me to my hotel, then went home to his own apartment in rue Thierry. I entered the room on tiptoe so as not to alert Khadija to my arrival, ignoring her repeated insistence that I wake her up; sleep would do her good, I thought. I didn't even turn on the electric light, but made do with the light coming in from the street. Gradually, my eyes grew accustomed, and I could make out the room and its contents, and all the while she slept on.

I didn't find out that she wasn't asleep, but gone, until I lay down by her side.

She had had a heart attack while I was at the club. The Angel of Death had taken her by the throat while I was out having fun.

Chapter 31

As much as the weak suffer, the strong suffer too. I had never seen Sheikh Munji the way he was yesterday, when we put Khadija in the earth, or today, when we sat accepting condolences. His face was furrowed with grief, his shoulders bowed as he sat on the chair. He didn't speak, his eyes bleary and swollen with his misery. His friend, Sheikh Bu Mikhla', whispered in my ear, "Take care of him, son."

"I will, God willing," I murmured.

He passed a hand over his beard. "I was sitting with him in his shop. We were chatting, and he swore that I must go up to his apartment for dinner and then look over the zakat ledgers. We prayed, had dinner, and picked up the ledgers. We talked and talked, and before we finished, my boy . . ." He paused; it appeared he had noticed that I was abstracted, not concentrating. He nudged me and went on: "Life and death are the province of God, my son. There is nothing we can do to change what is written. God Almighty is the only one who does not die." His face furrowed in concentration. "What was I saying? What, what? Ah, yes, I remember. I was saying, my boy, that before we were done with the ledgers, the telephone rang. It was you. Munji took it well at first, stoically, accepting that God had taken her back; but something in him was shaken afterward, Galal. He leaned on me, saying, 'Help me, help me, Abu Mikhla'.' He gave a sigh like a moan, and his fingers fumbled with the prayer beads lying in his lap. You know he has high blood pressure, so we rushed to give him his medicine, and he almost came out of his stupor, only Umm Khadija, God forgive her, started wailing so loudly and beating her head against the wall that he rose to quiet her down, screaming at her, 'Stop these things that anger God, you woman of little faith!' But then he collapsed and fell to the floor like a dead thing." The man muttered unhappily: "Sheikh Munji, whom we thought as strong as a mountain, Dear God!" He leaned back into his chair, preparing to listen. "And you, my son: tell me everything that happened in Nice. Tell me in detail."

I knew that there was no use arguing with Sheikh Bu Mikhla'; he was kindhearted but garrulous, and had no clue that silence and holding one's tongue was his duty in the circumstances in which we found ourselves. I decided to leave his side at the first opportunity; in fact, I made to rise on the spot, but he gripped my wrist. "Where to? Where to? We're not done talking."

It appeared he'd forgotten that he had asked me a question, for after he made me sit back down he started to speak again. "And God bless that grandfather of yours."

He gestured toward my grandfather, who happened to be looking in our direction, and thought Bu Mikhla' wanted him for some reason, so he rose, heading in our direction. I hurried to him, saying, "Nothing, nothing, Grandfather." I looked around me in search of a vacant seat, but there were none; there was nothing for me to do but to return to Bu Mikhla' once again.

As soon as I had sat down, Bu Mikhla' said, "Yes, God bless your grandfather. I went upstairs to him quickly. He was shocked, and kept asking me questions, his face pale: 'Good God! When did it happen? Where are they now? Khadija? Khadija dead?' And I calmed him down, and said, 'Get dressed immediately, Uncle, and let's go down to Munji, I left him in a terrible state.' And before we ran down, my boy, he called to your grandmother while he was at the door to call someone named Shamoun to catch up with us immediately." He didn't spare me, but went on, "Who's this Shamoun, my boy?"

I said, unable to hide my displeasure, "My uncle, Sheikh. My uncle, my uncle!"

"Your uncle? That's your uncle's name? Lovely, lovely! So, my boy, when we were on the stairs, I told your grandfather to take care of the sheikh with me. He said, astonished, 'What's this, Bu Mikhla'? Do I need you to tell me to take care of Sheikh Munji? He's my relation by marriage, and if God had blessed Galal with a child, we would have been its grandfathers.' Bless this grandfather of yours. Kindhearted and gallant."

Something seemed to occur to him as he was chattering, for his eyes widened and he looked cautiously at the man sitting by our side, finding him a sheikh like himself, not one of the Jews come to offer condolences; reassured, he leaned closer to me, and said in a whisper, "Why don't you invite your grandfather, my boy, to enter into our religion?"

I fell silent. Perhaps he thought that this had not occurred to me, for he beamed at me, proud of his idea, as he passed a fingertip over his mustache. "Isn't he your grandfather?"

I didn't answer, of course, for he knew the answer; plus, I thought it was a rhetorical question, and that he expected no answer. It was different for my interlocutor, though; he was waiting for me to answer, and actually said firmly, rephrasing the question, "Is he your grandfather or not?"

I was flabbergasted. I felt I was in the presence of a policeman interrogating me, not a man of the cloth, and retorted, "Yes, he is!"

"Do you love him, and want what's best for him?"

"Yes, I love him and want what's best for him!" I said in a rush, for fear that he would do what he had done in the previous question.

Then, he leaned so close that the tip of his turban was touching my head. In a soft voice, he said, "Then let's move fast, and get God's reward for converting him, instead of the deluded perdition in which he now wanders."

I said to myself, "You son of a monkey! Why all this circuitous conversation?" I was a little annoyed by his way of conducting a conversation; I also didn't like the way he was dealing with my grandfather as though he were his guardian or keeper—never mind the fact that we were at a funeral and the departed was my wife! I wanted to shut him up, or at the very least say, "Be quiet, Bu Mikhla', there's a time and place for everything," but I held my tongue. He must have interpreted my silence as approval, because he leaned over me again encouragingly, whispering in my ear.

"Think about it, my boy. Your grandfather is advanced in age, and he has one foot in the grave. Let us save him before it's too late." He even egged me on, lightly squeezing my shoulder, and said, "Think about it, my boy. Think about it. And we'll sit together, God willing, and plan it, and think how to introduce the idea to him." He slapped my knee and said, "That's enough about your grandfather. Tell me everything that happened in Nice."

A boy was moving toward us bearing a tray of hot drinks. Seizing the opportunity, I hurried over to him and helped him hand them out to the mourners.

We were holding the funeral at the rue des Écoles. We'd emptied the hall of furniture, and arranged some chairs and tables in rows, finding it the most suitable place for the men. For the women, we prepared a spacious room and supplied an additional row of chairs. One of Sheikh Munji's female relatives volunteered to play hostess to the ladies and see to their needs.

We seated Sheikh Munji on a chair in the hall, roughly in the center, and the mourners would bend and greet him. They came and went while he sat there, lost, distracted, muttering incomprehensibly from time to time. When he did raise his head, you couldn't make out his eyes, tense behind lids that had settled into a state where you never knew whether they were open or closed. A number of his cleric friends sat somberly by his side, their sympathetic eyes finding him every so often; some of them moved their heads in appreciation of the verses of the Quran emanating from the tape recorder placed on the table between our room and the room where the ladies paid their respects.

My grandfather followed Bu Mikhla''s recommendation; he never strayed far from Sheikh Munji's side unless absolutely necessary, and patted him on the shoulder and consoled him. The sheikh bowed his head in gratitude.

Bu Said, the sheikh's nephew, was manning the tape recorder. He started with the Sura of the Compassionate, recited by Sheikh Mohamed Rif'at, with his sweet voice, full of the awe of God, then verses recited by Sheikh Damanhouri and Menshawi and Sh'eisha' and Mustafa Ismail. Everyone was silent and still, overwhelmed with the awful presence of Death, and the wonder and dread inspired by the recital of the holy verses. Not a word, no idle chatter nor even acknowledging aloud the skill of the orators and the beauty of their voices. Nothing but a few scattered coughs and perhaps someone whispering in another's ear as Bu Mikhla' had done with me. Even the Jewish mourners observed the traditions, not smoking during the Quran recitals, nor leaving the funeral except in between segments of the Quran, signaled by the reciter saying, "Sadaqallahu al-Azim (God speaks the truth)."

At the instigation of Bu Mikhla', a Tunisian serving boy in the traditional garb of his homeland walked among us, coming and going while murmuring prayers, holding in his hand a chain attached to a metal dish containing lit coals and incense, fragrant smoke wafting from it. He went to the women's room afterward, and when he finished, he disappeared into the kitchen and stayed there, topping off the incense and relighting the coals, occasionally poking his head out, waiting for Sheikh Munji's instruction to start making another tour of the mourners.

Whenever a Quran tape drew to a close, Bu Said would allow a break, so that those present would have sufficient time to speak among themselves or smoke or use the bathroom. At that time, my grandfather would seize the opportunity to make the rounds of the mourners with his pack of cigarettes, offering it around to them as people used to do in old-time Egypt in the traditional tents erected for funerals. My Uncle Shamoun gestured to him to desist—we were in Paris, after all, not al-Hussein or al-Khaleeg Street—but my grandfather paid him no mind and urged the mourners to accept his cigarettes. He bustled into and out of the kitchen, calling for the Tunisian serving boys to supply the mourners with hot drinks: he bossed them around, ordering green tea for Mr. So-and-So, and Turkish coffee for this fellow, and Nescafé or a cappuccino for that gentleman over there. This attracted the puzzled attention of some of the sheikh's relatives; those who did not know him would turn to their neighbors and ask who he was, and nod appreciatively and respectfully when they received the answer.

My grandfather, though, was not acting out of a desire for approval or any such thing. To him, it was a matter of duty and the right thing to do; since Khadija was his granddaughter-in-law, well, then this funeral was his, and the apartment where the funeral was being held was his home, being the apartment of his own Galal, and by extension, these mourners were his guests and he their host. This was how he had been raised, and what he had learned during his life in Egypt among the people of that country.

My grandmother arrived, swathed in black. She walked in to where Khadija's mother sat, followed by my mother, my aunt, and Rachel, all dressed in mourning. Some of my grandfather's acquaintances attended as well, Egyptian Jews who used to attend the soirees at Mr. Yacoub's apartment. The only one who didn't attend was Elephant-Tusk—I mean Elephant-Trunk. He didn't so much as send a telegram. Mr. Yacoub came for just ten minutes, puffing rapidly on his cigarette, then decamped in haste with the excuse of an important appointment.

It was late at night. The last of the mourners had gone. We went downstairs together, my family and Khadija's close family, headed up by Sheikh Munji, leaning on my Uncle Shamoun!

I locked up the apartment, handing in the key to the French doorman, Pierre. "You still have six months left," he said. "Your contract was for a year."

"The lady of the house is gone, Pierre," I said. "Whom have I got to stay for?"

I drove my grandparents home, with two of the sheikh's daughters. My grandmother hadn't forgotten her usual nature, though: she said to my grandfather that tomorrow would be a black day for her friends Samaka and Hanouna who lived in Belleville. "Spare me. What on earth for, Yvonne?"

"They didn't come to the funeral. It's our family's funeral, isn't it?" And she went on to say that she'd gone to the funeral and done her duty when their relations, So-and-So and So-and-So, had died.

"You're within your rights," said my grandfather.

He wasn't saying it to humor her, or to shut her up as he used to do. He meant it. He patted my hand as it gripped the steering wheel. "Only God lasts forever, my son. It wasn't meant to be. May God have mercy upon her soul, and upon ours too."

When the household was fast asleep and I found myself alone in my old room, Khadija floated before me, her body wasted by death. I remembered the first time I had seen her in Sheikh Munji's home, and our conversation on the airplane on the way to Nice, and our laughter at the anecdotes of the exploits of her uncle, Mustafa Bu Saf.

I began to ask myself about this mighty force to whom all must humble themselves, to whom the heads of king and beggar bowed alike. The mystery whose depths cannot be plumbed, whose location cannot be discerned. The deep, dark void whose door we enter, never to return. The silent, invisible thing we think is far, yet is near, only separated from us by a small isthmus—a break in the breath, a trembling of the body, a rush that steals away the soul.

What was it that had made Sheikh Munji, so strong and stable, fall like a leaf in the autumn? What was it that had brought my mother's family there in their black clothing? What is this, that brings together near and far, that makes of an enemy a pitying visitor, that transforms us from one state to another, making us bow our heads, grim and silent, leaning on one another, bringing out the best in us to present to our fellow human beings?

I had known it when young. At first, though, I had not been acquainted with it in the form and nature in which other people knew it—I had only known it by the tears my mother shed whenever my father was mentioned in conversation. She would be sitting with her lady friends, and they would start speaking; then I would see a change come over their faces and glimpse their tears and murmurings. Silence and grief would reign, and a different atmosphere that my young mind could not comprehend. Or a neighbor would meet me on the stairs, pat me on the back, and say to whoever was with her, "This is Galal, the son of our neighbor Camellia, who lives on the third floor. Poor boy, he's an orphan."

I'd ask my mother the same question, confused. The question that preoccupied me at the time was, I thought, a simple one. I thought that it was my mother who was stalling and refusing to answer me; refusing to tell me why she alone was with me, and why my father wasn't there. When she lost patience with me, she said, "He's dead, Galal. Dead."

I still didn't understand. Though I was even more confused, it never once occurred to me that this meant he wasn't coming back. Maybe I thought at the time that he was hiding somewhere, or understood her words literally, not metaphorically, when she said, to console me, "He's gone up to where God is, in the sky." I took to looking at the breadth of the sky, saying, "Wherever is he? Which part of the sky is he in, exactly? And how can we go up to him? Or is he the one who'll come back?"

When I started to understand, I would ask myself: Do animals, too, know that they're going to die? The ewe, the pigeon, the female crow, seeing her mate lying unmoving, does she know that he's dead?

And he who dies: does he have a world, too? A body, a family, friends? And this world of his, where is it in this great Creation we inhabit, and does he miss us as we miss him? Does he see us as we see him in dreams? And he who dies in the blink of an eye, no preludes, no fading, in an accident or a sudden coma: does he know that he has died?

I had never met this tyrant face to face, not until I came back from that evening out with Mr. Mustafa Bu Saf. I called on Khadija; she didn't answer. I lifted her to my chest, and she fell from my arms.

She was gone. The body that had been warm a while earlier was gone, the heart where I found my home, the mouth that said, "Wake me, Galal, when you get back."

Chapter 32

Abul Shawareb's face lit up when he saw me coming into our office in Saint-Michel. He leaped up from behind his desk joyfully and took me in his arms, yelling to the employees in a voice that rebounded off the office walls, "Mr. Fouad! Harfoush! You, boy! Madame Renée!" He paused, clarifying, "Madame Renée is new. We hired her when you were on leave." Then he went back to bellowing: "Bu Lehya! Come here, you bald old coward! Where are all of you? Galal is back!"

I had stopped going to the office since Khadija had died. For nearly a month, Abul Shawareb had been calling me on the telephone and urging me to come: the season had arrived, and we had stock we needed to unload. My grandfather, too, was worried at my prolonged absence. It wasn't in my hands, though; I wasn't one of those who could easily cast their troubles aside and regain their zest for life. As soon as something serious happened, I would lock myself in my room, and give my misery free rein, whereupon it would grasp me by the throat as though I were a puppet in its hands. A second self would stand before me, now to ridicule, blame and goad, now to hurt and prick, all the while pulling out of the past a host of torments that I had thought long dead and buried in the flotsam and jetsam of time, regurgitating them one by one, moment by moment, word for word, down to each and every glance and outward sign of feeling. It was like a spool of guilt and misery, unwinding in slow motion.

I would swear that at that moment, I would be overcome with the sensation of being not one person, but two. And one of these, not satisfied with raining down punches upon the other, was determined to draw blood. This was how I was when my mother married her bridegroom out of the blue, and after what had occurred between me and Rachel. Indeed, it was how I was in Egypt, when I was a boy.

Whenever the children said something that hurt me, I would stay in my room for a week, hardly going out or even eating. My mother would be at her wits' end, sitting grim and worried, or coming into my room and sitting by me on my bed. She would think that the Evil Eye had struck me; she would rest my head on her chest, rubbing my back, her forehead rising and falling with her mutterings that seemed like prayers. When she was done, she would smooth my hair, murmuring, "Amen. Amen." After this, she would walk around our apartment with a copper dish filled with incense—a traditional Egyptian defense against the Evil Eye. She would wave it in circles above my head, then under the bed and inside the closets and in my grandfather's room. He'd rush to open a window, and huddle entirely under the quilt—the smell of incense stopped up his nose and made him cough. My mother, ignoring him, concentrated on me and my room, all the while ceaselessly reciting prayers to banish demons and evil spirits, by the power of Moses who parted the Red Sea, and Solomon whom God gave dominion over the spirits and the wind.

My grandmother used to watch her, saying, "The bathroom, too. Go over it several times, and pay special attention to the drains, and the crack under the door."

My grandfather, in hiding under the quilt, would poke his head out a little, appearing unconvinced. "My dear girl, forget this stuff. Go comfort the boy and find out what's wrong with him. It's not the Evil Eye or any such bunk. What stupid thing would anyone want to envy us for? I think, and God only knows, that one of the kids said something to upset him at school."

"I tried and tried, but it's no use," she would retort angrily. "You know how he gets, all blue, and not a word out of him and not eating, either."

After the incense-swinging was through, she would leave my door ajar, comforting me with stories from here, there, and everywhere, careful not to ask me a direct question; she knew that I didn't yield easily, and only ever said, "Nothing, nothing's the matter." The poor woman would come at me this way and that; I was aware of her intentions, though, and all her attempts to draw me out were doomed to failure. For what in heaven's name could I say to her? Was I to say that the schoolboys spoke ill of her reputation? That they stripped her before me every morning?

Not all the boys, of course. It was just that unclean, unscrupulous Saadoun, the son of Uncle Zakareya, the shirtmaker in the building next to ours. He was the only one who plagued me, and spread rumors about me. Was I to tell her that he put it about among the boys that Jewish women had no religion to keep them from promiscuity, and that they were, in the final analysis, whores, every day in the arms of a new lover, and that my mother was such a one, and that my grandfather was a fatheaded dupe without a scrap of manhood in him, who didn't leap to the defense of his womenfolk's honor like any normal redblooded male?

The only time I did let something slip was the incident in which that boy spread a rumor about my Uncle Isaac. He spat on the ground several times and said to a bunch of boys who'd gathered around him in the schoolyard, "You know that kid, Galal?" As they nodded, he went on, "You know his uncle?" Paying no mind to their silence, he continued, "That Jewish guy who blew on out of Egypt and headed straight for Israel."

One of the kids who lived in my street remembered him, and went along. "I know him! I swear I know him! His name is Isaac."

"Yeah! Yeah, you've got it! Well, this Isaac, the minute he landed in Israel, they're all, "Welcome, khabibi—"

The strange word drew the attention of one of the boys. "Do they speak Arabic like we do?"

"Do they! I'll say! They all speak Arabic, but it's all confused and they talk like foreigners speak Arabic over here. So they say 'khabibi,' and 'rabuna' and 'al-nafukh bita' al-ana' and stuff like that."

One of the boys, losing patience, said, "We got it already! Then what?"

"The minute he landed, they asked him, and he said, 'I want to volunteer in your army!' And where did he want to volunteer? In a powerful division, with lots of bombs and machine guns!"

"He said that?" the boy responded. "Oh, that dirty son of a bitch!"

"Not only that. He only volunteered on one condition, that they should give him a huge machine gun! A super-duper gun!"

"And they gave it to him?" asked another boy.

"Sure, they let him have it. Not just one machine gun! Two! With a dozen cartridges into the bargain!"

"What a traitor to the people he broke bread with. And then what?"

"What do you think? The fucker got down to shooting and shooting and killing and slaughtering all the Egyptians in 1967!"

"Oh my God, the bastard!"

I have no idea what his source was for all this classified information, in detail that would baffle an organization more powerful than the FBI!

I didn't know what to do. All I could do was cry and swear up and down to the other boys, "He's lying." I didn't even know at the time where my uncle Isaac was, whether or not he had gone to Israel, and, if he had, whether he had joined the army.

I knew nothing of all this, perhaps because I was so young and these were adult matters that they kept to themselves, and yet I swore and swore that it was all lies! I swore it, without thinking or making sure of the truth of what I said. I swore on instinct— instinctive fear! Instinctive defense! Any old instinct! I was protecting myself. Warding off danger. Defending myself, my own security. Defending Galal, never mind my Uncle Isaac! My body, trembling as I defended myself, cared not a whit for my Uncle Stupid, but for itself, standing before the other boys, and my tongue's only concern as it swore up and down that it was all lies, was to protect me from their force and allow me to live among them in peace!

Hassan, my brother whose mother had nursed me, always stood by me. I shall never forget what he did for me, the day he brought his father's small copy of the Quran to school, and he and I placed it upon our eyes, and took to swearing on it that Saadoun was a liar, by God Almighty, a liar, by this sacred copy of the Holy Quran, a liar, a liar, a liar.

But who could stand in the face of a rumor such as this, sharper than a knife? Was it I, with my motley crew of defenders: just Hassan and another boy or two? My thin body, swimming in a thin linen shirt two sizes too big, short pants, and long socks that dangled down over the tops of my shoes, the broad elastic round their tops drooping.

I asked my mother through my tears, and she burst out, "God will punish him! God will punish him and anyone in the whole world who wants to upset you or hurt you."

My grandfather flushed with rage. He marched straight down to Uncle Zakareya, Torah in hand. He reminded him of every man's duty to his neighbor, and swore before him that my Uncle Isaac was still in Morocco and hadn't yet set foot in Israel. The man set aside his scissors and threw down his measuring tape and stormed out in search of his son Saadoun. He kept kicking him until he admitted to it, and dragged him to us by the ear like a goat, yelling at him, "If it wouldn't have caused a scandal, you son of a bitch, I'd have made the kids follow you through the streets clapping and yelling, 'Liar! Liar!'"

My grandfather, upset, pulled him off Saadoun. "Now then, Usta Zakareya! Lighten up on the boy. He's learned that what he did was wrong, and it doesn't mean anything, it's just kids' idle talk."

"No, indeed, Uncle Zaki, I'm not going along with you. I'm not fudging the issue and saying it's kids' idle talk that doesn't mean anything! What he said is no small matter; it can ruin families. In any case, I owe you satisfaction, and I'll do whatever will give it to you. First thing tomorrow morning, I'll go to the boys' school with you and prove that what he said isn't true."

They went to see the headmaster together; the end result was that the man apologized to me and my grandfather, and clapped for the janitor, al-Boshi, to come, and told him to call the Arabic teacher and the religion teachers to come to his office immediately.

They came: Sheikh Zaki al-Tawil, the kind, decent man, who knew the spirit, not the letter, of religion, and that human beings were judged by their hearts and deeds, not their appearance. The man knew me well. I had long sat before him in the religion class, and he often called upon me to read from the Quran, for my voice was sweet and stirring in those days. He patted my shoulder comfortingly, and the next day he took me out to stand by his side as he lectured the boys at the morning lineup. He started out by speaking of religious tolerance, the faith that was not complete unless one believed in previous prophets: Abraham, Ishmael, Jacob, Isaac, Moses, Jesus, and the rest of the blessed prophets and messengers. He called upon the boys to repeat after him, "Religion remains incomplete unless . . ." saying that a true Muslim was one who believed in every one of God's messengers and prophets, starting with Adam, our father, up to Mohamed son of Abdallah, peace be upon him, and anyone still belonging to a revealed religion or creed other than Islam was one of Ahl al-Kitab, and had rights. He called down curses upon those who spoke ill of others falsely, for tolerant Islam, as revealed to our worthy Prophet, would never condone any deed that caused harm to another human being, be he Muslim or non-Muslim. He paused suddenly, calling in his sonorous voice and pointing with a finger, "You hear me, boy?"

A boy craned his neck forward, pointing a finger at his own chest: *Who, me?* But the sheikh made a gesture of negation. "Not you, not you. The boy on your right, wiping his nose on his shirtsleeve."

There was a ripple and a muttering in the line of boys; the physical education teacher cut it short by making the boy in question take a step forward, accompanied by another boy called al-Latkh who stood at the back of the row, whispering to the boy next to him, thinking no one noticed. I was standing there, under the protection of Sheikh Zaki, following his pointing finger, and staring in awe at his dark-skinned face and white turban and the collar of his caftan, buttoned high around his neck. Before the sheikh finished his lecture, he said, "Even if the uncle of this boy was as you say," and he bent to kiss me in front of all the boys before continuing, "even if the gossip you are bandying about were true—and I have learned that it is not—even if it were, our dear God says, 'No one shall pay for another's sins.' So, my children, cease doing that which displeases God."

And he gave me a little push, saying, "Now run along to class, and if anyone does anything to you, come to me at once—I'm like your father, after all."

Those were the days. The bitter disappeared amid the sweet. Peace be upon you, our sheikh, for I entered the classroom thereafter with my head held high, after the boys' tyranny had brought me low!

Abul Shawareb and I had paused our conversation, becoming engrossed in other things: he in a long telephone conversation, and I in my mind that had wandered far from there, to Saadoun and Sheikh Zaki and my grandfather, who had been worried until I'd come home from school that day, and didn't calm down—indeed, the whole household didn't settle down and get back to normal until I told them, "Thank heavens, it's all fixed, thanks to Sheikh Zaki!"

"And Usta Zakareya too," my grandfather responded, "people here aren't stubborn, they admit it when they've done wrong, and God does dwell inside them."

Abul Shawareb finished his telephone call and moved to sit on the couch opposite me, smiling: "Welcome, man, welcome back." He asked after my affairs and how Sheikh Munji was doing, and after the health of my grandparents. Little by little, his formal greetings trailed off, and he started telling me stories about his life with his wife, Umm Bahlool, and that he had, heaven help him, when he was fast asleep, suddenly felt that he was at his last gasp, his breathing cut off! He opened his eyes to find her kneeling on his chest, shaking him violently and yelling at him, "Get up, you coward! Wake up, you brute!"

Under her arm was the stick she used to discipline the children. Terror-struck, he rose; a word from him and a punch from her and he found out what the matter was. She had heard him talking in his sleep and calling for a woman named Jeannette, opening his arms wide, embracing and kissing the pillow in his arms!

Abul Shawareb was overcome by a fit of coughing. After he was done, he went on, chest heaving as he panted, "What do you imagine I would do with this old woman? I jumped out of bed, running from her. Whenever she took one step forward, I took two steps back, to keep at a healthy distance, and it was such a to-do. And when she made to leap on me and twist my arm, I beat it for the storage room, and grabbed a big stick—thick as a chair leg!"

"Whatever for, Abul Shawareb?"

"What kind of question is that? Self-defense, man! Mashallah, she's as big as a whale, and if she ever caught hold of me, she could break me in two!" With little-boy enthusiasm, he went on, "I feinted, again and again. I came from the right, then the left, until she grew exhausted and left the room."

I asked him who Jeannette was. "Don't you know her?" he groaned. "The Portuguese girl, my boy! Her eyes are divine, her lips are like wine, her laughter is roses and music so fine! Rest in peace, Nizar Qabbani—you alone know of the fire that rages in my heart!"

I felt that Abul Shawareb wanted to amuse me, so I went along. We chatted until the conversation turned to our company. "I'm meeting a client, Faizy Agaweed, at noon, at the Le Fouquet on the Champs-Élysées." I frowned, trying to remember him. Abul

Shawareb caught me thinking. "Faizy Agaweed! Did you forget him? The Turkish businessman who claims to be a descendant of Sultan Abdülmecid, the last of the Ottoman Sultans."

"Yes, yes," I smiled, "I remember him." He suggested we go meet him together.

Faizy Agaweed was sitting on a cane chair, leafing through *Le Figaro*, the poor chair groaning at his slightest movement. On the table before him was an ashtray full of ash and cigarette butts, a half-empty family-size bottle of Birell, and a coffee cup with just a sip left in it. The new thing was the upside-down tarboosh we could see on the chair beside him, containing his spectacle case, a gold keychain, and an ancient ivory-handled fly-whisk.

We had only seen Faizy in hats before, or else bareheaded. When we asked him about this change in fashion, he answered, tapping his fingernail on the tabletop with pleasure, "There's a story in that, a long story! I found this tarboosh and the whisk among the posses-sions of my late great-grandfather, Agaweed Pasha, may he rest in peace. I looked at them this way and that, and took a shine to them. I said to myself, why not let my great-grandfather live on in them, and do as he did?"

He blew his nose violently, with loud explosions, his proboscis and the cotton handkerchief rising and falling in an unfortunate dis-play. He pounded on his chest, taking a deep, whistling inhalation. "The two of you know, of course, that this effendi called Atatürk—"

We interrupted him, reminding him that Kemal Atatürk had been a pasha and not a mere effendi. He knocked on the table angrily, protesting, "I called him an effendi, so an effendi he'll stay." His face was flushed as dark as cumin as he repeated it. "When Faizy Bey says that Kemal Atatürk is an effendi, that's what he is! Understood?"

He would have actually ended the meeting then and there, but we raised our palms in apology, saying placatingly, "All right, all right, we get it. Let him be an effendi."

His anger appeared to have made him forget what he had been talking about, so he asked me. When we reminded him, he started to speak of this Kemal Effendi Atatürk, who had issued a decree forbidding his great-grandfathers to wear the tarboosh, and that this decree was still in force. Suddenly, he slammed the heel of his hand down on the table, knocking over the Birell bottle, and making the ashtray and coffee cup tremble. The smart, respectable people sitting there all stared at us, thinking we were fighting; Abul Shawareb had scooted backward with his chair for fear of being splashed with Birell. Mr. Faizy wasn't even aware of what he'd done! Fingering the upturned tips of his mustache, he went on: "I said, right! Why not take the tarboosh with me and wear it on my travels, which, thank heaven, are many? What do you think of that idea, then?"

We answered in unison, "Gosh, what a brilliant plan! Bravo!"

He took off his spectacles, wiping his fat, flabby eyelids. "That way I kill two birds with one stone: I did what I wanted, and I put one over on the Turkish government at the same time—I'm wearing a tarboosh and they're none the wiser. What do you think, eh?"

We replied with congratulation and praise.

It appeared he was pleased with his accomplishment, playing this trick on the Turkish government; he leaned back and burst into uproarious laughter, laughing on and on, the chair shaking, his eyes sparkling. The café patrons began to stare at us once again, disapproving of the loud noises we made, embarrassing Abul Shawareb and me. His guffaws couldn't possibly have been coming from his throat alone; I could have sworn they were emanating from another place, where some noisy orchestra resided: his belly perhaps, or maybe his small intestine. I met Abul Shawareb's eyes, but we made no comment. We were aware that not only did Faizy Bey laugh at his own jokes and the things that he had said, but that he was also a chatterbox, and we had agreed to give him a half hour to say what he pleased, before putting a stop to his talk and getting down to business. So we let him talk on, of the dam that Turkey was building over the Euphrates, of the Iran–Iraq War, digressing here and there; after his time was up, we forcibly dragged him to where we wanted.

We found out that he wanted to expand his business into Albania, Bulgaria, and Serbia, which he still insisted on regarding as provinces of the Ottoman Empire, and that he was prepared to sign a two-million-franc contract with us for purchase of goods. After we had agreed upon the arrangements, he suddenly began to speak of his grandmother, Zarkash Hanem, who owned two thousand feddans in the Anatolian plains all to herself, and used to grow cucumbers, turnips, and watermelons. Abul Shawareb and I exchanged another glance that said, "Now our deal is closed, why not let this nutcase say what he pleases and let our ears take in his ramblings?"

When I made to go, Abul Shawareb tried to dissuade me, inviting me to lunch. I begged off, saying I was meeting someone at the Deux Magots café in Saint-Germain. I looked long and hard at Faizy Bey Agaweed, strutting out of the café in his double-breasted suit, starched shirt collar, and tarboosh, which he had tilted to the left at a jaunty angle, and the fly whisk, which he was flicking this way and that, to say nothing of the watch chain at his waistcoat pocket. He looked like he'd stepped out of the last century. I wasn't the only one looking at him; everyone in the café looked up to stare after him as he walked out the door, and it's only because there were no horse-drawn carriages in Paris that I didn't call him a chaise to convey him to his destination.

I didn't really have an appointment; I just told Abul Shawareb that I did. At least, it wasn't a regular appointment, I just handed over the reins of my self to my heart, so it took me there. That foolish organ nagged at me, forced me to come to the Deux Magots café, and sat at the table where Khadija and I had sat one day.

It wanted her to feel my heart beating from her place in Heaven: its beat that it had withheld, and she had wished for, in life. It appeared to me that the pain that swept me away and engulfed me was not only the pain of parting; that it was not all of the type that fades with the days, growing distant with the passage of time, but was joined within my heart by another pain, another melancholy. At first I thought it to be blame, reproach, and censure—I had been Khadija's first love, and her last. Her first husband and her last. She had loved me in public and private, with her heart and her body. I, though, had only wanted a peaceful helpmeet, to care for her with the kindness mandated by religion and its strictures, but there was no ruling my heart! When I was accosted by some imagining, I would console myself with the thought, "There's nothing I can do. Perhaps my heart will come to love her in future."

I had never tried to control this heart, not once, nor even reproached it nor thought of some trick to seduce it! I never did. I left it to dream of what it pleased. Khadija motioned to it, held out her palm for it to alight there, but it was obstinate; it turned its head and flew away. When Nadia's visage appeared, even at a distance, it fluttered to her, and bent its wings to her will.

I had put my trust in time. I had said to myself: "Perhaps my heart will forget her. Perhaps Khadija will displace her. Perhaps, with time, anything can happen." It never occurred to me that there might be no time left.

Death took Khadija away, and my pain was twofold: the pain of parting, and the pangs of conscience. And now I asked myself if these were the pangs of conscience alone. Was my choice of this table only motivated by the pangs of conscience? Was my seat upon the same chair, at the same spot where Khadija used to sit, merely the pangs of conscience? When the waiter was taking my order, a moment before, I remembered that she had had coffee and I had had tea, and told him, "A coffee." He'd asked if I wanted it black, or with cream. "With cream," I said, for she had ordered it so. Was this merely the pangs of conscience?

What was this that had taken up residence in my breast? Was it love? Was it yearning? Had my obdurate heart realized its error, and started to pine for her? Only yesterday she had been within its reach, a body of flesh and blood, whispers, a pulse, living veins. This foolish heart, had it only started to long for her now, now that she was become a shadow, a pulse of light?

The previous day, I had heard a knock at the door. My heart leaped as I heard the voice speaking to my grandfather, asking, "Where's Galal? I want to come in and see him."

Yes, my heart leaped. Not just because it was Sheikh Munji, but because it was Khadija's father. I had started to long to see anyone related to her.

We sat together, he and I and my grandfather and my grandmother. "Why have you stopped going to work, my boy?" he asked. "Does your religion allow you to cut yourself off from the world that God created? Does your own faith allow you to refuse to accept what God has written?"

I was unable to make a counter-argument. I did not dare to tell him, "It's not what you think, Sheikh Munji; there was an altercation between me and my heart."

After a silence, he continued, "I spent three days at home, but then I went out into the world, met people, and got back to work. What's in the heart doesn't change; I only ask God to lighten the burden, and give me the patience to endure the pain of parting."

My grandfather was alert, listening. "Tell him, sheikh! Open his eyes. Make him see."

"Galal's a sensible young man, Uncle Zaki. Starting tomorrow, he'll go back to work and come to keep me company at my shop."

It was the first time he had called him "Uncle Zaki," or reached out to take a cup of coffee from my grandmother's hand. I suddenly heard her saying to my grandfather, "We really should try Sheikh Munji's meat. I've quite an urge to try it. What do you say, Abu Isaac?"

My grandfather's face lit up happily. "I'd love that! I'd love it!"

But I was struck with a sudden worry; I looked at the sheikh out of the corner of my eye. I think he understood, because he asked my grandmother to come by and choose whatever cuts of fresh meat she desired; top round if she wanted escalopes, and if she wanted to make a casserole or stew, well, then he had center-cut, or else he could prepare a couple of whole tenderloins especially for her.

It was only then that I thanked God that he had excluded *that* fridge, the one whose contents he set aside for customers who were slow to pay!

Before the sheikh left, my grandmother said to me jokingly, "If you stay at home after this, son, and don't listen to our master the sheikh, tomorrow I'll go there myself, until you come to your senses! I've got a BA and I'm a mean accountant. Don't you think so, Zaki?"

Alarmed, my grandfather said, "Easy, easy! This isn't some thing that a university graduate can do. It's business, buying and selling, import and export—big business. It's not your thing. Besides, you flunked out of college!"

"Quick, my boy," smiled Sheikh Munji, "before your grandmother storms the company and gives the employees and the workers hell, and demolishes what it's taken you years to build!"

"Sheikh Munji!" I laughed.

I was as good as my word to the sheikh; out of my deep affection for him and Khadija, I did as he said. I began to go and meet with Abul Shawareb and Faizy Bey, then my steps would turn to the Deux Magots café. Khadija had brought her father and my grandparents together in friendship, but only now that she was gone. And I, at long last, realized that I loved her, also now that she was gone.

Chapter 33

I was panting, the words coming out of my mouth at intervals. "What happened, Grandfather? When? She was fine this morning when I left . . ."

His face was dark; he caught me as soon as I came closer. "Barely two hours after you went out, she got up to make us a cup of coffee, and there! She hadn't gone two steps before she dropped." His eyes filled. "An aneurysm, they say. We can only hope for the best."

We were on the second floor of the Saint-Louis Hospital, in the critical care unit. The long corridor was painted a light salmon pink. At the end there was a wall clock, saying it was five minutes before noon—and rooms, rooms, rows of rooms facing one another, closed doors with numbers on them and wood-framed signs, some of which said "No Entry."

On the door of the room two steps to our left, a red light the size of a cherry flashed on and off. A tall, thin, sharp-featured nurse came out from behind her station in the center of the passageway and hurried toward us, answering the call. My grandfather nervously guided me forward by the hand, afraid she would rebuke us for being here in this sanctum where no visitors were allowed.

We saw a gurney speeding toward us from the end of the corridor, pushed quickly by two orderlies accompanied by two nurses, one holding an IV affixed to a pole on the gurney, as well as a fat man and a girl in her early twenties, whom I supposed to be the family of the person on the gurney. All were running. The fat man lagged a little behind; the second nurse had gone on ahead and pushed open one of the closed doors, and the gurney charged through it. Then they closed the door, leaving the man and girl behind. They stood there for a moment, serious-faced, staring at the closed door, then turned with a heavy tread and disappeared down the stairs.

"That's how things are done here," my grandfather said. "When a critical case comes in, they snatch them up at the door and rush into the operating theater—or somewhere else, I don't know. Like they're in a race with death." He turned toward one of the rooms, I think the one my grandmother was in. "That's what they did with me. I found them waiting at the door to the emergency room, and they whisked your grandmother out of the ambulance doors and fairly flew off, and it was ages—maybe half an hour—before I heard them calling out on the PA system. I ran to the desk, and they asked for her details. 'Details?' I said. 'Where is she, then?' They said, 'What do you mean, where? The doctors have been working on her for an hour. Where were *you*? Go on, now go on home.' I said, 'Home? What are you talking about, home? I'm not budging from here.' And I called you guys, and here you are."

My gaze gravitated to my grandmother's room.

"What are you looking at? Come on, come on, let's get out of here. You think they'll just let us stand here in the corridor? There's a waiting room on the ground floor for folks like us who just won't leave, and in another two or three hours they'll be closing that down too, and 'everybody out'! It's just that I come upstairs every now and then, and pretend to be lost!"

"So I can't look in on her?"

"Look in on her? Good grief! You want them to call security on us? Come to the waiting room, there's a sensible fellow. The family's there, one and all."

We found them all there; my mother, Aunt Bella, Rachel, and my Uncle Shamoun, accompanied by his wife Sarah. We exchanged somber greetings, unsmiling except for my mother, who managed to turn the corners of her mouth four millimeters upward.

I looked round without meaning to. My mother thought I was wondering where the others had got to, and said, "Uncle Yacoub and Haroun Bey have gone to Egypt." She stretched her arms restlessly. "I don't even remember how long they've been gone. Mom's illness has gotten me all mixed up."

"They went on Sunday afternoon, and today's Thursday," my aunt said helpfully. "So . . . so . . ." She took to counting on her fingers in Hebrew, muttering, "ahat, shnayim, shalosh, arba . . ." before she said, "Today they'll have been gone four days. And Isaac left Israel to meet them there as well." She went on sadly, "He adores his mother. If he knew, he'd cut his visit short and come running."

In spite of the circumstances, I asked, "Egypt?"

"Not exactly Egypt," my mother said. "They've gone to Sinai. They're meeting in Sharm al-Sheikh."

My grandfather was listening, and looked up in irritation. "And just where's Sinai? In the Congo? Or maybe in Brazil? It's in Egypt, isn't it?"

Ignoring him, my mother went on. "They're only going to be gone for a week all told. We thought we shouldn't call them so as not to upset their plans, unless things go downhill, God forbid. The first one we must tell is Isaac."

"With the grace of God, if their affairs go smoothly, they should have finished the preliminary contract on the land in Neama Bay," said my aunt, and she and my mother put their heads together, whispering.

I could hear most of what they said, though. My aunt was claiming that her husband Haroun, might he never prosper, would not let Mr. Yacoub or her brother Isaac come in as partners unless they paid their share at the new price, for land prices there had skyrocketed. He alone, they said, should be manager of all the casinos in the hotel they planned to build there. My mother, meanwhile, was affirming that if that was what he planned, her husband Yacoub would reject the offer, for he had told her before he left that the main casino, or at the very least the secondary one, must be under his management. "But," my aunt answered, "what does Isaac get, then, since each of them's got his eye on something right from the start like that?"

Sarah, my uncle's wife, was sitting nearby, staring at them intently, straining her ears to hear what they were saying, but failing. She dragged her chair a little nearer, till she bumped into the seat my grandfather was sitting on. He gave her a puzzled look, making a gesture of bemusement at her actions. She quite openly craned her neck toward them, but my mother quelled her with a glare, and she returned to her original position. My grandfather, Uncle Shamoun, and Rachel remained silent, unconcerned with what was being said. I, seated right next to my mother, could listen unimpeded; my curiosity was such that I was careful not to say a word, for fear they would interrupt their conversation, depriving me of the opportunity to find out what those people were doing in Sharm al-Sheikh!

Two hours: that was all they gave us. Just as my grandfather said, they turned out the lights in the waiting room and closed the doors. We left in separate groups. My grandfather and I went to a fast-food place, after which we sat at a small café at the junction of Saint-Michel and the rue des Écoles. A glass of juice, a cup of coffee, while my grandfather smoked one cigarette after another until some of his tension drained away and he began to regain control of himself and guide the conversation: he spoke and I listened. He was worried about my grandmother, and what would become of him if she should pass on, and reminisced about old times: the first time he saw her with her mother, Sitt Zuleikha, at a wedding held on the roof of a building in the Megharbeleen District. The host was a Muslim man by the name of Hajj Yaqout, the bride his daughter. My grandfather's family, and other Jewish families, were among the guests. His eyes shone. "The roof was packed, Galal, all mixed, men

259

and women, Muslims and Jews. Hajj Yaqout, God rest his soul, had a silversmith's shop in al-Zawya al-Hamra. Half his master craftsmen were Jewish, and he invited them so they wouldn't feel left out.

"That night, I saw your grandmother for the first time, with her mother. When the dancing started, she danced. With the singing, she sang. When the bridal procession started, she took part in the traditional celebration with the rest of them. I asked and asked, and finally I found out she was the daughter of Usta Sawaris, but that she was flunking out of school; she'd failed her BA exam three times, but 'Wow,' they said, 'she's a brilliant seamstress and great at embroidery!' Tablecloths, scarves, sheet borders, and the like—she had golden hands. She made them at home, and sold them to the stores. 'But careful,' they said, 'she's hardheaded and likes to pick a fight, and once she split a store owner's head open and they were all taken to the police station and there was no end of trouble.' I don't know why I set my cap for her, but I did, and the rest is history."

He tapped out a cigarette from the pack, contemplating it and raising the tip to its nose, inhaling the scent of its dried tobacco, and lit it. "Those were good days, Galal. You couldn't tell a Muslim from a Christian from a Jew. No resentment, no ill will, no judging by My Creed and Your Creed. Every neighborhood stuck together, and God didn't just belong to Cohen or Ali or Nassif; God was for everybody," he said. "I don't know why the world has changed so much, why it's less kind."

By his expression, I could tell he had noticed that I was curious or needed clarification. "I'm talking of what I hear from the people who visit from Egypt these days. They tell me of the troubles in al-Zawya al-Hamra, Ain Shams, and Asyut, and I don't know where else, but our days were good days. We never had anything like that at all."

He coughed suddenly, and looked accusingly at the cigarette. "These French smokes are so full of nicotine and tar, my word—you can't smoke two of them in a row. Anyway—in the old days, we used to attend one another's weddings, and go to each other's funerals.

Why, at the circumcision of your Uncles Isaac and Shamoun," he laughed, "I circumcised them both in one day, you see. That day, the men and women who attended were mostly Muslims! And my word! Our rabbi would send telegrams wishing the important sheikhs a happy Eid al-Fitr, and happy Eid al-Adha, and at the start of Ramadan! And they'd return the favor on Passover and Yom Kippur. Mustafa Nahhas Pasha, God rest his soul, came to visit our synagogues on religious holidays. Many's the time he went, he and the important men of the Wafd party, Serag al-Din, Ibrahim Farag, and Mohamed Salah al-Din." He shook his head, a faraway look in his eyes. "Why, even Muhammed Naguib, when he was president, came to visit our main synagogue! The revolution had just happened. It had just happened, and the world was still good. Those Zionist whippersnappers, with no decency or shame, hadn't yet done their dirty deeds and blown up stuff and ruined everything.* They made our lives a misery, may God bring misery to theirs. Because of them, the Revolution officers hurt the innocent along with the guilty!" He paused. "Say, do you know if Mohamed Naguib's still alive?"

"I don't know, Grandfather."

"You don't know! Right. That's what I get from you, I don't know this and I don't know that!"

There was a long silence. My grandfather lit another cigarette and lapsed into the requisite bout of coughing, but insisted on finishing it. "Where do you think, if God wills that it's your grandmother's time, that should we bury her?"

I gave him a surprised stare, and patted his hand where it lay on the table. "God forbid! Just pray that she recovers."

"God knows how much I want her to get better. But you see, if you'd been there this morning and seen her, you'd forgive me for

---

* The grandfather is referring to a number of terrorist acts committed by Egyptian Jews working with Israeli intelligence. The main post office in Alexandria was blown up, as well as the Egyptian Railway station and the American Cultural Center and what is now the American Library, in addition to a number of movie theaters. This operation was later termed Operation Susannah, or the Lavon Affair.

saying that. Her eyes, so alert, suddenly just *went*. Blank. She was just rambling, saying things from all over the place." In a lower tone, he said, "I don't know how she's going to get through this."

We sat there in somber silence until the waiter came by. I stopped him and asked for a lemonade for me and another for my grandfather. He gestured impatiently, "Forget the juice! I want coffee." After a fresh cigarette, he said, "I'm just asking to find out what you guys did when Khadija passed, God rest her soul."

I wasn't able to give him any useful information there, either; Bu Mikhla', that astute man, had taken care of all the arrangements by himself. I knew that he was like a guild leader for the Tunisians who lived in Barbès; he was the first to arrive when someone died, and the one who presided over the arrangements of preparing the corpse and the burial, the funeral, and going to take out the official forms and death certificates. He also arranged all the weddings and circumcisions, and he was a member of the zakat committee. No occasion, happy or sad, went by without Bu Mikhla''s presence, and he always had a hand in arranging it. All this he did out of the goodness of his heart. I told my grandfather, "Would you like me to ask Sheikh Bu Mikhla'?"

"No, no," he said, "he might think we're in a hurry for it to happen." He passed a hand over his chin. "My boy, as far as I know, the graveyards here aren't anything like the ones in Egypt, one for Muslims and one for Christians and another for Jews. France, my dear fellow, is a secular country, and everyone's mixed all together, alive or dead. I'd never thought of getting a plot ready, nor ever thought that any of us would be buried here." He looked far away. "I thought . . ." And he fell silent.

I recognized the source of his pain, but I had not the strength, at least right then, to open the subject of Egypt, so I took refuge in silence. It was he who finally resumed. "So, you think if I went to the folks at the embassy and petitioned them to have her buried in Egypt, would they say yes? At least she'd be buried next to her mother and father and the rest of her family."

I wanted the conversation to be over. "What do you say to a spin in the car before we go home?" I suggested. "It's three-thirty now, and everyone is still at work."

I believe he understood me, for he said, gathering up his things from the tabletop, "Is that so? All right then, and God will provide when the time comes."

I took him for a drive in the car. We started at the rue Saint-Michel, where we had been, and drove through Emile Zola Street and JFK Street; he gazed at people's faces and the shopwindows with a still, almost sleepy face. When we arrived at the spacious Place Charles de Gaulle, where the Arc de Triomphe stands, with its ancient aspect and sturdy structure, he reclined his chair and leaned back, closing his eyes. I thought he was asleep, so I clicked off the tape recorder, cutting off Abdel Wahab's introduction to Karnak, where he says

A dream appeared before sleepless eyes,
In a passing fancy it approaches, flies;
It fluttered in the silence of the mind,
Connecting the past to the present's hand.

"Why?" he said, eyes still closed. "Why turn it off? Listen to your heart's content, my boy."

So I turned it back on, driving in a circle around the Arc de Triomphe, and another, then another, going slow. The Champs-Élysées beckoned with every circuit, off to the left, wide and mad and treelined, with its old buildings and its cafés with their awnings, and I was overwhelmed with a wave of melancholy—sweet, pleasant melancholy. Abdel Wahab was suffering, saying

When night threw a lifeline to the light
And dewdrops shed their tears on the sand,
Did the dawn hear wailing, I wonder,
Among the melodies of the perfumed palms?

There were so few cars that the square itself appeared wider than before; the only vehicles in it passed practically without a sound or the hooting of a horn. The only disturbance came from a mini school bus; the little boys and girls, on their way home from school, poked their heads out of the windows and yelled at us, while their voices rang out in unison from inside the bus, in what sounded like a song. Even the staid old driver caught the bug, and wouldn't stop honking his horn! A traffic cop stopped him, and motioned to me to stop behind him. He delivered a long rebuke, the man sitting there before him like a statue, nodding every so often, without blinking or saying a word: traffic tickets in this country have no mercy, and the rules of the road hang over everyone's heads like a sword! The children, sensing it, pulled their heads inside and sat quietly. The bus started off again without a scrap of noise; the policeman drew near me, and my heart pounded.

He asked me why I was driving slowly, and asked about the old man by my side: was he really asleep, or unconscious? He reminded me to go at a decent speed like the rest of the traffic, or else! And he raised the book of tickets in his hand threateningly.

My grandfather awoke, wiping away something like drool that had appeared at his mouth while he was sleeping, and asked me, "What does this fellow want?"

"Nothing. He's making sure you're all right."

"Ah. They're like fighting cocks, those! A word from them and they'll have your license, whether you're a duke or a doorman."

Avenue Kléber was closest, so I escaped into it away from the cop, and we drove through the streets until I found myself in Saint-Michel again. My grandfather looked around. "Oh, no! Not again!"

"In fifteen minutes we'll be home."

"Fifteen minutes, half an hour—it's not like we've anything urgent." And he fell asleep again, as I drove through Saint-Michel, cutting across the intersecting rue de Rivoli, followed by Saint-Martin, and thence toward the Pigalle, where the Moulin Rouge stands. A few paces after that, but on the other side, I caught sight of some of our Levantine brethren, standing outside the Rat, their favorite club! I thought of Abul Shawareb, drunk, pounding on a table in that miserable club, wanting to pick a fight with anyone.

My grandfather stretched, opening his eyes for a spell. "Do you think when one dies, God will be good to one, and let one into Paradise?"

I understood how troubled he was, ever since my grandmother had gone into the hospital. "God grant you health and long life," I said, in a bid to cheer him up. "You're a good, kind man, and Heaven was made for people like you."

"You think?" He said it with fear and trepidation, putting out his match and taking the first puff of his twentieth cigarette. "You see, my boy, Paradise is like the stars in the sky. The ones high up in the heavens. Only the blessed can reach them—the ones who let go of everything, who only care about God's favor. Who never do others an injustice, nor harm the weak. Who always offer help and comfort—who never so much as idly twist a tree branch, or shoot a bird out of the sky for sport." And he exhaled heavily. "The prophets, Galal, starting with Adam, and all the way to Mohamed, did their duty, and went away to a benevolent God, and none of us has any excuse. Each one of us is responsible for his own actions."

I rubbed the bridge of my nose and said slyly, "So you do believe, then, that Mohamed is God's prophet?"

"Did I say otherwise? Of course he is! Sometimes you ask the most unnceccessary questions! At my age, with everything I've been through, a few steps till I'm in God's hand, do you think I still care who your prophet is and who mine is? All I care about now is how to please God. And just to set your mind at rest, I'll tell you a simple thing—it's simple, and the simple Egyptian folk said it long ago. When God wills you to go back to Egypt, take a walk through any crowd of people, or at any saint's birthday, and you'll hear them say it: "Moses is a prophet, Jesus is a prophet, Mohamed is a prophet. Let's hear you invoke blessings on all your prophets!"

Chapter 34

Sheikh Munji and his bunch didn't let me down. They all came to visit my grandmother in the hospital, headed up by him, accompanied by Abdalla Mamadou, wearing a tunic the color of eggplant, and followed by M. Raoul, our neighbor from the Barbès apartment house, and Sheikh Bu Mikhla', moving slowly, rosary in hand, an odd perfume emanating from his abaya—a sickening scent that, in Egypt, we used to call "spice-store sweepings." A little while later, Abul Shawareb arrived, accompanied by his wife Umm Bahloul. My grandfather was filled with energy, bursting with happiness, for they had told us in the hospital that some of my grandmother's nerve centers had started to respond, and in a week at most she would be coming out of the coma and back to her old self.

The visitors came to the waiting room, sitting in two rows opposite one another: my grandfather and Uncle Shamoun and three of our Jewish acquaintances, and my mother and aunt and some women facing them. Abul Shawareb had wanted Umm Bahloul to sit with the women as well, and motioned to her to do so, but she paid him no heed and sat among us with her legs crossed at the knee, while Sheikh Munji made a face, wondering at these women who did not obey their husbands, and at Abul Shawareb, this tame ram without horns!

We occupied the lion's share of the seats in the waiting room; only one seat remained empty. Two others were occupied by

Frenchmen, who turned up their noses at the noise we were making and left the room. It appeared that the hospital management was displeased with our number, and our lack of compliance with hospital etiquette, so they sent a security man to tell us politely to gather our things and leave; one or two visitors were enough: the hospital wasn't a café, and the waiting room was for everyone, not reserved for one patient's visitors.

Sheikh Bu Mikhla' took offense. Raising his voice, he said that this was the height of impertinence and disrespect, not to mention ill-breeding, and blatant racism against us on the part of the French.

My grandfather was concerned about the consequences of the sheikh's intervention—particularly after Bu Mikhla' had dared to wave his hand in the security man's face, saying, "What's this, man? Do you take us for just anyone, you and your despicable countrymen? Wake up, wake up! We're people of dignity and will not bear humiliation, and we have teeth that will chew through iron!"

He had the support of Sheikh Munji, who said, "And don't you dare overstep your bounds, young man, with so much as a word. Don't you dare! You are in the presence of two clergymen."

The security guard was baffled, staring at these loud-mouthed sheikhs girding their loins for battle, while my grandfather and Uncle Shamoun slowly died of embarrassment. They had words, and finally M. Raoul left so as to mitigate the problem, followed by the Jewish ladies, led by an old hag with a face, God help us, like that of an ogress. I asked my Uncle Shamoun as I watched her leave, "Who is she?"

"Hush!" he said, leaning over and whispering in my ear. "Shut your mouth and don't look at her like that. She's your grandmother's closest friend. That's Madame Samaka, and if she notices you looking at her like that she'll have you for breakfast—she's even worse than your grandmother! She has a tongue three feet long."

I discovered that it was not only I who was staring at her, but everyone there—even the security man, who had left us after my grandfather had told him quietly that we'd behave!

The conversation started up again, quietly and in decently low tones; but the yelling and gesticulating soon resumed. We spoke of practically everything: the war currently raging between Iraq and Iran; Ronald Reagan, the new American president; and some of the Gulf countries that assisted Saddam in public and Khomeini in private; and the incendiary statements issued by Georges Marchais, the leader of the Communist Party, at Charles de Gaulle Airport, upon his return from the inauguration ceremony of Konstantin Chernenko in Moscow.

Abdallah Mamadou was just about to speak ill of the Jews, but Sheikh Munji's elbow silenced him; he still offended the company, though, by blowing his nose loudly, and speaking of things that he knew nothing about, and that were none of his business. When he took to belching loudly, Bu Mikhla' leaned over to Sheikh Munji. "Who is this creature you've brought along? What on earth has this buffalo eaten today? Accursed man, he has no manners or decency whatsoever!"

"This, brother Mikhla', is one of the crosses that one must bear. If prayers for harm were answered, I would have prayed to God for a bolt from the blue to descend upon him immediately and relieve us of his presence."

After a while, Bu Mikhla' rose and left the room, crooking a finger at me to indicate that I should follow him. Taking me by the hand and guiding me to a place some distance away, he said, "Have you spoken to your grandfather, my boy, about embracing Islam?"

"Heaven spare us!" I said. "Don't you see what's going on, sheikh?"

"Hurry it up, my boy," he said, "or would you prefer me to do the job?"

"No, no, Uncle Bu Mikhla'," I said, "leave the matter to me, please."

We returned, and the session lasted for more than two hours, with talking and loud laughter, the hospital not knowing what to do with us, the security man poking his head into the waiting room from time to time. Finally, they left, Sheikh Munji embracing my grandfather warmly. They kissed on both cheeks.

"What a world this is," my grandfather said afterward, addressing Uncle Shamoun. "Sheikh Munji turned out to be a decent sort. If we'd become friends long ago, we'd have avoided so much heartache and fighting and ill will."

"You're just naïve," my mother said. "He's a meddling home-wrecker."

"Why don't you do us all a favor and shut up? Mind your own business, you and your Yacoub, and that lousy Haroun, and the gambling and all the hanky-panky you plan to get up to."

"What are you saying, Dad?" she protested. "It's business and trade and investments."

"Business? Oh, really! Why didn't you build a factory there? Sugar, cement, textiles, or something, or reclaim land, my fine folk, like our great-grandparents, who built wherever they settled? That's what I call business, my fine lady—not throwing dice and con tricks and razzle-dazzle and smoke-and-mirrors."

He and I left. "What do you say to a spin like yesterday?" I told him as we got into the car.

"No, no, bless you. Straight home. I'm tingling all over, and I'm exhausted."

He didn't even have dinner. We went into our respective rooms; he went to bed, and I performed my ablutions and prayers, then sat in front of the TV until nearly midnight.

Once in bed, I lay down and leafed through *Le Monde*. I had the urge to go to the bathroom before bed; when I did, I noticed his door ajar, unusually for him, and the light on.

He was panting, lying on his back in bed, eyes staring vacantly, with no strength to move a muscle. He didn't even notice that I had come in. I screamed his name, and rushed to the box where his pills were—he would take one under his tongue. Then I moved to unfasten the top button of his pajamas, which were choking him. I bent over the buttonhole, my fingers fumbling and failing time after time, until the button came off in my hand. His collar-bones stood out, and the entire area between them, the length of his neck, vibrated with his bursts of gasping. I found myself pulling the socks off his feet, and rushing to fling the window wide. I rushed to the refrigerator for a glass of water. I was moving entirely on instinct, without thinking what I was going to do next or even any awareness of what I was doing. He remained as he was, neither awake nor fully conscious. After a moment, he closed his eyes: I held him to my chest and called to him in terror, but he didn't respond.

He drifted away. First he started to call for people as though they were in the room with us; they could see each other in a field beyond that of vision. I felt it, not through any clear words, but by his gestures and mutterings, now quieting, now heightening, as though he was being approached by shadows that answered his call, and he responded in turn and did as they did. They were closer to him than I was. He wasn't aware of my presence, but of theirs; they were almost touching, but something stood between them and still separated them. It was a light thing, a transparent thing, an isthmus like a wisp of smoke perhaps, or a billow of fog. Their hands reached into him. You would think they could go straight through, but they could only try.

He was in a strange state. My eyes were misty; I could not tell whether my grandfather was alive and speaking to the dead, or dying while they appeared alive. The state did not last long.

I didn't want to cover his face as people do in these situations. I left his face uncovered, after closing his eyes. I don't know why my eyes moved to the Jovial watch on his wrist: it read 2:10 a.m., the big hand over the little hand, almost obscuring it. The face of the watch was devoid of movement, filled with meaningless numbers that indicated nothing. My grandfather was still, his arms resting on his chest, no trace of death on his face. I imagined for a moment that he had exhaled, that his eyelids were moving. I went back to staring at him, then called on God for protection, and rose to retrieve my copy of the Holy Quran that I always kept under my pillow. I brought it and sat at my grandfather's head reading it. I started at the beginning. I read the Fatiha over him seven times, and the Sura of the Cow, then al-Omran, until I arrived at the holy verse, "He selecteth for His mercy whom He will. Allah is of Infinite Bounty." I repeated it dozens of times. Then I went to the telephone, to tell my mother and Uncle Shamoun.

Chapter 35

No one stood by me as Sheikhs Munji and Bu Mikhla' did. They were with me every step of the way: when we put my grandfather in the ground, and the night of the funeral. Bu Mikhla', especially, did a wonderful job; I shall never forget what he did for us; how he saved us from a tricky situation and, within a few hours, found a graveyard where we could bury my grandfather. He did practically everything for us, from A to Z.

It was an unusual sight to see his stocky body in his abaya, the scarf of his turban wrapped around his short Moroccan tarboosh, as he muttered prayers a few steps away from a Jewish rabbi in a black suit, yarmulke on his head, both nodding their heads as they recited their respective prayers for my grandfather. Abul Shawareb slipped in among the Jews, as did Abdalla Mamadou, and Mr. Fouad. Umm Bahloul and Sitt Zahira Bu Saf stood by my mother's side, draped in black.

Sheikh Munji stood a small distance away, leaning on his stick, his eyes roving the gravestones before him, a great sorrow in his eyes. Khadija must have been on his mind. The poor thing was lying alone with no one to keep her company. She was the first of the Munji family to be visited by the Angel of Death. We had laid her in a plot that, as luck would have it, was not far from my grandfather's; perhaps her stricken father, from where he stood, could see her gravestone. Perhaps his nose could smell mother's milk on her lips as she reached up with her little hand to play with the edges of his beard and coo at him. Perhaps he remembered the days when she used to press her finger down on the doorbell and never leave off until they opened the door, barging inside in her school uniform, running here and there, her black hair pulled back in something like a ponytail, and when she used to . . . so many things! He had a far-off look in his eyes, his strength useless; his soul, too, was defeated, leaning, like his body, on a staff.

I approached him, patting him on the shoulder. "I'm all right, my boy, thanks be to the Lord. Go to the rest of your mourners—I'm family, you don't have to pay special attention to me."

It was a sad sight that day, the women with no makeup or finery, weeping or hiding their faces behind sunglasses, looking like a flock of ravens in their black clothing. The men had their hands folded over their chests, or else looked down somberly, avoiding meeting each other's eyes on the pretense of being busy. As soon as the rabbi left, the hats went back on, and everyone turned and left more quickly than they had come.

My grandmother knew nothing. She remained lost in her coma, until she died a few days after my grandfather. Mr. Yacoub indicated that we needed to call Bu Mikhla'; he came, accompanied by Sheikh Munji, and they did what they had done at my grandfather's death. With their charity and chivalry, they earned the admiration of my grandmother's Jewish relatives; even Elephant-Trunk, the low-down Zionist, bid them a friendly goodbye and shook their hands warmly when it came time for them to leave.

Mr. Yacoub took Bu Mikhla' aside, offering him a sum of money for his services; he took offense and pushed it away. "What is this, sir? Do you take me for an undertaker? I only do this to please the Lord and be closer to Him."

Sheikh Munji, who had been following the conversation, stepped in, saying angrily to Mr. Yacoub, "Do you think my brother

Bu Mikhla' is doing this for money? God forbid! We are doing what religion tells us to, which is to assist the destitute."

"Destitute?" wondered Mr. Yacoub.

"Yes," he said, "for the destitute are not only those in want of money, but every person who needs to accomplish something but lacks the experience and know-how to do what is necessary. Bu Mikhla' does not want a reward for what he does, or even your thanks, for his recompense and the reward he earns will be from God our Lord."

Yacoub and Elephant-Trunk didn't get it.

I remained alone in the apartment, contemplating my grandfather's things. His spectacles, his old newspapers, the Jovial watch he had brought from Egypt, which had remained on his wrist until he died, and my grandmother's gallabiya, thrown over a chair by the bed. I shook it out a couple of times to get the dust out, then folded it up.

This time, I didn't lock myself in my room as I had when disaster struck, or when I felt some inner pain—for if I did, who would come to see how I was? I used to wait for my grandfather to open my door and comfort me, indeed drag me to the dining table by main force; if I remained stubborn, he would bring in a tray of some dish I liked and stay with me for hours, until I grew ashamed and came out of this state.

I met my Uncle Isaac for the first time.

He was short and fat, just as I had imagined him; his face, though, was noticeably puffy, so much so that I thought he must be taking cortisone treatments. I was repulsed and intrigued by him at the same time. I shook his hand reservedly, but he embraced me, so I gave in and kissed him back. Gradually, the curiosity grew, the revulsion dwindling. However, I grew cautious of him as soon as he began to pay special attention to me; for some reason, I remained alert and careful about what I said with him. When he was distracted, I would look at him: his gestures; his measured, calculated smiles; his cigar, his diamond-encrusted Piaget watch, and the silver chain with the Star of David around his neck. He looked rich to me, compared to my Uncle Shamoun, but they occupied vastly different places in my heart!

He asked me if Cinema Misr in al-Geish Street was still standing, and asked after Hussein Sidki, the old-time movie star. He said that he remembered him, with his fellow actors Ali al-Kassar, Nagib al-Rihani, and Bishara Wakim. His eyes roved the room, then he said he had seen a Hussein Sidki movie called *Determination* a few days before he left Egypt, starring Sidki and the Jewish actress Negma Ibrahim.

I had seen that movie many times, so I corrected him, "You mean Fatma Rushdi, not Negma Ibrahim."

He wasn't aware that the Egyptian Gulf Street, near our house in Daher, had been renamed Port Said Street. He asked about Groppi's Café downtown, on the corner of Antikhana Street; puzzled for a moment, I asked, "What street? Antikhana Street?"

"Yes, Antikhana Street. Groppi's, opposite the statue of the Frenchman, Suleiman Pasha."

"Ah!" I said. "You mean Talaat Harb Square? Yes, that café is still there."

"Did they replace the statue?" he asked, astonished.

"Replace it? I'll say! Talaat Harb is a great man; he liberated our economy from foreign powers."

He grimaced.

Before the mourners had left, Mr. Saul Aslan, the manager of the Hôtel de l'Arcade, took me aside quietly and said, "I shall await your presence tomorrow for an important matter."

Mr. Saul gave me a warm welcome. As soon as I sat before him, he said, "Your grandfather always spoke very highly of you." He gazed at me for a minute, then said, "I've never seen a grandfather like yours, loving a grandson and privileging him over his children, even though . . ." He fell silent.

"Even though I'm a Muslim."

"No, no, no, I don't mean that precisely. I mean, even though you are not of the same religion." He scratched below his earlobe, still gazing at me. "Indeed, God knows, religion is one thing, and the heart is another. These hearts of ours, my boy, are one of God's secrets. And those not united in creed can be united in having a pure heart, connected to God. All of us, starting from Adam to the smallest newborn, have something of the spirit of God breathed into us, whether we're Muslim, Christian, Jewish, or even other religions, as long as we're God's creatures."

I leaned forward, eager for more. He seemed to enjoy my rapt attention, for he came out from behind his desk and sat before me. "Yes. A breath of God's spirit that He placed in us, growing day by day from when we float in the womb. Without it, the world would have fallen to ruin, and we would be at each other's throats, like beasts. Whatever the religion, my boy, we are all God's servants; whatever the book, we are all siblings, sons and daughters of Adam and Eve." He took to telling me the anecdotes and stories that the Jews used to tell about my grandfather when they sat together, so fond of him they were. He told me that someone had said to him jokingly, "Why not become a Muslim? We'll be rid of you, and you can relax and continue loving Galal."

Saul rose, going to a metal safe embedded in the wall; he withdrew an envelope and handed it to me. Inside it was a letter from my grandfather.

My son, Galal,

Life and death are in the hands of God. Who knows how much time I have left in this world—a minute, a year, or part of a day? I believe that God has written that my death shall be here, in this strange land. My boy, I beg of you, for God's sake don't leave me here all alone. Bring my body back to Egypt; we have a plot in Basateen. Ask where it is: it's in the name of my father, Isaac al-Azra'. The key is enclosed. Do what you can. Go to the embassy. Send a telegram to the minister. To the president. To any human being. Tell them that Zaki al-Azra', the stranger in death, wishes to return. If you can't manage it, visit me once a month. If you do go back to Egypt for good, come to me, even if you have to come especially from there. This is my first plea.

My second plea is this: Withdraw everything from my bank account at the Société Générale. I have about 300,000 francs in there. I had thought of giving you a third of that sum, and that's written down in an earlier will, as you know. But your financial situation is reassuring; all you need is something to remember me by, not money. So, withdraw this money and give half of it to your grandmother, and half to your Uncle Shamoun; they're the ones who need it most. Enclosed also is the bank card and the code number.

As for you, keep my gold ring and the Jovial watch, and give my spectacles to your Uncle Isaac.

Until we meet again, my boy, in a kinder world than the one we lived in.

Your grandfather, Zaki

January 7, 1985

I wiped away a tear that clung to my lashes, and said to Mr. Saul, "What shall I do with my grandmother's half?"

He thought for a moment, then said, "Give it to your Uncle Shamoun as well."

I didn't spare any effort to fulfill my grandfather's wish. I paid several visits to the embassy, and sent a packet of telegrams; no one seemed to notice, or if they did, they certainly didn't acknowledge it.

When my Uncle Isaac learned of what I was doing, he called me up. He asked me to drop everything and come immediately to my Aunt Bella's apartment. I tried to beg off or even defer the summons, but he spoke so nicely that I dropped what I was doing and went there, to find the whole family waiting for me. Elephant-Trunk, Uncle Isaac, Uncle Shamoun, Aunt Bella, and Rachel. With them sat an effeminate boy with his hair in a braid and an earring with a blue bead in his left ear. They told me his name was Simon, a Moroccan Jew: Rachel's fiancé.

A one-armed man came into the room. He was unusually short, practically a dwarf. He must have been in the bathroom when I arrived. As I shook his wet hand, they said his name was Chaim, the son of their Aunt Dalal, currently living in Lyons. Uncle Shamoun told him I was Camellia's son. He didn't hear him; Uncle Shamoun repeated it twice but the man still didn't hear him, staring at me and at him. Finally, Shamoun bent close to his ear and bellowed, "He's Camellia's son. Camellia, Camellia!" He turned to us, saying, "Well, this is a nice start to the day! My throat's sore already! What ears!" and he took hold of the man's ear again, bellowing once more, "Camellia's son! Camellia! CAMELLIA!" until the man got it and smiled at me. Then he shook my hand again and sat silently on a low chair they had brought especially for him so that his legs would reach the floor.

It didn't occur to me that it was a trap, a court convened to judge me; the charge being that I wanted to transfer my grandfather's body from here to the family plot in Basateen. The talk started out pleasantly enough, veiled in politeness and courtesy; it was on the tip of my tongue to say to them, "My countrymen in Egypt are dragging their feet in this matter, and I doubt that they will let it happen," thus ending all this talk and discussion. However, I stubbornly refused, and gave them to understand that I would do whatever I had to in order to fulfill my grandfather's wishes. They all bristled, turning against me. My uncle Isaac actually said to me, "Stay away from our father. His affairs are none of your business."

"They're a thousand times my business," I said, "and I have a will in his handwriting as well."

"This paper you have doesn't mean a thing to us. Who's to say it wasn't fabricated to trick you?"

"Ask Mr. Saul," I said.

"He doesn't mean a thing to us, either."

My Uncle Isaac took long drags on his cigar. He blew the smoke in my face. "The long and short of it is, we're planning to move your grandfather's body to Israel, so please stay out of our way."

"Israel?" I said. "I swear, if that's true, I will fight you every step of the way. Israel? My grandfather refused to visit it in life. Will you take him there against his will now that he's dead?"

He waved me off. "What are you saying? Israel, in the final analysis, is our country, the Promised Land."

"I do not get you people!" I cried. "Promised Land or no Promised Land, it means nothing to me! What I do know is that that will happen over my dead body!"

The argument escalated almost into a fight; they all stood against me, even the one-armed deaf man who was his cousin jumped up from his seat and tried to physically assault me, while I wondered how this pygmy had understood our conversation, given that he was deaf. Elephant-Trunk raised his left eyebrow and said to me, "If your mother Camellia wasn't dear to us, we'd have killed you." I was on the verge of coming to blows with him.

The only one who stood by me was my Uncle Shamoun. He took my arm and led me outside, and we walked downstairs together, cursing the lot of them.

I feared, though, that they would do it. I went to Mr. Saul, who flew into a rage and said, "What a bunch of hooligans! I'm on your side, and I'm prepared to bear witness that your grandfather entrusted me with that letter!"

Taking Bu Mikhla' with me, I started to go around to the government offices in Paris. They reassured us, "It's not that simple. There has to be a registered will, or an agreement from all the children. Plus, who is to bear the expenses of the transfer of the body? And before all this, the Israeli Embassy has to grant approval."

I thought of this issue day and night; my heart gave me to feel that it was like killing my grandfather, and that I was defending him. I took Bu Mikhla' with me again, and we hired a lawyer.

The lawyer who took our case was a lighthearted Frenchman. "Is this a fifth war between you and your kissing cousins?" he asked with a laugh. "In any case, I shall start a file as soon as I get a written complaint from Monsieur Galal. I won't take any action now, though; I'll wait until the French Foreign Ministry issues a decree, and then contest it."

We agreed.

It was a struggle between me and them, or so I thought; I imagined that they, too, were rushing about, from their embassy to the French Foreign Ministry, or any other official body with the power to issue a decision, to expedite the process of moving my grandfather's body. Seeking to glean news, I went to see my Uncle Shamoun; I also wanted to urge him not to sign anything.

"You actually went around to all those offices?" he said with a laugh. "You really are gullible! You don't think that old cabbage-faced Isaac would actually spend a single franc on something like that, or that he even cares? He was just hazing you, silly!"

"Hazing?"

"Yes, hazing. To draw you out, and make you give up on getting him buried in Egypt, in return for him giving up what you thought was his plan to have him buried in Israel. Only there was nothing to give up, because he wasn't going to do anything in the first place. That's what I learned later, from your Aunt Bella."

"What an old devil!"

"You said it! You, man, are still new to the game."

Since all my efforts with the Egyptian Embassy had failed, and to stop the bloodshed with this accursed uncle, I had to be content with doing what I could, namely, to visit my grandfather's grave.

I used to go to see him and my grandmother after prayers on the first Friday of every month. The Muslims were the majority on that day, and the place was full of them. Some were new to Paris, and came with small baskets of dried foodstuffs, imagining that they would meet the little boys who hang around gravesites waiting for such things; finding no one, they would carry them back, or give them to their children, of whom the full complement accompanied them, in their best clothes, as though they were going on a trip or as if it were a holiday. Naturally, no flower or bloom was safe from these; they ran to them and picked and tore them off, and the gravekeepers were out of breath chasing them hither and thither, hardly able to wait until we left and they could close the doors.

I came bearing three roses; I would bend and place two by the marble headstones of my grandfather and my grandmother. The third was for Khadija. Once, I met my Uncle Shamoun there. "It's Friday, not Saturday, Abu Saul!"

"I'm on a shift system," he said, "and sometimes I get Thursday and Friday off, not Saturday and Sunday." When he was done with his parayers for his mother and father, he asked me out of politeness, "Have you been to Khadija's grave yet?"

"No, not yet."

"I'll come with you."

Her grave was close by; from it, I could see my grandparents' graves. We stayed a while; I recited what verses of the Quran I knew by heart, and he closed his eyes and nodded, reading prayers for her soul from a small holy book in his hand.

Chapter 36

My mother had been away in Argentina with her husband Yacoub, visiting his son who lived there. Her return completed the circle of my displeasure.

The doorbell rang in quick nervous bursts; I opened it to find her standing there frowning. He was next to her, smiling, in a straw hat and a loud yellow shirt with a parrot on the front. She asked me eagerly, while still at the door, about the letter my grandfather had left.

"Yes, of course," I said. "Just come in first."

I went to my room to get the letter; I could hear her speaking, upset with me and my actions, saying that I was either a fool, or masquerading as one! With repressed anger, she was saying that she had wasted her life on me, raised and suffered and put up with everything, and what did she get in the end, Yacoub? An ungrateful son who wasted his mother's birthright, not even consulting her before doing what he did. He was trying to quiet her: "Hush, Coucou, hush, now's not the time."

I hung back to hear more, not sure what she was referring to. Was she angry, like my Uncle Isaac, at my attempt to move my grandfather's body? Or was this because of the money I had delivered to my Uncle Shamoun, which my Aunt Bella had hinted at when I was at her house? It seemed, though, that she was uneasy at my long absence, for her loud voice came to me: "Where are the papers, son?"

I gave her the letter. She read it aloud, muttering reproach between the lines for my grandfather's deeds. Then she addressed herself to Mr. Yacoub: "Father, rest his soul, is so contrary. He doesn't want to stay here with us—he didn't even have any sympathy for anyone but Shamoun!"

He dropped his eyes. "May he rest in peace. He was a kind, trusting soul, and naïve. He didn't mention me once! And shouldn't he have addressed the letter to Isaac, the eldest son, and if he wanted something done, told him to do it?"

I choked down what had been said. She pulled out a cigarette and lit it. "Fine. It's Shamoun's to do with what he pleases, may God give him joy of it. But what about my mother's share, that was in the letter?"

"That went to Uncle Shamoun too."

Her face flushed. "Your uncle who? You gave him all the money?"

"Exactly."

"The three hundred thousand?"

"Three hundred and ten, as it turned out, and he's had it since then."

"Ah, you stupid idiot! You just did that of your own accord, without consulting anyone or asking anyone?"

My blood boiled, but I controlled myself and said to her quietly, in clear, measured tones, "Yes, that's what happened. I did that of my own accord. I never consulted or asked anyone."

Mr. Yacoub intervened, pouring oil on the troubled waters. "Don't be upset at what your mother says, Galal. I wish my own mother was still alive and shouting and insulting me, yes, and hitting me as well. I would take it all with pleasure." He patted my mother's hand. "And you, Coucou, what's come over you? What is this, asking about money? You don't need money, do you? Praise be to God, we're blessed, and we have plenty."

She answered in indignation, "Yacoub, this boy has no gratitude. No sticking up for his mother, no 'This is my mother's money, this belongs to my mother.' Instead, His Excellency goes and gives everything to Shamoun! And Shamoun is henpecked—it's his wife Sarah who's going to grab it all for herself! I deserve it more than that scarecrow, who'll blow it all on herself!"

I made no comment, but she started up again in the same vein, blaming, rebuking, and reminding me of all she had done for me. I remained silent, my fingers reaching for Mr. Yacoub's lighter, lying before us on the table, turning it over and over, idly lighting it. I leaned back and crossed my legs, overcome by a strange pleasure, tickling my heart and comforting me. It was a dark enjoyment indeed, a joyless enjoyment at my mother's expense, but it was still pleasure, and it increased the more she waxed indignant against me. Part of me enjoyed it, and the part that didn't went by the board. It was an unpleasant enjoyment, God protect us from such; it was the pleasure of one who avenges himself, who gets his own back, who does something that has to be done. Then what? It brings him no joy, and he may disapprove of it, but the fact remains that he is more at peace when it is done.

She was my mother, but my heart rejected her. She had insulted my father. She had insulted him in my presence, and in the presence of this gentleman who was sitting between us, this aged feline before whom she bared her body every night. She had forgotten my father, forgotten me, washed her hands of the world we used to live in, but she had allowed her tongue to insult what must never be insulted.

I could have explained to her that I had tried to get Grandfather's body moved to comply with his long-desired wish, but even this was of no concern to her; here, Basateen, Haifa, or Tel Aviv, it made no difference to her. What mattered was money, money! Even with regard to this money with which she was obsessed, I could have explained to her that my grandfather had written this will when my grandmother was in full health, and that she had died without knowing anything about it. The money was my grandfather's, and it had gone, in the end, to the person he felt needed it the most. I don't know what your religious law says, Madame

Coucou. All I know is, my grandfather left something to be done after his death, and entrusted it to me, as though he were alive—and that I asked the advice of your relative, the wise, prudent Mr. Saul, who advised me to do as I did.

I could have said to her, as well, that this creature she had married had towering piles of cash, hoards of gold, whereas my Uncle Shamoun was a poor unfortunate who had no fixed salary and worked day to day. I could have told her many other true things, or even falsehoods, to extinguish her desire for this money; or I could have risen and kissed her head as we do in Egypt to apologize, and kissed her hand, and thus ended it all and cut out her resentment at the root. But I didn't. I could have; I almost did. But something inside me took hold of me and stopped me from doing it.

The session only cooled down after a long time. A long, uncomfortable period passed without speech, each of us stealing glances at the other when the other wasn't looking, or doing trivial things like tying a shoelace, scratching an itch, or sipping at a glass of water.

We finally resumed our conversation, but talked of other things, uttering commonplaces that people might say to one another chatting at a café, or meeting by chance in the street. She gathered up her cigarette case, her glasses, and her keychain and asked me, as though to clear her conscience, how my business was doing, and the company, and how Abul Shawareb was treating me. "Fine," I answered, "everything's fine."

She suggested, as her parting advice, that I move out of this place and find an apartment more suited to my status, and all I said was, "Fine, fine." She then went on to say that I should gather up "all this garbage"—my grandfather's bedroom set, the dining table, the broken chairs and kitchen utensils—and sell it to the doorman or even take it to the flea market and sell it there.

"I wouldn't sell these things for all the money in the world," I said. "They were my grandfather's." Unable to hold my tongue any longer, I said, "Anything else, Madame Coucou?"

285

The words came out unconsciously. I said them without meaning to, and instantly regretted it. I had betrayed myself with my words; not my whole self, just the angry part of it, while the other part, the part attached to my mother, wasn't strong enough to keep it trapped inside my mouth and banish it back to my depths.

Her face darkened. Mr. Yacoub coughed delicately, then placed his cigar in his mouth, bringing his lighter up to it. His eyes weren't on what he was doing, and the lighter went out. He lit it several times in succession, staring at my mother, then at me, expecting a fight to break out. Nothing happened, though, and the smoke finally came out of his mouth, disgusting and harmful.

She stared straight ahead. It wasn't a vacant stare. It wasn't a far-off look at all, but the kind of stare that follows a striking realization, like a snap of the fingers followed by a silence in which one's eyes light up as if to say, "Why on earth didn't I think of that?" Then she leaped to her feet, followed by Mr. Yacoub; I thought this was a prelude to storming out, and readied myself to catch her arm and kiss her hand, or even her foot. But it didn't happen that way. It was as though she hadn't even heard the "Madame Coucou" crack, or had heard it and didn't care. The line that had had this effect was "Anything else?" It reminded her of the thing she had forgotten, and drove her running into my grandmother's room, fumbling in the shelves of her wardrobe. She returned, bearing her jewelry box, her eyes shining with joy, while Mr. Yacoub trailed after her.

It wasn't a box as such; it would be a shame to call it that. It was a treasure chest, not unlike Ali Baba's, overflowing with jewelry of every form and color: earrings, rings, bracelets, and anklets that must have been part of the original trousseau prepared by her father Sawaris. There was light gold and dark gold, pieces with stones and without. I was stunned; I had never seen these things, in all these years. I had seen scattered pieces, now on her wrist, now at her throat, or sometimes hanging from her ears. Where had she been hiding all this? My grandmother never showed it to anyone; she had been hiding it for a rainy day. The poor woman never knew that the rainy day was to be her daughter Coucou, who'd lived with her day in and day out!

Mr. Yacoub put out his cigarette. She closed the box, then pushed it a few inches to the side until it lay before him, and said to him, "Keep an eye on it. I'll just be in the bathroom a minute, and we'll go right away."

She disappeared behind the closed door. He and I sat there, neither of us saying a word to the other, until we heard the creak of the bathroom door as she came out. He rose, bearing the box and saying, "All done, Coucou? Right, let's go, then."

And he headed for the apartment door.

"Where are you going with that?" I asked.

No one answered.

"I know I've no right to it and it's not even any of my business, but my Uncle Shamoun's share . . ."

My mother took hold of the door and it swung shut behind them.

Chapter 37

Months passed after my grandfather's death; the world had lost its brightness in my eyes.

There was no beauty or life left in the world. The streets weren't the same, Abul Shawareb wasn't the same, even Sheikh Munji wasn't the same, and the house was desolate and depressing. My grandfather's seat was empty, his bed was empty, and my heart was empty too.

If only I had just been lonely, if that had been all! Loneliness, if it be merely loneliness, is bearable; but I was overcome with desolation, destroyed with grief. It truly destroyed me; I nursed at its teat against my will, slowly, with a bitterness that cut off any hope for the world, and any trust in its nature. Many was the time that my eyes opened to face a new day, while my heart remained disbelieving—surely it was a nightmare, surely my grandfather was still in his room, and would come in and speak to me, and I to him! Then I would close my eyes as my heart ached, bereft.

My grandfather had not been just a grandfather; he had been more than that, much more. Despite his weakness and powerlessness, and his age—he had been nearly ninety—he had been my world, my family, security, aid, and comfort. He had been the one good thing in my life, and I don't think he had left a void in any of his children's lives the way he left a hole in mine, and none of them was struck to the heart as I was. He left me lost in a gaping void that was hateful and certainly painful.

A light went out in me after his death; I closed in on myself, forgetting that there was such a thing in the world as laughter. Who did I have, now that he was gone? My mother? She used to be; her name was still written in the box reserved for that name on my birth certificate. Or Rachel, who now flaunted her Beatle fiancé in my face? And my Uncle Isaac was fragile, a man of glass; I was not of his world, nor he of mine. As for Mr. Yacoub, he definitely did not enter into the equation. Gradually, they drifted away from me; I forgot to ask after them in time.

Ramadan came, then the Eid al-Fitr, then the Eid al-Adha, but nobody asked me where I was. And their feast days came, holiday after holiday, and I didn't even dial their number. We became like strangers. My motivation to ask after them cooled after my grandfather's death; they were the same. I was oversensitive about calling my mother, in particular. "She'll call today," I would say, and wait; "Tomorrow," I'd say, and wait; "The day after tomorrow," I'd say, and wait, and all the while the wall between us grew higher.

One world was gone, and here I was, on the threshold of a new world.

I had been in a world whose center was my grandfather: I saw him every morning as I went out, he used to call me a couple of times when I was at the office, and we would be together when I returned, eating and chatting and laughing and going out, and I might even tease him once or twice. We sympathized with each other, and gave each other comfort. We were never grandfather and grandson, but part and whole. He saw in me a part of him, and I saw in him all that I had. The part melted into the whole, and the whole enfolded the part. Even my grandmother's annoyances I had grown used to; if a day should go by in which she forgot her querulous nature, I would provoke her until she remembered it.

And here I was, before another world. A world I didn't want to enter. A world with Yacoub and Elephant-Trunk and Isaac and everyone else, and smoke and mirrors, and an accursed business, and heavy, stagnant air that clogged my throat and made me cough. A world where I was no longer a man, master of himself, but a boy, a first mate, a man who is led. And "Let's spend a couple of days with Golda, Yacoub's daughter, in Eilat, or at your uncle's in Haifa, and why don't you dissolve your partnership with that person and come in with us as a partner in Sharm al-Sheikh?" And "What on earth did you do to Rachel? What? What are you saying? Raise your voice a little? You say, honor and things you were raised on? Damn the four-legged beasts of whom you are one! What honor, ignoramus? Honor and chivalry are that you not walk out on your wife on her wedding night, not what's in your head." And "We saw you the day before yesterday sitting with that Sheikh Garbage, who used to be your relation by marriage, and that undertaker Bu Mikhla' was with you! Aren't you ashamed of yourself when you sit with these people?"

And lots of other words, like thorns, from Madame Coucou, sorry, I mean my mother, and her husband Yacoub by her side, smiling with satisfaction, busying himself with something else when I glared at him, as if what was being said was none of his business and meant nothing to him.

All that was left of them for me was my Uncle Shamoun. He was meek and affectionate, and had a certain pathos; nobody paid him any attention due to his poverty and low status. They had come to consider him a burden, not a brother. Sometimes, too, I went to visit Mr. Saul, listening to him and being reminded of my grandfather; however, he could only be seen by appointment, and our visits were constrained, half-hour slots, after which each of us would go about his business—like flowers, beautiful and cheering, but nothing lasting.

I even grew tired of Paris. It meant a luxury car, the good life, and money increasing in my bank account. What was the good of all this without a heart to rejoice at your joy, eyes to watch over you, a hand stroking your forehead as you complained?

I started to remember things that hadn't occurred to me in years. I took to asking myself, "I wonder if Uncle Ibrahim is still alive? How about Imam, my paternal grandfather's valet, who was always kind to me?" What about my half-sister, my father's daughter, in Mansouriya? Did she still remember me? And Khaleeg Street, and the alleyways of Daher, and Abu Ouf's café? And my old friends, Hassan and Ali and Fouad? Even al-Leithi, our funny friend who had flunked his secondary school graduation exam three times, followed in his father's footsteps, and was now a master trades-man in the Rod al-Farag market. In addition, there was the journey through the land of questions every night before bed; questions that wearied the heart and stole sleep away. Who are you, young man? Whose son are you? Mahmoud Effendi who planted your seed, or Zaki al-Azra' who took you in and raised you? To whose branch do you belong, now? Your family in Mansouriya, of whom you know nothing and who know nothing of you? Or your family here, who are like them, or worse?

With whom do you belong, then?

How many francs do you own now, sir? Can they make the finger, nay, the fingernail, of someone who loved you the way your grand-father loved you?

I found nothing for it but to leave behind everything I owned, and return.

Not to my family there, but to my country. To the old world; to the old streets; and to "Let me have a cup of tea, Amm Labib, and make it koshari 'ala maya beida," and "How are you, Galal? Where have you been, man, and how's the world treating you?" and "Do you plan to stay here in Daher, or move to Heliopolis?" and "How's So-and-so?" "Well, thank God." "And So-and-so?" "He's passed on, but his children are a delight! How about we go visit them after afternoon prayer tomorrow, and you can use the opportunity to offer them your condolences?" "Agreed, Amm Abbas!" I missed that world, and wanted to return to it. To go home for a day, for a year, to the end of my days, I didn't know, but to go back. Back home.

I surprised my mother one day with a phone call from Orly Airport.

"Hello, Galal! What's up? Where have you been?"

"In the world."

"Join us for dinner tonight. We're having a small soirée at Maxim's. A little thing on the occasion of the signing of the contract in Sharm al-Sheikh, and everyone's going to be there: your Uncle Haroun, Isaac, Yacoub, and Rachel. All of us, all of us."

"And Uncle Shamoun, is he invited as well?"

"Shamoun? No, Shamoun's not coming. No one told him."

"I'm not coming either. I'm having dinner with Umm Hassan tonight."

"Umm who?"

"I'm waiting to board the plane for Egypt."

"For Egypt? What's this? And you didn't tell me!"

"Uncle Shamoun knows. He and Sheikh Munji drove me to the airport."

"Shamoun and Sheikh Munji? Well . . ."

There was a silence. Finally her voice came over the line. "So? Are you moving there for good, or will you be coming back?"

"I don't know."

"What about your business and your work here? Are they still going on?"

"Yes, still the same."

"You want me to fill in for you until you get back? Look out for your interests with that Lebanese partner of yours, what's his name . . . his name . . ."

"Abu-Shanab."

"So do you?"

"No, I don't."

The line went dead.

The waiting room was a hubbub, a hive of activity. The day after tomorrow was the Prophet's birthday, and many people from here, North Africans in particular, wanted to make it home for a quick visit, a couple of days and then back. The speakers were calling out for dozens of flights: flights to Akkra, Dakar, Casablanca, and Tunis. My ears were peeled for these announcements; as soon as they announced the Egyptair flight to Cairo, I picked up my carry-on bag and headed for the departure hall.

It was the first bag I had packed the night before. I started with the pajamas my grandfather had been wearing when he died, then a long-sleeved gray shirt he favored, the gold ring, and the Jovial watch; I had placed the tarboosh in a cardboard hatbox, which I carried in my other hand. I wanted to bring these things back to keep in his old closet.

Glossary

Abdel Rasoul A Muslim name, meaning 'servant of the Prophet.'

Abu Hasira A saint formerly much celebrated by Egyptians. His popularity declined after the government restricted the festival of his birthday to Egyptian Jews in the wake of Camp David. Originally Yacoub ibn Mas'oud, he was a rabbi of Moroccan origin who lived in Egypt in the nineteenth century. The 'Hasira' of his title means 'straw mat,' a reference to the supposed miracle of his use of a straw mat as a boat on the high seas.

Abu Lehaf 'He of the Quilt,' or 'Mr. Quilt.' Similarly, 'Abu Mkhadda' means 'He of the Pillow' or 'Mr. Pillow.'

Abul Shawareb, Abu Shanab Both mean 'He of the Moustaches' or 'Mr. Moustache.'

Ahl al-Kitab Literally 'People of the Book,' the term refers to Jews, Christians, and Sabeans, explicitly mentioned in the Quran as believers in Abrahamic religions and thus having rights under Islam.

"Ahlan ya Hajj" Loosely, 'Hello, sir' to an older gentlemen. Literally, a Hajj is a man who has performed the pilgrimage to Mecca.

Akta' A play on Zaki's surname: Azra' sounds like the Arabic word for 'arm' and Akta' means 'one-armed.'

Arab Unity, the Strategic Dimension, the Homeland from the Gulf to the Ocean Nationalist slogans espoused by the regime of Gamal Abdel Nasser, president of Egypt from 1954 until his death in 1970 and a vocal proponent of Arab unity.

al-Atrash, Farid Singer, composer, and musician of Syrian origin who settled in Egypt. He was a prolific star, recording dozens of songs and appearing in dozens of movies.

Belmont Egyptian brand of cheap cigarettes popular in the 1960s and 1970s.

bey Although used as a rough equivalent of 'Mister' since the 1952 military coup, 'bey' was originally a title conferred during the Egyptian monarchy. By the 1980s, it was used mainly in reference to the police, the military, and the nouveau riche.

blessings on all your prophets It is customary for storytellers at public gatherings to promote unity by calling for blessings upon the Prophet, a call-and-response action engaging the crowd. This saying was the Egyptian way of getting around—indeed, working with—the fact that listeners at such gatherings were invariably religiously mixed.

castour A heavy cotton fabric, one of only a few kinds of fabric available during the Nasser era. It has become to some extent synonymous with modest means, although this was not always the case.

Damanhour This city was once known for its thriving cotton trade, which necessitated a lot of administrative work.

Damietta Egyptian coastal town, still a center for furniture trading.

dishdasha Flowing white outer garment worn by men in the Arab Gulf states.

Ebeid, Makram Egyptian politician in the 1930s and 1940s.

effendi An old-fashioned word for a middle-class person.

Eid al-Adha Muslim holiday, commemorating Abraham's sacrifice of a sheep instead of his son. Muslims slaughter animals and donate most or all of the meat to charity.

Eid al-Fitr Feast celebrating the end of the holy month of Ramadan

Fatiha Opening verse of the Quran, often recited to seal a transaction. To confirm an engagement, the families of the bride and the groom recite it together. It is also recited in memory of someone who has died.

fatta Bread soaked in meat broth and topped with rice, traditionally eaten at the Eid al-Adha.

feddan Unit of land measurement roughly equivalent to an acre.

feseekh Preserved, salted fish, considered inedible by some but consumed traditionally by many on the spring festival of Shamm al-Nesim.

gallabiya Traditional Egyptian one-piece gown for men.

halawa A sweet made of sesame seeds.

handprints Five is a number that is supposed to ward off the Evil Eye; five-fingered handprints in the blood of a slaughtered animal are considered especially effective.

hanem Female equivalent of the title 'pasha.'

Hosny, Dawoud Musician of the 1930s.

Ibrahim, Negma A star of black-and-white movies, of Jewish origin, best known for her role in *Rayya and Sikina*, a movie about two real-life sisters who terrorized the Alexandria shopping area of Zanqat al-Sittat, kidnapping, robbing, and murdering women in the early twentieth century.

iftar Meal eaten at sundown to break the daylong fast during the holy month of Ramadan.

"Izzayak ya Bey" Loosely, 'How are you, sir?' ('Bey,' from Turkish, is a title for an upper-class man.)

khabibi Mispronunciation of 'habibi' ('my dear').

khawaga 'Foreigner,' but formerly used as a title before the name of a Christian or Jewish man.

King Fouad University Now known as Cairo University.

koshari Egyptian dish, a mixture of rice, pasta, and lentils.

koshari 'ala maya beida A method of preparing tea in which loose tea leaves go into the cup or glass first, and then a layer of sugar; the sugar thus forms a barrier between the tea and the water so the water stays clear until the glass is stirred.

al-Latkh An epithet meaning 'Mud Stain.'

ma'allim A title conferred on a tradesman who owns a business and has apprentices working under him.

markaz Literally 'center'—the capital of a rural administrative division.

Mashallah A common phrase in Egypt, literally 'What God wills.' Used when giving a compliment—"Mashallah, you have shiny hair!"—as it is thought that expressing admiration for something without invoking God may bring down the Evil Eye upon the recipient of the compliment.

menein Type of flour cake taken to graveyards as charity.

Mizrahi, Togo Film producer of the 1940s.

Mohamed and Mahmoud and Khalil Muslim names, expressing the fact that there are no Jews left in the speaker's old town.

al-nafukh bita' al-ana Broken Arabic for 'my head.'

Naguib, Muhammad First president of Egypt after the 1952 military coup. He was deposed in 1954.

Nahhas Pasha Egyptian politician from the 1920s to the 1950s. He served as prime minister for various terms during this period.

the Nightingale Nickname for Abdel Halim Hafez, Egyptian singer in the 1960s.

pasha An honorary title under the Egyptian monarchy, higher than 'bey.'

prayer hall A room or a one-room structure that has the attributes of a mosque but is too small to be called a mosque.

Qabbani, Nizar Syrian poet. "Her eyes are divine . . ." is from his poem "The Fortune Teller."

Quran on the eyes An old belief says that if you lie while placing the Quran on your eyes, you will go blind.

rabuna Mispronunciation of the Egyptian Arabic word for 'God.'

Rushdie, Fatma Famous stage and screen actress who performed a number of Shakespearean roles and was nicknamed 'the Sarah Bernhardt of the East.'

Sagha Gold-trading area in the bazaar district near al-Hussein Mosque.

Sahat al-Hanatir Literally 'Horse-carriage Plaza.'

Sannu', Yacoub Journalist and founder of the modern Egyptian theater.

al-Sayyid, Lutfi Egyptian intellectual who was the first head of Cairo University.

semeet A type of traditional Egyptian bread.

Sheikh Salamouni Abu Gamous Abu Gamous means 'Buffalo Owner.'

Suleiman Pasha Frenchman who lived in Egypt during the late nineteenth and early twentieth centuries; helped train the Egyptian army.

Sultan Hussein Kamel Ruler of Egypt during the First World War.

sura A chapter in the Quran.

ugal Headdress worn in the Arabian Gulf states.

Umm Bahloul, Umm Hassan People are traditionally referred to by the name of their firstborn. 'Umm Hassan' means 'Hassan's mother.' 'Bahloul' means 'jester' or 'clown.'

uncle Respectful form of address to an older man, not meant literally.

Usta Informal title for a master craftsman.

zakat Mandatory sum paid to charity by observant Muslims.

Zawya Hamra, Ain Shams, Asyut Zawya Hamra and Ain Shams are districts of Cairo; Asyut is a governorate in Upper Egypt. During the period of this novel, there were tensions between Muslims and Christians in these area.